I0637175

THE DETERMINED

RACHEL RUECKERT

KENSINGTON
PUBLISHING CORP.

kensingtonbooks.com

KENSINGTON BOOKS are published by

Kensington Publishing Corp.
900 Third Avenue
New York, NY 10022

Copyright © 2026 by Rachel Rueckert

All rights reserved. No part of this book may be reproduced in any form or by any means without the prior written consent of the Publisher, excepting brief quotes used in reviews.

All Kensington titles, imprints, and distributed lines are available at special quantity discounts for bulk purchases for sales promotion, premiums, fund-raising, educational, or institutional use.

This book is a work of fiction. Names, characters, businesses, organizations, places, events, and incidents either are the product of the author's imagination or are used fictitiously. Any resemblance to actual persons, living or dead, events, or locales is entirely coincidental.

To the extent that the image or images on the cover of this book depict a person or persons, such person or persons are merely models, and are not intended to portray any character or characters featured in the book.

Special book excerpts or customized printings can also be created to fit specific needs. For details, write or phone the office of the Kensington Sales Manager: Kensington Publishing Corp., 900 Third Avenue, New York, NY 10022. Attn. Sales Department. Phone: 1-800-221-2647.

Kensington and the K logo Reg. U.S. Pat. & TM Off.

ISBN: 978-1-4967-4756-3 (ebook)

ISBN: 978-1-4967-4755-6

First Kensington Trade Paperback Printing: March 2026

10 9 8 7 6 5 4 3 2 1

Printed in the United States of America

The authorized representative in the EU for product safety and compliance
is eucomply OU, Parnu mnt 139b-14, Apt 123
Tallinn, Berlin 11317, hello@eucompliancepartner.com

For my dear friend, Carol Ann—a self-taught sailor in every way who lets me tag along.
For all of my fierce, female friendships.
You know who you are.

As to the Lives of our two female Pyrates, we must confess they may appear a little Extravagant, yet they are never the less true for seeming so, but as they were publickly try'd for their Pyracies, there are living Witnesses enough to justify what we have laid down concerning them; it is certain, we have produced some Particulars which were not so publickly known, the Reason is, we were more inquisitive into the Circumstances of their past Lives, than other People, who had no other Design, than that of gratifying their own private Curiosity: If there are some Incidents and Turns in their Stories, which may give them a little the Air of a Novel, they are not invented or contrived for that Purpose, it is a Kind of Reading this Author is but little acquainted with, but as he himself was exceedingly diverted with them, when they were related to him, he thought they might have the same Effect upon the Reader.

—Captain Johnson, preface to *A General History of the Robberies and Murders of the Most Notorious Pyrates*, London, 1724

AUTHOR'S NOTE

Mary Read and Anne Bonny were real women who sailed during the Golden Age of Pirates. They feature in several records, including an essential text for pirate studies called *A General History of the Pyrates*, a tome published over three hundred years ago under the name of Captain Charles Johnson. All three of these individuals appear as characters in what follows.

These pages reflect extensive synthesis and research—field visits, careful study, countless conversations, and my own imagination. Though this is a novel, a remarkable amount of this tale comes from sources. In the afterword and cast of characters sections at the end of this book, I separate out fact from myth, history from legend, and say more about my process of excavating these women from the sands of time.

Until then, "go boldly," and may the winds be in your favor.

THE DETERMINED

CHAPTER I

Spanish Town, Jamaica
February 1721

Spine pressed against the prison wall, Anne rested her hands on the swell of her stomach. The cloth of her breeches—the same ones from the night of their capture—clung to her damp skin as she sat on the unforgiving stone floor. She could still smell the grapeshot and gunpowder. She wore the same shirt too—*his* calico shirt. The bitter memory pierced her like a rapier.

Not even the child had energy to move. Nothing had energy to move in Jamaica's heat.

Anne didn't bother to glance up at the hush of men speaking outside her cell, the sound of their shuffling boots. Among them, she made out the voice of the burly guard who brought her daily water.

"I insist on supervising," he said. "She has no shackles."

"Are you suggesting I am unable to protect myself against an unarmed woman?" asked an unfamiliar voice.

The guard huffed. "She is no woman."

"I can hold my own," the stranger said. "I assure you."

Anne stiffened, aware of her vulnerable position. But if this visitor dared to touch her, he wouldn't be able to hold his own bowels when she was done with him.

She resolved to betray no nerves. A silence followed, heavy as the humid air in this godforsaken garrison.

"Do consider—"

"Surely, my good man, you have heard of my reputation?"

The guard relented. "I'll be down the hall. Call if you need assistance."

Not until after the squeal of her door opening, then closing with a decisive click, did Anne tuck a strand of red hair behind her ear. She lazily lifted her gaze up from the straw-covered ground.

"Good afternoon," the gentleman said, clearing his throat and removing an ostrich-feathered tricorn. He wiped beads of sweat from his wrinkled forehead with a kerchief—clean as snow—before placing it inside the leather bag he carried. Anne watched without blinking as he scanned the dim room: the saggy cot, a three-legged stool, a rancid bucket, the streak of sun from the slash of barred window above.

Then, finally, at her.

"I am sorry that a young woman of twenty-three, in your condition, must bear these difficult circumstances." He arched a brow, as if ready for a reaction—any reaction.

She looked away, hiding a stab of despair.

Sighing, he pulled the wooden stool from the corner and placed it in front of her. "May I?"

Anne balked. She couldn't help it. She'd known a life of pleasantries and politeness once, and she could still see through them.

"I don't have to ask who you are, since on that everyone is clear. Or *are* they?" He paused. "But you can call me Captain Charles Johnson. Yes, I know my way around a ship—circumnavigated the globe by my twenty-seventh birthday, if you can believe it."

"What I believe is that you're a rat spying for Governor Lawes." The sound of her own voice, loud yet raw from eight weeks of solitary confinement, startled her.

"No, miss. I assure you, I come on my own business."

At this, the baby kicked. Hard. Her hand flew to her side. Jesus, Mary, and Joseph. She still had two months of this feisty thing waging war in her womb.

The captain smiled, probably thinking he was making headway—the fool. He took a seat, then pulled out a small oak desk from his bag, along with a quill and some parchment. He rested a crystal inkwell on the floor.

No weapons. No objects of torture. Anne felt her muscles relax and eyed the writing materials with a surge of longing.

But still, this gowl—whoever he might be—deserved nothing.

"You have no reason to fear me," he said.

"I don't fear you," Anne lied.

Johnson inhaled, nodding. She didn't like the way his eyes lit when she spoke.

"I'm a writer as well as a captain," the man said, inking his quill. "I traveled far to see you. And your friend."

Mary's face flashed before her.

"I am compiling a book. The world is eager to understand you, to learn how—"

"No," Anne said. *No, no.*

No.

Anne placed a firm hand on the wall to pull herself up, to yank herself out of the upswell of desperation that flooded her chest and threatened to drag her under. She did not want to sit below him—to be pitied, judged, or exploited by this blunderbuss. She folded her arms over her belly and glared at the desk balanced on his knees. Her fingers twitched with yearning as she imagined wielding the quill herself.

"If you help me," Captain Johnson said with practiced patience, "I might be able to help you."

Of all the many lies she'd ever been told, it was the most beautiful one she'd ever heard.

CHAPTER 2

Kinsale, County Cork, Ireland
1705

"It's *mine*."

"Says who?" taunted Anne's friend, Seán O'Brien, holding the stick higher.

"Says me!" Anne roared, her fingers swiping at the air. Blood rose to her cheeks, the fury Mam warned could cause more freckles.

"*Dul go h-olc ort*," Anne swore. Bad luck to you.

The boy laughed at her curse. "You must make your *máthair* proud with that mouth. Obedient as a fiend, too—skipping your lessons again."

Anne balled her fists. How dare he bring up Mam? Or her dreary lessons? Da's efforts to teach Anne his trade, a last attempt to redeem her worth in the eyes of the granny and granddad she'd seen but once, were proving disastrous and dull.

Bloody hell, Anne *hated* dull.

And that miserable Seán O'Brien at the moment.

She swung again for the stick. It had been a double-edged sword in her mind a few minutes earlier as she and Queen Maeve battled Furbaide. If Anne still had the fallen branch, she would have used it to knock Seán into the River Bandon by now.

Anne threw all her force into his chest, toppling Seán into the soggy grass.

"Dirty papist," he shot, scowling at the stains on his trousers.

She smirked and folded her lanky arms. "I'm not the one covered in mud, you filthy bastard."

Of all the wonderful curses, this was Anne's favorite. Perhaps because she knew of no insults for the Protestants. Or maybe because *bastard* was the worst word of all. Da had told her off for using it. He warned her never to utter it in his presence again and, most importantly, never to say it to anyone else. Should she have occasion to talk to anyone else—a habit he and Mam generally advised against. The less people knew about their affairs, with Da's wife run off and Mam being a Catholic, the better.

But what did it matter? Everyone already knew the truth about her. And besides, Anne enjoyed winning her fights. Her friends never shunned rough play or swearing:

Go dtite tigh ort. May a house fall upon you.

Buinneach dhearg go dtigidh ort. May you have red diarrhea.

Then, of course, Anne's second favorite curse: *Go ndéana an diabhal dréimire de chnámh do dhroma ag piocadh úll i ngairdín Ifrinn.* May the devil make a ladder out of your bones to pick apples in the garden of hell.

Anne lunged for the stick and Seán gave up the battle with a torrent of snide insults. She scanned the pink-orange sky and the waning sun before heaving a victorious sigh.

"Well, I know something you don't," Seán said, scrubbing at the stains on his sleeves. "Aoife's *dadaí* is back from Cork—brought her back something you'd fancy to see."

Anne's heart leapt. "Go on."

When he saw he had something over her again, he flashed a wicked smile. Anne exhaled, then reluctantly offered him a hand. He took it.

"A sap whistle."

Anne gaped. Mam had gifted her a sap whistle for her eighth birthday last winter, but Da had taken it away after she'd shot peas at a passing carriage.

"Liam and Fionn will want to see it, too," Anne said. She and Seán began the walk along the riverbank toward the quay, her stick now a powerful scepter—no, a druid's magical staff—that she used to part the greenery as she journeyed. As they strolled, she plucked primrose, buttercups, and fuzzy purple sheep's-bit to make a clumsy bouquet for Mam. The enormous rock wall of Charles Fort, her friends' usual meeting spot, shrank behind them as they neared the heart of Kinsale.

Anne's skirt snagged on a thistle.

"I liked you better when you wore trousers," he said.

Anne yanked the linen hem free. "Not even the Devil cares what you think, Seán O'Brien."

He laughed in reply. The moment word began to spread a few years ago that Anne was not a Cormac heir, especially given the dubious circumstances of her birth, Da had declared that the ruse was over. The dresses soon followed.

By the time Anne and Seán reached the city center, the merchant shops were closing for the day. Ships and smaller fishing boats lay at anchor in the crowded harbor, their mighty sails the color of clouds. The smell of sea bass and huss wafted from the docks as men and women haggled.

"*Slán*. See you tomorrow, same time and place," Seán said, snatching the staff back before dashing away.

Anne stood and watched Seán go, his bare feet flying. She often wondered what would happen if she were to follow him to the poor side of town. Where did he live? What was his home life like? But she never pursued him. She wouldn't want Seán—or Aoife, or the rest of them—knowing the same of her. Anne's parents weren't keen on company. Or friends. Or her, at times.

A pair of redcoats walked past, deep in conversation, causing Anne to snap her attention to the time. She had to beat Mam back to the house. Clean off her boots. Hide the evidence of her folly. Present the flowers. Anne never quite knew which Mam she might get: the frail but playful mother who was all games and trilling laughs and teasing, or the strong mother who guided their family like the brightest of stars, knowing just what to do and say and how everyone else should act, or—on rare but terrible occasions—the firebrand mother who could lance Anne straight through with a single, hateful look.

The bells of St. Multose Church bellowed as Anne sprang across the road for home.

Anne skidded to a halt when she saw the commotion outside her house. In the fading light, a crowd gathered below the lowest gable. Neighbors. Parishioners. She didn't have to attend service with them to recognize the pinched faces. They muttered with pursed lips as they stood before the front window where Da kept his law office.

What was *left* of the front window.

Taking a step, Anne felt a crunch beneath her heel.

Glass.

She jerked her boot back. Her eyes darted from the road to the dozens of gawkers. Her breathing—already labored from the dash home—became shallower.

Mam.

Where was Mam?

"Mind yourself," someone said when Mrs. Doyle arrived with a broom.

"I'll mind what I please. These Penal Laws violate the laws of God and man both."

"Hush!" a man retorted. "Do you want to be next? Branded a 'West Brit'?"

"God?" a white-haired woman huffed. "They've no respect for the Good Lord. That hussy had it coming."

Anne's mouth went dry. Her heart hammered in her chest and she dropped the bouquet clenched in her fist.

Mr. O'Neill leaned forward on his cane to better inspect the damage. "Did anyone see who dealt the blow?"

Mam.

Find Mam.

Before anyone spotted her, Anne slipped through her secret slot in the blackthorn hedge near the carriage house and sprinted for the entrance to the servants' quarters.

Flinging open the door, she froze on the front step, remembering her boots. The muck. No one used this entrance. No servant would work for such a "family" as hers. She'd leave a trace. Mam could spot a pinprick of dust.

Find her.

If she's alive, she can flay me later.

Anne's pulse sounded in her ears as her feet pounded up the stairs. She pushed through the last paneled door, spilling into the drawing room and searching for her parents. No candles. No smells of dinner in the making.

"And how are we supposed to survive if your law practice fails?" came a shout from upstairs. "If they kill you and drag me out onto the street? Or haul me back to jail?"

The hair on the back of Anne's neck rose.

Firebrand Mother.

Mam was very much alive.

"I would never let that happen to us," came Da's calm but passionate rebuttal.

Anne sagged with relief. They were safe, and she was safely forgotten—again. If Anne could make it to her own bedroom, past Mam and Da's argument, she'd hear everything in the morning without getting in the crossfire. She could clean the boot prints off the stairs before Mam noticed.

She removed her shoes at last, holding them by the laces, and tiptoed up the stairs.

"Stop acting the goat, William. They'll bring torches next. We can't go on like this. Me, living in the house. Our child will be the death of me—growing taller by the hour, wild as a feral dog. It's bad enough she robbed me of my health, that my belly landed me in prison. You'll never know what I endured there, the nightmares I still suffer."

Anne stopped in her tracks midway down the hall.

"If she masters my trade, if I present her again—"

"Do you think I was born yesterday? Has she given any indication that she is capable of letters in all her eight years of mischief? That she cares for books and legal ledgers? Your parents will never spare us a ha'penny for a child like her. Take heed of the truth. We're on our own. Even the kitchen mice keep better kin."

Anne's fingernails bit into her palms. She should be anywhere else but here.

"Meanwhile, Mrs. Cormac—" Mam spat.

"I don't want to hear her treacherous name in this house."

"As long as your wife still lives—even if it's with another man a world away—she haunts every room. And don't go blabbering about coverture and the Common Law either, William. Even if it isn't legally sound, she plagues every corner of this home. And not a person in this godforsaken town will let me forget it. For all we know, she returned to throw that brick herself!"

A silence. Anne held her breath.

"Calm yourself, *mo chroí*. You are the *bean an tí* of this house. You are my heart and soul, the very bones of me. *You.* There is no one—and there never has been—anyone else but you. Your spritely spirit is too much for your body."

They might have been kissing. They were always kissing. But Anne swallowed and the braver part of her soldiered on, ear angled toward the door.

"There'll be holy murder to pay," her mother said, her voice quieter. "It's time, William. It's time to leave Kinsale to the wolves. Make for London. Anywhere. Anywhere is better than here."

Anne felt the earth shift in the pause that followed.

"For you, Peg?" Da said.

"For us."

"Consider it done." Da's voice softened. "There's nothing you and I can't do together."

When the words ended, replaced by strange sighs, Anne padded toward her own room. Her heart galloped and her fingers shook. Once inside, she reached for the water basin.

Leave?

Leave Ireland?

She couldn't. *They* couldn't.

Anne placed her boots inside the white porcelain bowl, the heels still sticky with clover and mud. Liquid spilled over the side.

And how are we supposed to survive . . . ?

Has she given any indication that she is capable . . . ?

Anne reached for a towel and scrubbed. Her eyes burned. She knew she lived in a house of secrets. She knew Mam ran the house despite her frailty and that they couldn't employ servants—that Mam had once *been* a servant. She knew there was a reason why her parents kept her inside, away from her mysterious granny and granddad, away from churches and festivals, away from anything of interest.

But until now, Anne hadn't known that Mam's failing health—and that rumored time in prison—was all her fault.

Our child will be the death of me . . .

The towel stained as she rubbed at the laces. Starting tomorrow, things would be different. Anne wouldn't meet Seán or Fionn or Liam. She wouldn't see Aoife or her new sap whistle. Not even for a few precious hours of fun.

She scoured the boots until her knuckles were as red as her hair. Starting tomorrow, Anne would be good.

And with that sobering knowledge, Anne knew the first thing she had to do.

CHAPTER 3

Three days later, Anne faced the Cormac estate where her granny and granddad lived. She stood taller than the pines framing the iron gateway of the imposing stone arch. A lioness statue perched atop its center, glowering down at her with empty pupils.

Anne swallowed the knot in her throat. She'd risen hours before the sun, put on her boots, then made for the road. Blisters now boiled on her heels. Though two years had passed since she'd confronted this place, Anne knew the path. She'd never forget that morning her family had climbed into the carriage: Mam's rose-water perfume, Da's new cravat, how they arrived at what Anne could only assume was a castle.

Then what followed: Mam, paler than a ghost. Da, kneeling before the strangers—pleading on behalf of her, a child, who should not suffer for the sins of "his" parents. The old woman whose painted mouth fell open at the sight of them, pale eyes watery as they fixed on Anne. A wrinkled man, scowling with thick gray eyebrows beneath a powdered wig.

The eruption of curses. Da's ear-splitting fury when Granddad called him a "*bréagadóir*," a liar. Mam's bone-white face before she fainted, crumpling to the floor.

Now, standing before the iron gate, Anne blinked away the awful memory. Her best dress, tight around the stomach, left her slightly nauseous from swirling nerves. *Damnú*. There would be no use hiding the filthy hem. It wasn't as though she could have asked to borrow the carriage.

If her parents had lost everything on her account—if Mam's poor health was Anne's doing—she owed her parents this much.

And maybe, just a wee bit, she owed it to herself, too. For she could not, *would not*, lose her lovely Ireland.

Anne spit into her palms and smoothed out her hair, frizzy from the damp air. She only had to slip through the bars, cross the Cormac grounds, announce herself at the door . . .

It needed to work.

Da and Mam had explained their own plan after the brick incident. A new family secret: they would move under the cover of night, taking one sea chest apiece. They would leave behind the debts. The rumors and ill-wishes. It would just be the three of them: Da, Mam, and Anne.

Da held Anne's hands in his as Mam stroked her hair. "We've run out our luck here, my little lass," she cooed, the very picture of Strong Mother—all traces of Firebrand gone. Mam embodied all the power of the sun. When she radiated approval and affection, the house glowed like the longest day in summer.

And without the light of that sun, they all withered.

A lump formed in Anne's throat. "But what if I don't like London?" She hated the selfish words. How dare she resist a plan that would ensure her Mam's health and safety? Da's happiness and secure employment?

"I know you'll miss Kinsale," Da said, his face soft with love as he knelt down to her level.

Ma crouched beside him. Her brown curls piled atop her head like a crown. "I will, too." At this, Mam's sapphire eyes, the same color as Anne's—flooded with tenderness.

"But what if we had the money to stay? Or to not move so very far?" Anne asked, her chin quivering.

Da rubbed the backs of her knuckles. "I wish we did. More than you know. But we'll mind what we've got." At this, Da threw an arm around Mam and Anne, pulling them close. "And we have a lot. Everything we need, right here."

Anne gripped the rungs of the gate. She squeezed her eyes shut, summoning courage and rehearsing her lines. *"Je suis honoré de vous rencontrer."* She knew to call the woman *Seanmháthair* and the man *Seanathair*, to tell them she'd read a whole shelf of books and could recite John 14 in Latin—that she was capable of learning, that she would make a worthy heir despite the unfortunate case of her sex. She'd retained more of Da's lessons than anyone might suppose. She was not such a hopeless cause.

Anne felt the width of each bar for the best way through, then shimmied through the slats.

She could just make out the brass knocker of the grand doorway when a bark startled her.

"You there!" someone shouted.

Anne whirled to face the voice. Her knees trembled.

"How'd you get in here? You've no business begging in these parts." The bald man held a rope. A large dog pulled at the leash, growling.

Anne opened her mouth, but no words came out. Each bark from the mutt made her shrink.

Taking in the state of her dress, the groundskeeper paused. "Thieving from the kitchen won't get you far. Away with you!"

"I'm . . ."

The hound snarled, and she hated how she flinched. Her ankles seemed shackled to the grass.

"I'm here on family business," Anne tried again. "My granny and granddad live here."

The groundskeeper laughed. "Haven't heard that yarn before."

"My name is Anne Cormac," Anne all but whispered, her eyes fixed on the dog's yellow teeth.

"Oh? And my mam's the Queen of Bloody England. Be gone, you scrawny cat. You'll not get a crust."

She should've run for the door by now. Burst inside. Created a scene if she had to.

Why the Devil couldn't she move?

Three sharp barks shook her to the bones. Unable to budge, Anne forgot her words, her French, her pleasantries.

Her mission.

"Are you daft?" the man yelled, loosening his grip on the leash. "Out with you!"

Before Anne could see whether he would drop the rope, she sprinted in the direction of town and the home she would now most certainly lose.

CHAPTER 4

Mam exhaled with triumph when they spotted England's shore a week later. Anne stood at her side on the bow of the ship in the brisk dawn. Mam, bundled in a shawl, rested her hands on Anne's shoulders.

"Good riddance to our mighty troubles," Mam said, head thrown back and eyes closed as sea mist clung to the gray air. The brine burned Anne's cheeks. "I hope the Devil cannot swim."

Anne laughed in response, though she knew her heart to be broken forever. Served her damn right. This was her own doing, her own fault. That dog had not charged her, had not snapped its teeth into her flesh. She'd run away, fled, within sight of the door, chased by her own pathetic fear. "All will be well," Anne muttered. She stared into the waves, the way they crashed relentlessly against the hull. "Da promised to take care of us."

Mam glanced over her shoulder to where Da stood, engaged in conversation with two men, then she whispered into Anne's ear. "Remember to never call him *dadaí* in public. We must strive to leave all traces of Ireland behind, especially Irish."

Anne nodded dutifully, remembering her new vow to be good. She peered up to study Mam's face. Her expression glowed with health and light. Mam heaved a great breath, causing a small cough. Then she ran her fingers through Anne's hair. "Come, turn around. I'll be fixing your wild mane again."

"Sorry," Anne offered, allowing her mother to plait her thick tresses. She was sorry for everything. She'd never tell her parents what she'd done, where she'd gone. And she'd never forgive herself for freezing. Failing.

A gull called overhead, circling before making its way back toward land. Had this gull ever been to Kinsale? Seen the sails of ships unfurling in the harbor at dusk or the emerald of a new spring? Sat atop Fort Charles, in whose shadow Seán and her friends might be playing even now?

A poignant silence settled as the wide ocean brimmed all around them.

"Heed this moment always," Mam said thoughtfully, dividing Anne's tangled hair into separate strands. "You'll be a woman before you know it, my Anne. There are certain things every woman must know."

Anne's stomach knotted. Mam tugged as she formed the start of a tight plait, but Anne did not wince.

"Your father is a fine man," she whispered. "As fine as the Good Lord makes them. But his being with me wasn't always so clear. When your father made his intentions known, under the nose of that cold-hearted Mrs. Cormac, there was another. A blacksmith from the market who used to fancy me."

Anne stiffened as Mam told her, for the first time and with a strange, secretive quality to her voice, about this blacksmith. His fine eyes. How she'd fancied him. His flowers and nice compliments. It was a difficult story to follow, something about how the blacksmith—learning of Da's growing attachment to Mam—had come to the Cormac estate and stolen some silverware that somehow, later, ended up in Mam's bed while she served as the Cormacs' maid.

"The bitter fool," Mam lamented. The case of the missing silverware, in addition to Mam's suspiciously untouched bed in the servants' quarters while living with the gentleman of the house, was what sent Mam, with Anne in her belly, to prison. The spurned blacksmith, in a rage, had set her up. Da's legal wife, Mrs. Cormac, discovered the silverware and pressed charges. Mam's health had never been the same since her six months in jail.

"They locked you in the gaol because of me?" Anne asked, confirming what she already knew.

"Because of *Mrs. Cormac*," Mam corrected.

Anne feigned a glower meant for the wench she'd never met, though from this tale, she wondered why Mam did not condemn the blacksmith. These strange details only made her insides coil. She knew Mam spared her the worst truth: that Anne, growing in her mother's belly, had made life so difficult. Unbearable. Had almost killed her then and so recently again. Maybe starting anew, losing everything Anne loved, was the only way forward.

Her mother deserved that horizon.

Mam's voice grew wistful. "It's hard to know sometimes, which way my life might have gone, had I not been a young maid in the Cormac house," Mam said, tying off Anne's plait. "Don't misunderstand me, though. I'm grateful. Not all men in your father's position would have stuck around. And I love him better than any other—and only more so with each passing day. He worships me like a queen, never minding my lowly beginnings." She turned Anne around and faced her, tucking stray hairs behind her ears. "I'm only saying you need to watch yourself. The world is not kind to women."

CHAPTER 5

Spanish Town, Jamaica
February 1721

Anne awoke from a dream with a jolt. The verdant green disappeared, replaced by impenetrable black. Sweat dripped down her face, and her bulging stomach felt wet with it. Damn heat—like the hell this truly was, as if a dog panted unceasingly in her face. She longed for fresh air. A salty gust and the sound of a sail flapping. Or relief in the form of an autumn breeze through the heather. What she wouldn't give for a cold compress like the kind she used to apply to Mam's forehead.

From her cell, Anne could hear the mutter of voices and the shuffle of irons somewhere down the corridor that must have disturbed her sleep. A new prisoner? It certainly wouldn't be that blithering Captain Johnson at this hour.

Mary?

Anne's heart leapt. She listened closely with a spike of hope that they were moving Mary nearer. But she did not hear her friend's voice from among the sounds.

Anne heaved her body up, pissed for the thousandth time that day, then returned to the cot. She rubbed her temples, where a headache pounded, and scanned the slit in the wall. No moon. It had to be after midnight, but what did time mean to her? Here, she slept more than a cat. There was little else to do, little motivation to stay conscious.

She lay on her side, her oversized shirt sticky as it clung to her skin. Mother of God, the *smell*. The white cloth of the shirt had grayed since her capture. Every muscle in her body ached, but her lower back throbbed.

The faraway voices remained vague and distant.

Closing her eyes, Anne tried to recall her dream. Kinsale. Sleep always carried her to that happy place. Never to those unremarkable years of toil in England.

Anne wrapped her arm over her belly. The corner of her lip tugged up, remembering more than just a dream. Remembering Mam. Each night after a successful lesson with Da, she'd clutch a coverlet to her chin and listen as Mam's voice—deep for villains, vibrant for heroes—took her mind to wondrous heights. But Anne had a favorite.

"Tell me the story of Grace O'Malley."

"Not that one again," Mam said with mock exaggeration. "Lord have mercy."

"Please," Anne begged.

And so Mam began: the story of the infamous Gráinne Ní Mháille, who traveled and traded with her father, Black Oak, training as chieftain and learning the laws of the land and sea. How a rival clan had slaughtered her husband, Donal O'Flaherty, snatching up his land until Grace took back his castle with a force only love could explain—the same force she showed when, only an hour after giving birth to her son on the deck of a tossing ship, she swaddled the child and stood tall on the ship's bow, her head shaved, leading her loyal crew and admiring followers as they seized an enemy ship. How she later met face-to-face with Queen Elizabeth, prepared with a list of demands for her clan—demands the English queen ignored, unsure whether to see Grace as a heroine and equal or as an unruly thief and threat.

"And she was real?"

"Real as strong ale after a long day."

Anne would then sink deeper into the bed—a soft bed, a *real* bed—her eyes half-mast. "I want to be brave like Grace O'Malley."

At this, Mam always laughed. "A bald lass to embarrass your old da?" Kissing her on the forehead, she reminded Anne to say her prayers before wishing her a peaceful, dreamless sleep.

Anne rolled onto her other side. The baby did not stir, though she felt its heat like a bonfire. According to the court, she wouldn't live long enough to pass on Mam's stories. But curse the child all she might—for its foolish father and all the discomforts of being in the family way—Anne knew her situation was not the baby's fault.

How Anne could know this fact clear as the Caribbean Sea but still blame herself for Mam's hardships and fate, she didn't know. She snorted and might have laughed if she hadn't been so parched. After weeks of rotting in this gaol, how had it never occurred to her? Like Mam, she too was a woman proved with child, tossed into a filthy cell.

Different circumstances, Anne rationalized. Her belly had saved Anne's life.

For now.

CHAPTER 6

Spanish Town, Jamaica
February 1721

"Right this way, Captain," an apple-cheeked soldier said to Johnson the next day, escorting him to the other end of the garrison. The second female pirate in custody was also rumored to be with child. What *scandal*. Johnson could hardly fathom his luck. Every account mattered to his growing manuscript. But these women, he knew, would tip the scales.

"I follow your lead," Captain Johnson replied, his bag gripped in hand. He was no simpleton. To make good on his promise to Rivington in London, to have a manuscript that would make up for his last three failures at the press, Johnson needed something remarkable. Something that would appeal to the sensibilities of old salts, readers of novels, and even the most uptight of priests.

Something that would sell as well as pirate trial pamphlets.

The subject held inherent intrigue. Johnson, a seafarer with a natural interest in these rovers and a proclivity—obsession, really—toward the particulars that come with research, knew what this chance meant. Debts stalked him like shadows. He could scarce show his face in society. But if he was honest with himself, even without profit on the line, Johnson would still be here in the Caribbean. Nothing fascinated him more than sea rogues. It had been so since the moment he took his first steps aboard a ship half a lifetime ago. What memories! Some fond. Most fonder in hindsight. The ones he avoided scrutinizing emerged in occasional nightmares.

"Right in here, sir."

Johnson gave a slight bow to the soldier as the cell creaked open. The smell of vomit caught him in the gut. He saw at once why there had been no fuss about supervision as there had been with Anne, and his earlier elation flitted away. Mary lay shivering under a tattered blanket.

Shivering in this heat?

"This gentleman is here to see you," the guard said to Mary, curled up on the straw floor. Her brown hair spread around her shoulders. She did not move or speak.

Johnson turned to the guard and lowered his voice. "Good heavens. Has a doctor attended to her?"

"The day before last."

Johnson tried not to look alarmed. "Bring the doctor again. The woman needs medicine."

He hoped he was not too late.

Johnson shuffled inside, careful of where he stepped. The guard remained outside the door—in no hurry to carry out Johnson's requests.

"Make haste, man!" And only then did bootsteps sound down the corridor.

Breathing through his mouth, Johnson found the three-legged stool in the room. He tentatively scooted it closer to the woman, unsure how best to proceed. She lay on her side with eyes closed. She was not a beautiful woman, and Johnson guessed her to be in her mid-thirties—ten years older than Anne, at least. She too wore a man's loose shirt and trousers. She had little by way of curves save for the swell of a stomach he spotted under her blanket. The only other feminine feature worthy of note was her sharp cheekbones, emphasized by what must have been hunger.

What an unpleasant business. "Miss Mary?" Johnson tried.

To his astonishment, her lids slowly opened.

Johnson composed himself. "Excuse my intrusion. I am . . . Well, there will be time for that later." He felt heartsick at the sight of so much misery. "How are you feeling?"

Mary's eyes fixed on him, and something about her direct gaze felt unnerving. Like she mocked him, or perhaps even pitied him. Though drenched with fever—it didn't take a doctor to see that much—she seemed surprisingly alert.

"Just as you might surmise," she answered through raspy breath. Her voice was low and quiet. Distinctly English, West County.

"I'll have the guard bring more water."

Mary gave a slight nod of thanks. But she did not speak again.

"How far along is the child?" he dared to ask, wondering if this might be the way into the conversation.

For a long time, Mary said nothing. Her dark eyes and lack of response put him on edge. Johnson wondered if there might be a more opportune time for a visit.

Perhaps she'd gone mad.

At last, she spoke. "If you are not a doctor or a soldier," she said, pulling the blanket to her chin, "or a priest who has come to take a confession, or a saint here to release me from my pain, why are you here?"

Johnson set his bag down but paused before removing his writing desk and papers. He was practiced at exercising proper distance between himself and his subjects. But in Mary's cell, the fraught reality of his task nagged at his conscience. This was not like trying to claw trust from that stubborn Anne, nor was it like listening to the typical desperation of accused pirates or the prattling of gentlemen he'd interviewed.

For a moment, they just watched each other. Something flickered in him, not attraction and not judgment—but also not that familiar flutter of writing something he knew would cause a stir. Something about this woman disarmed him.

"I'm a fellow countryman here to listen," Johnson said at last, by way of beginning.

$\mathcal{C}$HAPTER 7

London, England
1695

Mary was eleven years old the day she learned she was a girl and wasn't named Mark.

Mark's stomach had ached that morning, like a mouse was chewing on his innards. But he'd ignored it as he picked up the baskets filled with fresh loaves. He clutched one wrapped loaf to his stomach. The heat seeped through his threadbare shirt, warming his blood and soothing his cramping belly.

A crowd of competing hawkers had gathered outside Mrs. Dalton's bakery. Mark stood with Ma at the front of the line. If they could be the first to reach the north side of the harbor, they could sell eight baskets of provisions between the two of them and return home before dinner.

"Move it along," jeered a snaggle-toothed man.

Ma did not betray any sign that she'd heard him. Instead, she calmly handed coins to Mrs. Dalton before shouldering her own baskets filled with hardtack. Her linen dress was the same pale color as the sky. The color of the Thames on a foggy London afternoon.

Ma stood tall despite her tattered skirts. The roped baskets hung from a staff across her back. Her dark hair appeared smooth as silk no matter the weather. She was so beautiful, and Mark suspected she didn't know it. Or maybe she didn't want to know it.

"Off we go, then," Ma said with her usual brightness, striking off with a fast clip. Mark trailed a few steps behind. With their brisk pace and well-honed route along the Thames, they arrived at the buzzing docks ahead of the other hawkers. Salty air wafted toward Mark, rustling his straight dark hair tied with a simple leather cord. The sight of the tall ships always took his breath away. How did they manage to avoid crashing or tangling their anchors? To stay afloat even during poor weather?

His stomach seized. He hoped it would go away soon, this case of bad milk.

"Bread?" Mark offered an approaching fishmonger. The man reeked of rotten cod. "Fresh made this morning," Mark added. The man shook his head. So did the next one, and the next, until—finally—two sailors took a loaf to split and Mark pocketed the money.

"All of London seems to be out," Ma said, returning from a deal with Captain Southwick, one of their regular customers. "Fine fortunes today. The good captain bought two bags of hardtack." Sweat gleamed on her brow, and her eyes danced with delight. "I reckon we'll be home early. Might even have enough sugar for a little cake."

But Ma's grin faded in an instant. Mark followed her gaze down the wharf until he landed on a sailor saying farewell to a woman. The lovers clasped hands, the man's forehead pressed against the woman's, and Mark could see the sailor's lips moving. He didn't need to hear to understand. The woman sobbed into his chest before his superior shouted for him to board.

Ma sighed before turning away and scanning the horizon. Mark couldn't be sure, but sometimes he wondered if Ma waited for his father to return from one of his voyages. To return from the dead.

Having never met the man, Mark did not think to miss him. But Ma's eyes brimmed whenever Mark asked questions.

"My darling child," his mother once said when tucking him into bed, "the greatest joy and greatest mistake of my life was loving a sailor." Ma sang songs as she worked, as she scrubbed clothes or carved spiraling skins off of pale potatoes—songs of fishermen's wives, songs she'd learned from seafarers, and songs so old that no one knew where they came from:

> *Found me a man who cut his heart in three,*
> *The wind, the waves, and sometimes me.*
> *One in two sailors make widows new.*
> *I raise a cold cup to my ocean of sorrow.*

Mark's innards squeezed, and he could no longer ignore the pressure in his gut.

"I'll be back, Ma," he said, leaving the bread in his mother's care. She nodded absently, understanding, as Mark scurried off to find a place where he could squat out of sight.

He clambered down rock stairs to the underside of a bridge. Then, as Ma insisted, he checked to make sure he was completely alone. When Mark pulled down his trousers, he froze.

Red. He was sticky with blood, his inner legs stained like a butcher's knife.

His breath hitched.

I'm dying.

His pulse hammered. Ma praised Mark for not being easily frightened—not of the dark, not of strangers, not even of Mr. Robert's feisty cat who lived on the opposite side of the thin wall.

But now, Mark was terrified.

I'm not ready to die!

Forgetting his urge to urinate and the pain in his abdomen, Mark yanked up his trousers. Blood had soaked through the backside, a cold feeling made all the colder as he sprinted back to the wharf.

Ma was haggling with a merchant. Mark repressed every impulse in his body to not interrupt the sale until it was complete.

"Thank you, sir. Good day," Ma called after the buyer, that slight singsong quality to her voice fully returned.

How Mark longed to stay quiet. To not burden his mother with this news. It would break her heart. It would break his own heart to leave her.

"Ma," Mark said, his mouth dry.

Her face fell as she took in his distress. She knelt down.

Mark drew close, whispering into her ear.

She snapped upright, gaze darting in both directions.

"I'm sorry, I—" Mark said.

"None of that rubbish. It is *I* who am sorry," Ma said with gentleness. She rooted through the bags and baskets until she removed a tattered shawl. "You're not dying, darling," she said, with an urgency so quiet that Mark alone could hear it. The firm confidence put Mark at ease. Ma wrapped the shawl around Mark's shoulders, gauging the length.

"Ma?"

"Listen closely," Ma said. Their mirroring mahogany eyes were level, serious. "I'll explain this—all of it—tonight." Her eyes pooled, like she did whenever she spoke of Mark's father. Her unmistakable remorse left Mark feeling unsettled. "Go home and wash. Don't let a soul see the blood. You understand, my dear? Clean yourself up, then start on dinner." Ma exhaled, then glanced at the remaining baskets. She smiled a sad smile as she placed a cool hand on Mark's cheek. It was tender enough to make his eyes water. "I'll return as soon as I've sold the rest. And not a moment longer."

Later that night, Ma took Mark's hands in hers. "Do you remember," Ma said, her eyes intent and her back facing the crackling hearth, "all the times I've said that you are different from other boys?"

"Yes," Mark said, cradling his knees on his sleeping mat in their rented single room. Ma had reminded him of this difference often and urged discretion about this mysterious point. His difference had remained unnamed, but Mark knew enough. To avoid questions about his parentage. To dodge gossip about his and Ma's circumstances. To avert his gaze from bathing bodies. To squat away from any prying eyes while other boys urinated against the wall or into open gutters with body parts that looked altogether different from Mark's own.

He'd known. Hadn't he always known?

Had he not *wanted* to know the truth? If not knowing made Ma happy?

The bowls from the fish stew Mark had made were cold and untouched on the table. At his feet lay a neatly folded towel and a wash bin. Mark was "on the rag," as it turned out. Not dying.

"And this . . . menstruation . . . is what makes me no longer a boy?" Mark asked, staring hard at the floorboards. This unpleasant queasiness felt more like a painful inconvenience than a grand rite of passage. If he wasn't dying as he'd feared, why was it this, of all things, that required everything to change?

Ma winced. "Not exactly. This was my fault—a ruse to protect you. Our survival depends on the goodwill of a distant relative who thinks you are a son, not a daughter. It's a long story. But I didn't want you to carry the weight of a constant lie—the haunt that eats me alive every day. It seemed too cruel a thing to ask a child to do. I see now that deceiving you was a fool's errand. Your bleeding reminds me that this fantasy cannot go on. I fear I've done more harm than good."

Silent tears dripped off Mark's chin. Despite the shock, another part of him felt a sense of relief, like he might no longer feel itchy in his own skin. That he'd not been wrong in watching sailors' wives at the docks, wishing he too might wear a long skirt that rustled as he walked. Or that he'd desired, since before he could remember, to be seen as lovely like Ma—without knowing in full what that meant.

Ma pulled Mark into a hug, rocking him with soothing sounds.

"I'm so sorry, darling. I thought we had more time. I saw no other way. But I was wrong."

Mark felt his heart swell with a mix of affirmation and sorrow, all tinged with anger. *Anger?* Had he ever been angry at his mother? He'd trusted Ma completely.

"Do you want to eat?" Ma asked.

"No," Mark said, rubbing his nose and puffy eyes.

"Do you want to rest? I can tell you more tomorrow."

"No, I'm ready," Mark said, trying to sound as old and wise as she was. "Tell me everything."

Ma kissed the top of his head. "Very well, there is a lot to say," she said, taking a deep breath. "But to begin, your name is Mary."

The sound rang like a bell, vibrating from his ears to his toes. *Mary.* The name that Ma had given him—no, *her*. As Mark—*Mary*—huddled against the drafty hearth and listened to Ma that night, she missed nothing of Ma's words, committing each startling phrase and revelation to memory.

There had been a firstborn, a son christened as Mark. The real Mark. A legitimate child.

A brother.

There had been not one, but *two* sailors. A husband lost to the depths in a storm. Then, a lover—Mary's father—lost to the noose for piracy. Ma was with child when the news spread. She, along with a group of forty-seven other women, begged Queen Anne to pardon the men, speaking to their skills and goodness. But it all came to naught. That mental image of a man dangling from the end of a rope caused Mary to shudder.

Ma had moved herself and the first baby Mark in with friends living in the country, where she could give birth to a new baby in secret so that her husband's distant family, whose charity she relied upon, would not withdraw their aid when they learned about her illegitimate child.

A bastard, Mary translated. A common enough insult at the docks.

"Do you understand?" Ma asked, explaining her firstborn's

early death to fever shortly after Mary was born. The floodwaters of grief. How Mary had been dressed and brought up as him for a crown a week—the thing that paid the rent even now.

"Can you forgive me?" Ma whispered.

Mary nodded. Her anger toward Ma felt foreign, like a bee-sting welt, and she longed for it to fade. Her mind snagged on the particulars as each piece moved into place, like all those ships taking berth at the dock. Finally, an honest accounting of her life.

A brother dead. To be missed forever.

A father lost.

"I have made many mistakes in my life," Ma said. "But you were never one of them."

A crown a week to survive.

"Say something?" Ma urged, wiping away a fresh set of tears. "You can hit me if you wish. As hard as you like." But the joke made little sense, as Ma had never raised so much as a finger against her.

Mary blinked, dazed but suddenly quite hungry. This change would take time to absorb. All the rules of a baffling game that she'd believed to be unchanging.

For the rest of the night, Mark was too exhausted to be Mary, to learn *how* to be Mary. He took a seat at the table, and Ma followed. His mother appeared pale and nervous in a way Mark had not seen. His heart ached for Ma. For all the losses she'd suffered. The pain from a sea of secrets.

He hoped he made Ma's life better—for Ma never once made him feel like a burden. That despite it all, the two of them could be enough. A family. Even as a bastard daughter.

"What do we do now?" Mark asked before picking up a spoon. His stomach still pained him, and he wasn't sure how much was due to hunger, this newfound ache called womanhood, or Ma's accounts.

Ma leaned back in the chair and ran a finger over the rough grain of the table. "I don't know. There's still much to teach you about the world and a woman's place in it—things no child should have to hear. But no more secrets between us. This time, whatever tomorrow brings, we'll decide on the path together. You have my word." Her voice broke as she reached out a hand. "And my whole beating heart."

CHAPTER 8

London, England
1697

"Are you a simpleton, lad?" the butler hissed in Mary's direction. "Take Lady Barton's horses to the stable."

Mary's attention snapped up from the dark eyes of the gelding at the front right of the carriage's team. She'd been struck by the lovely eyelashes and gentleness of the beast, much more so than the noblewomen who now greeted them outside the estate.

"Yes, sir. My apologies," Mary said quickly. She made it a point to avoid the butler's stern attention. Mary kept her head down and led the four hackney horses—their glossy, chestnut coats shining in the rare spring sun—toward the carriage house. The sound of their hooves and the cart's wheels on the pebbled path felt as rhythmic and calming as a heartbeat.

Mary had spent the past two years grappling with her situation. The fact that she was a bastard, had a brother who died, and would now cramp and bleed for nearly a week out of every month—a rubbish bargain, even if Mary's bleeding was inconsistent. Ma had been clear that they could start fresh, with Mary trading in her trousers for a secondhand dress. As a girl, Mary could have continued to scrimp by at the docks, or she could have sought hire as a maid in a fine house. But Mary's lean, thirteen-year-old body was in no hurry to become a woman's, and she made twice as much coin as a stable boy for the Goodwins than she would have as a maid. Very little, but still. She and Ma needed money more than ever. To Mary, the choice to continue dressing as a boy was obvious. The relative of Ma's husband had passed away, taking the crown per week payment with them to the grave.

And yet, Mary now knew herself to be a girl. She felt the ache of others not seeing her as one. But she'd settled on this disguise for now. She had gone by Mary at home these past two years, but in public she was still Mark.

The horses snorted as they reached the carriage house. Their noises made Mary smile. Such beautiful animals. She felt more at ease with them than the people she worked alongside. Mary was soon met by the head groom and two other stable boys, who unhitched the cart. The stable team removed the harnesses, wiping them down with leather oil before putting them away for the duration of the Bartons' one-week stay.

"A fine meal soon," Mary cooed to the gelding, patting his muscular neck as she finished brushing him down. As the other boys saw to the rest of the horses, she led the gelding to a stall with fresh hay and a brimming bucket of water. Closing the stall behind them, Mary looked over her shoulder, saw she was alone, and pulled a skinny apple core out of her pocket.

The gelding, velvet nose buried in hay, would not be bothered.

"Such politeness, and this after I saved that final bite for you?" she tsked. She tossed the sweet treat into the heap, wiped her sticky hands on her trousers, then went to find a shovel. She needed to muck out the other end of the barn.

That's when her eyes alighted on something shiny in the straw in the far corner stall. She stooped and picked up what appeared to be a woman's wedding band. She turned the gold ring over in her palm. Her eyes bulged, taking in its brilliant sheen.

What would something like this cost?

Enough for Ma to rent a better room. Enough to buy boots that didn't soak Mary's feet when it rained. Meat with every meal.

She exhaled. Before she could stop herself, Mary ran to find the head butler. She knocked on the grand door of the Goodwins' estate. The butler excused himself.

Once the door shut behind his heels, his eyes found her and his tone changed. "What is the meaning of this?" he roared. "I'm attending to Lady Barton and her daughters."

Mary gulped but stood tall. "Sir, I found this." Extending her hand and explaining, she saw the fury in the butler's beady eyes extinguish.

"You discovered it in the barn?"

"Yes, sir." How such a lovely possession came to be there, she could only guess. But she was not hired to speculate on the Goodwins or their visitors.

He studied the treasure, then looked at her anew. "The Goodwins appreciate your service, and so do I." He shifted his weight, arms folded over his tight gray waistcoat. "How long have you been with us, Mark?"

"Just over a year, sir."

A smile crossed his thin lips. "Well, Mark. I think it is far time we gave you a raise, then. And how about the rest of the day off? How does that sound?"

"Thank you, sir," Mary said, suppressing a grin. She bowed to the butler before the door clicked. She counted one heartbeat, then two, before bolting to tell Ma.

An hour later, Mary rounded the corner onto the dense housing block where she and Ma lived. She panted, her head spinning from the run. Catching her breath, an arm reached out and yanked her into an alley.

Mary yelped. "Ma?"

"Shh," Ma said. "Did they find you?" Her eyes were wide with panic. "Did they come looking at the Goodwins'?"

They?

"I don't understand," Mary said, eager to wipe away Ma's unease. Why wasn't she at the docks, where Mary hoped to surprise her? She leaned into her mother's chest, the comforting smell of fresh bread, sweat, and sea air. "The butler sent me home early. I got a raise!"

Ma heaved a sigh, which confused Mary. "I thought I'd have to wait until nightfall for your return," Ma said, cradling Mary close and smoothing her hair. "Everything is all right, my dear. But I need you to listen carefully." Ma whipped her head around, saw they were alone, then opened the bag at her feet. She pulled out some oversized men's clothes, including a wool cap and a brown leather jerkin. When she looked up, Mary saw tears in Ma's eyes. "Quickly change, darling. We are not safe here anymore. I'll explain on the way."

They took the long way to the wharf, along curving side roads. The ribbon holding Mary's straight dark hair had fallen out. With one hand, Ma clutched Mary's hand tighter than Mary had ever known—even as a young child—and with the other hand, Ma held a scarf that shielded her face. Mary lumbered forward in the new clothes, cap bouncing above her brow and heart pounding, as Ma told her the details of Mr. Robert's betrayal.

"Mr. Robert?" Their neighbor? Mary had taken pride in finally befriending his fussy cat.

"Walls have ears—and more heart than greedy men," Ma whispered with a distinct bite. "He knows who you really are and that he'd fetch a fine price for the knowledge."

"For knowing who I am? Why?"

"For telling my mother-in-law's heir." The conversation cut off when they spotted a pair of redcoats. Ma led Mary off the path into a blacksmith shop. The thick smells of red-hot iron and singed horse hooves greeted them at once.

"What'll it be?" growled a man with a thick drawl.

Ma studied the weapons through the smoke. Her eyes lingered on a knife.

Mary kept her mouth closed, trying to fathom Ma wielding a blade. But Ma dug into her pockets and counted the few coins in her palm.

"Nothing today," Ma said to the blacksmith before uttering a prayer. Mary heard her mother's voice crack. Ma's voice never cracked.

They left without buying anything. She turned to Mary. "Will you hold this for me, darling?" And before Mary could answer, she'd slipped the coins into her pocket.

After the soldiers had passed, Ma and Mary ventured through the street with renewed haste. Mary wanted to throw her arms around Ma. She wanted to go home and make shortbread biscuits. But her boots moved, and she breathed through the fear.

"Miss Marlow tipped me off—found me after the brutes broke in and tore apart our room," Ma said. Mary noted how much calm she tried to summon through this retelling. "The living relatives are demanding the money back in full."

"But that's impossible," Mary said, louder than she intended.

Ma tightened her grip as they strode forward. "They favor throwing us in debtors' prison. Or selling us as indentured servants. Mary, I'm sorry, my dear girl. I'm sorry for it all."

They passed carts and shops, carriages and idle fishermen, the smell of the harbor growing stronger as they neared.

"But they can't. Surely they can't do that," Mary said. "What about my raise? Will it not help?"

"Hard earned, I know, my darling. You've turned out so well, so good. No one will haul either of us away if I can prevent it," Ma said with a determination that could make God himself shake on his throne. "And I can. I *will*. No more mistakes." This time, there was no question. Ma was crying.

"Ma?"

Hearing Ma's pain made Mary's own eyes spring with tears, never mind that Mary was breaking the unspoken rules—crying in plain view while wearing boy's clothes.

Men's clothes.

But Mary and Ma were off again, the topsails of large ships visible from the bridge.

"Wait here," Ma whispered once they reached the waterfront. "I'll stay close." Ma kissed Mary on the brow, lingering there a moment, and pulled Mary's cap so it sat lower on her forehead. Then, adjusting her own scarf and wiping away her tears, Ma set off with the intensity of a hunter.

Mary folded her arms over the jerkin covering her new shirt, large and baggy even with the cuffs rolled. She felt silly, drowning in her new attire. She knew Ma would have a reasonable explanation. Even now, with Ma's strange behavior and terrible tales, as hawkers and fishmongers eddied around her with their pungent catches, as if this was any ordinary day.

A strong swell knocked into the pier. Her chest tightened, the warm glow from the butler's praise long gone. Maybe she should have pocketed the ring. Where would she and Ma go now, with so little coin? Ma's countryside friends, who'd attended to her in Ma's hour of greatest need, had moved years ago without leaving word of their new address. And everyone on their London block would recognize Ma or Mary—or rather, Mark—and might seize the opportunity for a petty reward. Who could they trust?

Trust Ma, Mary told herself as a gust of wind slammed into her. *Ma will take care of us.*

When she returned, Ma smiled and exhaled with what appeared to be relief, though her mouth was lined with sorrow. "I have a plan," she said firmly, taking Mary's hand like she had years earlier, when Mary was still a young child accompanying her to sell bread. Ma led her through the press of bodies until they reached the top of the docks and stood in front of a familiar vessel flying England's colors.

Ma knelt down, still clutching Mary's hands in hers. "Captain Southwick," Ma said, "has agreed to take you on his merchant ship."

A shadow crept into Mary's heart. She glanced up, where she could make out the figure of Captain Southwick, the older gentleman who'd always bought hardtack from Ma. "What about you?" Mary asked.

More tears filled Ma's eyes, and Mary collapsed with despair into her arms.

"Shh," Ma soothed, rocking Mary in a hug and speaking softly. "Listen carefully, my baby. My darling, darling girl. I know this isn't easy. I know this is a moment both of us will carry for the rest of our lives. So remember, please remember and hear what I have to say. Maybe someday you will understand."

Mary could form no words. Ma pulled back for just a moment and held Mary's shoulders firmly.

"These clothes were your pa's. Your *real* pa. A good man, I'll swear it until the end. God rest his soul."

Mary's lip quivered.

"Captain Southwick was a friend to your pa. He too is a good man, someone of influence—an educated fellow," Ma continued. "A kind gentleman who runs a good ship. We can put our faith in him. He can make something of you."

Finally, Mary's flood of emotions became words. "When will I see you again?"

Ma's face crumpled, but then she put on a smile and threw her arms around Mary, enveloping her like a blanket warmed by the hearth.

"This is the hardest part of what I have to say," Ma said at last, with pinched deliberation. "But I need you to listen. Are you listening, Mary?"

She nodded furiously, not minding that Ma called her by her true name in public. Because to Mary, there was no one else in the world except her and Ma.

"I tried to give you everything I could in this life, and it hasn't been enough."

"It *has* been enough," Mary said as tears flowed down her cheeks, her head resting on Ma's shoulder. "We have everything we need. We have each other."

Ma exhaled. "Heed everything I have to say, darling. There

are better jobs, more secure ways in the world, for a boy than a girl. I've told you this is so. But you'll never rise to any station as a stable boy, coming home to me and worrying about our basic welfare at every opportunity. And now, we have a debt on our heads."

"I don't want any other job," Mary cried. "And I'm earning more now."

"I know, my dear. But as God lives and granted me the gift of being your mother, I want you to *live* a life. Not just survive one. Not just scurry from fear to fear, in search of a place to rest your head and troubles. If I'd been born a man . . ." At this, Ma choked, and then began again. "If I'd been born a man, there's so much more I could have done to prevent this heartache. But I am not a man. Just as you are not. But for now, my love, my heart, you *can* be—for a precious few more years. And I need you to promise me something."

Mary held Ma like it was answer enough.

"Promise me, my child, that you will not come looking for me. That you will not come back."

"I can't promise that," Mary said at once, shaking her head and smearing tears on Ma's scarf. "I won't do that. Never."

Ma rocked her in her arms. "The trouble of being a woman, Mary, is that women take care of everyone else before ever getting the chance to start their own lives. And a woman like me? In my circumstances?" she huffed. "There is no climbing up. I am a risk to both of us. But for you? A ship's boy making a modest wage, making his way in a proper trade? By the sweat of your own labor, *you* might have better. *You* might get a wonderful chance to truly live. Not just the life that was handed to you, in this hovel corner of the world. But the life I wanted for you. The life you deserve. One with choice. Freedom. Until the day when you no longer need or want to pretend. When you can be safe and also true to who you are."

Mary's breath snagged and she struggled for air, but she heard every troubling word.

"I can do this and still come back. I'll work hard, then return to look after you. I'll pay the debt, I will! I'll find you."

"I know you would," Ma said, with another embrace that threatened to crack the earth in two. "That is why you can't. That is why I must flee—somewhere where these brutes won't find me. And most importantly, where they will never find you."

"No," Mary said, shaking her head again.

No.

Ma took Mary's hand and led her to the gangplank of Captain Southwick's ship. Mary felt limp, like her soul had been dragged out of her. But she followed her mother's sturdy steps as they boarded the merchant vessel. How did she dare move? Mary did not know. She would spend years looking at this moment, replaying it in her mind. The trust between her and Ma stretched out like a taut rope, invisible, and yet a powerful tether all the same. Mary fought to breathe. She tried and tried to breathe as she absorbed her surroundings: men pulling at lines thicker than snakes, another man shouting orders to take in the aft sail, a circle of others pushing their full force against a wheel to lift the anchor chain. The deck rocked beneath her, an unsettling motion. She'd never been on so much as a rowboat.

"Welcome to the crew, Mark Read. We're so pleased you've joined us," Captain Southwick said. He wore a tricorn and a blue waistcoat with brass buttons. "You've arrived just in time; we are ready to make way. My second-in-command will show you to your hammock and give you a tour of the ship once we leave the harbor."

Mary looked up and blinked, taking in his wrinkles, his gray wig, and his well-fed belly. She'd never studied him, never truly seen him. He had only been the kind man who purchased Ma's supplies. Did he know her father well? Did he know where she'd find Ma again?

I'll find you, Mary vowed, whirling to face her mother.

"Take care of my son," Ma said, holding her chin high and

speaking with authority. "Watch after him, Captain. Care for him as if he were your own."

"I'll do everything I can," Captain Southwick said, clapping a hand on Mary's shoulder.

"Ma," Mary said. She pulled away from the captain, and, trembling, fell back into her mother's arms. She didn't care if it made her appear weak.

"You'll learn to be a man now, Mark," Ma said. And Mary winced at the shift. "Be brave. You are, and always will be, the greatest joy of my life. Remember what I said. What I taught you. I love you. Don't look back."

It was Captain Southwick who finally pulled Mary away from Ma. Mary felt as if her head were underwater. She could make out none of the final words the captain and Ma exchanged before Ma descended the gangplank.

Mary ran for the rail, staring down at her Ma with shock and disbelief as Ma began to walk away. The shouts of the crew and sounds of the moving ship surrounded her.

Look back, Mary begged. Her vision blurred from weeping.

Her mother moved on through the crowd, slow and heavy. Mary wiped her eyes and squinted, careful not to lose sight of her.

Please look back.

"To your positions," a man behind her barked at the others. Someone blew a whistle. The ship lurched forward, and Mary gripped the rail to keep her balance.

"Come with me, lad," Captain Southwick said with tenderness, suddenly at her side. "It's no use pining."

She didn't hear him or his steps moving away. Instead, Mary stood frozen at the rail, staring at her mother shrinking, until at last, Ma did turn around.

Scarf clutched to her chin, Mary watched Ma tremble, a finger pressed to her mouth. They locked eyes, or so Mary imagined, as they moved farther and farther away from each other.

Ma raised her hand, extending it out. Mary raised her own with a limp wave, the baggy sleeve falling down her forearm.

Ma did not move again. She stood steadfast and watched, fixed forever though the distance grew. Mary's throat burned. Waves crashed against the hull. Her head pulsed and her raw eyes burned from the briny air.

But Mary did not budge. Not for minutes, maybe hours. Not until the dock was a gash of dark against the gray-blue horizon.

Only then did Captain Southwick return. "This way, lad," he said softly. "I'll introduce you to the crew and Master Tansley, my first mate."

Mary peered up at him.

He considered her in silence, then beamed. "I remember well the day I set out on my first voyage," he said. "It gets easier, lad. I promise."

Mary blinked and remembered to breathe again. She wasn't sure how long she'd been holding her breath. It was only then that Mary realized the coins were still in her pocket. What about Ma?

How would she live?

"You'll start off working in the galley like all cabin boys," Captain Southwick said. "But if you are anything like your pa, you'll serve best with a ring dial and a sounding weight in hand. I'll see to your training myself."

"Sir?" Mary managed to utter.

"Time will tell, lad, but keen navigation runs in your blood."

CHAPTER 9

Atlantic Ocean
1701

Mary panted against the ropes, her back horizontal to the ship's deck forty feet below. To fall from the mainmast from this height, she knew, would be instant death.

She would be a fool to let her fear show. Men—she'd learned in her careful study—came in every shape and size and temperament.

But masking fear? This seemed a common feature.

Settling her nerves, Mary steadied her pulse and pushed her strong legs into the spiderweb of slanted lines, climbing a horizontal ladder. She'd breathe easier if she hadn't bound her small breasts. The shirt she wore, her father's shirt, fit better than it had four years earlier. She wore it sparingly now, a threadbare treasure for days when she needed luck or when her other shirt sorely needed a wash. A red kerchief covered her tanned neck, and she kept her dark hair tied at the nape.

At last, she flung her body onto the maintop platform. It wobbled under her weight. *Another trip aloft, another day alive.*

"What do you make of these shoals, Mark?" shouted Captain

Southwick from far below. Captain Southwick stood beside Master Tansley. It had taken years for Mary to notice the pleasant quality of the brooding first mate's face. But now that she had, she'd never allow herself to study it again.

Mary's empty stomach lurched as she used the spyglass to squint at the variants of blue in the sea. They'd waited days in this windless stretch as the sun beat down like a tyrant. They were supposed to arrive in Provincetown weeks ago to deliver their liquor cargo and pick up a load of timber due in Liverpool. The whole reeking crew was restless, stricken and weary with heat.

Mary studied the ominous shadows on the water. The bright sun overhead created glares on the surface, but the captain relied on Mary's vision. She'd risen from cabin boy to serving in Tansley's defense drills by sprinting from cannon to cannon as a powder monkey, running black dust to the gunners. Finally, at seventeen, she'd mastered her navigation training and become the sailing master's best assistant. Mary had beheld America's shores during vibrant, wooded summers and stark, bitter winters. She'd seen ports across all of England, but they all blurred together in her mind with their grit and gray and fish and fog. Back and forth, back and forth. She'd developed calluses on her palms and strength in her otherwise thin body. She was at least a foot taller—a young man now, according to the crew. She'd learned to shape the naturally low resonance of her voice to speak with more monotone and less variation, moving the source of her voice downward into the deepest cavern of her chest. Her livelihood and chance of finding Ma someday depended on her performance. Not a day went by that she didn't think about Ma. Alone, Mary practiced dropping her pitch on more difficult sounds by using a mantra of her own making: *This work is often awful, but not always.*

Often awful, but not always.

"We're so damn close," Master Tansley cursed as he looked up at the limp sails. Mary felt the crew's eyes bore into her with anticipation.

All these years of hiding bloodied rags and concocting creative schemes to urinate, and still no one had guessed her most guarded secret. Not even the generous Captain Southwick. She'd dedicated years to investing in a lie, and the weight pressed on her like an anchor.

"Too shallow in patches," Mary yelled below with calm clarity, knowing well the rumors of Cape Cod waters. This knowledge was more powerful than all the pressure to press ahead, more important than her own pining for a bath and a proper meal. "We can't risk this route, Captain."

Captain Southwick groaned and removed his tricorn, fanning his red face. But he didn't challenge her. "We'll sail for deeper waters and approach the harbor from the south."

"Very well," she heard Tansley say in a tone indicating that he found this not very well at all. Mary felt relief in his disapproval. Her stomach squirmed at the thought of his *approval*, which was out of the question. But Tansley and the ship's leadership, along with Captain Southwick, were no halfwits and had little interest in running aground.

Mary climbed down the swaying mainmast as Tansley oversaw positions and the bosun whistled for order. Much as she hated delivering bad news, Mary knew somehow that practicing caution sharpened her instincts, even and especially when impatience, urgency, and human frailty were present in a situation. Those qualities had the same blinding effect as fear. And fearful people made terrible decisions.

Step by step, Mary lowered herself until her feet touched the smooth planks.

She could afford no mistakes.

When they finally arrived in Provincetown Harbor a week later, the wharf hummed with energy. Hawkers approached with more than their usual goods.

"Did ye hear?" one man yelled, waving a broadsheet newspaper at incoming transport boats.

"War! England is at war with Spain!" another shouted down the pier.

War? Mary stepped from the rowboat onto the pier and tried to wrap her mind around the faraway-sounding word. The only war of her short lifetime was the War of the Grand Alliance against France, though she'd never seen its evidence while it raged. *War,* she repeated. She felt nothing: no fear, no excitement. Nothing but a strange void in her chest. But maybe she'd feel more once she had a corncake in her belly, one slathered with honey.

With a single look, Master Tansley silenced the murmurs. He turned to Captain Southwick, who wore his usual blue waistcoat and appeared unsurprised by the development. The two leaders exchanged hushed words. After an agonizing wait, Master Tansley read the names of the men who were to stay behind. Mary, to her relief, was not among the first guards. Another set of sailors hefted and rolled the cargo onto the wharf and into the care of a buyer.

"Off with the rest of you," Tansley said to the remaining crew. The men sprang into motion. A few snapped up newspapers while others laughed and hurtled their way toward Great Island Tavern or to secure beds at the Black Sands Inn. Mary waited for the stampede to slow before moving. Captain Southwick put a hand on her shoulder.

"Mark, might I have a word?"

Mary tried not to think about corncakes. The smell of seagrass. Priceless privacy. But something in her beloved captain's face, the creases in his forehead, commanded attention. "Of course."

He gave a coin to a gap-toothed man distributing newspapers and pocketed the parchment. They walked toward the gray-shingled cottages in town as wispy clouds trailed overhead. Captain Southwick peered around. When they passed the throngs at the Wren's Inn, where most seafarers stopped, he finally spoke. "If it is true what they say, swift change is upon us."

"Sir?" She tried to puzzle out Captain Southwick's behavior. Though she saw the captain as a kind of grandfather, they were not equals. He respected her, but in front of others, he did not confide in her or ask her opinion beyond navigational matters. To show preference would breach rank and sour the crew toward her.

White sand blew onto the long road connecting the entire town. Through the grimy window of the Eight Bells Tavern, they saw a middle-aged barmaid mending a curtain. No patrons sat inside.

"Come, I'll buy you a drink," the captain said, opening the door.

A musty odor permeated the room. Captain Southwick ordered two mugs of ale. Though Mary was well-accustomed to alcohol as part of a sailing diet on a liquor merchant ship, she disliked the way it burned her throat and left her thirstier. Ma had said that too much liquor made even good men lose their minds. Mary had seen as much among her fellow sailors, their slurred speech and sharp words, and felt little inclination to join in their excessive drinking.

But maybe resentment tainted her opinion. She couldn't afford to drop her guard, her attention, her position. She couldn't afford the privilege of escaping into a mug. A second of irresponsibility could cost her, and Ma, everything. She could not be like the other men. Because she wasn't one.

"What do you know of world affairs, Mark?"

"Not much. Everything I know of the world I learned from you or aboard your ship."

"Have you followed the gossip regarding the Spanish king's death?"

She'd heard some tales at various ports and the musings of fellow sailors. But what did the lives of kings have to do with her? She avoided politics and strong opinions; those only drew attention. "No, sir."

The barmaid set down a pair of tankards with disinterest before returning to her mending. Captain Southwick took an enormous gulp, then stared off as he continued. "King Charles II left no heir to Spain's throne. Rotten timing, with world powers playing chess—and more than a dozen nations fancying themselves the rightful rulers." He caught her eye, maybe detecting her unease. "I don't say this to scare you, Mark. But this is no trifling matter." He leaned forward on his elbows. He had that paternal look with a furrowed brow that Mary had come to recognize—affection from a man who'd taken her in. "This will be a war among many nations. Not just any kind of war. One fought on land and sea. Do you comprehend the significance?"

A shiver ran down her spine, and she took a sip. "No, sir." She might have pretended more knowledge with anyone else, but she didn't need to with Captain Southwick. "That is, I don't understand why you are telling me this."

Only then did he remove the newspaper from his jacket and spread it out on the table. Mary scanned the bold letters. Though she could read a compass, she couldn't read this.

"It's as I feared. I wouldn't be surprised if a third of our crew were to join the Royal Navy once we reach England," he said with a sigh. "I did as much as a boy. How old are you?"

"Seventeen."

"I joined the Royal Navy a few years younger than you." He circled the ale in his mug. "Despicable place, a navy ship. Overcrowded. Cruel superiors. Frequent food shortages. Irregular pay at best. Vicious punishments."

Mary feared corporal punishment above all; it would expose everything.

"I saw more than a few decent men die from lashes. And illness. Oh, the illness on a ship like that." He shook his head and his eyes seemed to water at this confession. Mary looked at her hands in case this display of emotion caused him shame, as seemed the custom for many men.

"I promised your mother I'd look after you as if you were my own son."

Ma. The mention of her made Mary's insides squeeze.

"Don't worry about me, Captain," Mary said, eager to dismiss his concerns. "I have no plans of leaving your crew. This ship is my home." In truth, the ship was more than a home. It was everything. The source of her wages and structure and friendships, however guarded. The place where she savored hard-won satisfactions and honed her skills and mind. The ship was her nights and days that inched her closer to financial freedom. For her, Ma, and whatever they might do, wherever they might go together.

Captain Southwick's eyes crinkled. They were still a bit damp with feeling. "If you were my son—and understand me, Mark, nothing would make me prouder," he began again. "I would not have you stay on my merchant ship for a scrap of pay for every ocean crossing. I'd want something more for you."

Mary felt herself falling, though her body remained rigid in the chair with a grip on her cup. Falling into an old pain, an old memory.

No. Mary wanted to say. Scream.

Not you, too.

Captain Southwick ordered another ale, making sure the barmaid was out of the room before talking again.

"I will speak candidly. War is a curse as well as an opportunity. For a young man like you, with your training, it might seem obvious to join the navy. But don't throw away your life on the sea. Not even another year."

"But my talents, my trade?" Mary protested. She no longer had Ma at her side, but she clung tight to her advice.

He held up a hand. "Hear my reasoning first. For an attentive young person like yourself, there is another path I'd advise you to consider: the cavalry."

"Fighting on land?" Mary imagined herself holding a weapon, charging an enemy line. It revolted her.

"On horseback."

A faint ember in her glowed at the mention of horses, but it quickly extinguished.

"Holland will be far enough from the enemy lines," Southwick continued. "Assuming those hold, there will be no safer place to join." He tapped the broadsheet with a finger. "And no swifter way for a clever, clear-eyed young man to rise through the ranks."

"Why not the navy?"

"The sea battles will be much bloodier—and they were wretched in my youth. So many countries will engage this time." Captain Southwick leaned back, lost in what must have been memory. "Besides, the navy is too rigid, too old. Too many numbskulls at the top."

Mary took a swig of bitter ale.

"Trust the words of an old man who's seen more than enough. Do not repeat my mistakes. You'll always have me, as a friend or an employer whenever you need one. Not even the king has use for an old sea dog like me in a war like this," he guffawed. "But do me this favor: Join the cavalry when we return to England. Apply that sound head of yours to making something of yourself. Rise to your full potential."

This kindness, this *seeing* her, made Mary want to sit up taller. She trusted him. A whisper of her believed his words. Another part wondered what he'd really believe about her if he knew the truth.

Or rather, her lie. That constant guilt lodged deeper inside her chest in the presence of the captain's care.

"Do it for me and for your ma."

His words were both a knife twist and an unshackling. She inhaled, dropping into that deep, calm place inside her. She didn't know how many more years she could successfully wear this disguise. But if it brought her more savings, more freedom for the unknown future? More comfort and security for her and Ma?

With Captain Southwick's blessing and confidence, she'd take her chances.

CHAPTER 10

Ink blotted Captain Johnson's parchment and stained his hand. He'd been sloppy, his swan quill flying as he captured Mary's words. Her tale proved even more extraordinary than he'd anticipated. A girl posing as a boy, moving through the world as a young man, undetected for so long? This female pirate business was proving to be a enterprise indeed. Who could resist such a tale? Beyond the shock, he felt something more in the story, something more in her. A surge of compassion. The genuine curiosity that drove his endeavor.

It didn't hurt if he could spin a profit from such an account, he comforted himself.

At that moment, he realized Mary had stopped speaking. She stared with unflinching dark eyes at the prison wall. Her shallow breathing reminded him of her present suffering and delicate condition. The stench of vomit returned him to his senses. The stiff, three-legged stool below him.

"Might I fetch you more water?" he asked, hoping he might urge her to continue. "I did call for a doctor." He needed this woman to carry on, at least for however many days or weeks his inquiries took. He rather hoped she'd pull through and live.

She's a convicted pirate, he had to remind himself. Regrettably, if she didn't die here of prison fever, the gallows would finish the job. He shivered.

Focus. He had to focus on his work.

"Did you join, then?" Johnson asked.

"Mmm?" Mary mumbled, followed by a long silence.

"Did you do as Captain Southwick advised?"

No answer.

"Did you join the cavalry in Holland?" he tried, a bit louder.

But she was already asleep.

CHAPTER 11

"You again." It was a statement, not a question. Her lower back ached and she did not rise from her cot. This scum didn't deserve it.

"Good morning, Miss Anne," Captain Johnson said in a chipper tone.

By the Devil's ass, was this buffoon capable of exhibiting any other emotion?

The captain welcomed himself to the rough-hewn stool, perching like a guest in a parlor. He carried the same leather bag of writing materials as before.

Clearing his throat, Johnson watched Anne covet his possessions. "I brought something that might cheer you up."

Anne's gaze narrowed, not betraying her growing interest. She knew his world and his game. She could outwit him.

He retrieved a guava from his bag, then held it out to her.

Whatever she'd expected, this wasn't it. The sight of anything beyond a pale crust of bread registered as a growl in her stomach.

"Local to Jamaica," Johnson said. "The name 'guava' comes from a Native word, I'm told. Slightly sweet and good for health."

"You can't buy me like a whore, Captain," Anne said, sitting up and folding her arms. Sweat circles drenched the armpits of her putrid, baggy shirt.

Your move.

To her annoyance, he did not react to the insult. Perhaps he thought she actually was a whore. It wouldn't be the first time someone assumed as much.

"It's a gift. No cost," he said.

"Everything has a cost."

He sighed with exasperation. Anne lifted her chin and stared at the chipped stone in the corner. She'd spent many hours studying that gray speck of rock.

"You don't have to say a word in exchange; you've made your disinterest in an interview clear. But do consider your unborn child. Your diet here is—"

She snapped her attention on him and cast daggers. "Less than favorable? Unsatisfactory? A disgrace to the oh-so-mighty Christian hearts of mine rock-hurling accusers?"

This, she noted, did surprise Johnson.

For a moment she said nothing. Then, she snatched the fruit from his damp palm and bit into the green skin. The tangy, pink meat inside did not disappoint. She sucked the pulp and tried to hide her delight.

"I had the privilege of meeting your friend."

Mary.

Mary, who'd been right about Captain Rackham. Who'd been right about everything.

Anne stopped licking the residue off her hands and watched him. Her heart hammered. They both knew the advantage had shifted in Johnson's favor. Damn him.

"How is she?" Anne asked with forced steadiness. She folded her arms atop her belly and held back the flood of words and questions.

A shadow of sorrow crossed his face. "Not well, I'm afraid. She claims the fever comes and goes."

Anne stiffened. An image from the last time she saw Mary, after their trial two months ago: Mary's dark eyes dazed, her whole body shivering despite the heat, the guards separating them and dragging Anne away.

"Tell me everything," Anne demanded.

To Johnson's credit, he did not withhold or negotiate. He gave his full, troubling report.

"She. Cannot. *Die*." Anne fumed between gritted teeth. She stood and paced the straw-covered floor. She clenched her fists and resisted the urge to scream.

"She needs constant care, I grant you that." Johnson shook his head. "These conditions are not meant for women in a delicate state."

Anne continued to pace. She detected genuine pity from this man, and she no longer knew what game the two of them were playing.

"Mary never deserved to be here," Anne said, head pressed against the stone. Her hair—the only physical feature she'd always tended to with a degree of vanity—now looked like the mane of an animal. A trapped, pathetic, vicious animal. Why was she talking? And of all people, to this blithering gombeen?

It's your fault she is here.

It's your fault Mary joined the crew.

Jesus, Mary, and Joseph. She needed Johnson. Not just for the paper and ink she hoped to procure—the price of her eventual cooperation with the captain. She needed his help now. Immediately. Until Anne could get them both out.

The baby kicked.

Right. Bloody hell. There were more than two lives to spare. Mary had understood that far longer than Anne.

But now it was too late.

Was it too late?

"What do you want from me?" Anne said, whirling on the captain. She stood above him, towering and attempting confidence. She had to at least pretend to drive a hard bargain.

He studied her carefully. "I already told you."

She huffed.

"Mary had no quarrels talking about her life," Johnson said, rubbing his palms on his knees. "She was quite frank."

This was the friend Anne knew. A woman who took no interest in hiding anymore.

"As a result, what she shared moved me, and I believe it will move others." Johnson paused. "Do you not think stories matter?"

Anne stifled a laugh. What practical use did stories have? But the question hit her like a blade to the gut. Her childhood in Ireland. Mam tucking the coverlet to her chin, rewarding a successful daily lesson with a bedtime story.

Stories were fiction, Anne retorted. *Lies.*

Mostly.

"If Mary departs this mortal realm, is it not better that something of her lives on in words?" Johnson continued. "Maybe forever?" His eyes gleamed in a way she didn't altogether like. "Would it not be better to give something of the truth about her to the world?"

"I've read enough to know stories have little to do with truth. Especially ones written by meddling pricks. Men who twist facts to suit their wicked fantasies disguised as righteous, rigid beliefs."

His brow arched. "You were educated. Brought up by a gentleman. That much is clear. So how does a young lady like you, at the onset of her life—and proved with child—end up here?" he said, gesturing around the room.

Anne sat on the saggy cot again. She placed her hands on the round of her stomach and stared hard at the ground.

This was her chance, her move.

"If I talk to you," Anne said. "And I mean *if*," she emphasized. "There are two things I require."

His posture shifted. "I'm listening."

"You must do everything in your power to convince the vermin who run this garrison to attend to Mary and her unborn baby."

"I called for a doctor."

Her eyes flashed. "I don't mean 'call for a doctor.' I mean *get* a doctor—even if that means you have to drag him by the bollocks. Ask Mary what she needs. Get it for her." Anne closed her eyes, wishing she could give Mary immediate freedom. She had a plan. But until then, what she'd give to offer a word of comfort. Anything to her friend.

Johnson raised a meaty finger to object.

"And I need evidence that you did more than try."

Lowering his hand, he nodded.

"That is my first request."

"That was," Johnson paused, counting, "technically three requests."

She scowled, though he seemed to have meant it as a joke.

Johnson cleared his throat. "Very well. The second request?"

Be careful, shouted every instinct in her body.

Trust is earned.

The last thing she wanted was to endanger more people than she already had.

"Paper," she said with boredom.

"Paper?"

"Yes. Paper and ink."

"What for?"

She shrugged.

Cards close to your chest.

Hook him like a fish first.

"I have a right to know."

"Then maybe I've had enough questions for one day."

He exhaled but looked more smug than outright concerned.

"We have a deal," he said, extending his sweaty hand.

Anne feigned disinterest, counted a few breaths, then shook it. She tucked her swollen bare feet under her and stared hard at Johnson while he took out his paper and inkwell, then balanced the desk on his lap.

"What grand tales do you wish to hear?" Anne asked. "Bargains with the Devil? Horrific murders and splendid plunders? Unchecked female depravity?"

Johnson's wiry brow shot up, almost touching his tricorn.

"That is what you are here for, is it not?" Anne said. "To write something salacious?"

He reddened. "I told you, Miss Anne. I'm here for your story. No matter what that entails."

She balked. "And if it's far more boring than you and your readers might hope?"

"I very much doubt that. If helpful, I'll pose a starting question: How did you get the name Bonny?"

Anne thought again of Mam: her ability to create a story out of thin air. Anne could imitate Mam if she tried. She could provide Johnson with entertainment. It mattered little to her—so long as Johnson upheld his end of their deal.

In the end, she decided to tell something like the truth. If memory can ever be called that.

CHAPTER 12

Charles Town, South Carolina
1716

A *thwack* on the desk startled Anne back into her history lesson.

"*En quelle année la guerre a-t-elle commencée?*" asked her new tutor, Monsieur Perrin, without a trace of impatience.

Anne blinked. The dappled leaves on the laurel oak outside the window disappeared as the face of her Huguenot tutor came into view. His gentle russet eyes behind spectacles. She'd longed for a tutor for years, realizing now how she'd glorified those days in Da's office when she was a child. Had she forgotten what serious study entailed?

Difficulty, however, did not diminish an education's importance—a wisdom Anne had at nineteen that she'd not enjoyed eleven years prior. And at her late age, she hadn't a moment to lose.

"Can you please repeat the question?" Anne asked. She worried this lengthy lesson might delay her first outing with Ellen Fulworth. The young lady had extended an invitation to shop for finery in preparation for her family's upcoming ball. "A real honor," Mam had declared.

Anne still didn't know what to wear. The proper way to style her red hair, which frizzed something terrible in South Carolina.

Monsieur Perrin offered a small smile. "Your mind seems elsewhere today," he said in English through a thick nasal accent.

"I'm sorry, sir," Anne said as a knot of shame coiled in her chest. Da invested significantly in these lessons now that he'd opened his law office in Charles Town last month. The loan, he assured, covered all manner of luxuries. Mam had the finest dresses—Anne, too. The lost years of struggling in London seemed a world away, replaced with parlor visits, sugar-dusted cakes, long church services on Sundays, and a doctor to cure Mam's cough. The supposed "London of the Low Country" boasted a varied society, though the Irish clung together like thistles.

"*Très bien.* Enough for today. We can continue the Hundred Years' War tomorr—"

"Thank you, Monsieur Perrin!" Anne was already gathering her books.

To Anne's relief, she arrived before Miss Fulworth at the agreed-upon spot. Smoothing down her hair, Anne observed riders on horseback and barkeeps sweeping thresholds. The roads here stretched out in long, straight rows. Buildings with multiple stories housed residences on the upper levels and businesses on the ground level. The butcher smoked meats while clusters of rough men swayed outside the Red Star Tavern.

A few feet to her left, Anne watched two dark-skinned women who sat beside a stack of baskets. Their fingers flew as they braided long strands of grass. One weaver leaned in to whisper something, which made the other let out a peal of laughter.

Were they cousins? Friends? Did they work for the same estate? She'd never seen people of such varied skin tones in Europe.

Anne felt her pocket, where she kept the money Da had given her. "Shopping for finery," as Ellen had called their planned excursion, clearly meant something beyond picking up supplies to make dinner—a task Anne still needed to do for Mam. And in her haste and fuss about clothes, she'd forgotten a satchel to carry her purchases. She could use a basket.

Anne took a step closer. "Are these for sale?" she asked.

The two women stopped speaking at her approach. One looked down while the other—who'd laughed earlier—held Anne's gaze with flashing eyes. "They can be." She named a price.

Anne took a small coin and, in return, the woman gave her a basket. Anne tied it to her belt, then studied the lovely weave. "I've never seen anything this intricate. What's the material?"

"Sweetgrass," the weaver said. "Sometimes bulrush. We use these to harvest rice."

Anne turned the basket over, surveying the tan-and-brown pattern. She'd become quite good at embroidery, but nothing to match this skill. "Where did you learn?"

"Mother to daughter, for generations. We—"

"There you are!" came a shout from across the street.

Anne turned to see Miss Fulworth hurtling toward her, one hand clutching her straw hat.

Offering a quick shrug of apology to the weavers, Anne dashed across the road to meet her.

"I thought you'd gotten lost," the young lady said, her violet-blue eyes dancing. "I searched the neighboring shops." She hooked an elbow through Anne's and steered her toward the wharf. This close, the beautiful Miss Fulworth smelled of lilies and ash soap. "Is your family settling in?" Her attention snagged on Anne's basket. "Ah. What do you think of Charles Town?"

How much to betray, how much to conceal? Anne stiffened, too aware of the arm wrapped effortlessly around hers. Anne hadn't experienced much opportunity to form friendships. With Da and Mam properly—secretly—married by a South Carolina preacher who knew nothing of Da's former wife, Anne had been elevated from bastard to gentleman's daughter. They were the Cormacs now, of the distinguished Cormacs of Ireland. Miss Ellen Fulworth of fine English breeding would not be impressed with the prejudice or financial suffering they'd experienced before arriving, and Mam—who'd bloomed in this society like a rose enjoying a late-summer growing season—wouldn't want the town knowing either. "The green reminds me of Ireland," Anne said. Her heart pulsed with recognition of that truth. "I'm sorry my lessons went long, Miss Fulworth."

"Ellen will do. What lessons?" She pulled a face as they threaded through the backstreets. Her expression didn't match her perfect, ebony curls. As the youngest daughter of a wealthy merchant who ran a warehouse filled with furniture, spices, cloth, and other coveted treasures, Ellen surely modeled what all refined ladies did.

"History. French. That kind of thing," Anne said with a dismissive casualness. Da had gone to great lengths, including debt, to support this dream. Why did she feel the need to minimize it for Ellen? The realization tasted sour on her tongue.

"Sounds dreadful, especially at our age," Ellen said as a gust pelted them from the harbor. A brigantine was sailing in, and the Ashley River sparkled beneath the lowering sun. "I went through countless governesses before my parents gave up. The only one I liked, they dismissed." Ellen threw her head back to laugh—far too dramatically—and Anne steadied her friend to keep her from crashing into a man pushing an apple cart.

Anne bit back a curse. "I never had a governess."

"Is it also true that your household doesn't employ help of any kind?" Ellen said.

Anne detected an evaluating tone in Ellen's words. "My mother is suspicious of servants." That felt safer than explaining Mam's past or that Mam—once a servant herself—had never let go of the pride of maintaining her own home. Anne fulfilled all the chores when Mam was too ill. But what did Ellen care?

"Such a curiosity," Ellen said with what sounded like relief. "You're nothing like the others here. It's about time I found a best friend like you."

Best friend? Her stomach flipped. Before Anne could come up with a response, Ellen stopped abruptly. She tugged on Anne's arm and untied her hat.

"Are you ready to 'shop'?" Ellen giggled.

Anne followed Ellen's line of vision to a pair of young sailors. Ellen dropped her black lashes as they passed. "Oh, no!" Ellen burst. Then, to Anne's confusion, Ellen knocked her own hat into the breeze.

"I have it," the taller of the sailors hollered as he chased the hat down the docks. The other, a sullen fellow with stringy blond hair, merely watched.

Anne's cheeks burned. She wondered what Mam would say about this brash behavior. What would Ellen's parents think?

If she wasn't so ashamed, Anne might have admired the hell out of Ellen. Anne hadn't been that untamed since her days of running with Seán O'Brien's pack.

"For you, Miss Fulworth," the tall sailor said, presenting the hat to Ellen on one knee as if she were a queen. Dimples punctuated his boyish grin.

Ellen removed her clapped palm from her lips and extended her hand. "How very kind, Mr. Taylor."

"Anything for you, Miss Fulworth," he beamed.

Anne shifted her weight, trying to make sense of a game she'd never played before. *She'd* been played. A pawn. A safe accomplice for this spectacle.

Did she mind, if these silly antics got her out of the house? Earned her a friend?

The sullen man looked at Anne, his gray eyes widening with sudden interest. He might be decent looking after a bath. But Anne broke his gaze, distracted by Ellen's theatrics.

"Ah, forgive me. Where are my manners?" said Mr. Taylor. He gestured toward his companion. "Ladies, this is Mr. James Bonny."

"A pleasure," Ellen said. "I haven't seen you before."

"I'm new to this port," Mr. Bonny muttered. When Anne finally glanced up, he was still staring at her.

"My dear friend is also recently arrived," Ellen said. "May I introduce Miss Anne Cormac?"

"So pleased to make your acquaintance," Mr. Taylor said while Mr. Bonny nodded, unable or unwilling to say another word. He tucked a strand of oily hair behind one ear.

"Will you be in town long?" Ellen probed, securing her hat atop her head as she stared hard at Mr. Taylor.

"I certainly hope so," he said with a deep bow. They locked eyes for a heartbeat longer than necessary before the sailors continued on.

Anne's flimsy facade of refinement cracked as Ellen stared after them. "Jesus, Mary, and Joseph," Anne whispered, forgetting to leash her cursing. "This is what you call 'shopping for finery'?"

"Precisely." Ellen's face shifted from stupid flirtation into a look of complete satisfaction. "I invited you here today not because I think you'll make another pretty friend—I've had enough of those—but because you're not a fool. You've just confirmed my hope. And besides, I'm desperate to escape my family by any means necessary. Particularly my brute of a brother."

Anne opened her mouth, then closed it. She truly did not understand friendship.

"I'm bored to tears, Anne. But mostly, I'm angry. *Really* angry." She reached out and touched the basket tied to Anne's belt. "This place isn't what it seems. My father talks of moving to the Bahamas, taking his trade with him. I can't imagine what my life might look like on some hunk of sand in the middle of the ocean. I long for a new city—a real, liberal-minded city. Only the Devil could stop me from trying to break free."

Anne crossed her arms. She didn't know whether she should be irritated by this spoiled young lady or impressed.

"You're bored too, don't deny it," Ellen said. "I've seen you at church; your face betrays your every thought." She huffed. "You're an only child, stuck half the day with a tutor, and the other half spent alone while your father works and your mother makes visits or keeps to her bed."

At this, Anne's blood boiled. "You know nothing about me," she snapped. How did Ellen, or anyone, know of Mam's condition? "What gives you the right—"

Ellen held up a hand. "Don't be defensive. It doesn't suit your complexion—not with *that* hair. How long have you been here—two months? Three? People talk. Your mother sees the wrong doctor. Your father is trusting the wrong people. Maybe my eavesdropping can finally be of use. I can help. And in return, you can help me."

Wrong doctor? Her guilt and protectiveness of Mam reared like a spooked horse.

"You're insufferable," Anne growled. She wasn't sure if she wanted to hate Ellen, love her, or *be* her. To her annoyance, Ellen seemed only more pleased by her reaction.

"Challenge me. Fight me. Swear your pretty Irish head off, I don't care," Ellen said. "It's all better than the alternative."

"The alternative being . . . ?"

"Pretending," Ellen exhaled, her fire extinguished, replaced with sorrow. "Like all these other masquerading hypocrites."

Anne unclenched her fists. Ellen looped her arm through Anne's again, holding her chin high as they strode home, the chimney smoke from cooking fires wafting.

"If I'm lucky," Ellen continued, this time with bitterness, "I'll snag a husband who can take me away from this horrid place and family."

Anne preferred this version of Ellen to the earlier one. With this Ellen, Anne needn't hold back. "I trust what you say about your family. But there are more horrid places, I assure you," Anne said.

Ellen gave her a hard look. "I'll give you a *proper* tour if you call on me tomorrow."

CHAPTER 13

"Tell me the name of the best doctor," Anne said the second they were alone in the Fulworths' manor the next morning.

The corners of Ellen's lips turned up as she did her needlework in the parlor. "I knew you'd come." Ellen's voice had a demure lull that made Anne want to throw her cup of tea at her.

"It's urgent," Anne said, heart hammering as she sat primly on the sofa. Light filtered through the lace curtains and over the cherrywood furnishings and spotless room, which embodied the opposite tone as the previous night: Anne had awoken to the sound of Mam's violent coughs, followed by cries of frustration. When Anne had flung open her parents' door, she had seen Mam shove Da away when he tried to stroke her cheek. Her mother continued to scream—which only worsened the cough. Then Mam had fallen with convulsive sobs into Da's chest.

In that moment, Anne's eyes landed on the bloodied kerchief beside the bed.

Anne tapped her fingernails against the porcelain cup.

"I propose we call on Dr. Ashby," Ellen said, pulling at a pink thread. "We can stop there before our tour."

Anne's tea sat untouched. She hadn't slept a wink.

"You look pale. Are you feeling well enough to go?"

Anne rose by way of an answer.

Arms linked, Anne and Ellen strode through Charles Town.

"I'm sorry about your mother," Ellen said as she pointed to a green door. "This is where Dr. Ashby lives."

Anne bit her lip. Da was protective. Fiercely so. "My father will want to make the request."

Ellen tilted her head, scrutinizing Anne's face before yanking her up the stairs. "Then we'll say *I* sent him." Anne did not object.

When the butler answered, he reported that Dr. Ashby was on a visit. "But I'll urge him to see Mrs. Cormac at the soonest opportunity."

Anne, unable to speak her gratitude, merely curtseyed as they left.

"My family will see no one else," Ellen said as they took to the streets again. "Dr. Ashby once pulled my brother Peter back from the cliff of death."

"Your brute of a brother?" Anne asked with caution, recalling yesterday's mention.

"Not *that* one," Ellen said, her grip tightening. She paused, looked in both directions, then rolled up her sleeve. The skin on her wrist had purpled, with yellow and green patches.

Anne's eyes widened with horror. "He . . . did this to you?"

Ellen stiffened and yanked down her sleeve. "That and far worse. Nathaniel is a monster." Ellen shuddered. "I know secrets about your family. It's only fair you know some about mine."

Anne reached for Ellen's wrist with tenderness, but Ellen brushed her away and linked arms again. The resumed poise in her step seemed to say the conversation was over.

"You can trust me," Anne said, her mind unable to move on from the bruise. Was Ellen safe? Were her parents aware? What else did this older brother do to Ellen?

"I know I can," Ellen sang. She spun around, her rosy cheeks and pinned black hair a portrait of happiness. "I don't know how I know it; I just do."

Anne blinked. She didn't understand how Ellen could speak of such things and maintain proper appearances.

"Wipe away your scowl. I promised you a tour, and a proper tour you shall have. The butcher's wife is watching. She's a terrible gossip. My pa's reputation protects me for the most part, but few are immune to her verbal lashings."

Anne plastered on a tight smile. "For someone who hates pretenders, you seem to have perfected the art."

"To spot the fakes, you have to master being one." Ellen batted her eyelashes. "I learned from the best." She gave a slight nod to a two-story brick building. "See that place there? It's a black-market warehouse for smuggled goods. Almost everyone is in on the enterprise, brushing shoulders with pirates. My pa, from what I've gathered, leads it all."

"Pirates?" Anne swallowed. Men who rampaged and ravaged and murdered and stole to their heart's content? "In Charles Town?"

"Oh, yes. And that house on the corner just there? Mr. Bull runs a gambling ring. He entertains a dozen mistresses there. But Mrs. Bull in turn keeps herself occupied with the captain of a fishing vessel," Ellen tsked. "I saw the two enjoying a naughty little tryst a few months back."

Anne raised a brow. Mam had told her candidly how it was between men and women. But she'd never heard it spoken about like this.

Gulls scattered as they neared the edge of town, their wings disappearing over the Ashley River.

"That's not the half of it," Ellen said, stepping in front of Anne and blocking her view.

Anne folded her arms.

"We can't appear like we're quarreling. If we are to be friends and help each other, at least *look* like you are pretending."

"Sweet Jesus, I'm trying!" But Anne uncrossed her arms and resumed her smile. This was a lot of work, being Ellen's friend.

Ellen pointed east. "That dock brings in human beings to sell."

Anne's mouth dried. In London, she'd heard of such things happening in the Caribbean and on plantations throughout the colonies. But here in town? "I don't understand."

Ellen stared at Anne with flinty hardness. "My Lord, you really don't know a thing."

Anne felt heat rise in her throat. But this time, she held her tongue.

"Come. There's something I have to show you."

In silence, Ellen and Anne walked to the far end of Tradd Street, which was flanked by the river. When they reached a bridge in front of a brick redan, Ellen stopped.

The square was empty. But only recently so. A pungent, unidentifiable smell seared Anne's nostrils. Two gentlemen exchanged ledgers across the way.

Bare footprints covered the ground. One set was the size of a child barely old enough to walk.

"Our wholesome town calls this 'the usual spot,'" Ellen said. She strode forward, surveying the sails of small sloops and fishing boats that moved up and down the river. "It's as if they can't bear to give it a name, an unspoken acknowledgment of their shame. You recall the one governess I liked? The one my pa dismissed?"

Anne nodded. Her throat tightened.

"She was a Quaker. She and another Quaker fellow—a good man she later married—sneaked me here on a number of occasions. They taught me the truth—that the rich thrive because of the free labor of the enslaved."

Anne's veins iced over. She could not take her eyes away from the child's prints in the dirt. Then she spotted something gray in the dust. She stooped, picking up a coin-sized circle that read "Lot 4."

A number instead of a name. A metal merchant tag.

On a human being.

"Most sales take place on the decks of the galleys, death ships that transport kidnapped Africans and treat them worse than cargo. Cruel cannot begin to describe what these people endure. Some sales happen on plantations or through private contracts. But the most successful method? Bring them to Charles Town before the hordes of wealthy white planters. The crime happens right here—by way of a *vendue*, a public auction. The French makes it oh-so refined." She scoffed. "A seller sets a minimum price." Ellen motioned her head in the direction of the men across the road. "That shorter brute is the vendue master. He facilitates each sale and takes a significant commission from each life sold. Watch him count his profits."

Anne dragged her gaze to the men. Their smiles and congratulations as they shook hands.

Ellen's glare shot daggers. "I've seen infants torn from mothers. Husbands from wives. Neck shackles. People so ill they couldn't stand while the masses shouted bids. Lash wounds that would make even Satan faint. They snatch Natives too—the people of this very land—then trade them like gambling chips."

Anne dropped the metal tag as if it scalded her. Her eyes burned and overflowed. The exhaustion of a sleepless night, the severity of Mam's condition—the condition Anne had caused—and now this.

Her new home. The supposed safe place she and her family had believed in. *Needed* to believe in.

"I've cried my share of tears, too," Ellen said, pacing. "But tears don't help. They don't change minds. My tears and yours are wasted on people like my pa and these so-called Christians who enslave people to run their households and plantations. The townsfolk wash their hands of guilt like Pontius Pilate and declare it God's natural order."

Bile coated Anne's throat. The faces from town, their various shades flashed before her. The two weavers. Their unease at Anne's approach. The flashing eyes of the young woman who'd crafted Anne's sweetgrass basket.

In some small way—as a bastard Irish Catholic—she'd known what it meant to be different. To be despised and treated worse for it. But *this*?

The reason families like hers could talk of freedom? Could start fresh in hopes of eventually prospering? Anne understood, all at once, how naïve she'd been.

A team of horses forced Ellen and Anne to leap out of the road.

"I'm not afraid of being damned," Ellen said as dust rose in their faces and stuck to Anne's cheeks. "As far as I can tell, everyone here already is."

CHAPTER 14

"How is she?" Anne asked Da, entering her parents' bedroom upon her return. Her hands shook from exhaustion, from all she'd seen and heard.

Da put a finger to his lips to silence her. He sat in a chair by Mam, a towel across her forehead as she lay in bed. An empty wine bottle rolled on the floor. Da's.

Anne forced herself to look, really look, at Mam's weakened condition. Her cheeks had lost all the luster they'd gained. Her always-pinned hair fell like a nest on the pillow.

"With rest, she might improve enough for the Fulworths' ball," he whispered. "You know she longed to go."

Anne shifted her weight, her eye snagging on the new teal dress draped over a cedar chest.

"Did anyone call today?" Anne remained standing and kept her voice low. She would let him bring up the doctor's name. Da, fortunately, had already mentioned the Fulworths.

Da ignored her, staring down at Mam's sallow face.

"Da?"

He exhaled, then tore his attention away from Mam.

"Yes. A *Sassenach* by the name of Dr. Ashby," he said with red-rimmed eyes. There was a sleepless quality to them, an edge and danger. Like a wounded animal.

"The Fulworths recommended their personal doctor?" Anne feigned surprise and awe, ignoring the Irish insult about the doctor's Englishness.

"He insisted on seeing her. Said he'd heard a troubling report."

Anne clenched her teeth. *Pretend better*, she could hear Ellen whispering into her ear. "I don't see why our neighbors should meddle in our affairs. The Fulworths must especially want Mam in attendance," she paused. "Did he have anything useful to say?"

He grunted. "Yes. But nothing to trouble yourself with. Your mother needs rest; it's the only time the coughing stops." Rising, he walked Anne to the door and closed it soundly behind her.

With the hardwood door inches from her nose, Anne stood alone for a full minute. As her mother declined, her father followed like a shadow.

How would she ever tell Da the rest of what Ellen told her, about who he could and could not trust? About the great evils of Charles Town?

Anne swallowed, then turned toward her own, echoey room.

The following Saturday, everyone in high society gathered at the Fulworths' manor for a midsummer ball.

Everyone except Mam.

In the dusk, punctuated with fireflies, Anne ascended the steps in satin slippers. She clutched her green matura, the French-style dress with a lacy stomacher and train, looking more like a woman than she ever had in her nineteen years. If her heart wasn't laden with sorrows, she might have felt beautiful. Anne could not help but study the African men attending to carriages, leading away horses, and opening doors for the laughing, pink-faced guests. The sight made her gut churn. She couldn't unsee what Ellen had revealed, couldn't unsee the rot of pretending to be good and virtuous.

Da lumbered beside Anne in a new waistcoat Mam had insisted

he wear. Da had not changed his clothes in days and smelled slightly of ale. Between work at his law practice and tireless hours caring for Mam, he'd little desire to be anywhere else. But Mam, upright in bed today and in chipper spirits, had begged him to go.

"You must send my regards to Mrs. Fulworth!" she'd said, taking a pause to cough. "Be my eyes. I want to hear every detail."

When Da refused, saying that Anne could do the task just as well, Mam pursed her lips. "And risk not being invited again? Don't be daft. You must go as Anne's chaperone, and I won't hear another word against it."

"But *mo chroí*, you need me."

Mam let out a string of curses and threw her pillow against the water basin. The porcelain fell to the floor and shattered. Anne's body went ramrod straight. *Firebrand Mam was back*, after being dormant for so long. Then Mam's fire dissolved in a fit of coughs.

Only then did Da relent and agree to attend.

"A fine evening, Mr. Cormac," said a gentleman in the foyer.

"Oh yes," Da said without feeling. "Fine, fine."

"How's business?" asked another, this one wearing the red uniform of a soldier.

After a flurry of introductions, Anne caught sight of Ellen hiding near the orchestra. Her pulse leapt and she made her way toward her. Anne didn't always know how she felt around her friend, the strange tension in her body and her constant position of defense, but at least Ellen told her the truth.

"Have you seen Mr. Taylor?" Ellen whispered, stuffing a sweet into her lovely mouth.

Anne scanned the scene—the couples, the banquet table, the fragrant gardens with white buds.

"He said he would be here," Ellen growled. "I wanted him to meet my pa."

Anne was not at all sure that Mr. Taylor, a common sailor—however uncommon his smile—would feel welcome. "There's still time."

"That's why I like you," Ellen said, her chin pointed and stiff.

"You're a terrible liar. And I, alas, am a fool. My 'shopping for ball-worthy finery' came to naught." Were it not for the slight wetness to her eyes, anyone would have guessed that Ellen was delighted. "Come, let's get punch." She hooked her arm through Anne's, and when Ellen's ruffles slipped up to her elbow, Anne spotted a new bruise.

"Ellen—"

"Sister, who is this enchanting companion of yours?"

Anne and Ellen turned toward the speaker. He had dazzling green eyes and ebony-black hair, just like Ellen's. He towered above the other men in the room, and a smirk graced his lips.

"Find your own dance partner, Nathaniel," Ellen grimace-laughed. "Miss Cormac was in the middle of telling me a story."

Nathaniel. The name felt like a spider crawling down her spine. Anne tried to tug Ellen away.

"Pleased to make your acquaintance, Miss Cormac," Nathaniel Fulworth said, the pinnacle of manners.

Ellen stepped between Anne and Nathaniel, resuming her singsong. "Oh, don't mind my oldest brother. He loves to dance with every lady in the room."

"But as I was saying—" Anne began, pretending to continue an engaging tale, just when another young man approached and tapped Nathaniel on the shoulder.

"Do me the honor of the next dance?" Nathaniel asked Anne with a wink before turning toward his friend.

When the men stalked away, Ellen gave Anne a glass of punch.

"What the Devil just happened?" Anne asked.

"The wolf found the prettiest girl in the room and pounced," Ellen said, sipping her own glass.

"I can refuse," Anne said, despite knowing the stir it would cause to reject a member of the family hosting this ball.

Ellen's eyes pleaded. "If you decline, he'll only try harder. He may even suspect I've told you . . ." Ellen shifted the pearl brace-let on her wrist.

"I understand." Ellen's secret would remain safe. But Anne was loath to be so near the person who'd hurt her friend.

"Pretend you are a complete bore—and don't resist," Ellen said, taking a huge gulp. "He feasts on a fight. A challenge."

Anne tasted acid when the French minuet came to a close. She felt Nathaniel behind her before turning around to face him.

"Shall we?"

Anne's fingers twitched as she handed her punch to Ellen. She forced a dull smile as she looked up at Nathaniel and noticed the emptiness in his pupils. He bowed, then placed a too-firm hand on her waist to escort her to the floor.

"I'm a poor dancer," Anne said, avoiding his vile stare. She'd had few occasions to practice. She hoped he'd suffer from his choice of partner.

"I'm sure you're being modest." He clasped her hands as the orchestra began an English country dance.

"I'm not." She decided to forgo efforts at form and to step on his feet as much as possible.

"Just follow my lead."

The cheery music began and Nathaniel swirled her in a circle. At the cue of a swell, they took the hands of their neighbors. They held their arms up in arches, then took turns moving between rows like water under a bridge.

"Your hair is lovely," Nathaniel said between movements. "Like pure fire."

Anne felt her cheeks burn with rage.

"And a lovelier blush," Nathaniel said.

Damn him. Anne stumbled as the orchestra and dancers continued. Nathaniel forced her into motion again.

"Do you like fire, Anne Cormac?" he said as they turned in unison.

Anne's temples ached. She wanted to yell. To call for Da. To end this ridiculous whirling as Nathaniel led her around the floor. To shut out the claps and fast tempo. For a moment, she was eight again, outside her grandparents' estate, stunned and unable to move. The snarling dog's teeth. The crush of failure. The inability to control the outcome, let alone her fear.

They twirled. Arms up. Arms down. Anne felt dizzy. She said nothing. *Nothing.* Instead, she peered into his flat eyes, trying to spot the monster lurking within. By some stroke of grace, the music stopped and the dancers clapped with merriment.

Nathaniel bowed. Anne did not curtsy.

"Shall we have another?" He leaned forward, his gaze raking over her collarbone. "Or perhaps you'd prefer some fresh air?" he whispered.

At that moment, another man cut in—a lanky gentleman with soft eyes and a pocked jaw. He'd been dancing with his wife beside them. Perhaps he saw Anne's distress. Perhaps she just imagined his kindness.

"Give the rest of us a turn, Mr. Fulworth," the gentleman said, taking Anne's shaky hand and leading her to the opposite end of the room. The way he said it, Anne knew that he knew. She felt a wave of relief and forced herself to breathe again.

CHAPTER 15

"How is your mother?" Ellen asked with caution as they walked toward the docks the following week.

"Worse," Anne managed to say. But Holy God above—Mam was *more* than worse. "She hasn't broken a fever since the night of the ball." Mam hadn't even been well enough to hear the details that Da and Anne had carefully gathered for her.

Not that Anne would have told Mam about the worst part of the night. Her skin prickled with the memory of Nathaniel's hand on her waist, his hunter's stare.

"I'm sorry to hear it," Ellen said with uncharacteristic softness. No lectures. No admonitions to pretend better.

"Thanks," Anne said, shuffling her feet along the wharf. Maybe she and Ellen had moved beyond needing things from each other. Maybe their friendship was settling into something sturdier. The crisp sea air rested on her heavy eyelids after another long night. "Dr. Ashby has been coming daily." The doctor was troubled by the blotchy rash on Mam's abdomen and her refusal to eat. Mam wobbled whenever she tried to stand and complained of a headache. She needed the chamber pot every hour and moaned in her sleep, waking the whole house with her fits and coughs.

Most troubling were the hallucinations.

When Anne had entered her parents' bedroom the night before, she'd stared at Anne like she'd seen a ghost. She raised a white finger and pointed at Anne with something like an accusation. The room itself seemed to spin. Mam's pale lips trembled, but no words came out.

"It's only Anne, *mo chroí*," Dad soothed. "Only Anne."

Yes. *Only me.* Then, Mam's old words rose in Anne's mind like a curse.

Our child will be the death of me.

Da turned his head, bloodshot eyes narrowed with clear instructions: Leave. She needs peace. She needs *me*.

Mam continued to point and mumble. When Da laid her down, she threw her fists against him and screamed.

"You," she slurred at Da with accusation. "*You* did this to me."

Tears sprang from Anne's eyes. She could not bear to see Mam, all light and blaze, reduced to embers and delirium.

As Anne stewed in her hellish memories, Ellen lifted a gloved hand at Mr. Taylor, who hastened his approach. Mr. Bonny followed behind him.

"Do you think Mr. Taylor will soon make an offer?" Ellen said through her pearly smile.

Anne blinked. Before she could answer, Ellen and Mr. Taylor were exchanging lengthy greetings.

"And so good to see you too, Mr. Bonny," Ellen said.

Bonny gave a curt nod. A skullcap covered his hair today. His gray eyes surveyed her. Anne didn't care to flirt or "act" today. Not with everything going on at home.

"I hear you're sailing back to the Caribbean. Or is it home to England soon?" Ellen asked the sailors. "I have always longed to see London—so much livelier than this backwater. I wouldn't mind living there. Wouldn't that be wonderful, Anne?"

Anne remembered the years she spent moving around with Da and Mam all too well. The horse dung in the roads. The scorn the English cast in her direction. How they mocked her Irish accent until it was ground down like wheat into flour. The overcast days and damp evenings, the never-enough money, the no-jobs-for-the-Irish years for Da.

"London is awful," Anne said.

Ellen spun, her lips pursed in a warning. In lightning time, Ellen giggled and played it off like a joke. Mr. Taylor laughed in response. Anne's shoulders tightened, and she had the strong urge to abandon Ellen—no matter her urgency to find a husband. She longed to go back to the place where she was not allowed to be, the place she was banished from: Mam's sickroom.

"Miss Cormac, Miss Cormac!" came a voice from down the pier.

Everyone turned to see Dr. Ashby's youthful assistant barreling toward them.

Anne's stomach plummeted. Her throat constricted.

No.

Please no.

Ellen searched Anne's face as the assistant stood before them, panting. His heavy gaze lifted.

Not here. Not now.

Never.

Anne felt the earth tilt.

"Your mother," he said, removing his cap. "I'm sorry."

Rain fell unceasingly on the day of Mam's funeral. After a modestly attended service, the priest presided over the burial. The ground turned sticky with mud as onlookers huddled together against the weather and listened to the final rites.

Da was not there. Inconsolable, unrecognizable, and absent.

How could he let me face this alone?

Anne stood, stone-faced in the downpour, listening to the sounds coming from the priest, but not the words. She stared at the wooden cross on his rosary.

"May she need faith no longer, but see God face-to-face," he said.

"Amen," the others spoke, moving forward to mutter prayers and drop a handful of sod onto the coffin. Some offered a word of comfort to Anne while others patted her shoulder or squeezed her frozen hands.

All she felt was the rain. The emptiness. Bouts of forgetting why she was there, followed by full-body chills.

"Anne," came a familiar voice to her right.

Ellen. At least Ellen had come. However strange that friendship, Ellen was—if anything—an example of someone Anne wanted to be: strong and self-assured. And Anne needed these qualities more than ever.

"Would you like to say goodbye?" Ellen whispered.

Anne lifted her quivering chin, catching the pain in Ellen's violet-blue eyes. No acting. No tricks. No humor. And even then, Anne knew what she would remember most about this day. Not what was said, but who was there.

And who was not.

Da's absence burned like a hot coal down her throat.

"Come," Ellen said, gently taking Anne's arm and leading her to the edge of the grave.

Anne curled her toes inside her boots and swallowed a sob.

Ellen said nothing, just squeezed her hand.

Anne blinked back tears and rain. What could she possibly say?

I didn't mean to make you sick.

I don't accept—cannot accept—that you have left me.

What will I do without you?

Then worst of all:

Who am I without you?

Anne's arm shook as she lifted the clump of dirt in her fist. Mam had crossed lands and oceans, exchanged a cramped jail cell for high-society ballrooms.

Mam. Lovely like Ireland. Wind and air. Water and bread and honey. Life itself.

Anne opened her fist, unclamping her grip finger by finger, and let go.

CHAPTER 16

Charles Town, South Carolina
1717

Da made it clear that Anne was a walking mistake made of blood and bones. In the five months following Mam's death, he took offense at the sound of her footsteps, at her gentle probing about his appetite apart from strong drinks, at the way she opened or shut the door to bring him a cup of tea. The last time she'd brought him a letter, a business request, he'd buried his face in his hands. The way Da behaved lately, the disarray of notes and ledgers—even after selling off the treasures he'd bought for her and Ma—Anne did not imagine her lessons with Monsieur Perrin would last much longer.

"What's wrong, Da?" Anne asked, still holding the most recent letter. Her chest tightened. Her sorrow for Da, though oceanic, had become heavy with salt.

"Enough," he slurred, massaging his temple. "I'll not be nagged by a witch in my own house."

"Is this not my house, too?" A house that she ran alone without Mam. Was there no room for her own grief?

She'd *make* room.

He snapped his head toward her. "Don't you question—"

"Oh?" She felt her tongue sharpen. "Was it not *you* who taught me how to question, how to think, in the first place?" Where was that Da from her childhood? Her first teacher? "You can't go on like this." Anne's voice rose. She gestured around the filthy bedroom and placed the letter atop a pile of others. "You don't even look at me anymore."

His red-rimmed eyes narrowed to slits. "Did it ever cross your womanly mind that you look a bit like her? That you are here and she is not?"

"After France's victory and the House of Valois seized the throne, what did England lose?" Monsieur Perrin said one day in his nasal English.

Anne copied his words onto her paper, not registering them as a question she was meant to answer until she paused at the end of the line. God have mercy. She couldn't remember the past five minutes, let alone the past hour of lessons.

Monsieur Perrin did not thwack the desk today, nor had he in the months since Mam's funeral. Lately, he hadn't even challenged Anne by using French.

"How about a story instead?" Monsieur Perrin said after a long pause.

Anne's eyes widened with horror. *No.* No more frivolous, childish stories. Not if Mam wasn't here to tell them. Nothing good lasted. As if to prove it, the Fulworths had announced their move to the Bahamas. All eyes trailed Anne whenever she drifted through town to visit Ellen, perhaps due to Da's strange behavior and absence from society.

"I can finish the lesson you've prepared," Anne answered Monsieur Perrin.

"I think you will like my story," Monsieur Perrin continued, unfazed by Anne's response. He removed his spectacles and placed his books aside.

Anne hunched over the desk, then finally returned the quill to the inkwell.

"In my country, during the Hundred Years' War, there was a remarkable young woman called Jeanne d'Arc. She was, and remains, a great hero of France. At the age of seventeen, she led the French Army to victory." Monsieur Perrin studied Anne with a paternal quality that made her miss the Da she used to know.

Without noticing, Anne sat up a little straighter. "A girl?"

"Yes."

"You're telling me that a girl younger than me led the French?"

"To *victory*." Monsieur Perrin continued his story about Joan of Arc, born in 1412 in some forgettable village as a farmer's daughter. She believed she heard voices from angels and female Saints, a calling from the Lord, telling her to rally her people—to put a man named Dauphin Charles on the throne and to drive the English from French lands. When she turned seventeen, she embarked on a great journey. She cut off her long tresses and dressed like a man to travel, then met in secret with the noble Dauphin Charles. After a series of tests, she earned his trust. "Joan the Maid," he called her. She took up training in arms, like any other soldier—clad in metals and wielding a sword. She mastered military strategy and led charges, scaled burning ladders, and survived an arrow to the neck.

A pang walloped Anne, the memory of Mam's bedtime stories of the mighty Grace O'Malley—her strength and command on both land and sea.

"What happened to her?" Anne asked, more alert than she'd felt in months.

Monsieur Perrin peered out the window, as he'd advised Anne against so often. When he turned back and met her gaze, she saw the sadness in his eyes.

"Tell me."

Mr. Perrin winced, wanting to end there, on the happy note, the marvel. "Enemies traded her to the English. They held a trial and accused Jeanne of heresy. She evaded their arguments. Infuriated, her accusers drew up seventy offenses—including blasphemy, dressing as a man, and witchcraft."

"They found her guilty?" Anne asked, beating him to the bad news.

Monsieur Perrin cleaned his spectacles. "She rejected their accusations until the end. She had a chance to live out her days in prison, but she refused to relinquish her men's clothing and sense of the divine. They burned her at the stake, and she was made a saint at the age of nineteen."

Anne sank back into her chair and clenched her teeth. Her limbs felt heavy. Her heart sore. What a terrible ending. Was Joan of Arc a hero? A bloody fool? "Why did you think I would like this story?" Anne demanded, verging on defense. There was enough death and unfairness in her fraying world.

Monsieur Perrin blinked away his confusion. "I'm sorry, Miss Cormac. I meant no harm. And perhaps it is improper to say this." He put his spectacles back on and cleared his throat. "But something about you reminds me of Jeanne. *La sainte patronne de la France.* You ask thoughtful questions and resist simple answers. Standard conventions, such as those found in my lecture methods, do not serve you best. I hope you will remember this lesson and what Jeanne inspired in her people, commanding them to, *'Allez hardiment!'*"

"Go boldly," Anne repeated.

He began to pack his belongings. "I do not pretend to know the difference between heroes and heresy, as history writes and determines those answers." He paused to catch her eye. "But I would be a failure of a tutor if I did not tell you, at least once, the rare quality of your mind."

Anne's heart thumped with equal parts bafflement and curiosity. Monsieur Perrin had evaluated her difficult situation, the whole of it and her, and offered her this unexpected gift. She had a mind. Listening, Anne recognized that she also had a heart.

And despite everything, it still beat.

CHAPTER 17

"Take me with you," Anne begged Ellen for the hundredth time.

But now, standing at the docks in the colorless morning as men paraded sea chests aboard a Fulworth merchant ship, it would be the last.

"My family is not one worth joining," Ellen said through gritted teeth, squeezing Anne's hands.

"Careful with that!" Mrs. Fulworth roared when a sailor dropped a trunk. Mr. Fulworth busied himself with double-checking the manifest as the Fulworth children readied themselves to board the ship bound for the Bahamas.

"My father has become impossible," Anne whispered. She'd already told Ellen of his latest behavior and erratic plans. Too unstable to continue law, Da had arranged for another loan, with interest, to buy a plantation away from town and pay back his debts.

A plantation run by enslaved people.

Anne had argued with Da, using Christianity and the flimsy comparison of Irish oppression to appeal to his heart. Where was his compassion? His conscience? Enraged, he threw a bottle at her, which shattered on the wall behind Anne—a mere foot from her head.

Ellen had been right about the futility of tears. But Anne could not—*would* not—bear his sins any longer.

"Say I am your sister. 'Anne Fulworth.' Isn't that lovely?"

"Drop it, Anne," Ellen said with exasperation. "If you want to run, at least run in the right direction." Her violet-blue eyes shone with regret. "Don't be like me, wasting time on pointless schemes like pursuing Mr. Taylor."

Anne shifted her weight. Mr. Taylor was nowhere to be seen on the docks today, though she'd spotted his crew and his friend, Mr. Bonny. Mr. Taylor had not made an offer of marriage—whatever his true feelings and Ellen's clear willingness to abscond. Anne thought Ellen had understood why Mr. Taylor would not ask for the hand of a woman who was so obviously above his station. She suspected that Ellen *did* understand in her better moments. But anyone could be blinded by hope.

"Children, come!" Mrs. Fulworth called.

Anne stared at her feet. She'd cried enough in the year since Mam died to last a lifetime and had no more left to give.

"I may not be an heir, not with two brothers and five sisters," Ellen said. "But you, Miss Anne Cormac—an only child—*are*." Ellen scanned Anne's face for understanding.

"But we've sold it all. And the debts—?"

Ellen held up a finger. "Play the game better than the rest of the hypocrites. A marriageable man doesn't have to know the details."

"Isn't that a lie?" Anne whispered.

Someone cleared their throat, causing Anne and Ellen to jump.

"You startled us, Nathaniel," Ellen said in a false tone as she smoothed her dress and stared at her boots.

"I'll miss you too, Ellen," Nathaniel said.

Anne's gut squeezed. She looked at Nathaniel's smug expression, then back at her friend.

"You're not—?" Anne began to say.

"I'll follow the family in a few weeks, but my main operations will remain here in Charles Town." He paused. "How lonely we'll be without my sister's company. Shall I call on you soon to see how you're faring?" His finger flicked her ass before he stalked away.

Did he just—?

Did she imagine it?

Nathaniel would stay behind. It was only when Ellen shook her shoulder that Anne came back to herself.

"Listen, Anne," Ellen said with increased urgency after Nathaniel left them. "You're clever, more clever than you give yourself credit for. Stop underestimating yourself—it's irritating—and quit studying everyone like a starved pet in need of affection. People aren't worth your groveling, so find your food elsewhere. Feed yourself. I wouldn't be your friend if I didn't tell you the truth, no? We have always told each other the truth."

"I am *not* a damn dog," Anne said.

But Ellen continued on, silencing her with a raised hand but looking pleased at Anne's response. "For God's sake, run, but with your head on your shoulders. Aim your shot and don't miss." She hugged Anne one last time. "Don't be like me."

Anne was not Queen Maeve fighting Furbaide. She was not the fierce Grace O'Malley or the brave Joan of Arc. But Ellen made Anne feel that she could be more.

Jesus, Mary, and Joseph. Why were there always so many goodbyes? "I don't even have a gift for you to remember me by," Anne said.

"As if I could forget my first and only true friend," Ellen said, somewhere between a scold and a sob. They held each other until Mrs. Fulworth pulled Ellen away.

Dread pooled in Anne's stomach with each day that passed. She refused to receive any visitors. For a week, she spent most of her time outdoors, visiting Mam's grave or staring at the river as she pondered Ellen's words. At home, she studied Da's papers whenever he was away.

This afternoon, she occupied herself by writing a letter to Monsieur Perrin in the drawing room. Though Da had dismissed him as she'd anticipated, she wondered if Monsieur Perrin might recommend her as a governess. Where did people post such positions? Could she be a teacher of any kind? He might laugh, if her tutor was capable of laughing. But being laughed at was hardly the worst of her problems.

She'd take anything. Any way out of this situation with Da.

Footsteps sounded outside the door. She covered her writing materials with a shawl. Da was home early. Too early to finish her day's goal. She had to start on dinner.

Then came a knock—it wasn't Da.

One rap.

Two.

The hair on the back of Anne's neck rose. To her horror, the door to the drawing room swung open.

She'd locked it. She *swore* she'd locked it. Anne's stomach plummeted at the visage in the entryway.

"Good afternoon, Miss Cormac," Nathaniel Fulworth said warily. He scanned the drawing room. "Forgive my imprudence, but I'd heard you were most unwell. And with circumstances as they are, and my dear sister gone, I thought you could use a friend." His attention flicked to the staircase. "I had especially hoped to catch your father, to lend him some advice. He is, I understand, not home?"

Anne felt her cheeks burn, aware it sent the opposite message than the one she intended.

"I'm feeling terribly unwell. If you don't mind—"

But Nathaniel was already shutting the door with a click. The sound of a coffin closing.

Her breathing stopped.

"The town speaks of your Da's neglect." He glanced at the papers and inkwell peeking out from under the shawl, then moved forward to see what Anne was working on. "Ah, are you writing to Ellen?"

She didn't answer him. "I'm sure my father would be delighted to talk about business—and his duty as my father—another time."

She stood from the desk, her fingers brushing against a paper knife for opening correspondence.

No, for this.

Anne tucked the blade into the pocket of her skirt and moved away, creating distance between herself and Nathaniel. "I think you should—"

But before she could finish her sentence, he pressed his mouth against hers. She gasped. "I knew what was between us," he breathed when he finally pulled away. "From the first moment we met." Nathaniel's voice was heavy with longing. He pushed a hand through her hair. "That fire in you."

Anne's heart raced with terror, and her eyes darted around the room. The door, blocked. The window, impossible. Then Nathaniel kissed her again, hard. She ripped away, and he held her wrist with a force that made her wince.

"Let go of me," she demanded. "I'll—"

He leaned in, pressing her back against a wall. Moving against her, his mouth trailed her throat where no scream emerged. "You don't have to hide your reason for all those visits to Ellen." He ran his hands through her hair, then dragged them down her chest. She shrieked with fear, and he sighed with pleasure, his mouth on hers, stealing her air away.

Every nerve of her screamed. And yet her body stiffened, rigid with fear. Frozen in place. Like a trapped animal.

No, like a little girl. Standing in front of her grandparents' estate. Unable to speak. A dog lunging but never pouncing. Her treacherous feet moving, running. Away from the home she might have saved.

"Shh," he smiled. "I won't hurt you."

Anne squeezed her eyes shut as Nathaniel ran his hands over every curve of her dress.

A cry from the little girl inside her.

Not this, Anne thought.

Never again.

"No," she said aloud, squeaky and quiet, but a no all the same.

This seemed to embolden Nathaniel, who fumbled with the laces of her dress.

Act, Anne thought, forcing her eyes open. *Think.*

Nathaniel moaned and found her mouth again, biting her lip. She tasted blood—metallic and bitter. She twisted in his grasp, kicking and fighting, but it only seemed to encourage him.

You are clever, Anne told herself, channeling Ellen. What would Ellen do? What would Ellen say?

Ellen, with her bruised wrist.

She couldn't be Ellen. She couldn't be any person but herself.

Be watchful, like Mam warned.

Be cunning, like Grace O'Malley.

Her pocket.

The paper knife.

Fight, like Queen Maeve.

Trust yourself, like Joan of Arc.

Nathaniel tore off his shirt. Flustered by her gown's many laces, he hiked her dress up and gripped her ass. Anne clenched her teeth hard enough to grind bone. She reached for the knife.

Nathaniel groped one of her breasts. She wanted to vomit at his noises. Her trembling fingers closed around the paper knife.

Anne didn't have time to reconsider. She breathed in, exhaled, then used all her strength to plunge the metal into his stomach.

Nathaniel bellowed as if shot, but Anne was already racing for the door, flying down the stairs, the road, her heart hammering like a battle ax as she sprinted for the docks. Her feet knew where to take her, even as her mind struggled to keep up.

Anne found Mr. Bonny loading cargo onto a ship alongside his crewmates. Mr. Taylor was nowhere in sight. But perhaps that was for the best. Whatever his feelings toward Ellen—even if Anne never saw her friend again—she would never seek out Ellen's intended.

Mr. Bonny looked up when she approached. She would turn away if she had anything to turn back to.

Go boldly, she thought, remembering Monsieur Perrin's lesson.

"Mr. Taylor isn't here," Mr. Bonny said. "He joined a man-of-war headed north."

It took Anne a moment to register his meaning. "I didn't come for him. Can I have a word?" she asked, heaving and wild-eyed after Nathaniel's attack. She could only imagine what she looked like: unchaperoned, unruly hair, blood wiped on the inside hem of her dress. The limited traces of red said what she already knew: she'd not dealt a serious blow to Nathaniel—she'd barely punctured his skin. Nathaniel would be after her. With a tale of how she'd welcomed him into her house.

Mr. Bonny's companions laughed. One slapped him on the shoulder as he rose.

"You remember me, then?" Anne said, her arms folded to keep herself together while they stood on the far edge of the wharf. She could smell the sweat drenching his armpits.

"You'd be hard to forget," Mr. Bonny said, gray eyes fixed on her.

She studied him carefully. "But do you know who I am?"

He shifted his weight and scratched his ear. "The lawyer, Mr. Cormac's daughter."

"His *only* daughter," Anne said, remembering Ellen's words. "His only child."

His forehead wrinkled as he studied her anew. "What are you saying, Miss Cormac?"

"I need immediate passage from Charles Town," Anne said. *An escape route without a trace.* She hoped, with everything in her body, that he would not ask her to explain why. She would fall apart at the seams.

"We leave for Nassau under Captain Eford tonight," Mr. Bonny said, gesturing toward the ship.

Was it enough time? It would have to be enough. With any luck, Anne might even find Ellen once she got to the Bahamas.

"My father has fewer means than others in this town." She looked him over, his threadbare clothes and oily hair. "But he does have some." She cleared her throat. It was not a lie, though it was not the full truth. "We would dissolve the union as soon as possible. You could go your way, and I would go mine, but you'd have more shillings to show for your troubles."

"You are actually proposing that—"

"Yes. I am proposing."

His jaw dropped.

"Will you marry me, James Bonny?"

CHAPTER 18

Spanish Town, Jamaica
February 1721

Captain Johnson's pulse thumped. A woman, making her own offer of marriage? He'd never heard of such a thing. Would readers believe it? He'd make them believe. He inked his quill again, eager to capture the pirate's next words, when suddenly Miss Bonny ceased talking.

He looked up, expectant.

But Anne, her red hair tied atop her head and sweat glistening on her brow, did not return his gaze. She massaged a cramp in her foot.

"What happened next?" he asked, exasperated.

"You asked me how I got the name 'Bonny.' I was rather generous, as you can now ascertain why I sometimes used the alias 'Fulworth,' too."

Captain Johnson set his jaw. He had to have this story. He *must* capture it first. "Generous?" He repeated with frustration. "To pause there?"

Anne narrowed her eyes.

Johnson cleared his throat. He had revealed too much

excitement—a blunder. He'd need to exercise more patience, coming as often as necessary. Be more affirming. Consoling, perhaps, in dealing with the fairer sex in this delicate state. If Anne could be called delicate. Though surely she once was? "It is only that I am anxious, on your account, to know if matters resolved."

Anne guffawed. She leaned against the stone wall, her hands folded over her belly.

"Did your father approve of the marriage? Did you find Ellen?"

Anne considered him in a way that made him feel like a petulant child. It was all rather unpleasant. But he held his quill at attention.

"No, and no."

He should've left by now, but Johnson couldn't stop himself. "What happened to Mr. Nathaniel Fulworth? Did you intend to kill him? Was he all right in the end?"

Anne scowled with more hate than he knew was possible in such a pretty face.

Or was that hurt?

"Go attend to Mary," she ground out, turning away with finality. "As you damn well promised."

CHAPTER 19

Flanders
1705

"We picked the wrong queue," Mary said, craning her neck to see the holdup at the front of the line. A pack of men waited impatiently for their issued weapons.

"Shall I find you a ladder, Read?" Henry quipped.

Mary shot him a good-natured glare. If her older brother had lived, the real Mark, she imagined he might be like Henry Danby—silly and imprudent but the best of companions. What Henry lacked in looks, with his pimple scars and early balding, he made up for in loyalty. He towered like a spindly beanstalk over not just Mary but all the men there. When Mary and Henry first met in the infantry four years earlier, he'd mocked her height in a way that made her stomach squirm. At night, after unbinding her whisper of breasts, she would lie awake with fear that he suspected her secret. But Henry teased everyone, his humor a tonic stronger than anything the military offered. When other soldiers got deep into their cups and sneered at Mary's shyness, he defended her. She often studied his confident posture—his lifted ribs and direct eye contact. She scrutinized his behavior and tried to mimic the self-assured way he held himself and spoke with authority. Thanks to him, she'd never gotten into a brawl. "I wouldn't do that if I were you," Henry warned any potential opponent. It was Henry, not Mary, who boasted of her impeccable aim with a musket and deadly precision with a sword. "Mark Read here's got a chilly calm that'd make the Grim Reaper turn coat and bolt."

Being noticed was something she'd avoided for most of her twenty-one years. But being noticed for her accuracy in battle, thanks to Henry, had led to esteem and promoted her from infantry cadet to the ranks of the cavalry.

"I don't need a ladder," Mary growled.

Henry raised his hands in surrender. "My apologies. It doesn't take vision to see that Father Time himself has taken up distribution of the rifles."

She laughed, along with the soldiers within earshot. Would Henry, her best friend since leaving Captain Southwick's ship, treat her differently if he knew the truth about her?

Of course he would. Sorrow lodged in Mary's chest. Captain Southwick had dropped her off directly in Holland, not allowing Mary so much as a chance to search for Ma.

As Henry engaged the soldiers ahead of them in conversation, Mary frowned at a scuff on her secondhand boots. She *would* find Ma someday. She refused, despite the eight years that had passed, to give up hope.

"We're from Bristol. You?" asked the fellow in front.

Henry turned to Mary. She wished he would answer for them, as he tended to on most occasions. "London," she said, keeping her voice low. She could sound so much like a man now.

"Been there once as a boy," one said.

"Hideous place," Henry retorted.

"Compared to Flanders, every place is hideous," said another.

Mary had to agree. This country, with its white-beach shores and carpets of bright wildflowers streaking the countryside, would be another sight to describe in full to Ma. How could something as ugly as a war be fought on such beautiful plains? Mary didn't know, but she was grateful for Captain Southwick's foresight in encouraging her to stay clear of the sea battles. She *had* been safer here, all while pocketing a modest salary for her future.

"Do you have your horses?"

"Not yet," Henry said. "Who in town should we deal with?"

"Brought mine from home." The soldier shrugged, moving as the line inched forward.

Though Mary had not been on horseback before, she looked forward to her training in Flanders. She'd never forgotten how much she loved the horses she'd worked with as a stablehand. She imagined she might feel more powerful, more capable, on the back of one. With reins in her palms and all the power of a steed below her, she could be free.

After what felt like ages, Henry and Mary reached the front of the line. Mary approached the table first.

"Full names?" said the man in a faint Flemish accent as he checked a long list. He lowered his chin, and a shock of blond hair fell into his face.

"Mark Read and Henry Danby," she said.

"Former cadets?"

"Yes, sir."

When he looked up, Mary's heart caught in her throat.

He was the most beautiful human on God's green earth.

"This isn't the infantry. Here, we issue pistols, short muskets, and sabres," the Fleming said, his eyes the color of high tide as they settled on Mary.

Mary forced her slack jaw shut. She should say something. Her lips should be moving.

Henry laughed from deep in his throat. "Read can wield anything you put into his hands, I assure you. I'm not half bad myself."

Mary nodded, remembering Henry was there—remembering that the world still existed. "I can hold my own," she said. Much as she disliked shedding blood, she'd done it plenty in her four years in the infantry. "And I'm a quick study."

The man blinked, his gaze studying Mary a little too intently.

She held her breath. He looked from Mary, to Henry, then back to Mary. "I have seen two hundred men today alone, and each assures me of the same." He leaned forward, and Mary stared at the vein along his throat. "But you have not yet charged into battle like this—never faced a hedge of bayonets or swung a sword at an enemy clambering along the ground who is unable to meet you as an equal."

Mary swallowed. Her head swam, whether from the sound of his voice or the horrors he recounted—horrors she already knew to some extent—she did not know. If a soldier could be female, could a siren be male?

"Officer Van Acker, a word?" someone interjected before stooping to whisper into the Fleming's ear. Whatever he said made Van Acker sigh.

"Very well," he said with a huff, scribbling something on his ledger. "Welcome to the cavalry. Sergeant Gorst around the corner will see that you get your proper weapons."

Henry moved, but the soles of Mary's feet dug into the grass.

"Is there a problem?" Van Acker asked.

"No, sir." She could feel her cheeks burn as she darted after Henry.

But there *was* a problem.

Mary no longer had one, but two secrets to keep. If her mild fancy for Master Tansley during her sailing days had been a hazard, this threat was a blazing forest fire. Mary had to survive this war in more ways than most. And to do that, she had to stay far, far away from Officer Van Acker.

CHAPTER 20

For three months of training, Mary never saw Officer Van Acker. Sergeant Gorst headed their regiment and kept them busier than sailors taking in canvas during a storm. Mary and Henry, like the other soldiers without horses, acquired them from neighboring villages. Henry found himself an old Spanish-bred gelding he called Arthur while Mary took home a true prize—a brown Thoroughbred she'd named Merlin.

Merlin's agility and spirit won her over at once, though his hot temper cooled in her presence. His high spirits allowed her leverage in the negotiations. Ma would have been proud, seeing her strike the bargain. Merlin was sixteen hands tall and utterly gorgeous. Mary hadn't meant to spend so much of her savings, but she needed a horse. It might have colic or break a leg, leaving her penniless, but a deeper part of her said otherwise—that she could trust this creature despite the risks. She would have a better chance of rising in the ranks on the back of a fine, capable horse like Merlin. To do so would secure a better future for herself, and her mother. Any day, any second—Mary knew—this could all come to an abrupt end.

Mary's mind was all training—bonding with Merlin, learning swordsmanship on horseback, practicing how to maintain and quickly assemble her weapons, and participating in drills. Drill after drill after drill. Her legs and buttocks ached in places she didn't know they could. She had all but forgotten Van Acker existed when he rode into camp one April afternoon.

"Oh look, it's Father Time again," Henry said. He leaned in his saddle and grinned at Mary. "Think he can do us a favor and slow down our training schedule?"

Mary's mouth went dry. Merlin's dark ears pricked and he stamped his foot.

"At ease!" Sergeant Gorst yelled at the regiment, his jowls shaking.

Officer Van Acker dismounted and bowed to Sergeant Gorst. Mary couldn't make out their words, but Sergeant Gorst showed clear displeasure. His lips formed a tight line as he read a letter Van Acker handed him.

"Soldiers!" Gorst shouted. He held his chin high in the bright sun. "Today is your last day of training. Tomorrow, we join Van Acker's regiment and move west."

This was it? Superiors never had to explain their orders. This was war. This was battle. Not just the defensive fighting she'd learned on Captain Southwick's ship or the marching and minor skirmishes she'd dealt with as a cadet. Real war.

A murmur rippled among the men. Mary tightened her grip on the reins, feeling slick sweat on her palms. The moment she looked up, Van Acker caught her eye. That glaze of blue, the shock of white-blond hair. How he looked atop a horse. Mary immediately glanced away, feeling a burn down to her toes as she shifted in her saddle.

"Dismissed for the day," said Gorst. "Rest. We move at dawn."

"To Queen Anne!" one English soldier said, holding up a flask as they sat around a fire that night.

A few toasted with enthusiasm. Others were slower to follow. Mary swirled the liquid in her cup, knowing she'd dump it out at the first opportunity. Keeping a clear head remained her greatest asset. Her stomach roiled from nerves, or maybe it was the slop served at dinner. Officer Van Acker's regiment had joined them, but there would be more—thousands more—in the days and weeks to come. She looked around at the lit faces of her companions against the black of night: mostly young men, some old. Mostly English fighters like her and Henry, but also the Dutch. A few Austrians, Hanoverians, Prussians, and Danes. A handful of Scots, Irish, and Swiss. Captain Southwick had been right about this being a world war.

Had he been right about this being the safest way forward?

"You're awful quiet tonight, Read," Henry said to Mary, elbowing her in the ribs.

"Because I'm normally such a talkative fellow," Mary said.

He tsked. "Don't be testy with me. If I perish, you'd regret it terribly."

The humor left Mary's face. "Don't jest about that."

Henry sighed. "Very well. What is there to jest about in war?"

Mary shook her head. Henry had a new pimple on the bridge of his nose—stress did that to him.

"Officer Van Acker, over here," one soldier hollered, waving his arm.

Mary went rigid. With one breath, then two, she stood up to make her escape. Unfortunately, she slammed right into Van Acker.

She gasped, sounding too much like a woman. "I'm sorry," she muttered, moving to leave again. Only her feet, her miserable feet, would not move.

Van Acker angled past her without a word and stood in the fire's glow. He crossed his arms. Mary was beginning to feel her feet again when the interrogation began.

"Is it true?" someone asked.

Mary turned to listen.

Van Acker exhaled. "I fear so."

Henry shot Mary a look, gesticulating for her to return to her seat, but she did not budge.

Someone handed Van Acker a drink, and he downed it. His muscles flexed under his loose white shirt. After wiping his mouth on his sleeve, he sat with the men who watched with expectation. His white-blond hair fell loosely to his shoulders.

"What's true?" Henry finally asked.

"We anticipate skirmishes as we travel," Van Acker said. He drew his brows together, and his jawline appeared even starker in the dancing flames. "But the true goal is to battle Marshal Villeroi and the French troops in one month's time."

"How many on our side?" asked a Scot.

"As many as we can get. All the guards, dragoons, foot soldiers, and artillery companies on the continent. Civilian contractors, too."

The men searched each other's faces. Some flickered with anticipation while others paled.

"Can we win?" Mary asked. The words were out of her mouth before she could stop them.

All eyes turned to her. She immediately regretted speaking—all this attention from him. From everyone.

Van Acker rose slowly like the smoke and Mary squared her shoulders.

"Draw your sword," he said.

Someone gasped. Mary's heart thumped with fear. "Is that an order?" she asked.

"I am not your commanding officer."

Henry laughed nervously, and the man beside him kicked Henry's boot to silence him.

What game was this? Mary's hand shook, but she reached for the blade at her side. She unsheathed it. Van Acker did the same.

He took his stance. "Your name, soldier?"

Mary gripped the sword tight. "Read."

"And where do you hail from?"

"London, sir."

His lips tugged up at the side, then he turned around to meet the gaze of onlookers. "How many of you here are also from England?"

Half raised their hands.

Van Acker spun back to Mary. "And how many of you here, other than Read, thought to wear your sword at all times?"

Mary's stared at her weapon. She'd been sleeping with a knife since joining a ship, never sure when she might have to defend herself or her identity.

Van Acker lunged, and Mary blocked his blow. He smiled. How Mary hated that smile. This man was a risk to her, to every battle she had to fight on an invisible field. She wanted him to leave her alone. She wanted him to disappear.

She struck from above, and he parried. Foot over foot, they went again. Metal against metal, the way Southwick had taught her. Mary's heart pumped and her blade swirled and there was nothing but ringing and grunts and a hum in her bones.

At last, Van Acker faced her, close enough to feel his heavy breathing—his blue eyes close enough to see the smolder in his pupils. He flicked his blade in a movement that threw Mary's to the ground. She stepped on the handle and flipped it back into her palm—an old trick from her sailing days. Her chest heaved and she bared her teeth. What was wrong with this man? How dare he pick her out of a crowd and challenge her?

How dare he exist?

Van Acker sheathed his weapon, then raised his hands in surrender. "With a battalion of soldiers, brave and always prepared like Read from London," Van Acker said, eyes kindling with intensity as he studied first Mary's blade, then the gathered men, "yes, we can win." He paused, his voice quiet and flinty. "We *will* win."

She fumed as the men cheered. All Mary wanted was to storm away into the night. Disappear. Sleep and put to rest the uncharacteristic anger pounding inside her skull. Instead, she forced herself to wait. Two minutes, then three, until enough soldiers had left so she could slip away like a fog.

CHAPTER 21

"Victory!" came the wallops from around camp that night after they'd seen to the wounded and buried the dead. "God save the Queen!"

Mary was no queen, but she had at least saved herself during the ambush. She'd also protected the undefended in the camp: a group of fifty women traveling at the rear of the line—the camp cooking staff as well as an officer's wife, Mrs. Lambert, who'd been in the throes of labor for two days. Mary happened to be in the right place when the skirmish struck. She'd longed to be near them—but not *too* near. To listen to their voices, their gossip, and their troubles. What sorts of things did women talk about?

It startled her, at times, this distance. She was no man, but she'd never had the chance to learn how to be a woman.

What *was* she?

The same women now passed out food, pressing Mary's hands with thanks. "Bless you, soldier," they said. One didn't let go of her grip. "They've taken Mrs. Lambert to the village for a caesarean," she whispered. "If, by some miracle, the lady survives and bears a living son, she vows he'll be named after you."

Mary couldn't speak. She took the bread without meeting the woman's eyes.

Henry smiled as he took an extra portion without fuss. "You might use this to your advantage, Read," he said, one brow arching as he surveyed the female staff.

Mary rolled her eyes and carried her meal to a copse of ash trees so she could eat alone.

Henry followed her. "I only meant you could have asked for another ration!" he corrected. "A hero's bounty."

Mary sat on the hard ground and tore into the crusty bread. Her clothes still reeked from the fight. She hadn't felt safe in her skin since the ambush.

Her friend settled in beside her. "The whole camp is singing your praises."

As if she hadn't noticed. "It was a group effort—I won't say it again," Mary growled. She curled her toes in her boots. This skirmish was nothing. In a few days, maybe a few weeks, they would join with more troops—countless more. They would fight wars that the red poppies in the field would remember for centuries.

There was nothing here worth remembering. She begged for it to be true.

"Congratulations, Read," came a voice from above.

Mary's gut clenched in recognition. Van Acker stood before her, his blond hair disheveled and his gray tunic stained with sweat and blood. It seemed he also hadn't bothered to wash or change. "I've never seen such levelheaded thinking in a pinch. The way you baffled the enemy, driving the line together again. Is it true you employed a naval battle strategy?"

"I did what any man would do," Mary said, though Captain Southwick's drills for operating under confusion and disorder had risen like instinct.

"Leadership like that will be rewarded."

She choked.

Henry whooped and elbowed her in the ribs.

"Can I sit with you?" he said with more casualness than she'd seen him exhibit before. Henry assented, and Mary stared ahead. She could feel the heat of Van Acker's body, and it made her skull buzz as if invaded by a swarm of flies.

Van Acker stretched out his muscular legs, then picked at the scrap of bread in his dirt-caked hands. Why did he choose to eat the standard fare rather than the superior meals reserved for officers?

Never mind. It didn't matter. She couldn't waste a single thought on him. It took her entire, constantly thinking mind to survive a single day of her secret life.

"Sergeant Gorst took a hit," Van Acker said with regret as he chewed.

Henry cursed. "Will he live?"

"An arm wound. The lucky bastard will pull through. But in the meantime, your regiment needs a new officer."

Mary froze. She had wanted to rise in the ranks. She'd *wanted* this, *needed* this, to secure a life for her and Ma. But not so near Van Acker, where she was bound to make mistakes. Her stomach churned.

"It's already been decided, Read. There is no one worthier; you proved that yourself." His bright eyes lingered on her. "Am I right, Danby?"

Henry slapped Mary on the back. "You couldn't find anyone worthier." He continued with a list of her better qualities until Mary shot him a please-stop-talking glare. He raised his hands in surrender.

"Does Read snore?" Van Acker said.

Mary whirled. "What does that matter?" She could hear the sharp edge in her voice that betrayed her growing panic.

"Silent as a stone," Henry answered without missing a beat.

"Well, that will be an improvement. Gorst kept me up half the night with his nasal troubles." He laughed, a melodic sound she hadn't heard before—one that stabbed Mary between the ribs. "Eat up, Read," Van Acker said. "Then I'll show you to our tent."

* * *

Mary held her breath and shuffled her feet through the officer's camp. Bonfires had already been lit as dusk descended. Van Acker waved at a few men in the process of changing their war-soaked garments as they prepared for bed. Mary had seen enough naked men in her lifetime to know to look away.

This, she rationalized, would be no different. No different from the thousands of other times. But her heart dropped into a deep pit of her stomach when Van Acker opened the flap of a two-person tent.

"Yours is the left cot," Van Acker said. "Do you need help moving your effects?"

Mary swallowed and shouldered her single bag. "I have everything I need."

"That's all you brought?"

"It's all I have."

Van Acker studied her, then nodded. He entered the tent and Mary reluctantly followed. He tugged off his muddy boots, then tore off his shirt. Mary pursed her lips. The seared image of his bare skin, the ripples of his muscled back, sent a current through her. She ignored it, ignored everything.

"Nothing like a battle to beat down the body," Van Acker said.

"Mmm." Mary slowly unpacked her small bag. It was dim but not dark enough to change her clothes. She pulled a fresh pair of breeches and a clean shirt from the pack—her father's old shirt. It fit her perfectly now, at twenty-one years old.

Hugging the clothes behind her back, Mary left the tent. She found a clump of oak trees and changed, away from prying eyes.

When she returned, Van Acker sat in bed with a book in hand. He'd pulled his blond hair out from the tie and it hung loose just below his collarbone.

Mary swallowed and bolted for her cot. She got under the blanket and pressed her eyes shut. Though she usually removed the cloth binding her breasts once under the protection of the covers, she would not tonight. Or maybe any other night going forward.

Rolling onto her back, she felt her heart thunder. How would she sleep? She missed Henry already, his chipper nature, his comfortable presence, and his protection. As long as Henry quipped and made a fool of himself, people looked at him. Not at her.

"How are you feeling after today?" Van Acker asked, turning a page of his novel.

Mary winced. He wanted to talk about *feelings?* "Fine."

Van Acker huffed. "Fine? Just your usual ambush and combat after lunch?"

"Yes. Fine," Mary said, turning onto her side to face the tent wall. "Thank you," she added for good measure.

Van Acker laughed—that horribly beautiful sound from earlier. "Have I done something to offend you, Read?"

Mary gritted her teeth. "No." *Never mind the part where you exist. That I can't seem to think clearly whenever you are near, when caution and thinking are keeping me here and alive.*

That we now have to share the same sleeping quarters.

Mary dared a glance at him. He still held his book, but his ice-blue eyes didn't leave her.

She'd have to try a different approach since the former was having the opposite effect.

"What are you reading?" she asked. "Is it not a strange thing to bring to a war?"

"Why would it be strange?"

Was there no easy way out of conversation with this insufferable man? The easiest way to draw attention away from herself, she'd learned, was to ask questions of the listener. Men always seemed more inclined to wax on about themselves.

She was not used to questions being lobbed at her.

"It is of little use for victory." Though as she said it, Mary felt bitter envy.

"Do you only live for victory?"

"Do you only live for long-winded conversation?" Mary said, horrified the moment it came out.

Again, Van Acker laughed. "I knew you disliked me. Why?"

"I don't dislike you," Mary said, wishing the covers could make her disappear. "I'm tired."

"I understand," Van Acker said, flipping another page and squinting in the candlelight. "Forgive me. I'm an overcurious person—at least my father always said so. I suppose that's why I seek company in books."

At this, Mary softened. Perhaps she had been too hard on him. She resorted to her usual tactic. More questions. Better he talk than her.

"Do you get along with your father?"

Van Acker flicked a glance at her. "It's complicated. But my mother was wonderful."

Was. She noted the past tense and the bite of pain that accompanied it.

"To answer honestly, I love him well, and I know he cares for me. But sometimes I wonder who he might have been had he not been born 'Lord Van Acker.' If he wasn't a baron, perhaps he'd care for me beyond my position. I might have been a better fit for the clergy than the military. A scholar of sorts. I love languages." He paused. "What about your father?"

Mary was aware of the threadbare shirt she wore—her father's murky legacy, his skills as a navigator. The same skills she herself had honed and then abandoned. Just like she'd abandoned so many things and people she'd loved. "My mother was the person who raised me," Mary said. "She wanted me to have a life she couldn't have for herself."

The raw, blazing truth surprised Mary. When was the last time she'd told the truth?

"It sounds like she truly loved you," Van Acker said. The quiet but serious quality of his voice only deepened. Then he shook his head and closed his book. "My apologies. You said you were tired. It's been a long day."

"It has," Mary said, feeling her muscles relax. As they did, the fatigue in every muscle begged for sleep.

"Well, if you ever need company," he said, waving the leather-bound book, "this one came from my father's library. You might be surprised what the characters, despite being fictitious, have to say about our situation."

She should have said thank you or pretended to be asleep. Instead, Mary inhaled and told more truth. "I can't read."

Van Acker said nothing for a moment, then answered with a smile in his tone. "I can teach you."

Mary forgot to be terrified. A bolt of joy leapt in her throat. "How?" But when she asked, it sounded like an accusation.

Van Acker blew out the candle. "You may have noticed the tedious moments between riding, sleeping, eating, riding again, and the occasional battle and fearing for one's life. Plenty of time to learn in those moments."

Mary's stomach fluttered and she pulled the blanket to her chin like a child. What worlds might she know, which dangers might she avoid, with this knowledge? She was glad Van Acker could not see her it the darkness.

"I'd like that," Mary said at long last. When Van Acker did not answer, she assumed he was asleep.

"What is your Christian name?" Van Acker finally said a full minute later, groggy in a way that made his slight Flemish accent more pronounced.

The panic returned. If she sought to learn to read, Mary would have to be even more careful.

She *could* be more careful. Once she figured out how to speak to him without vehemence, stunned silence, or terror.

"Mark," she said with confidence. So much confidence that she almost forgot to play the game. "And yours?"

"Björn," he yawned. "Reading lessons start tomorrow, then. I'm glad to have something to look forward to. Because snuffing the light out of fellow human beings gives me no pleasure."

Mary did not move or speak again. She only allowed herself to close her eyes after she heard Björn Van Acker's breathing slow and was sure he'd drifted off to sleep.

* * *

Mary rose before dawn the next day. She rubbed her eyes and left the tent without sparing Van Acker's cot a glance. She set off to find Merlin resting with the other horses. Could she still ride with Henry? She hoped so. She had so many questions about this new position as an officer, and her right arm ached from sword fighting the day before. It would be another long trek, but this time—God willing—no skirmishes with the enemy.

Merlin and Arthur stood together in the field—the horses every bit as companionable as their owners. Merlin snorted when Mary approached with her hand outstretched and pressed the white diamond on his forehead.

"Good morning," came a voice from behind.

Mary almost leapt from her boots. "You," she said, her fists balled at her sides.

Van Acker frowned. "I didn't mean to frighten you."

"You didn't," she said, calming herself. She'd lived her whole life not only perceiving threats, but anticipating risks where there were none. She had to, she reasoned.

Van Acker—Björn—set off warning bells in every direction.

But that wasn't his fault. It was hers.

He raised his hands, one gripping a book. "I thought, if you were up early, we might get a morning lesson in first thing. Before the troop travels."

Mary blinked.

"I only thought—" he began again, then his chest fell. "I'm sorry. It's just that there's truly nothing I love so much as reading. Letters and thinking and, well, perhaps I'm lonely. Forgive my eagerness. But it isn't just that. You could memorize some of the lesson and practice it on the ride today. To make use of the time."

Mary stroked Merlin's velvet muzzle and tried to focus.

"Shouldn't you be teaching me how to be an officer? How to lead a platoon?"

The corner of Björn's lip tugged up. "Oh, there will be time for that. But based on what I saw yesterday, it should be you teaching me. You're born with it."

You wouldn't believe what else I was born with. Mary crossed her arms and stared toward camp, where she could hear the noises of the women preparing breakfast. She doubted very much that she would pass up her first meal as an officer.

"All right," Mary said, moving before he could see her smile. "Ten minutes, then food." Her stomach rumbled, loud enough that Björn could hear.

"Perfect." He handed her the book, then searched around for something on the ground.

Mary's brow rose as she examined the pages, the brown cover. She ran a finger along the fraying spine. The symbols meant nothing to her.

But hope leapt in her chest. Maybe, someday, they would mean something.

"Here," Björn said, returning with a stick. He stabbed it into the dirt. "We'll start with the alphabet. Wait, no . . ." He paused, shaking his head, his hair flopping into his eyes. "We'll start with this." He leaned forward and drew figures. After a pause, he went to a second row, then drew more.

"There," he said, arms crossed as he surveyed the scene with pride.

"And what is this?" Mary said. She studied the shapes, admiring the symmetry. Her stomach rumbled again, and this time, Björn laughed.

"Look closely," Björn said, pointing. "Because that, Mark Read, is your name."

CHAPTER 22

But it wasn't her name. Not her *true* name.

Mary shook her head as she rode alongside the troop under a relentless sun. In the three weeks since her first reading lesson with Björn—three weeks of traveling north, learning the rules of being an officer, maintaining weapons in the event of an attack, changing clothes in the dark, tromping off into the forest to urinate, and keeping her small but visible breasts bound day and night—why was *this*, the detail of her real name, the lie that bothered her more than it had in times past? Out of all the other lies?

Merlin had paused to snap up grass, and Mary gently lifted the reins. "Almost there," she soothed.

"You said that an hour ago," Henry hollered from behind.

Mary rolled her eyes. "You're like a child."

"And you worry about us like a woman."

Mary's stomach clenched, and she turned in the saddle to glare at Henry's sunburned face as he trotted Arthur on her left.

"Oh, come now, don't look so glum," he said as he passed. "Friends tell friends the truth."

She swiveled Merlin around and rode on, hiding a scowl that betrayed her fear and guilt. She was aware of the rest of her platoon watching, trailing her in the procession of a dozen other troops as their forces grew in number.

"I just mean you could afford to loosen up a little," Henry said. "You've been so agitated, so serious since your new promotion—even more serious than usual."

"Easy for you to say, Danby," Mary said, touting formality and her rank. "When you are in charge of a hundred souls, let me know how well you sleep through the night."

Though in truth, only part of her lack of sleep was over her troop. Despite their scrappy nature, they'd shown themselves worthy of fighting. Competent. She had total confidence in them. They had courage, raw and real. The skirmish had already proved it. They followed her without question, which was as strange as it was wonderful, and they rarely complained despite the hardship of training while traveling—all while knowing more battles loomed ahead. Their side was gathering, growing into an army unlike anything they'd ever seen.

And so was the enemy's.

Mary was not guilty of neglecting her duty. No. Her lack of sleep had more to do with late-night conversations in her tent, followed by late-night nerves once Björn fell asleep. Remembering those talks set her heart ablaze. The thrill that she was in over her head and, for once in her life, permitting herself the indulgence of toeing the line. Just the night before, after tracing the alphabet on the dirt floor of the tent in the last light of a candle, Björn had grabbed the stick in her hand, his callused fingers brushing hers. "Not like that," he said. "This is uppercase, and that is a lowercase *Q*."

Her whole body ignited as she held her breath.

"Try again on your own," he said with a brightness he never showed as a soldier. He rested his chin on his fist, one strong arm propped on his knee.

Mary forced her hand to redraw the shape.

"That's better." Björn beamed. "I'm sorry. If we had spare paper, this would be so much easier."

Mary stared at her work, the lines of letters, savoring the heat still tingling down her fingers. "Don't be sorry," she said.

Björn Van Acker could never know. He *would* never know. She could not put him at risk. And she refused to name this feeling, even to herself—something older than wars and countries, kings and languages.

A feeling older than names.

But it didn't need a name, much like Björn never needed to know hers. She could be content—more than content—with the knowledge of him: the constellation of freckles on the round of his right shoulder, the teardrop scar just below his ear, the animated way he read aloud the works of Shakespeare and Joost van den Vondel, Dante and Miguel de Cervantes—the prized treasures from home he lugged in his bag.

There was the way his jaw cracked when he yawned and the sound of his steady breathing throughout the night. His questions that she'd learned to answer with as much honesty as she'd ever allowed herself—stories about Ma, about her time as a stablehand, and what she'd learned as a navigator aboard Southwick's ship. Her plan to find Ma after the war and live a simple life in peace.

Björn seemed to care about all of it as much as she cared about his past—the youngest son of a baron, a young but bored child from a long line of war heroes, a boy with a knack for trouble and a facility with words and learning and people.

Arthur snorted, reminding her of Henry's presence.

"Fine. Keep your little secrets," Henry taunted when they spotted camp at last, then he laughed as Arthur took off at a gallop. "But only this once," he called out. Others followed him in a swarm, moving around her.

Mary and Merlin stood in the kicked-up dust, feeling the current of lives, the changes that had already happened as well as the changes she knew—like the breeze coming in over the too-green valley—were coming.

Henry was right; he usually was. Mary had changed, irrevocably. But they all would before this brewing battle was over. If she felt more fear, it was because she had more to lose.

"Listen well!" roared the Duke of Marlborough at the mass gathering of officers, sergeants, and corporals in front of his tent. He wore a red coat trimmed with gold buttons and a black bicorn hat. Mary marveled at the uniform—something she and her fellow soldiers did not have. The group accompanying the duke appeared clean and rested, unlike the men at camp. She hunched and felt out of place.

Mary stood next to Björn, his strong arm pressed into hers as more and more restless men joined the throng. She did not budge, and she relished the reassuring touch of him, the feel of anything good, while her heart pounded and told her something terrible approached.

"We gather here as allies," he boomed. "Tomorrow, we meet the French led by Marshal Villeroi." The duke's forehead wrinkled under his powdered wig. "We will give them a fight that will bring them to their knees, or their graves."

A few cheered while others crossed their arms. Björn looked down at Mary, offered a reassuring smile, then returned his gaze to the speaker. She wondered what Björn was thinking—if he would rather talk about anything other than bloodshed with such a gathering of travelers from such far corners of Europe.

"We have sixty-two thousand troops against their estimated sixty thousand, if our scouts are right. We will demolish this enemy in the name of Queen Anne and bring Spain back to her rightful place in the world."

Mary's knees ached from all this standing after a full day of riding. Her pulse quickened as the duke went over the weapons and marching orders, the overview of where the drums would sound. The drills needed for a successful charge.

"We are the British Royal Army!" the Duke said, spit spewing as he shouted. "The moment we cross the river, we ride to victory."

Mary exhaled as Björn whispered in her ear, "We'll stay together. Our troops have proven to do well side by side—our superiors know that."

Mary nodded, though her gut twisted at the possibility that they might be separated—a thought that had not entered her mind until now. A few men carried armloads of dark blue coats.

"Uniforms for all officers!" the staff called. A press of bodies moved into a queue, and Mary could smell the sour sweat on the man in front of her. Her slight height did not serve her here. The chaos and energy crackled, and she clenched her teeth while nudging her way to the front.

Björn tugged her arm out of the mass. Then he handed her a coat. "Here."

"How did you—"

He put on his own coat. A perfect fit on his sturdy frame. A startling match to the sea of his eyes, which held little joy.

Mary pulled on her own. It sagged a bit, as most of her clothes did—a preference to conceal her form. But it was notably smaller than the rest of the uniforms the others were trying on.

He knew the size of her body. Which made sense, she assured herself. Her height was no secret.

Or, at some point, he had studied her figure. She opened her mouth, then clamped it down again as they awaited further orders.

"Tell me again how we're supposed to do a synchronized dance with sixty thousand tired men and tired horses?" Henry asked.

He and Mary sat on the ground outside the busy armory, waiting for their swords to be sharpened. The screech of metal made her nerves scream. To keep busy, she meticulously cleaned every part of her musket and bayonet—a foolish task in the swift-approaching twilight. "We'll line up in rows, stretched out over two miles," Mary said. "Our seventy-four battalions and one hundred twenty-three squadrons will form an unbreakable wall and make the first move across the river barrier by tomorrow afternoon."

"Tell me not as an officer, but as a friend."

Mary stopped her tinkering and looked at Henry. His pimples, bless him, had flared again. Heavy circles shadowed his pale eyes. She wanted to pretend that everything was fine—to radiate her usual, resounding calm. She wanted to assure him that victory was inevitable. Just look at all the soldiers, gathered in this united cause.

But her insides churned. She no longer cared only for a secure future—much as she still longed for one and planned to honor her vow to find Ma. It was the agony of losing Henry, or any of the men she led. Any mistake she made was no longer hers alone to bear. The costs of bad intuition, a small blunder, the tiniest of slipups, could be the end of the people in her charge. People she loved.

Loved?

"Still here?" came a voice to Mary's right.

She gazed up at Björn.

"Might be here until dawn," Henry said, stretching his arms. "I'm not fighting the damn French without my sword. Should've just kept it blunt."

"Not an option," Mary shot back, her fingers fumbling over the parts of her gun. "I'm not sending you into battle without the best of chances."

"Read?"

The sound of her name, in Björn's voice, nearly undid her.

"Why are you attaching a bayonet blade upside down on your musket?"

She froze. She hadn't noticed this thoughtless error. It was only then that she saw her fingers shaking.

Henry reached over and grabbed her hands. "It's all right to be a little nervous, Read."

"We'd be halfwits not to be," Björn added.

Mary pulled her hand back. "I'm not nervous," she said. She couldn't be. She couldn't fret and worry "like a woman," as Henry had rudely accused her of not long ago. She was not, was *not*, a woman.

What was a woman—this great liability she'd been born with?

And what were the strengths of being one?

Male, female. What did it matter? She had to be more, she imagined, than who she was—more than she'd ever been before. She had to protect people. She had to return to that place of quiet calm, to access the deep well of tranquility she needed in order to fight well tomorrow.

She needed clarity, and her mind had turned to straw—had *been* turning to straw for weeks. She'd not only allowed it, she'd encouraged it.

Henry exhaled. Björn stood with his arms crossed and a look of concern on his face—saying nothing, just waiting and listening.

She memorized their faces. No. She would not. There was no need to. They would not, could not, die.

Mary's eyes watered. She sucked back the tears, pulled the emotions back inside and cleaned her weapons with renewed vigor. She was a sealed cask of secrets, watertight and unbreakable. There would be a day after tomorrow, a sun rising then setting over Mont-Saint-André in the west. There would be a day after tomorrow for all of them. But first, Henry needed his sword.

CHAPTER 23

Flanders
May 23, 1706

Horses stamped with impatience and soldiers shifted in their saddles, the brush of metal and weapons at the ready, when at last, the drums began.

Boom . . . boom . . . boom-boom.

Mary sat up straighter, robed in her blue uniform—the nicest thing she'd ever worn and wasted on such a cruel, messy occasion. Countless boots and hooves had trampled the grass into mud. She swallowed. Somewhere behind her, she knew Henry rode alongside the ninety-nine other men under her watch.

And far up and to the right, Officer Van Acker and his platoon gathered with other Dutch troops.

She could not see him—hard as she searched. She could not make out any individuals in the waveless sea of bodies. Thousands of men, thousands of rapid heartbeats.

And thousands more, the enemy, standing across the thin river ahead. A flimsy divider.

Mary swallowed and Merlin swished his tail with anticipation. She tried not to think about the enemy ahead, tried to wash her hands of compassion. But the words from Björn's reading of *Julius Caesar* the night before rang through her head: "In war, events of importance are the result of trivial causes."

Had she thought such nonsense before Björn? Questioned the world and its motives, beyond her desperate need to survive?

The drums quickened, like her pulse. The pounding set her teeth on edge.

She closed her eyes, inhaled. *Find the calm*, she told herself as her fingers combed through Merlin's black mane. Calm under pressure was her strength, her greatest weapon. *Do not lose your head.*

People are counting on you.

"Soldiers, forward march!" bellowed the Duke of Marlborough from the back of his gray horse.

And with that command, as if delivered by Moses himself, the sea moved.

The infantry regiments struck first, the fire of flintlock muskets announcing the point of no return. Smoke and screams erupted within an instant, and bayonets glistened in the sun.

"Steady," Mary whispered to Merlin as his ears stood to a point. Every second, every minute, was agony. She imagined she could taste blood. The air smelled of sulfur and iron.

Focus. Mary turned to check on the men behind her. Their orders were to offer a defense for the dragoons pulling the heavy artillery. It would be hours before her troop saw any action. Or, maybe they wouldn't have to fight at all. Maybe this would be over once the front lines tore each other to shreds.

"Sir!" came a sergeant in a red coat as he rode swiftly toward the duke.

Mary tried to read their lips. After a rushed conversation, the sergeant tore away.

"Isn't that Van Acker's superior?" Henry said, suddenly at her side.

Something whistled and crashed overhead. "Hold formation!" Mary yelled, covering her head and calming Merlin.

"Read, look," Henry said, pointing at the front as he recovered a spooked Arthur.

The English lines had been breached. The enemy drove like an arrow through them.

"Regroup!" the duke roared, shouting commands to individual officers. "Stay with the artillery," he barked at Mary, then rode off to the next officer.

She stiffened. Mary had a task, a job. She held firm to the reins and ignored the tingling in her toes, the thumping in her chest.

She ignored the desperate urge to look up, to look out.

Shrieks and bloodcurdling sounds rang out from the front. Inhuman in their horror.

Her eyes watered. Something broke in her. Something was wrong.

At last, she raised her chin and saw Henry—his mouth slightly ajar, his wide eyes fixed ahead.

She dared to look.

The enemy drove deeper, the knife digging into the lifeblood of the troops. As she took in the horror, two more sergeants atop their mounts raced toward the growing gash in the line.

Toward where that other sergeant had gone.

Where *Björn* had gone.

"Henry," Mary said, speaking before she realized she was speaking.

He snapped his attention back on her, his pale eyes haunted.

They had time. Hours, precious hours, before the enemy would draw near her troop's position—assuming they would make it this far. "Henry," Mary repeated, her heart flailing like a wounded bird. "I need you to take charge."

A blast from the battle sent Arthur on edge, his hooves dancing in the mud. Other horses did the same, shifting and snorting as men covered their own ears against the ringing fire.

"Hold steady!" Mary shouted, whirling Merlin around and backing up, backing away. She tore off her coat.

What was she doing?

She had a job. A commission. A purpose and orders.

But she also had time.

What of the rules?

The rules kept her safe, kept her protected.

Kept her alive.

"Henry Danby will direct this unit," she said, flinging her coat at him, "until I return." And she *would* return.

Henry's shock melted into an astonished scowl.

"Are you mad?" he mouthed.

"Stay with the artillery." Where he'd be safe. Where the entire troop would stay safe.

Before he could protest, before her better senses could stop her, before she could imagine all the ways she might be accused of deserting, Mary pressed her heels into Merlin and galloped.

Whizzing shots muffled the sound of Merlin's thundering hooves. Flashes of misery blurred past. A body rent in two. Another clutching the stump of a missing arm. The blank eyes. Someone dragging himself through gore. Moans that could make the earth crack open.

Where was he?

Where was his troop?

Mary pressed on, smoke stinging her eyes and acrid smells flooding her nostrils. One soldier lunged, and she unsheathed her sword and cut him down without looking back, without assessing the damage and the blood.

Another on a bay horse charged at her, and she dodged, flinging her blade out and slashing with all her might—what she knew to be a fatal blow to his stomach. Her elbow shook from the hit.

She rode on. On and on. Where was he? Where was Björn?

Then she saw two men dismounted, circling each other with blades. One of Björn's men.

His troop. This was his troop.

She held up her crimson-soaked sword and scanned the crowd with wild eyes. The chaos and confusion. The steel and crack of gunpowder.

She dared to scan the ground, the wounded and dead.

Be calm, returned that voice in her skull. *Breathe.*

Merlin leapt over a body and Mary sank into herself, into that well within her chest. An intuition, the navigation—that gift from her father pulsing through her veins.

Head clear, heart open, eyes alert.

Then she heard him.

She circled Merlin toward the sound. Björn in hand-to-hand combat, teeth bared as he rammed the butt of his musket into his opponent's chest. Blood ran down his thigh. The two wrestled, slamming bodies and metal, trying to take the advantage.

That moment of distraction cost her. Merlin jumped over another body, and Mary flew from his saddle. Pushing herself up, she leapt to her feet, slipping and sliding in the mud as her feet pumped, running for Björn. She gripped the hilt in her hand.

Then with a grunt, she saw the Frenchmen slam Björn to the ground, Björn's back in filth as the man stood above and raised a knife to slash—

Mary slit his throat before he knew she was there.

The Frenchman dropped to his knees with a whimper, then toppled over. Mary gulped air like water as Björn's unfocused eyes found hers.

Eyes she'd recognize anywhere.

"Read?"

She went to him, throwing his enormous arm over her shoulder and forcing him to stand. She did a quick scan: the limp, the blood, the muck in his hair.

"You're hurt."

"You're out of rank."

"Take a good look; there are no more ranks."

Björn winced as he stepped. Merlin, who'd stayed like some miracle, stood amid the battle, watchful and expectant.

She knew that beast was worth the coin.

Mary took his reins. There was no way she'd be able to lift Björn onto her horse.

"Your arm." It was still unscathed. "Can you pull yourself up?"

He reached for the saddle, tugged and groaned. A shot fired overhead, and he shuddered to put strain on his leg, but with enormous effort he flung himself and settled upright atop Merlin.

He reached out a hand, his gaze filled with a softness that melted her.

She took his hand, held it firm, then pulled herself up.

"Why?" he said, his stomach leaning against her, his hands wrapping around her waist.

She pressed her heel into Merlin. "Hold on," she said as they cut through the simmering battle toward the hospital tents. *Hold on to me. Do not let go.* "That's an order."

"Are you my commanding officer?"

That same line. He'd remembered. The smile was halfway up her face when a French soldier to her right drew his gun. Mary watched as the shot whistled. Björn, throwing her forward in the saddle, shoving her left with enough force to knock breath from her lungs as her abdomen slammed into Merlin's withers. Björn's body, a shield.

The shot slammed into him, and he slumped forward.

CHAPTER 24

"What you did was unspeakably stupid," Henry growled, stomping after Mary as she stormed toward the hospital tents.

"I did what was necessary," Mary tried to rationalize. "Then I returned to lead our troop, as I promised." After rushing Björn, unconscious, to the hospital tent, she'd rallied her shaky courage and galloped back to her position and duty, putting on the uniform coat again. Her troop had stood another hour, then came to minor blows before the smell of sulfur and iron cleared the sky, their victory declared by the Duke of Marlborough.

"Oh, did you now?" Henry fumed.

Henry. Furious and pimpled and alive. Very much alive, thank the Lord. As Björn was when she'd left him with the doctors.

Was he still?

"I escorted a fellow soldier to safety," Mary said. "Finished out the battle strong without losing a single man in our troop. We won, didn't we? No one is complaining or filing a grievance. Are you?"

Henry blocked her path. The path to Björn.

Mary folded her arms over her blue coat, as if that might keep her battering heart from bursting through her skin.

"Something's weird with you."

Mary glared as her head pounded. She massaged her temple. "I don't have time for your usual games, Henry. I'm tired. Bjö—Van Acker—could be dying as we speak."

For taking a shot meant for me.

Did he? Take a shot for me?

Henry held out a hand, stopping her.

"You know what the men are whispering now?" he hissed, quiet enough so no one else could hear. "About you and Van Acker?"

She really did not want to know. She could imagine and had stayed up many nights fearing it.

"I'm only trying to protect you," he said. "Think of your career. Your reputation!"

She shouldered past him, knocking him aside.

"You abandoned us," Henry called out.

This froze Mary in her tracks. *Abandoned?* She could understand his anger, but he didn't know the meaning of the word.

Mary balled her fists. She needed to get to Björn. She needed Henry to understand. She whipped around and stared at his torn shirt, the mud stains up to his knees.

"You abandoned *me*, your best friend," he said, this time with a hitch in his voice.

Heat rose in Mary's throat, but she steadied herself. Exhaled.

"I'm sorry, Henry," she said with intent. Pressure built behind her eyes. This day promised to break her, the emotion rising like a tide. "I hope someday I can explain, but right now, I have to go."

Björn. Get to Björn. Henry was here, alive. She could attend to his feelings later.

She turned to leave again. Her aching feet protested every step, but she ran anyway.

Pungent, animal smells assaulted Mary as she barreled into the officer's hospital tent. She suppressed a gag.

If these were the conditions for the war's leaders, what were the other tents like?

A doctor passed without giving her notice, rushing to a man strapped down for an amputation. The sight of the soldier's chewed-up limb, the bite stick between his teeth, caused her insides to revolt. She flew out of the tent to vomit.

Wiping her mouth, the sounds of men screaming, cursing, crying for their mothers like children, came in pummeling waves behind her. She knew which one came from the amputation.

She covered her ears and placed her head between her knees to steady herself. Her whole body shook. *Breathe,* she told herself. *Breathe through your mouth; repress the smell.* The dizziness abated. She had to find Björn. Even if it meant looking at every half-living body among the hundreds.

He had to be alive.

Mary inhaled, then plunged back into the distress and confusion, checking every cot. One man writhed in agony as a surgeon tried to pry something out of his ruined cheek.

She moved on before the images seared into her mind—the kind she would never tell Ma about. But Mary knew, she knew they would burn like a brand—much like the dreams of earlier battles she'd fought. Lives she'd extinguished.

Her heart pounded as she glanced at the faces. What was left of the faces. The stink of death. Fear.

Inhale. Exhale.

Shattered bone. Next man. Next bed. Where was he? Why did he do it? Why, why, why did he do it?

And then she halted. She'd know that mess of white-blond hair anywhere. He rested on a cot. His boots had been removed but his leg had not yet received attention. Someone had wrapped a cloth, already bloodied, above the shot wound she knew had lodged in his chest.

Mary rushed to his side.

"Who are you?" came a gruff question from a middle-aged nurse—a woman who'd darted in to check the bandage. "Are you trained in medicine?"

Mary took a step back, watching the nurse unroll some fresh cloth more quickly than lightning.

"I . . ." Mary began, not knowing how to answer. Who was she to Björn? Not kin, not a member of his platoon, not even a fellow countryman. "I'm his friend," Mary said at last. "And no." These confessions sounded small, too small. She did not blink as the severe nurse with gray-streaked hair checked the dressing and swore.

"Shouldn't he be awake?" Mary asked. "Do you have anything for the pain?"

"Blood loss. He's unconscious."

Mary reached for Björn's hand, then paused. She bit her lip, then cupped his fingers in hers. They were still warm.

"Stanching won't help for much longer, not with this wound," the woman growled. She glanced behind. "There aren't enough doctors. Numbskulls. Did they learn nothing after Blenheim?"

Mary heard the words but not their meaning. It startled her to be talking with a woman like this. A woman who appeared to be an expert, calm in the heat of crisis. Who was she? How did she end up here? Mary recognized her strength, one altogether different yet similar to Ma's.

To hers.

What did it mean to be a woman? Mary didn't know, but this one somehow seemed more capable and determined than the many wide-eyed doctors she'd passed.

"I'll need your help," the nurse said decidedly. She removed the soaked bandages on Björn's chest, throwing them into a bowl. "Do you have a strong stomach?"

Mary nodded despite her doubts. She stared straight into the angry hole below Björn's collarbone. She could feel his pain like the shot had hit its true target.

"It went clean through the right side," the nurse said. "He's lucky. Missed the vein. But we have to cauterize it, front and back. Stand here and stanch. I'll get the hot iron."

Mary did as she was told, pressing a new cloth to the wound. She could feel his heartbeat—faint, but present. She studied Björn's face, pale and beautiful despite it all.

"Live," she said as tears sprung to her eyes. An order.

* * *

Mary perched on her cot, staring at Björn's empty one.

Three days had passed. Mary waited, like the rest of the surviving soldiers, for orders from the Duke of Marlborough and the highest leadership—maybe direction from the queen herself. It was a marvel to consider: a future, *more* battles, after so much fighting and bloodshed. Who still had an appetite for this war?

Would it go on and on like this, until they were all dead? She couldn't continue. Never mind the rank and coin it once promised.

Henry had refused to speak to Mary after their argument. She didn't blame him. He needed answers—*deserved* answers. No one seemed up for talking except for a few soldiers bragging at meal time. Others huddled by the fires, fingers trembling. Some of the men from her troop glared at her, whispering as she passed.

Mary's gaze drifted from Björn's empty bed to his books, an inkpot, his nightshirt crumpled on the floor. Mary would be with him rather than here if she'd been allowed to stay. But the nurse had sent her out when Mary began to sway after the cauterizing. She'd ordered Mary to eat, to not pass out or vomit anywhere near the wounded, and to stay out of the way.

As much as Mary wanted to go on as before, nothing was the same—nothing could ever be the same again.

She removed her bag from under her cot and began packing.

Henry was right. She could not avoid these rumors; they were true. Her thinking mind had returned, and she had limited options. The men suspected Mary's attachment to Björn—that much was clear from Henry's remarks and their sneers. It was only a matter of time before an official complaint would be filed. Better to end this on her own terms. She'd be ready to slip out in the haze of the battle's aftermath—once she'd seen for herself that Björn had recovered. Desertion meant guaranteed death if she was caught, but she would put on women's attire before they could find her. Twenty-one was younger than Mary had hoped to quit this masquerade. But she'd pocket what she had saved, find Ma, and start fresh.

It would hurt, to leave Henry now—after everything. On this bitter note. Her men would be fine, more than fine, under another officer.

As for Björn, she'd done what she could. Now she only posed a danger to him. Leaving and protecting his reputation would be her final gift.

Mary stilled as voices approached the tent. In a panic, she dropped her bag and rolled herself under the cot. A medical assistant entered with Björn, supporting him with one arm while he leaned against a crutch.

He's alive.

Mary's pulse fluttered, and she clamped her teeth together to keep from shrieking with joy. She could slip out undetected now. She'd seen him one last time.

"Is this all right, sir?" the assistant asked, helping Björn to his cot.

"Yes," Björn said, masking any pain. "Thank you for your kindness."

The assistant bowed. "Shall I blow out the candle?"

"No, thank you."

Mary winced, wishing he'd snuffed it, as she listened to his receding footsteps.

"Read?"

She stilled.

"What in God's name are you doing down there?"

Mary hit her head on her cot, then pulled herself out. "Dropped something, is all."

His stormy eyes bored into her before trailing down her body, at the dirt smeared on her knees, then glancing at her opened bag.

For a long moment, they said nothing.

"I'm glad you're well," Mary said, summoning stiff formality. "You gave the men a scare."

He surveyed her face with pinched pain. "Why did you do it?" he asked.

Not this again. She couldn't answer Björn any more than she

could answer Henry. "I need to fill my waterskin," she said casually.

"Read," he said in a wrenching tone that stopped her at once.
"Please. Stay."

"I'll be back soon," she lied, not daring to look at him as she
stuffed everything within reach into her bag. Never mind the rest.
She had to keep moving, keep walking. She had to free him, and
herself, and with every second this would only get harder. "You
should rest," she said, pushing through the tent flap.

Tears formed the second Mary felt the air on her face. Stars
pricked the moonless sky like a thousand stab wounds, but her
boots pressed on through throngs of crickets as she made for Merlin in the camp's pasture. She followed her feet, the only thing she
could trust. They moved when every part of her begged her to
stop, to turn back, to tell the truth.

She had never been allowed to risk the truth, and the cost tore
into her heart.

Her feet shuffled mindlessly beneath her until she reached the
pasture. It took her minutes, too many precious minutes, to find
Merlin in the dark among the other horses. At last, she pressed her
wet face to his forehead before tossing a saddlebag over his strong
back. She threw a leg over him, then rode toward the black curtain
of forest, the boundary, the border of no return.

Not fifty feet away, she stopped. The saddlebag was
unbalanced—a rushed job. As she dismounted to readjust, Mary
swallowed a sob. She would disappear. Soundless. Nameless.

"Don't go."

Mary spun and reached for her sword, only to realize she hadn't
brought it. She didn't need to see his face to know that voice—
however weakened—that shattered frame that had limped to
where he knew he could intercept her.

"What are you doing out of bed? Your wounds—your leg! You
fool, you need—"

"Don't go."

If she'd only been quicker. If she'd only been able to find Merlin faster. "You don't understand," Mary said. "I have to."

He leaned on his crutch and surveyed her, then took a labored step forward. Then another. "If I let you go, will you first answer me one question?"

Mary squeezed her eyes shut and berated herself for being defenseless. "That depends."

"I can start," Björn said, taking one step closer. He stood a head above her. "If I were to make a report of my companion, I might start with the quality of Read's mind."

Mary coughed out a laugh, then covered her mouth. What if someone heard them? Found them before her escape? More tears rose.

"—Read's talent for learning, but even more so for listening. For watching. Read is very cautious. More cautious and considerate than anyone I've ever known. But braver for it, too. Beautiful."

Every nerve in Mary turned aflame. This examination had to stop. But when she opened her lips, no words came out.

He took another step. He stood close enough now that she could feel the heat of him. It took all her power not to step backward, to retreat.

"—Read also has some curious habits, I'll admit." He took a deep breath. "Like dressing under blankets. Trailing into the woods to urinate." He swallowed. "Hiding bloodstained rags before washing them in the river."

No.

She turned to Merlin, but Björn's hand grabbed hers.

"Please, Read. *Please.*" The urgency of his plea stopped her cold.

She whipped around, startled and furious. He knew. He couldn't know! No one could know. "Let me *go,*" she ground out, but it sounded more like a wail. She pressed her fists against his chest and leaned into him, watchful of where she knew a wound meant for her had branded him instead.

He wrapped one strong arm around her, the other supported against the rough-hewn crutch. "I will do anything you say once you answer my question," he begged. He raised a shaky finger as if to wipe away a tear on her cheek before checking himself and lowering it again. "No matter what you say or do, I could never cause you harm."

How long had he known? Mary rested her head against him, believing him, then nodded. "Only one."

Then, she would be gone. And he would be safe.

"Why did you do it?" he asked, his voice caught in his throat. "Why did you save my life, after I'd convinced our superiors to tuck you and your troop away from the front?"

She stepped back with shock. Did his face mirror hers—fear and . . . vulnerability? It was not the question she expected, the more obvious one about her sex.

Her resolve began to snap, buckle by buckle.

"For the same reason you saved mine," she said. A guess. A hope. A half answer.

The last tether to a life of hiding.

He lifted his finger again, tracing her ear and jawline, then the hollow at the base of her throat. She inhaled sharply, the sweet touch of him coursing down to her toes—a feeling new and wholly hers. Natural.

Too natural. It wasn't too late to escape.

"And what reason *is* that, Read?" he asked, breathless.

She raised her chin, her gaze meeting his. She wondered what her own eyes said, if they already betrayed the biggest truth she'd ever known.

Then she pulled his lips to hers, and let her body say the rest.

CHAPTER 25

Henry said nothing, his mouth hung open with horror, his face white as a bandage.

In the four years Mary had known him, he'd said many things. Never had he said *nothing*.

"I know it's a lot to take in," Mary said, clearing her throat and standing a healthy distance away—from Henry and his potentially loose fist, as well as from the camp. "But I thought . . ." She bit her lip. What had she thought? She'd warned Björn, as they'd made their plans to leave together, that Henry might not take well to this.

But Björn believed in Henry, and in her. And she knew he was right.

"I just thought I owed it to you," she continued. "As your friend." His accusing eyes, after saying she'd abandoned him, still seared.

Henry huffed and rubbed the furrow between his brow. "I'm just supposed to accept that my best *friend* is a—"

"Complicated person? With reasons for choosing such a difficult path?"

He sucked air through his teeth.

"The *same* person you've known for four years?" she tried.

"You've seen me naked! How many times have you seen me dress and bathe and . . ." He buried his face in his hands and swore. "Who else knows?"

"No one else but Van Acker. And no one else *will* know. Do you understand?"

Henry rolled his eyes. "I'm not going to rat you out, Mark—er, *Mary*," he said, visibly squeamish. "But don't forget that it's *you* who smashed the basic rules of trust." He pointed in her face, then shook his head, backing away and kicking a rock. "You lied to me. You lied to all of us! You've violated the basic laws of nature."

Mary said nothing. Though not prone to temper herself, she'd seen enough of Henry through the years to know that his fury would take whatever course it needed to take. He'd burn through it like gunpowder, then he'd be back to his jovial self with little memory of the offense.

But she didn't have a long wick to work with. One afternoon. That was all the time she had to make this right. Björn, who'd been honorably discharged due to his injuries, was seeing what he could arrange for her dismissal on similar grounds. Internal wounds, or lunacy if they had to.

If it couldn't be worked out, they knew what they had to do.

"Women aren't supposed to bear arms," Henry said, pouting and kicking more rocks as he spouted off various other points of nonsense. "They aren't supposed to fight like men—or be half as good at it as you are."

Mary considered leaving mid-tantrum. But his barbs did little to hurt her. What could, after a night like the one before? Björn. His lips soft, then rough and urgent against hers. The cool of night against the heat of her skin. His fingers through her dark hair, hers trailing his face with a gentle reverence.

Her standing tall, unwrapping the tight cloth that had bound her breasts, night and day, for years.

His asking: "May I?"

Her uncomplicated "yes" as he touched her.

The swell of giving up, of giving in, against the impulse to control.

The sounds of hunger that followed as they kissed—from her, from him. The forest and stars and wilderness the witnesses.

Her: "I love you."

Him: "Will you marry me?"

Marry?

Mary.

Her name. On his tongue. Even though he didn't know it yet. Not until he spoke the word aloud and she saw herself, and an entire future that included that full self, did the world burst open. He wouldn't bed her then—not that she would have allowed it, even if he'd asked.

But tonight, she would have him all. An irrepressible smile crept up her face.

"Are you mocking me?" Henry said.

Mary exhaled, returning to the present and recovering from her embarrassment. "No, Henry. And I'm sorry—for lying and hurting you. I'm just . . ." She laughed, and this seemed to unnerve him all the more. "I'm also *not* sorry. Whatever suffering you feel is nothing to what I've endured. I'm happy. I hope you never know the weight of holding in a secret all your life—the heft of that impossible weight." She lifted her chin up at the bright sun. "But how good it feels to be free in this moment."

"You are truly happy, then?" he said.

When she caught his eye, she noticed a slight shift. Shivery and subtle, but there.

"More than I've ever been," Mary said. "It'll be a simple service, late tonight at the church in the village. Me and Björn."

"And then?" Henry asked.

She shrugged. "I'll take the coin I've saved, he'll bring his, and we'll build a life."

We'll find Ma.

Start a family.

Make a home I'll never have to leave.

Henry nodded with more solemnness than she knew him to be capable of.

"Very well. I can't say I am glad for this new information, but I am glad to have known you." He began walking away. "Whoever you are."

"Henry," she called after him. Her heart squeezed. Her joy felt so easy, so light. Why could he not hold this with her?

"Goodbye, Read." He waved without looking back. "I'll tell no one what you told me. I owe that much to the good man I used to know."

Mary dismounted Merlin and faced the simple stone church. The night was soft and gentle, though she worried something bad awaited—for how could something this good be happening to her? To *her* as she truly was, as Mary Read? It was far easier to anticipate pain than to clean up the dust of crushing disappointment.

After tying Merlin to a post and patting his shoulder, she glanced at her clothes in the darkness: breeches, muddied boots, and what was left of her father's shirt. She'd left her blue uniform coat behind, folded and hidden under the cot.

This attire was fine enough when she was Mark Read four days earlier, before the sky's possibilities erupted like a summer rainstorm, watering tendrils of her heart she hadn't dared acknowledge before.

Would the priest object and refuse to proceed with the wedding if she wore men's clothing? *Her* clothing?

She ached to feel beautiful. Mary fussed with her straight black hair, then thought better of it. What was the use? Taking a deep inhale to steady her shaky nerves, she entered the church where she knew Björn would be waiting. In case of encountering any difficulty, they'd left separately. He'd needed the extra time to make all the arrangements and see to their discharges while Mary packed up the remainder of their possessions for the journey. Mary insisted he let her do it all, given his condition, but he assured her he'd rest only after they were well on their way, together.

Closing the heavy door behind her, Mary inhaled incense and glanced through the dark nave. Candles flickered at the front where a robed priest stood next to not one, but two men. Her heart stopped.

The three men turned when they heard her enter.

"Henry?" She didn't know whether she should run toward him or away from him. Her pulse thumped as she looked from Henry to Björn behind him. Björn watched with a radiant expression of adoration that threatened to undo her. He seemed lit from within.

Henry answered for her, meeting her halfway. "I'm sorry for my yipping. But I've got two objections."

Mary pulled back as if stung.

"First, you didn't invite me," he said.

"I told you—"

"As I was saying, you did not formally invite me. My second objection: that foul piece of inappropriate clothing."

Mary frowned. Not this rigidness again.

Björn stepped forward, his injured leg stiff but sturdy. He held out a box with a grin. "This is for you," he said.

Mary opened the lid. Tears sprang to her eyes when she saw the folded fabric. She hesitated a heartbeat, then another. She touched the white linen and removed it, letting the skirt of the dress unfurl to the ground. It was simple. Clearly used. But it was perfect— everything she'd always wanted and wished she could wear.

It was hers.

"How did you . . . ?" Mary asked Björn, her voice so soft she wondered if anyone heard.

"Don't thank me, thank him," he said with a nod to Henry.

Mary whirled on Henry, the dress pressed to her chest.

"A gift, even though I never got a lousy invitation or much time to secure one." His gaze was soft with emotion despite the armor of his humor.

"Thank you," she said, throwing both arms around him with all her strength. His being here, for accepting her, was even better than the dress.

"You didn't think I'd miss my best friend's wedding?" he said, squeezing her back. He sniffed the top of her head and cursed. "Even if you do smell like a damn horse."

The priest cleared his throat at the front of the church.

"You paid him for discretion?" Mary whispered, reiterating the plan.

"I did," Björn said. "But there was no need, in the end. You've been formally discharged."

Mary searched Björn's face. "On what grounds?"

He grazed a thumb over her cheek. "Later," he said, firm but gentle. "We also paid for speed. We can't linger."

Mary beamed at Björn, then Henry, before finding a place to change into the dress. And with that gesture, she would no longer be a secret-keeper living in the shadows. She would be a wife, with a companion at her side. This was the utmost wish of her heart. She would find her mother. Make a future with someone rather than wait for an elusive tomorrow while the sand trickled out of her schemes. She would not need to be on constant guard. She could choose her life for herself, whatever that meant after a lifetime of hiding. The children would come. And life would be easier, so much easier as a woman. How could it not be?

Standing before the old priest, stating her true name and her consent to be the wife of Björn Van Acker until death did them part—his luminous smile, his kind eyes below that crown of gold hair, his marked strength despite his wounds—all in the presence of God and her dearest friend, Mary imagined nothing else.

CHAPTER 26

Spanish Town, Jamaica
February 1721

"Björn?" Mary called out. Her skin felt aflame. Wet. Like she'd been doused with water. Why was she lying on a mound of straw? Scratchy. Itchy.

A swollen stomach.

A baby. A baby! Her heart leapt, knocking tables over in its thrill.

A dream?

No. Not a dream.

She was with child. After ten years of trying. It would be here soon.

"We were discussing the Fleming officer. How your intense feelings clouded rational judgment and rendered you negligent in the army," came a man's voice.

She lifted her head. Tried to lift her head.

"Miss Read?"

Why couldn't she lift her head?

"I'm with child," Mary said in a thin sound she didn't recognize. "Will you tell Björn? Did someone tell Björn?"

"Yes, we know—nearly seven months along, a month shy of

Anne's condition. You told the court. You 'pled your belly,' remember? They agreed to spare you both until your time?"

She tried to push herself up, then collapsed. Why didn't her arms work?

"Miss Read. Rest. You need—"

She elbowed herself up. She didn't need rest, she needed Björn. She needed to get back to the Three Horse-Shoes. Someone had to put the soup on and change the bedding. The officers and other ranking soldiers enjoyed coming by for drinks in the evening. Good men. Friends.

She held out her hand for support. It shook. Why did it shake?

"The wedding. You were telling me about the wedding."

Her vision blurred, then focused again, this time settling on the man. His captain's hat with an ostrich feather. He held a quill. What was he writing? She could read it—she could read many things now.

"What happened after the wedding?" he asked.

"That is private," Mary said. What a question from a stranger. But this captain looked familiar. Had they met? Was he an officer who frequented the Three Horse-Shoes? She must have poured him a drink.

Where had she put his glass?

The captain yelled for help through bars. Iron bars.

"You're fevered, Miss Read," he said, turning to her. "Lie down. You're seeing things that aren't there."

"Björn," she wheezed.

The captain spoke with someone through the slats. She heard the word "doctor."

"I don't need a doctor. I need Björn," she said, calm and gentle and firm. "Where is he?"

The captain turned toward her again, this time with a look of caution. "I don't know, Miss Read. That was something you were just telling me."

Another man entered. A doctor? A surgeon? She swallowed a scream. She'd trained, all her life, to not scream like a woman.

She clutched her stomach. Her baby. This was her blessing to love and protect.

"She's mad with fever," the captain said to the doctor. "Do you have something for this?"

Mary held herself tighter and felt the world tilt.

"I'm not mad," she said, her eyes closed as she felt hands on her, adjusting her body. "I was never mad. Björn told the army that so we could marry—so I could be discharged. So we could make a home and make our fortune another way. The Three Horse-Shoes. Have you heard of it? The ordinary near the castle of Breda?" She stopped there. She did not offer an invitation, as she might have done otherwise. She was not sure she liked this company.

"Bloodletting should help," the doctor said, rifling through a medical box.

Blood? No.

"No more blood," she breathed. The metallic smell. The pools on the ground and color on her blade. The hospital tent and the amputee and the shot through Björn's chest. Blood, so much blood. Month after month after month. The crimson stamping her undergarments. The black clots in Björn's lungs. The coughing. The coughing that never stopped.

Until, one day, it did.

"Björn needs a doctor," Mary said, her pulse racing with memory as her eyes flung open. "Not me. Him!"

The doctor gripped her arm and made a gash. She gasped. Iron. Tangy. Thick. She knew it so well.

I'm with child, she thought, before everything went dark again.

Björn, I'm carrying a child.

We have to find Ma.

CHAPTER 27

Anne heard footsteps echo down the corridor the next morning. Captain Johnson seemed to prefer morning appointments.

She sprang to her feet. Jesus, Mary, and Joseph. Anne didn't know she *was* capable of "springing" in this rathole in her miserable condition.

The baby kicked, and Anne rolled her eyes. "It's not *you* that's miserable," she shot in an affectionate whisper. *Just the carrying part.* She'd rather kiss the Devil's ass than go through this again. One month left.

And then?

She couldn't think of it.

"How is Mary?" Anne said, arms draped over the boulder of her stomach. She hoped she didn't sound as desperate as she felt.

"Good morning to you too, Miss Bonny," Captain Johnson said as the guard locked him inside the cell. He wore a gray velvet jacket and the ridiculous, oversized tricorn she had come to associate with him.

Fools. What was the point? Anne wasn't going anywhere without Mary.

The gombeen perched on his usual stool and handed her another guava. His forced smile made her all the more anxious. He removed his hat.

She placed the fruit aside. "How bad?"

"Fever dreams. Some hallucinations, maybe. But she can speak—and does so when she is able. She told me some curious stories." His eyes grew at the memory, and he shook his head with lingering astonishment. "The doctor is doing what he can."

Anne turned away and cursed.

"I *am* doing what I can on that account. You may think many things about me, but I am a man of my word."

Anne looked over her shoulder and studied him. A gentleman? She'd known a few of those. Ellen's despicable brother, Nathaniel, being one.

But Captain Johnson was not of that sort. She believed him. Even if he only wanted her and Mary to live for his own selfish sake, at least they shared the urgency of this goal.

"Did she ask about me?" Anne asked.

Captain Johnson gave her a strange look. "No."

Anne bit her lip. A stupid question—she was a halfwit to ask it. But perhaps no word about her was better than any word against her. Anne would make it up to Mary. She would do anything it took.

"Miss Read told me about her marriage. There was nothing about her being wedded to a Fleming in the trial papers."

Anne paced. "There are a great many things not included in those trial papers."

"So I understand," Johnson said, steadying his writing desk on his lap and inking his quill. "Which is, might I remind you, the reason I am here." He peered up, expectant. Perhaps a bit too expectant. Anne had to remind herself that the next move was hers. God have mercy, she needed that quill and paper.

"Can you tell me what happened after she married the Fleming?"

Anne scoffed. "That's her story to tell."

"You're making this conversation unnecessarily hostile," the captain said, with more agitation than usual.

She paused to consider his words, and then continued pacing. "I promised you my story, but not hers. And you still owe me the second part of my bargain."

"I have not forgotten." He tapped his thick fingers on his knee. "I have also not forgotten where you left me in your own tale. While Miss Read's marriage is still a mystery to me—though your response has at least confirmed that, indeed, there *was* a marriage—your own marriage to Bonny is much more well known, despite your creative use of an alias."

Anne decided that she'd had enough of her pacing, so she picked up the guava and sat on the cot. She took a bite, trying not to show how delicious and appreciated it was. Gratitude would get her nowhere. Groveling and freezing and inaction had swallowed up too much of her former life, her former self.

And a lot of bloody good that old self got her.

"You won't tell me what happened after Miss Read married. I understand. But you *can* tell me what happened after you proposed marriage to James Bonny."

"Per our agreement, yes. But you still owe me something more." She bit into the guava and looked anywhere but at the damn quill he held in his hand.

"I forget nothing," the captain said. "Man of my word, remember?"

Anne tossed the skin into the waste bucket, with perfect aim. Then she turned to the captain. They were not exactly friendly, but she did feel that they were coming to understand each other. He took her seriously, and she insisted on nothing less.

"Another fragment of my life," Anne said. "Not the whole of it. But next time, you must bring what you promised—in addition to attending to Mary."

He leaned back, waiting for more.

"I will do as you say, on one condition," Captain Johnson said.

She glared so hard she thought her eyeballs might burst. "We already made our agreement, *Captain*."

"Yes, but there are certain challenges, as you might suspect, that come with your second request." He'd dropped his niceties, and Anne preferred it. "Questions others, and *myself* I might add, could pose. Timing is a delicate thing for you, but especially for Miss Read."

Anne swallowed at what he implied.

"I will expedite your request for writing materials, with no further questions, if you promise me one more thing."

Anne leaned against the wall, searching for strength, feeling the blow coming.

"If Mary Read is, for whatever reason, incapable of completing her tale, you must fill in the gaps as needed."

Anne shut her eyes and her head fell forward, her matted hair a curtain. "Mary will pull through," Anne ground out. Mary could fight her way out of anything. If not for herself, then for her child.

"Of course she will," Captain Johnson soothed. "But if—"

Anne held up a hand. "Enough."

He leaned back, the stool squealing below him in protest.

"I accept but will hear nothing more of that talk again. Do you damn well understand?"

He bowed his head like a perfect gentleman. "I understand." He dipped his quill into the inkwell. "Now," he said, clearing his throat. "Where were we?"

CHAPTER 28

Caribbean Sea
1719

As Anne scoured the starboard deck on her hands and knees, the *Swallow*'s ship dog pranced in circles, nudging Anne for attention.

"Enough, Mops," Anne laughed, moving her supplies out of the spaniel's path. The grit of the holystones had made her knuckles raw. "You'll knock me and this damn bucket over." Sun baked the back of Anne's neck and the lower part of her legs, where she'd rolled up the patched breeches she'd inherited from Alby. Her red kerchief—a gift from Dutton—held up her hair. Captain Elford had assigned her this job of swabbing the deck today, but it wasn't always her appointed chore. Anne's main job was to wield her female dress and innocent mannerisms to deliver suspicious packages to the Royal Gullet Tavern and Barrels & Bones. Captain Elford allowed no one but Anne to carry out these deliveries.

Ellen would be proud of her performances—if not the illegal methods of the crew. Ellen would also have no problem saying their crimes aloud: petty thievery, black-market liquor dealing, tax evasion.

Piracy.

Then again, Anne felt that Ellen would have understood her desperate situation. Ellen, whom Anne had still not found in all her voyages through the Caribbean. Not in Nassau, Port Royal, Havana, Petit-Goâve, or Tortuga.

Mops pressed her wet nose against Anne's cheek, interrupting Anne's scrubbing. After two years aboard this sturdy, eighty-foot, two-masted merchant brigantine, Anne had proved her usefulness with canvas mending, cooking, and cleaning. She'd also managed to gain the small crew's trust, and they'd finally let her in on their secrets. She'd heard less and less of their vocalized superstitions about women aboard—and she worked harder than any man in their company. She'd filled a marrow-deep need to belong and had earned, at bloody last, the respect of everyone.

Everyone, that is, except her husband.

The dog licked the sweat from Anne's brow and Anne relented, tackling the dog and burying her face in Mops's auburn fur.

"I love you better than anyone," Anne cooed, scratching Mops's ears. "Mops" was short for "Toddy Mops," known in full as "Toddy Mops, Agatha, Belonna, Nosewise, Rumbullion, Sophos, Doubloon—Grand Duchess of the *Swallow*." The crew also called the dog "Parrot" when she wouldn't stop yowling, "Shark" when she nipped at suspicious sailors, "Barnacle" when she stood in everyone's way, "Mrs. Beans" when she got into the food rations, and "the Kraken" whenever the dog sprinted down the deck like a demon out of hell—nails slipping and sliding on the planks— once they announced that land was in sight. Mops, a great listener, paid constant vigil to Anne's bouts of grief: her guilt over Mam's death, Da's red-rimmed eyes and gutting words when he'd cut her off without a second look, the nightmares. Jesus, Mary, and Joseph, the *nightmares* of Nathaniel smirking in her doorway. The paper knife gripped in her shaking hand.

The dog rested her snout on Anne's shoulder, like a hug. Everyone—whatever they called the spaniel—adored Duchess Toddy Mops. She was their favorite captain. Anne never knew she could love a dog after what happened at the Cormacs' estate. She never knew she could love herself again. Maybe even for the first time.

And yet, here she was, arms wrapped around the most beautiful, perfect being that ever breathed. Even if Anne was less so. James would be the first to point that out.

As if on command, the Devil appeared. Mops's tail stopped thumping against the deck.

"Happy anniversary, James," Anne said without looking up. She quit her play and dunked her hands into the bucket, noting that the water matched the color of his unwashed scalp.

"A fine enough day," he said quietly, standing at the rail.

Anne watched as he gazed out at the opal blue and bit into a sugar apple. Did he find this day fine? How, and in what way? It was hard to discern what her husband approved of. She knew he appreciated sunsets over sunrises, took pride in his quick knots, and enjoyed curing his own salted meats. But what else? The crew clearly preferred her company to his sulky brooding, and they never made any inappropriate advances. She felt safe, a strange feeling she was beginning to identify in her bones. The men talked to her openly of their pasts: Alby and his troubled relationship with his father, Dutton's late wife, Murphy's home in Dublin and how it compared to Anne's beloved Kinsale.

A warm Caribbean breeze blew across her skin as she swabbed the deck, the *Swallow*'s sails snapping to catch the swell. "A fine day to remember our agreement," she said.

Two years. That was the bargain they'd made at the onset of their marriage: James would keep her safe in his care, and Anne would earn back the money he felt she'd robbed him of. He'd lied about the crew's involvement in small-scale piracy, and she'd concealed the truth about her nonexistent dowry after Da cut her off. The arrangement made Anne and James even.

Now, they could dissolve their union. They hadn't shared a bed in over a year. Anne had little interest in him or in carrying his child, and James—whether from his generally low appetite for such things, or maybe from knowing what evil had brought Anne to his ship in the first place—didn't press the issue. A mercy. Anne could be free of her obligation toward him and determine her next steps, with a bit of coin to her name, even if she was in no rush to leave the *Swallow*.

"There's something I need to talk to you about," James said.

Mops took off down the deck when she heard Captain Eford emerge from his quarters.

"Being...?" Anne disliked how, as the time drew nearer, James Bonny changed the subject whenever she brought up their arrangement. How he stared at her, with scowl marks etched into his forehead, whenever the others laughed at her snide remarks and jokes during lantern-lit meals. The jokes seemed to rise from nowhere, no longer trapped behind a wall of fear and restraint she'd known all her life.

She refused to believe his crusty mannerisms masked genuine feelings for her. Anne had no intention of getting attached. His affections, if real, would not change the terms of their agreement.

"In private," James added when Captain Eford was out of sight.

Anne bit her lip, cursing Mops for abandoning her. She stood, wiping her gritty hands on her trousers. She'd need to change into her blue dress for dinner.

Anne joined James at the rail and inhaled the salt air and wide horizon, vast and blue, limitless and unbound. The brine of the wind rippled over her like a baptism.

This view—the one James so detested, always complaining it wasn't a large farm or a piece of valuable property he felt like he deserved—never failed to sweep her off her feet.

"The king has issued an important proclamation," James said.

"And what could a king say that has anything to do with us?" Whatever her quibbles with James, she spoke her mind. He never hurt her beyond cruel words.

James moved closer, and she could smell his sour breath as he whispered. "King George is offering pardon and a reward for those willing to report certain offenses."

The ship swayed, but Anne held her ground. "What kind of offenses?"

"It doesn't matter. What does matter is—"

"What kind of offenses?" Anne repeated.

James growled. "Now you care to ask the hard questions, do you? Now that you're away from the pining lovers you fawn all over?"

Anne swallowed. "You and I both know that isn't true."

James seemed to try again, running a hand through his stringy hair. He moved to touch her shoulder, an uncharacteristic gesture that made Anne flinch. She heard him hold his breath, as if wounded, before dropping his arm to his side. "We wouldn't have to scrape together a living anymore. According to reliable whispers at the docks, the king is offering you and me a way off this ship."

Anne's stomach sank. "But I don't want to be off this ship."

"You'll do what I say. You're my wife. *My* wife."

"Under very specific and limited conditions, I'll remind you. Which are no longer valid."

He balled his fists and kicked the bulwark of the ship. "Damn you, Anne! Let's keep this simple. I am your husband. Where I go, you go. The king is offering a price far more than what we could make trading watered-down booze, and you're telling me you'd choose to remain? Hasn't it been you, all along, who has been groveling for more pay to 'start afresh' and other such nonsense?"

Anne felt the rage scorch up her neck and into her cheeks. "What does this price require?"

"The details don't concern you."

"If you expect me to follow you like a helpless whelp, you'll find that it does concern me," she said.

He growled. "Reporting certain criminal activities."

"Namely?"

He lowered his nose to her face, his contempt hot enough to smell. "Acts of piracy."

Her stomach twisted, and her pulse quickened. "Our activities, then?" There. She'd said it. She'd said it aloud.

James barked out a laugh. She wasn't sure she'd ever heard him laugh, and the sound unnerved her. "I've been in these waters, fighting for a living, longer than your pretty little head has been at needlework with your ass atop a fine cushion."

Anne bit her tongue, determined to decipher every word spoken and unspoken.

"So yes, Mrs. Bonny. You could say I know a few pirates. And I won't be sorry to see them go, or to fetch a coin for my troubles."

Think.

Act.

Which one is supposed to come first again?

"Understood," Anne ground out, forcing a tone of indifference. "And the sum is quite substantial?" How *could* he? How could he do this to the other men? Murphy and his intent to return to Ireland's emerald shores. Alby and the debts he owed after a life as a failed sharecropper. Dutton, that soft-spoken man, who wished to purchase a quiet farm in a village where he might die in peace. Even Captain Eford had simple dreams of a modest retirement near his children.

What other loyalties would James be willing to break?

He spun around. "You accept, then?"

"What choice do I have?" she feigned, her mind sifting through the facts and remaining choices. "I only hope you will pay the small share you owe me, now that my debt is paid. That we can settle things between us for good."

He huffed.

"You *do* plan to uphold our deal, of course." She shouldn't have said it, that extra cry for reassurance. But the tremor in her throat wouldn't swallow it down.

"We'll discuss all that later," James said, looking off to where Dutton now took the helm. "Tell no one," he said. "I've devised an excuse to return to Nassau tomorrow morning. Then, you and I will debark and arrange a meeting with Governor Woodes Rogers."

With that, he turned on his heel and made for the crew, leaving Anne alone with her jaw clamped hard enough to break teeth.

What could James do, at his absolute angriest?

She clutched her elbows and squeezed her eyes shut. Tomorrow, she would find out.

ℭHAPTER 29

The crew attended to their posts as they brought the *Swallow* around Hog Island to enter Nassau Harbor. Looking down, Anne could see every reed and coral lining the ocean floor. She felt a chilly calm as she tied off a line before helping Alby and Dutton drop anchor into the clear, turquoise sea.

"Mrs. Bonny and I will take the first rowboat to shore," James said. He carried a single bag and gave no signs of his plans to abandon and betray them. Anne had nothing of value. All she'd managed to smuggle was a handful of coins, shaved off the top of her illicit deliveries, and a knife for self-defense.

The dagger wrapped against her thigh was no bigger than the paper knife from two years earlier. She hoped her kerchief would hold the blade in place. But mostly, she hoped she wouldn't need to use it.

"Any special parcels to deliver, Captain?" Anne asked as Alby aided James in untethering the rowboat hitched to the side of the *Swallow*.

Captain Eford handed her a squat black bottle wrapped in cloth, just as Anne slipped him a note.

His wiry brows shot up, and Anne shook her head to signal silence. He gave a slight nod of understanding, then slipped the paper into his gray jacket. "Take this to the merchant who goes by 'Tom' at Beardsley's Barrel," Captain Eford said. "He'll be at the second-to-last business on Bay Street. We'll be an hour or two behind you."

Anne took a step back, surveying the familiar faces, the familiar shape of the *Swallow*. Murphy and his sunburned nose. Alby and his crooked grin. Dutton and the yellowing quality of his eyes. Her friends' tar-stained fingers from weatherproofing the lines. The smell of musty cedar. The ivory sails. The planks she'd scoured until her palms developed calluses.

Mops whimpered, and she scratched the spaniel's floppy ears one last time. She would not, *could not*, look at her without falling apart and betraying her plan.

"*Goodbye*," Anne breathed.

"Ladies first," James mumbled, gesturing for her to descend the ladder. He offered a hand, which she did not take.

"The governor's mansion is due south above Old Church Hill," James said once they logged the *Swallow* and reached shore. His urgency was palpable as he picked up his pace on the beach-covered path into the shantytown. A few drunken men passed, along with a horse-drawn cart and a pack of sheep wearing bells.

Anne did not move.

Study the sand, she decided, rooting herself to the earth. It was so bright that it glowed.

James flung down his heavy bag and glared. "Enough of these womanly sensitivities."

The sand was finer than sifted flour. The very opposite of gunpowder.

"We're wasting time."

We?

Anne lifted her chin and watched his eyes shift from her to the horizon. At the *Swallow* in the distance.

James lunged and knocked her aside with his shoulder, his

mouth agape as he watched with horror as the *Swallow* raised her sails, getting ready to make way.

He wheeled on her, eyes narrowed to slits. "*You.*"

Anne felt panic rise in her chest, but she steadied herself.

James shoved a finger in her face. "After everything I've done for you." He knocked the bottle Captain Eford had given her to the side of the road. The glass shattered against a rock.

"They are good men. They had a right to know." Captain Eford and her friends were not rogues and violent criminals. They deserved better than a hangman's noose. "You should be thanking me. If I'd told them before we left, they might have tossed you overboard. If anything, I've saved your life. We're even—more than even." She didn't love James Bonny, but that didn't mean she wished him dead.

"You've thrown away our chance! The captain alone would have been worth a hundred pounds."

"There is no 'our' anymore."

His eyes bulged and he shook with rage. Anne took a step back, remembering the knife hidden under her skirts. "I'm invoking Brehon law," she said, the rehearsed sentences on the tip of her tongue. "According to ancient custom, it is my right as a woman to end this marriage. I release us both from the bargain and will take what coin you owe me for my labors."

The louse of a man had the nerve to look injured. Then, his face twisted and he laughed. "Brehon law? You're not in provincial Ireland anymore. If it's divorce you fancy, you might better acquaint yourself with the laws of the English. I own you until death, and there isn't a thing you can do about that."

Anne's throat constricted, but she squared her shoulders. "You despise me, and my latest defiance should make my own feelings clear. I'll not be married to a turncoat coward. Let me be and go your own way. We can pretend this never happened."

She needed to pause, rein in her pride and rage. She needed money. He could sulk on his own time.

He stepped closer, his nose an inch away from hers. She stopped breathing, unwilling to inhale his foul breath. He stared at her lips, and for a horrible moment, she feared he might kiss her. "You won't find Nassau to be hospitable to an unaccompanied woman of a mere twenty-one years, Mrs. Bonny. Not with nine ill-bred men to every one woman skulking about. We'll see how you fare after a few months alone on this dune without a man to protect you. When I return for you, my *wife* as the town well knows, I hope you'll have returned to your senses."

"You're mad," Anne scoffed. She tasted bile.

"And you're alone—in a notorious nest of pirates. I'll find an honest crew to sail with by nightfall. You, on the other hand . . ." he scoffed. Then, without finishing his sentence, he stormed away.

For hours, Anne walked the sandy streets, avoiding glances and shouts from passing packs of sailors. Her whole body felt taut as a halyard line. Why hadn't she invented some excuse to take Toddy Mops for company and protection? She missed the spaniel already. She mentally counted the coins she'd managed to smuggle behind James's back, but she needed a miracle. The smell of meat wafted from a chimney. Her stomach growled and she ignored it. As the white sun traveled through the sky like an unblinking orb, her heart pounded at the threat of dusk. James, that horrible man, was right. She was alone—more alone than ever. The *Swallow* was her home and safety.

But no more.

Jesus, Mary, and Joseph. Her friends had better appreciate this sacrifice.

Anne did not bother to remove the sand that had collected in her sweaty boots. Holy God above, were there white grains everywhere? Sand in her hair. Sand in her ears. Sand in her teeth. She might ignore her blisters. She might ignore hunger. But her whole body demanded a safe place to rest for the night. And the night after that.

She'd never missed Ellen more. Where the bloody hell was she?

Anne turned onto a quieter street, reading the signs atop the shops, taverns, and brothels with names like The Pour House, The Poisonwood Tap, and The Coin & Cutlass. An image of Nathaniel invaded her mind, and she pushed it out, picturing instead the hidden knife.

"Would ya look at this firecracker."

"Say, you think her hair is that color everywhere?"

"How much for the hour, lass?"

Anne whirled, her heart pounding as she studied the two drunkards. "I am *not* for sale."

"Don't be like that, missy. Everyone has a price."

She pulled out the knife. It trembled in her fingers. "Stay back."

"Pussy has claws," one purred. He reeked of rum. The other put up his hands in mock surrender.

"That's enough, Boris," came a fierce, firm voice.

Anne spun around, her small dagger raised.

The man—Anne now saw it was a man who'd spoken despite the melodic timbre of the voice—did not react. He kept his striking dark eyes on the two men. "You and your lot know better. Hire a proper prostitute up the road at the Siren's Swig."

The two men muttered. "As you say, Read. An honest misunderstanding is all."

Anne gathered her nerves as she watched the men leave. Then her shoulders dropped and her whole body convulsed.

"Go home before the true brutes come out," the stranger said, his short, lean frame turning for the door of a two-story brick tavern. "It isn't safe."

"Wait," Anne said, holding up a hand.

The man turned, and Anne felt his steady mahogany eyes survey her disheveled appearance. "Are you a runaway?"

Anne shook her head, still fumbling for words.

"A pirate's mistress?"

Anne had no answer. She felt tears sting her eyes.

The man tucked a rag into his belt, then folded his arms. He must have been a barkeep. He was skinny, but strong, and he had an unnerving, poignant gaze, prominent cheekbones, and circles like he hadn't slept in all his thirty-something years. "I don't want any trouble, you understand? I've got enough problems of my own."

Anne nodded, finally putting away her weapon. But she did not budge. Neither did the barkeep.

With a long sigh, the barkeep opened the door wider. "Come in before I change my mind."

Anne didn't need to be told twice. Inside, an assortment of long tables and round tables crowded the large room with an enormous hearth. Pipe smoke lingered in the air. A bar ran along the length of one wall, and to the side of that, an entry to the kitchen. Opposite the bar, a set of stairs led to a second level.

The man moved to clear a table, and Anne followed. A few other tables were occupied with well-dressed sailors and plates of salmagundi—roasted fish, sliced eggs, nuts, and pickles atop a salad. Anne salivated. The men laughed, clinking glasses and swapping stories.

"Here," the barkeep said, handing Anne a basin of soapy water. "Ever worked in a tavern?"

Anne's nerves from the encounter with the men still pummeled through her, and she merely shook her head.

"Have you ever worked at all?" he added.

Something snapped back into place, and Anne felt her temper flare like a lifeline. "I'm a sailor." That, Anne hoped, sounded better than citing her experience with embroidery—even if the former sounded a bit absurd.

The barkeep didn't react.

"Read!" came a voice from the end of the room. "Another round of ale for these rascals."

He acknowledged the order, then returned to Anne. "You can call me Mark or Read—either suits. I've no power or influence with the owner of the Jubilee. But I can find you a corner behind the bar to sleep for the night." He flashed a ghost of a smile. "Keep your secrets safe. Anyone in this den of pirates has them. I'll not be asking you for yours."

He tossed Anne the damp rag, then sped away to handle the customers.

CHAPTER 30

"Just one night" of sleeping behind the Jubilee's bar turned into two, then three. A week passed, followed by another and another, and still Anne washed the dishes, scoured the floors, and mopped up vomit when customers got a little too deep in their cups. The manager relented to the arrangement. Anne's labor paid for the lodging and table scraps, but nothing more. She stayed busy and out of sight, only venturing outside to fetch well water or to make a purchase for the cook.

Anne studied the people around her. The head cook, Mr. Huxley, did not use full sentences until noon. The rat-faced owner came and went without introduction or notice of her, and no one bothered to mention his name beyond "sir." Anne had met two barkeeps and five barmaids. She liked Read best. He had a strength that reminded Anne of Ellen, but without the sharp edges. On more than one occasion, she'd seen Read break up a fight without so much as a blow. He had instincts like a cat and not a trace of fear. The customers in turn seemed to respect him with a kind of reverence. Read had little to say beyond the work of the day and, as promised, had asked Anne nothing about her situation. Out of loneliness, Anne had offered up bits and pieces about Ireland, a handful of stories about Mam, vague references as to why she could not return home, and select details about James Bonny and her current crisis.

"Sounds like he isn't worth a groat," Read said one day as they polished the silver.

"He's a gowl. Do you think he'll return as he threatened?"

Read paused before responding. In the two weeks of working together, Anne had gotten used to his silences. "Stubborn like that with a mind for greed? I fear so."

Anne's gaze flicked to the thin silver band on Read's ring finger. She dared to probe. "What's your wife like?"

Read froze.

"Forgive me, I shouldn't have asked," Anne said.

Read returned to polishing a pitcher. He was all angles with straight dark hair hanging to his shoulders. Read couldn't be more than ten years older than Anne. His quiet confidence seemed tarnished by sorrow.

"Gone," Read finally said, moving onto a candlestick with renewed vigor.

Anne nodded, understanding but not understanding. She wouldn't ask where Read's wife had run off to. Perhaps it was after another man. If she'd gone after a sailor or a pirate, always in and out of port, it would be pointless to guess anyway. For all of Da's flaws, Anne never appreciated how rare it was—his sticking by Mam through it all.

"Anne!" barked the cook, Huxley, from the other end of the room. "Just got word. Captain Rackham himself is dining here tonight—with a large crowd we'd be wise to impress. We're out of pork flank." The bulbous man placed some coins on the table. "Fetch us some, aye? And don't settle for a tough batch. Old Wentworth at the Hog's Wife can do better for an old friend."

A salty spring breeze teased her snarled hair, which she'd tied back with Dutton's red kerchief. The smell from the ocean made her miss life aboard a ship and the company of her boisterous companions. All except James, of course. She shivered despite the pleasant heat.

He can't be back already, she reasoned—assuming he'd return, let alone find her hiding spot. There was no possibility, on God's green earth, that she would run into James today. Or the next.

She pressed forward—past Dieter's Den and the Pewter Port, eyes fixed on her boots traveling the sand-covered path flanked by palm trees and sea grape shrubs—focusing on the task and familiar route to the butcher shop.

Why did I pry into Read's marriage? What is it to me?

Is Read one to take offense?

It was perfectly reasonable, Anne argued, to not know where Read lived, or how he lived, or why he ended up in this haunt for rogues. Hadn't his kindness been enough? Anne couldn't also demand friendship.

She hadn't had time to properly apologize before Huxley called her away. "Damn Captain Rackham and his miserable hungry cronies," she muttered.

That's when she collided into another person, hard enough to knock her off her feet. She landed flat on her ass.

"Jesus, Mary, and Joseph!" Anne bellowed, brushing sand off her skirts. "Mind where you're walking!"

"My apologies, miss. Are you hurt?"

The voice sounded genuinely concerned. "No." Anne relaxed her wince and tented her eyes at the sun's glare, where stood a ridiculously tall man. He offered a hand, which she ignored, then pushed herself up onto her own feet.

"I'm glad to hear it. That allows me the risk of pointing out that it was you, in fact, who ran into *me*. Headlong, I should add."

Anne patted her pockets in a huff. Read had warned her of various pickpocket techniques, and she wouldn't be swindled by this man.

And God Almighty. What a man he was. Dashing. Sun-bleached

brown hair. Loose-fitted, flamboyant red trousers. A dazzling half smile.

With . . . was that a fistful of wildflowers in his hand?

"I haven't seen you around these parts before," he said.

"As it so happens, I'm a new arrival."

He flicked a glance over her body, then continued on with his flower picking. "You nearly trampled this lovely lupin. Lucky I saved it in time. Isn't it a pretty blue?"

Anne scowled. "Do you make it a habit of plucking flowers right in the path of people going about their business?"

The corner of his mouth tugged up. He snapped up a stem of purple blossoms just off the path.

"And what business are you about, miss . . . What do they call you?"

"Anne." It surprised her to hear her own name, to hear herself offering it so freely.

"Is there a surname? A husband's name, perhaps?"

Anne blinked. An image of Ellen and Mr. Tyler on the docks back in Charles Town flashed through her mind. Was this flirting? "That doesn't concern you."

"Your business, or your surname?"

"Both."

"As you wish," the man said, stopping to pluck a sprig of red geraniums to add to his colorful collection.

"Are you a gardener?"

"Curious, are we?" he stood and took a step closer.

Anne cleared her throat. She was suddenly conscious of how long it had been since she'd taken a proper bath. "I told you my name. It's only courteous to offer yours."

He hesitated for the briefest of moments, as if gauging her seriousness. "Everyone here calls me 'Calico Jack.' But to you?" He paused. "You can call me by my true name, John." He held the purple blossoms to her nose, their natural formation a near perfect circle. "Care to smell?"

Anne raised a brow. He laughed. She stifled a laugh herself, then inhaled. Sweet, delicious, light. Her eyes shot open. "Vanilla?"

"A similar scent, I'll grant you that," John said, his youthful boyishness on full display. "But this is milkweed, in its flowering season—an essential plant to this region." He lowered the stem to his side and surveyed her face. "I see you are far from home indeed. I was thirty before I had my first brush with such finery as vanilla."

Anne patted her pockets again for good measure. The coins were still there.

"Care for an escort into town while you conduct your very secret business? I've gathered what I needed here."

It was only then, at last, that Anne came to her senses. She'd take her chances traveling to the Hog's Wife quickly, and alone. "I can fend for myself." And in that moment, she felt its truth, relishing the way it radiated through her core.

Did his face fall for a fleeting instant? She wanted to imagine so. "Suit yourself, Miss Anne," he said. He reached into his bouquet and pulled out a single yellow alder. "A buttercup, in case we never meet again."

She took it, twirling the delicate stem in her fingers. And before words returned to her, he was gone.

That night, the full Jubilee staff showed up in anticipation of the crowd. The owner himself arrived two hours early, dressed in a wig and a dapper green waistcoat with silver buttons. The rooms upstairs were emptied of prior guests, the beds fluffed and made with clean coverlets. The accommodations for Captain Rackham were ready, and no one could say how long he and his crew would stay in Nassau. The barmaids dusted and redusted every surface until it gleamed, and Anne swept what felt like the thousandth grain of sand out the back door. She had to admit, her brush with John had left her with an unpleasant fluttering in her stomach. But it also infused a bit of energy into her work. Ellen would have approved. Anne, having never found herself in this situation or in this state of feeling before, didn't know if she agreed. For her own sake, she was determined to pay the encounter no more attention. She had a job to do.

The other barmaids assisted Huxley as meaty smells wafted. It was enough to make Anne's mouth water. She hoped the men might leave enough leftovers for her to snatch a morsel once they retired.

"And the wine?" Anne overheard the owner say.

"Madeira. Nothing but the best. Rackham's favorite."

"Better be," the owner growled. "I'll be damned if the Black Jib steals any more of our prized clientele. Business hasn't been the same since they stole Ben Hornigold out from under us. The pissing turncoat."

After running around in a frenzy, the owner called the full staff together for a meeting. Anne took her cue, lining up shoulder to shoulder with the other barmaids. "Listen well," the owner said as he paced.

"What are we, soldiers on the front lines?" Anne whispered to Read. "How hungry could these men be?" She'd been trying to establish a friendly tone since her insensitive comment about Read's wife.

Read half smiled. "I've seen worse."

Anne took the smile as a sign of Read's forgiveness, if Read had been offended in the first place. No matter. It was time to put it all behind her: the impertinent question, Anne's longing for Ellen, the run-in with John—though she'd tucked the buttercup's stem into her braid. The silliness caught her off guard. But if the blossom only had a few hours to live, it would be a shame to let it wilt in her pocket.

"As you know, Captain Rackham is a true gentleman. Don't let his kindly demeanor deceive you. The man ousted the notorious Charles Vane from his own brigantine through an overwhelming vote from the crew. Then he took on a French man-of-war with staggering success. Few are more wanted by the sniveling Governor Rogers, but few are more feared, or respected, in New Providence. It is the greatest privilege of our establishment to welcome this leader and his men—to show him, and the rest of this town, that the puppet of a new governor has no real rule in these parts of Nassau, a kingdom of free men."

A few clapped and cheered. Anne joined, but she noted that he did not include women in his vision of freedom.

Huxley, visibly impatient with the owner's grand speech, interrupted. "He drinks like a fish and tips well, especially for generous service. You know what to do."

The staff around Anne seemed to decode this without problem. Did this have anything to do with the lower-than-usual necklines of most of the ladies in the line? Anne might have asked Read for clarification, but a growing noise swelled from the street. A cluster of laughing men approached, their shadows growing in the lanterns hanging outside the windows.

"Positions ready!"

The owner threw open the wooden door, his arms outstretched and his face instantly transformed from stern to warm and friendly. "It's been too long, Jack. You're welcome here."

"There's no place better for making up lost time with good friends."

That voice.

Anne didn't have to look, and she didn't dare. Her pulse skittered and her mouth hung open. She wasn't sure what horrified her more: that *this* was the famed gentleman she'd been told about or how happy she was to see him again.

She snapped her jaw closed and straightened as John—that is, bloody Captain Jack Rackham—entered with his men. Anne stared ahead, abreast of the other barmaids, hoping he would not see her among the others, and hoping like hell that he might.

Mother of God, you're married, Anne. Get a hold of yourself.

Not according to Brehon law. Not according to my conscience. I settled my debt.

Damn James Bonny if he thinks he is, or ever has been, a true husband.

What nonsense, Anne thought, gathering her wits. Her banter in town with Jack was a single, mostly unpleasant encounter—all things considered. Nothing more.

She was nothing. No one.

And didn't she mean to keep it that way? To be "just Anne" without a last name until she had enough coin, purchased some false papers, and made arrangements to get off this island?

"Would you be so kind as to put these in my room?" Anne heard Jack say, handing flowers to the owner.

"With great pleasure."

Anne stiffened. It was the wild bouquet. No doubt a gift for a lover, she realized now. As the patrons made their way inside, Jack stopped in front of her. He wore a new set of brightly colored clothes. Equally flamboyant, perhaps more so.

Lifting her chin, she met his golden-brown eyes directly. They danced with mirth under his black tricorn.

"Curious," he said, daring to touch, ever so gently, a petal of the yellow alder. Her breath hitched. He winked, then followed the rest of his men to the tables.

CHAPTER 31

"The bearded fellow in the corner needs more ale," muttered a barmaid juggling three plates as she made for the kitchen.

Anne bit her lip, then glanced left. The sailor in question sat at the same enormous dining table as Jack Rackham, though at the opposite end. The fellow raised a glass and threw his head back with a rancorous chortle. Was that gravy in his beard?

Anne had determined to spend the entirety of the evening—until the last man took to a bed upstairs or stumbled up the road to find a brothel—avoiding that table. It was one thing to encounter Jack when he was an equal in the street. It was quite another to meet him in a tavern as a waitstaff peon.

"No time for idleness," the owner snarled behind Anne before shouldering past her. The room roared with noise and festivity.

Anne grabbed a pint in each hand and gripped them hard. Sweat glazed her forehead, which she wiped against her forearm. She could deliver the ale, then flit away quicker than a hummingbird. Her heart pounded like the wings of one.

Dodging the jolly drinkers and angling between chairs, Anne slipped the ale in front of the bearded sailor and reached for his empty mug, just as the man grabbed her wrist.

"Now, who's this fine lass?"

Anne jerked away, but his fingers wrapped tighter.

A curse boiled in her mind, and she grimaced to keep from snapping. She felt a shiver down her spine, the bone-deep recoil left from Nathaniel. She couldn't react or speak her mind while the owner stood a mere ten feet away. Not with such "esteemed" company. She hadn't had the training or experience of the other barmaids on how to humor drunken, manhandling patrons. What the Devil was she supposed to do?

"Are ye from the emerald shores? Hair's a dead giveaway. I'm a Scotsman myself." He belched. It was then that Anne saw that it was indeed gravy congealed in his beard. "We've been too long at sea, too long without the company of a pretty face."

Her cheeks burned a hue that Mam used to warn would encourage new freckles. Anne hoped Captain Rackham wasn't watching.

If she could loosen the sailor's hand, appease his mood a little, she might succeed.

This isn't Nathaniel.

I'm with others. I'm safe, she tried to tell herself.

I'm capable.

"A Scot, you say?" Anne said, unclamping his thick fingers one by one. A nervous noise like a laugh came from her throat. "When was the last time you saw home?" If she kept his attention on himself, and not on her, she might sneak away without notice.

"Not since the uprising," he said, his face reddening. "Not since that 'Old Pretender,' James Stuart—"

"Good lady, excuse my interruption." She felt the heat of him, standing behind her. Rackham spoke loud enough to cut through the deafening merriment. "We need another round of punch. We're dry." He slipped her a half-filled bottle of rum. "If you would be so kind."

He placed a hand on the small of her back to turn her away, giving her distance from the Scot. She caught his gaze. His look asked, *Are you all right?*

She returned his stare with one brow raised. *I had it under control.*

Turning on her heel, she returned to the bar to fetch a fresh carafe.

"Anything else?" she said curtly when she returned to Rackham's seat. The Scot, she saw from the corner of her eye, had continued on with his tale to all who would listen.

Rackham, Calico Jack, John—whoever he was—snagged her attention for a second too long. "That'll be all for now."

She was striding back to the kitchen with her head held high when she bumped into Mark Read.

"If you approach men from behind, you can slip away faster."

Anne took a moment to respond. "You saw that?"

Read dodged another barmaid carrying steaming bowls of stew. The contents of one dribbled out the side, and Read dropped to mop it up with a rag.

Anne knelt, too. She wanted to tell Read all that had happened to her, to tell someone—anyone. Of Nathaniel. Of the shiver she felt at the slightest touch. She wanted to tell Read that she'd managed the situation better than expected. That she was alone and afraid and lonely. That she needed a friend.

Instead, Anne muttered, "Captain Rackham stepped in to help. That's something."

Read finished wiping the floor, then he stared Anne right in the eye. What the bloody hell did that intense look mean?

Then, without warning, Read gripped Anne's wrist.

Anne yelped. This time, she did curse, a sound muffled by the shuffle of chairs and rowdy conversations.

"Break my hold."

"What the—"

"Break my hold. Try to get out," Read repeated, calm as a waveless sea. "Pretend I'm a drunken brute and free yourself."

Anne recovered, then moved to rip away. She felt sensitive to Read's touch, and confused. She maneuvered right, then left, but Read's grip remained.

"Clawing at fingers will get you nowhere," Read said, dropping Anne's wrist and offering up her own. "Quick, grab mine."

Anne did as she was told, and Read moved fast as a blade: whipping his hand in a circle and breaking the grip in a single, powerful move. It was over in a blink.

"How—"

"Later," Read said. The two stood, reorienting to the boisterous party. Anne felt her line of sight drift toward Rackham, who sat listening to an animated sailor to his right. Read noticed.

"I'll see to that table for the rest of the evening," Read said, tossing the rag to Anne. "There's a shattered bottle under the barstool near the door. And Huxley could use some help preparing the dessert. He's in a mood."

The dining room of the Jubilee cleared out by four in the morning. Only a third of the guests remained behind, taking occupancy in the upper rooms of the tavern. The rest? Not even God knew. The streets of Nassau never slept.

And on this night, neither could Anne.

She curled up in her corner under the bar, as she had every night since her arrival a few weeks earlier. Her head pulsed and her mind raced in the quiet darkness. The smells of roasted meats and booze remained, mingled with the lingering tobacco smoked from clay pipes. Huxley had saved scraps of the feast to divide among the staff, but it didn't amount to much.

Anne turned onto her side and squeezed her eyes closed. Her shoulder ached against the hard floor. She tried counting sheep, as Mam used to do with her as a girl. She tried focusing on the rise and fall of her chest, steadying her pulse with even breaths. She tried screaming inside her head about all the reasons why she needed to fall asleep immediately, then—when that failed—she stared at the wooden beams of the cedar ceiling until all she saw was a ship, which brought memories.

At last, she undid her braid, hoping this might calm her headache. The yellow alder fell out, a delicate thing she'd forgotten about. With the scant light from the lanterns outside the windows, Anne could tell it had wilted into nothing more than spindly grass and shriveled petals. By the Devil's ass, Anne was terrible at keeping hold of anything. Or anyone.

She startled at the sound of footsteps coming down the stairs. It wasn't yet dawn. And after a long night, surely no one would stoke the fires until late morning.

She swallowed, remembering the knife she kept under her makeshift pillow—an abandoned, threadbare dress she'd found in one of the Jubilee's upstairs bedrooms.

Craning her head to peek behind the bar, she saw a figure with a candle. He stumbled down the last step, then righted himself with a curse.

Him.

If she didn't move, maybe he wouldn't see her. She held her breath as he ambled along the wall, then he stopped in front of the wine case a mere six feet away and rooted through the contents. She could see his sun-bleached hair in the candlelight as it brushed his collarbone, his bare feet, the faint sight of his toned muscles through a thin cotton shirt. He spoke so elegantly, so like true a gentleman, that it felt strange to see him looking like any other sea rogue in his nightshirt.

She closed her eyes, willing herself to disappear, to unsee what would only make this more torturous.

Don't turn around. Don't—

A decidedly ungentlemanly shriek told her the wishing hadn't worked.

"What the hell are you doing out of bed?" Jack wheezed, recovering from the shock.

"I'm not out of bed, you halfwit! This *is* my bed."

"Good Lord, you sleep here?" he shot in a whisper.

"Yes. You're intruding on my bed." She winced. She hadn't meant it to sound like that.

"I'm not technically *in* your bed," Jack said as he slumped against the opposite wall. He fumbled with the bottle, trying to uncork it. "You failed to invite me. I assure you, I would have remembered."

Anne huffed. "Didn't get enough to drink?"

"I can hold my liquor. Besides, there was too much catching up to do and minding after my surroundings"—he paused—"to properly relax." The cork popped, and he lifted the bottle in triumph.

"You're drunk."

"I know my limits."

He took a seat on the floor and faced her, his back against the brick wall. This was nothing like Da's tantrums and behavior, his slurred curses and cruel words, after a night of heavy drinking. Maybe Jack wasn't drunk after all. He set the candle down and surveyed Anne's modest accommodations. "Why are you sleeping under the bar like a barn mouse?"

"Why did *you* lie about your name?"

Jack smirked. "I didn't lie. John is my Christian name."

"The model of a proper Christian, no doubt."

"You're avoiding my question."

Anne folded her arms. "I take safe lodging where I can find it."

His brow raised and he took a swig. He passed her the wine and, after considering her pulsing headache, she pressed the bottle to her lips. The liquid burned all the way down.

"It's not right for you to sleep here when the Jubilee boasts about having the cleanest beds in town," Jack said. "I can bring this up with the boss."

"Please don't," Anne said with horror. *It's all I have. I don't want to be a nuisance. I don't want to be back on the street.*

"It's either that or you take up my bed upstairs."

She scowled.

"Without me! Good gracious, Anne, what an assumption," he teased, swirling the contents of the bottle. "I'd be more comfortable here, so near the hospitality on offer." He gestured toward the case behind him.

"I think the world might notice if we switched places."

"Ah, that's the wonderful thing about this town," he said with a devilish smile. "Welcome to Nassau. Nobody cares, and nothing is shocking. Come now. Get a night of proper sleep—just one night. I'll safeguard your precious sleeping quarters, Bon."

Anne snapped her head and gaped. "What did you just call me?"

"Bon. I quite like it. Suites you better than a dainty little name like 'Anne.'"

"You know." She felt her gut clench. How? How did he know who she was?

"Aye," he said, offering her another swig. "I made it my business to know. That's the other wonderful thing about this town—no secrets."

Anne stood and clenched her fists. She wasn't sure if she wanted to pummel him or kiss him. Bloody hell, had she ever wanted to kiss a man? What was this infernal madness?

Jack merely watched, seemingly delighted by her rising temper—which enraged her all the more. "So it'll be my bed, then?" he said.

"Answers. *Now.*"

He tutted. "Tomorrow. Get some rest; there will be time for all of that. You have my word. Besides, you know where to find me." He made a grand, sweeping motion to the floor.

Anne gave him a murderous glare, then stormed up the stairs. Miserable man. Miserable, beautiful, *infuriating* man. She entered the only room with an open door and an absurd flower arrangement by the window. Either they were never intended for a lover, or the lover had failed to come.

Damn him. She'd sleep guilt free. She'd sleep until noon. She'd sneak around his room and gather every single trace of information about him before she emerged with her wits about her.

Sweet Jesus, she was tired.

Head on the soft pillow, eyelids heavy, it was only then that she remembered, with a sudden jolt, that she'd abandoned her knife.

She inhaled—too heavy to care, too light to feel scared anymore—the scent of milkweed blossoms perfuming the air.

CHAPTER 32

A high sun nudged Anne awake. She stirred, flipped over in the gentle golden air, and smiled into her down feather pillow. Such a dreamless sleep. Such a deep, needed, peaceful—

Her eyes snapped open with sudden memory.

Scrambling out of bed, she noted the lighting and cursed. She'd slept late. More than late.

And that bastard owed her answers. What did he know? Was James already hunting her down?

Throwing on her boots, she scanned the room. Beyond the vase of flowers, nothing proved unique. No clues. Nothing of ill report.

Then she spotted his sea chest at the base of the bed.

A thrill moved through her, but she didn't move. She comforted herself with the fact that, unlike him, she could take the moral high ground. The less she knew about him, the better. He'd leave soon enough. And so would she.

Since when have I been a saint? She felt the leather and brass studs of the trunk, ready to rifle through it all, then frowned.

It was locked.

Racing down the stairs, Anne's heart lurched when she saw the empty floor under the bar.

"Good afternoon," came Huxley's voice. She jolted. He gave

her a once-over as he sat beside the hearth, then continued prying conch meat from a stack of pink shells. "Missed the breakfast shift—all three of our guests, that is, who managed to rise."

"I'm sorry. It won't happen again." She was acutely aware of her wrinkled dress, her mussed hair, her next budding question. Her cheeks flushed. This did not look good. But this was Nassau, not Charles Town. "Have you seen Captain Rackham?"

The cook's annoyance was unmistakable. "Be back before the night rush," he said, motioning his paring knife toward the door. "Said to find him at the docks. You'll know the *Ranger* when you see it."

Gentle waves bumped against the wharf as the sky vaulted in an endless celestial blue. In the distance, Anne saw a colony of flamingos. Black-headed gulls flapped overhead in a breeze that made the constantly wet air tolerable, even pleasant. Anne floated toward the sounds and smells of the open sea, a destination she'd avoided since her arrival. Every venture outside had felt like a risk.

But this? She closed her eyes and inhaled. This was home. The closest thing she'd known to it since leaving Ireland. And out of fear, she'd stayed away, hidden in the Jubilee.

It wouldn't be a mistake she'd repeat again.

Sure enough, she recognized Rackham's lovely ship immediately. A sloop with a needle-thin bowsprit and *Ranger* painted in gold lettering. It was modest, but fine—with a strong mainmast holding a mainsail and a jib.

"How'd you sleep?"

Anne craned to look at the honey voice above as she stood on the dock. Rackham waved from the raised quarterdeck of the stern. He leaned against the rail and propped his chin on a fist. He wore a loose pink shirt.

"I've had worse." She wasn't ready to admit it was the best she'd slept since before Mam died. "And yourself?"

He shrugged. "Well enough." He gestured to the ladder. She climbed, and he offered his strong hand to pull her inside. She hesitated, then took it, feeling the tingly heat of his rope-callused fingers.

"What do you think?"

She scanned the polished oak deck. A few crew members cleaned the bow at the other end of the sixty-foot sloop until it gleamed, and Anne couldn't hide the look on her face.

He beamed in response. "I'm glad you like it, Bon."

She turned to face him, crossing her arms and returning to her purpose. "You owe me answers."

"Which I'll be pleased to give. Shall we?" He offered his arm.

For a moment, she remembered her old life—the parties and balls, the society events back in Charles Town. But she was that woman no longer. Anne strode past him toward the elevated plat-form, where stood a compass and the most glorious helm she'd ever seen. She placed both hands on the handles, admiring the craftsmanship and brass inlay of stars along the spokes.

"How do you know my name?" she asked.

"You told me."

She rolled her eyes. "Don't be coy. I need to know if I'm in danger."

"Why would you be?" He placed himself beside her, then stole her fingers away from the wheel to redirect her attention to him. The places he touched singed as she dropped her hands to her side. His gaze had a new look, one she hadn't seen in the captain before. He searched her eyes. "You're safe."

What a presumption. For all she knew, he was deliberately se-ducing her with the beauty of this ship. Safe? With a man like Bonny on the loose? What empty nonsense. She almost laughed to cover the emotion that simple phrase could stir. He seemed to notice.

"You're safe," he repeated, and at last, she caught his stare with-out fear. He took a step back, then cleared his throat. "I meant what I said yesterday. There are no secrets in Nassau. This shanty-town is well-enough acquainted with Bonny in the ten years he's lurked about New Providence. But"—he paused—"it was you, in fact, who offered up your full name when Bonny listed the *Swallow* at port."

Anne shifted, her boots hard against the glorious polish of the wooden deck. She'd forgotten. She never thought it would matter. The only thing she cared about now was procuring forged papers to get off this island.

"My crew and I make it a point to know who is in town, and who is away. We have many friends and even more enemies. I have a deal with the name-takers and risk nothing."

"You don't strike me as a man of caution."

"Maybe not for myself," he said, leaning against the rail as he studied her. "But for others in my care and under my protection? I try."

Anne returned to tracing the decorative edging of the helm. He might know her name, but he knew nothing about her.

"And James Bonny?"

"Off island."

She sighed with relief, then studied the fore-and-aft rigging with closer attention, running her palms along the ropes.

"Are the rumors true?" he said. "Do you know your way around a ship?"

She grinned. "What about your own escapades?" she asked. "Ousting Charles Vane, running amok in the Caribbean as a fearsome, bloodthirsty leader, and evading capture at every turn?" She paused. "Are those rumors also true?"

He knocked on the boom above her head. "Not the violent part, not if I can help it—I've never been that kind of pirate." He made a dramatic bow. "Merely a gentleman at your service. I can make an exception for James Bonny, though. If he deserves it."

She huffed by way of sidestepping the question. Though she knew he was a pirate—like anyone else on this scab of land—it still made her squirm to hear the word spoken aloud. Had she not, herself, been a kind of pirate? James would have accused Murphy, Alby, Dutton, and Captain Eford of the very actions Bonny and Anne participated in while aboard the *Swallow*.

What did it mean to be a pirate? And when had she slipped, without a clear warning or border, into this murky life? She knew that it had consequences. "Why do you do it?"

He used his thumb to polish the standing compass. The front of his open shirt waved in the soft breeze. "You tell me. Why does the sea call to you?"

Because of the texture of salt air when it dries on bare skin. Because of the wind in my hair that calls me back to something older than myself. Because of the burning flame of a sunrise after a storm. Because it refuses to be small, contained, controlled, predictable. Because it has no care for names or pasts or marriage arrangements or sins. Because it's not afraid of me or who I might become, what I might say or not say, how I might act or fail to act in a moment of terror or weakness.

Because the sea didn't leave me.

Because it never will.

She rested against the wall behind the helm. "Surely loving open water and a fine horizon isn't the same as thieving and stealing."

He shrugged and rubbed his neck. "I've never met an honorable seaman. Merchants prey on the less fortunate and exploit and lie and cheat at every corner. Slavers are unworthy of even the deepest circle of hell. The navy beats its men into groveling ash, then invokes God to justify murdering fellow humans who speak another tongue. Privateers are pirates who call themselves noble and make deals with the worst of the lot—governors and royals. Pirates, at least, are honest—or the kind whose company I most enjoy. It is said that 'when a pirate sleeps, he dreams not that he has died and gone to heaven, but instead, that he has returned to New Providence.' You've witnessed enough to observe Nassau's particular freedoms. Stealing is a quicker way to make a coin, too. *But,*" he added with dramatic emphasis, "it might please your Christian conscience to know that I am reformed. Took the king's general pardon up with Governor Woodes Rogers last night before dinner. It's all settled. A life behind me and my men. A clean slate stretched out ahead."

Anne rocked on her heels, studying his face for any hint of lies. "So . . . you're not a pirate?"

"Not anymore."

"Then what will happen to your ship? Your crew?"

"I must be content to remain dishonorable in the same, ordinary ways as all the other self-proclaimed members of the 'civilized' world."

Jack, seeing Anne shift her weight, pulled up an empty keg for her to sit on.

"Thank you," she said, surprised and touched by the gesture.

"With pleasure. Now. Tell me of yourself."

Another hour passed, then another. Anne told Jack of Ireland and her parents, the bleak days of life in London, and a summary of her time in Charles Town. Da—heaven help her, the wound still stung. She surprised herself in telling him about Nathaniel and what drove her into marriage with Bonny. He listened—unlike her father, the only other person she'd told—and seemed to believe her. Imagine it! Sharing the story, however vaguely, helped release some of its hold on her heart. In turn, Anne learned about Jack's childhood in Bristol. Fishing in the River Avon. His overprotective father and over-doting mother. Breaking his mother's heart when he committed to a life at sea. How he came to be called "Calico Jack" on account of his preferred choice of clothes—a light calico textile akin to muslin, perfect for the hot climate—and why he felt little need to distinguish himself with stiff velvet waistcoats and constrictive jerkins. He had nothing to prove in dressing like a proper gentleman and wore every wild color under the sky, a trait Anne found rather endearing.

When the sun seeped into a buttery glow off the port side of the *Ranger*, reflecting off the crystal green water, Anne took her cue to return to work. "Are you coming?"

"In an hour or two. Need to settle a few things and careen my sloop with due haste." He adjusted his tricorn. "Save me a seat, Bon. One away from the Scot with wandering hands."

She bit her lip. Did she like this pet name? She hoped her cheeks didn't reveal how she felt knowing this wasn't goodbye. At least for a short while longer. It wouldn't hurt to have a friend, if she was foolish enough to call it that, who knew the town, who could help her find a way to escape before James returned. "Which, of your many names and titles, am I to call you?"

The corner of his mouth twitched into a half smile. "Anything you want."

CHAPTER 33

Jack Rackham didn't look at her, not once that night, though he stayed in the smoky main room of the Jubilee until only five men remained. His deliberate not-looking drove Anne mad. The remaining sailors in the tavern nursed another round of drinks while shuffling cards and gambling into the morning hours. The hearth fire had turned to ash.

Anne willed herself not to glance over at Jack as she and Read finished scraping hogfish off the plates from dinner. Was this the feeling of falling for someone, this constant, unpleasant illness?

No matter what it was, she'd treat it like seasickness. Best to keep an eye on the horizon ahead. Best to think of anything but the swirl in her gut. Outlast it.

"You can go home," Anne said with a jaw-cracking yawn. "I'll finish the rest." It had to be three in the morning.

"I went home early yesterday," Read said, drying off a fork and moving to scour another. He tilted his head to where Anne usually slept behind the bar. "Your turn."

Anne stiffened. Now that Jack knew she slept there, she didn't want to draw attention to it. Others could be watching who weren't so charming. And Jack, she already knew, would wage another siege and demand she find herself a proper bed. *His* bed.

It was too much to think about.

Read studied her, then put down the drying towel. "Come, give me your wrist again."

Anne's reflexes were slow, but Read grabbed a hold anyway. Again, it made Anne tense. "Do you remember what I taught you?"

Anne tried to mimic the swing of her hand, but didn't get far. They switched, with Anne gripping Read.

"Watch closely," Read said. "You can evade who tries to grab your arm by using their own arm against them." He demonstrated how to hook a fist behind the opponent's wrist, then follow through in a clean, sharp circle.

"Again," Read said, showing the move again, but faster.

"Let me try," Anne said. She took a breath, then executed the motion. It worked on the very first attempt.

"Half the battle is getting away. The other part," Read said, "is not escalating the situation. Move swiftly and decisively if you're backed into a corner. But if you are serving patrons, recover with a false laugh or a playful tickle—batting your eyes or offering a flirtatious compliment, if you can stomach it. Insulted men lash out."

"Where did you learn this?" Anne said, eyes wide. What if she'd known it the day Nathaniel assaulted her?

"On a ship a very long time ago."

Anne leveled a look at Read, and Read did not flinch away from her intense gaze. Had he always had such long lashes? They reminded Anne of Ellen's, leaving her a little heartsick. "Why do you always speak as if you're a hundred years old? You can't be more than—"

"Thirty-five."

Same age as Jack, Anne noted. "So ancient," Anne teased.

"Feels like it when you've lived a thousand lives."

They resumed the clatter of washing and came upon a full flask. "Need a nightcap?" Anne asked.

"I don't drink."

"Why not?"

"That's a personal question."

Anne gritted her teeth and picked up another plate. She felt almost scolded, like a child. What made that inquiry more insensitive than the others earlier? It was difficult to speak with Read when he clearly had no interest in revealing anything of substance about himself. It was the opposite of talking with Jack. So much openness. Connection. She admired Read, but why did he always shut her out? "Suit yourself. But go home. Truly, I insist. It'll only be another half hour."

After a few more utensils, Read set down his rag. "Anne," Read said, "there is something I've been meaning to tell you." Anne glanced to where Rackham and the others continued their card game. One man, from his wallop, had clearly won the round. "Has Captain Rackham made any advances?"

That, Anne didn't remark, was a *personal question.* "No," Anne answered as casually as she could. Her mouth soured at what Read implied. And her answer was, Anne regretted, the truth. "What would give you that notion?"

Read leaned against the bar with a faraway look, considering one of the lanterns with a burned-out candle. "Just be careful," he said. "Rackham is a known womanizer." He retrieved his jacket, making an exit through the back door.

Anne pulled her hands from the soapy water, noting the pruny skin and red hangnails she'd chewed raw after Bonny betrayed their friends and abandoned her.

She'd had such a fine day—a lovely, wonderful day. Why did Read feel the need to ruin it? Had he and Rackham been friends? Rivals?

Was Read *jealous*?

No. She felt in her bones that wasn't true, part of why she felt safer near him.

But did she *want* him to be jealous?

Anne dismissed the idea outright. A final shout from the lone table announced that the game was over. A gangly Swede took the winnings. They offered a mix of curses and congratulations, their chairs scraping against the floor. One man swayed like sea-grass in the wind. Anne held her breath, knowing Jack would have something to say to her before the night was over. She had little ammunition left.

The others stumbled up the stairs in their clunky boots and Jack, as predicted, lingered. "You've been washing that mug for a while, Bon."

"Before you say anything," she said, raising a hand, "I want you to know up front that I'm not sleeping with you tonight." It came out awkward and abrupt. But between Read's warning and her own inexperience with these pesky feelings of—she'd admit it—attraction, she wanted to make her stance clear.

"Well, I'll have *you* know that I'm not letting you sleep on the floor. I tried it. And it's a lousy bed. So where does that leave us?" He took the mug from her hand and set it on the counter. "Take my room," he said, a gentleness to his plea. "It'll destroy my honor to let you suffer on this floor another night longer. I'll stay here tonight."

Anne massaged her temples. She'd already thought it all through. "If the cook, or the owner, finds you sleeping here, they'll blame me. You're a captain and a favored guest. I'm nobody."

His face softened. "You're not nobody."

She dragged her palm down her face in exasperation. "Please?"

"How about a compromise?" Jack said. "And only if you agree. But hear me out. You say you will not 'sleep with me tonight.' If by 'sleep' you mean rest beside my person in the same bed, I take your point and respect your wishes. I have been known, on rare occasions, to snore. But, if by 'sleep' you mean 'enjoy the delights of flesh,' I think we can avoid such impulses and still set aside our current stalemate. We can reside in the same bed—a nice, comfortable, and appropriately large bed—both get an actual night of rest, and both put aside this impossible impasse."

Anne tried not to gape. It was entirely mad. Did she trust him? Did she trust herself?

"You swear you won't be dishonorable?"

"I give my word."

"Fine." She crouched down and retrieved her hidden knife. "But I'll warn you now—I'm bringing this."

Captain Rackham did *not* snore, Anne noted with appreciation. But lying in the cool dark, the ocean breeze making the glass panes tremble, she faced the wall with her mind ablaze like the sun at zenith. After three rest-filled nights of this sleeping arrangement, three nights where Jack had proved infuriatingly true to his word—much to her everlasting gratitude and confusing disappointment—she wondered if she might sleep better under the bar downstairs after all. An uneasy hunger festered in her.

A gust threw the open window against the wall, and Jack stirred beside her at the sound, tossing over onto his side—facing her.

She froze until his steady breath resumed without interruption.

Rest, you fool. Jack doesn't seem to have any difficulties sleeping. And your boss won't have compassion if you crumple over a table from exhaustion.

Anne squeezed her eyes closed. But all she saw was the past few days with Rackham. Days filled with banter, nights sleeping back to back with tension tight enough to snap a rope.

And that rope was fraying.

Anne had demanded he turn his back to her when she changed into her secondhand dress for the evening, and she allowed herself only one peek, on the second night, when he removed his calico shirt by reaching back one muscled arm and pulling it over his head with a single motion. Jack had a cluster of large freckles to the right of his spine and an inch-long white scar along his neck. The sight left her dizzy.

The wind continued to howl, and Anne silently cursed. That rattle didn't help anything. She placed her bare feet on the wooden floor, then crept across the room to close the window.

There.

When she turned around, she saw that Jack had taken all of the coverlet.

She gritted her teeth and padded to the bed as noiselessly as possible. Slipping back onto the straw-filled mattress, she held her breath as she tugged the blanket back over to her side. He looked far too innocent.

To her horror, he rolled over again, throwing a heavy arm around her while continuing to sleep.

Her jaw dropped, and she didn't dare breathe. He'd offered his hand three times before, once on the *Ranger* as she climbed aboard, once on its decks, and once to pull her away from the endless dishes. She remembered the singe of feeling along her fingers and her uneven pulse at his touch. But he'd never—Holy God above—*held her* like a lover.

And he wasn't even awake for it.

She spent a brave minute relishing the feel of his sturdy embrace before trying to wiggle away and free the coverlet. But the blanket was tucked under his weight. She sighed, loudly, then let her frustration loose. "Damn you, Jack. You're insufferable." She yanked on the coverlet and his eyes flew open.

His eyes, his face, not even six inches away.

Jack took a moment to register her presence, then he smiled. "Something the matter, Bon?" He reached out a finger, then tucked a strand of hair behind her ear.

Her stomach lurched so hard she thought she might faint. No words came. He must have felt her shudder. After an unbearable pause, he moved his hand to trace her cheekbone, her chin, the dip of her throat. Time skidded to a halt.

A breathy sound escaped her lips, and she leaned deeper into his touch. *This* was how it was supposed to feel? What she'd been missing with James? She needed more, *more*, of whatever this was.

But who was she fooling? She knew. Oh, she knew exactly what this was.

And she burned for it.

Lying side by side, watching him watch her in the faintest glow from the lanterns on the street below, Jack said nothing. He simply ran that single finger down her hot skin to the neckline of her dress. Could one die of delight? Anne arched involuntarily, and he placed his other hand on the small of her back, pulling her closer into his hips. Her breath hitched.

Then that wicked finger slipped from the cotton of her dress and moved down, brushing over the swell of her breast until his thumb nudged her hardened nipple, and he squeezed.

She responded with an unmistakable moan and pushed herself into him, her lips—at long last—finding his mouth. She leaned into the flame. He responded with more fire. They tumbled over, mouth against mouth, body against body. Jack pulled her onto her back, drawing away from the kiss to watch her face as she squirmed with pleasure, as one of his strong hands hiked up her skirt.

She melted into a glorious surrender—shutting her eyes to the room, her ears to the wind—and his hand found the heat between her legs. She gasped, digging her fingernails into his back and tearing off his nightshirt.

She tried to form words. To make a joke. To get on as they did. But this was a language without words. They ripped off clothes, and she gripped his hair. Skin warred against skin. A war against death and time and limits. A war against all the saints combined.

Then, with a skilled motion of his hand between her thighs, Anne's vision blurred, and the stars exploded into gold.

CHAPTER 34

Spanish Town, Jamaica
February 1721

"So," Johnson said, clearing his throat and loosening his cravat in the blazing heat of the cell. "Captain Rackham is the father?"

Anne snorted at his visible discomfort. She'd spared him all the best parts—including the wild nights that followed, first at the Jubilee and then in the captain's quarters on the open sea with nothing but the wind for direction. Those memories still burned bright. The days so long and ripe, bursting with promise. What might have happened if they'd never returned? If they'd never stepped foot on Nassau again after their year at sea?

But a woman, of course, should never refer to sex and admit, however vaguely, that she enjoyed it. Least of all to a gentleman like the old salt in front of her. Well, to hell with that. What did Captain Johnson know of actual discomfort? She rested her hands on the hard round of her stomach, the calico fabric of Jack's shirt sticking to her sweaty skin. "Yes," she finally answered. "Jack was the father of my first and also this feisty one."

The captain's eyes bulged with shock, but he kept his focus

on the paper in front of him, determined not to catch her gaze. "You . . . had another child with the pirate?"

Should she draw this out, maybe even lie? He probably deserved it. If he could survey her like a trapped bug, why couldn't she? No. She'd tell the truth, protect her heart, and he'd do with it whatever suited his purposes.

"I lost the baby," Anne said. She considered studying the stone wall, but instead, she stared without blinking at Johnson. A part of her wanted to force him to listen. To tell him of the night she realized she'd missed her monthly, of the shock and pit of nothingness she felt in the cellar of her heart when she first understood. Of the immediate dread that followed the nothingness, a fear that she was somehow not a real-enough woman because she felt more trepidation than excitement. But she was young, still so young, and without Mam. She couldn't tell him of the courage it took to tell Jack, how he picked her up and spun her around so long she nearly passed out, then his overbearing insistence that she disembark and take rest in Cuba. How he'd called her "delicate." How he'd refused to let her stay aboard the *Ranger* in her condition despite her protests. Of the night she awoke in a strange home with a sharp pain in her abdomen. The cramps that clamped and seized her insides like an unrelenting storm that brought her to her hands and knees. Of the blood like a slaughterhouse, how it covered the Spanish tiles. How she would have called out if she hadn't been friendless and alone. How only then did she weep, how only then did she feel the potential in the wake of the loss, the fear and the hope and the ambivalence all together, all at once.

But if she couldn't tell Johnson all of that, she would at least make him take note of the first pregnancy.

"Where did you last see the child?" he asked, still refusing to look up.

Simpleton. "I didn't 'leave' the child anywhere." She refused to diminish the experience by clarifying that the child made it only five months in her womb. "I did everything I could."

"Right, of course," he said, eager to escape the details. "And this time?" he gestured. "You're sure Rackham is the father?"

At this, Anne rose to her full height and glowered. A bead of sweat dripped down her forehead. "*Yes*. I'm sure," she spat.

"I only meant—"

"We're done here for the day."

"Miss Bonny, please, I didn't intend—"

She stood. "Consider your questions, then try again tomorrow." She gestured toward the corridor, like a grand hostess offering a polite farewell, as if she opened and closed the door of her own free will.

It didn't matter that it owned her—that these walls kept her inside while Captain Johnson went back and forth between cells as he pleased. It didn't matter that she'd lost everything and had made a thousand mistakes. She still had her dignity.

Johnson seemed to comprehend. He jumped from the three-legged stool and tucked away his possessions.

"My request for paper and quill?"

"I'm working on that."

"Consider better answers, too, *Captain*," Anne said. Though the fury had left her face, she still felt the angry hum of it throughout her limbs. "I might grow impatient."

"Of course," he said, offering a curt bow before the guards led him away, toward a cell Anne was not allowed to enter.

CHAPTER 35

New Providence, Nassau
July 1720

"Read, did you hear? The *Ranger*'s pulling into harbor," Huxley grumbled when Mary entered the Jubilee's smoky kitchen. "Spotted not thirty minutes ago."

"Mmm," she said without surprise, hanging up her jacket and tucking a rag into her belt. Rackham always returned after making stops to his mistresses at every port. Rumor said he had four in Havana alone. What had it been, a year? He was overdue.

"I figured you'd be interested in that morsel of news," the cook said, his tongue peeking out of the corner of his mouth as he chopped an onion. "I thought you were fond of the girl. You sure fussed after her enough."

"Assuming she's still with him," Mary said. "But yes, I am fond of her. Like an older *brother* would be," she emphasized, taking a place beside Huxley to dice the remaining heap of vegetables for the stew. The smell left her slightly nauseous. Was there rot in the potatoes? "But she's capable of making her own choices." In truth, Mary wasn't sure at all whether that fluff of red hair knew her way around the world—not with that tiny knife she wielded.

But voicing her concerns with Anne seemed to do little by way of impressions. And didn't the young deserve to learn their own lessons? She certainly had.

Besides, maybe her unflattering views of Rackham weren't fair—he'd taken up the king's plea, and perhaps other pardons, to reform and turn the *Ranger* into a standard merchant ship. Given up his womanizing? Doubtful, but possible. Since losing Björn and the inn when his father, Lord Van Acker, sold it away, Mary's shadowed view of the world clouded her judgments. She felt like a crystal decanter that had fallen off a shelf. Someone might try to reforge the glass—and it may still hold wine—but it would never reflect light the same way again.

There she went again. Björn, God rest his soul, might have appreciated the poetics. But Mary's own sadness bored her.

"And what of Bonny?" Huxley asked.

"What of him?" Though men might complain about gossiping wenches, Huxley—among many others Mary had known—delighted in hearsay. Two years of living in a pirates' den had taught her that much.

"You didn't hear?"

Mary, exasperated, pressed her palms to the table. Her silver wedding ring clanked against the wood. Thomas, whatever he was to her, disapproved of her continuing to wear it—especially when it could fetch some coin. But she'd be dead before it came off her finger, and he'd stopped bringing up the issue as they lay in bed.

"Hear what?" she asked.

"Bonny's waiting to intercept them and take back his wife," Huxley said.

At this, Mary turned. "Does Anne know?" How did Huxley know, for that matter?

"Seein' as he has the governor involved? I think not. Rackham won't like that a bit—having his woman snatched away, with Rogers sniffing around his ship."

She swiveled to face Huxley. "Has anyone tried to warn her?"

He shrugged.

Mary threw her head back and groaned. She was far too tired for this. But by the time Huxley could respond, she was halfway out the door.

Mary tore through the streets. She nearly knocked over a merchant leading a goat by a halter, then narrowly darted out of the way to escape the collision. Her heart pounded. It was odd to feel it pound like that again.

Don't be too late, an old instinct scolded.

Don't do anything impulsive.

Don't draw attention to yourself.

Her stomach sank when she saw the lowered sails of the *Ranger* already anchored in port. She ran the length of the pier, chest heaving. A crowd had gathered, blocking her view. She craned her neck and glimpsed a snatch of unruly red hair.

"Take your disgusting hands off me!" the familiar voice screamed. It ripped through the air like rent canvas. A soldier pinned down her flailing arms. Behind Anne stood James Bonny and Governor Rogers himself—looking grave in his red uniform. His left cheek bore that famed musket-ball scar from his privateering days. Or was it from his years as a slaver with the East India Trade Company? Vile man. Rogers had two dozen soldiers with him, the only way he'd dare to show his face on this side of Nassau. He'd gotten bolder since shutting down the uprising two years ago. This town of buccaneers, rebels, rogues, renegades, and freed men and women who'd escaped the horrors of slavery, all depended on the governor's absence and fear of them. The people had ruled themselves before Rogers arrived with orders to rid the town of piracy.

"What's the meaning of this?" Rackham shouted, his teeth bared. "By what right?"

"By the right of being her *husband*," Bonny spat, daring a step forward now that three soldiers stood guard around Rackham.

Rackham lunged and one of the guards caught his fist.

"You are *not* my husband," Anne said to Bonny.

The gawkers seemed to be enjoying the spectacle, Mary observed with distaste. Better someone else than them, especially a woman. They called New Providence a "free place" for all, but talk proved cheap. That phrase never gave Mary the confidence to give up her disguise as a man, which she'd taken up the year following Björn's death. It was a fearful decision, a retreat into a past she wasn't fond of. But she had been Mark before she'd learned to be Mary, and Mark paid the bills. Only the crew that had brought her here two years ago knew her true sex, before she'd gone back into hiding upon reaching Nassau.

Anne clawed and screamed as a soldier locked her elbow behind her back and led her away to a carriage. Mary tried to catch her eye, but Anne never stopped searching for Rackham.

"It'll be all right, Bon," Rackham yelled after her, his voice betraying his own despair. And it was, Mary saw, genuine despair. The raw anguish on his face stirred something in Mary. Memories. Björn's expression when he'd taught her how to read by drawing in the mud with a stick. The intensity of his look when he'd chased her to the outskirts of camp. The softness of his touch when his fingers curled around hers all those nights in their marriage bed. Those same kind eyes shifting to deadly daggers if any patrons of the Three Horse-Shoes so much as hinted at a sign of disrespect against Mary. She knew, oh how she knew—over the course of ten extraordinary years—what it was to be loved.

Perhaps Captain Rackham was a reformed man. Maybe he cared for Anne after all.

The crowd parted to make way for the procession of soldiers with Governor Rogers at the center. Bonny had the nerve to stay behind, flanked by guards. "Next time, whore about with someone else's wife."

Rackham's face reddened as the soldiers raised their bayonets to his throat. "Name. Your. Price," he growled.

The onlookers gasped. Bonny appeared small and lanky in the presence of a man with a reputation and build like Rackham's.

Bonny seemed drunk on the reversal of power. He huffed with satisfaction, then stalked off, leaving Rackham shaking with rage on the pier.

"It's all right, Captain," one of his men tried to say. "We'll get her back. We'll—"

Rackham swung around and tore at his hair.

Mary gauged the crowd, which had once again pressed together to watch the dramatic scene. It was, Mary admitted, one of the more exciting events of the summer. But she'd gotten distracted.

Don't do anything impulsive.

Don't draw attention to yourself.

And yet, her feet moved. Mary slipped away to be nearer to the carriage. To overhear, if she could, where Bonny was taking Anne.

CHAPTER 36

"Jack!" Anne screamed, kicking the carriage wall as James held her away from the window.

"Stop it, Anne," he said, settling in beside her. "You're making a scene."

A soldier thumped on the door with his musket, and the carriage pulled away with a jolt. The crowd stared after them, but Anne could no longer see Jack.

Anne cursed. "*I'm* the one making a scene?"

James—no, Bonny, for he deserved no familiarity from her anymore—slumped against the seat and loosened his cravat. He refused to look at her. This stranger wore gentlemen's clothes and a newfound confidence like a too-pungent perfume. The carriage shook as it picked up speed. Anne craned to look at the street, the white sandy road she'd have to return by.

Study the path, she vowed. *Think.*

She remembered the knife under her dress, in its usual place. She moved her hand to feel it under the fabric.

Anne could jump. But she wouldn't get far. Soldiers on horseback flanked the carriage.

She could stab Bonny in the eyeball for all she cared. He deserved no less. But that, also, would not get her far.

"You're a scoundrel," Anne said, biding her time. If he wanted a pleasant carriage ride, she'd give him one to remember.

"Oh? For doing exactly what I said I would? Returning for you and hoping you'd learned some manners? Some of us hold true to our word."

"You didn't honor our bargain."

"You changed the rules on me, Anne. So I did, too."

She punched the door and Bonny grabbed her wrist. "I told you, Anne. Enough."

He said her name with such casualness. Like he owned her. Glaring at his white-knuckle grip, she remembered what Read had taught her. With a sharp, circular movement, she broke the hold. "Don't you dare touch me."

Surprise etched his brow, but it disappeared in an instant. He snarled. "I could beat you. I've never hit you, never abandoned you for any other woman—can't say you've demonstrated the same degree of loyalty. I've protected you as I'd promised, been a good husband."

She scoffed. An image of Nathaniel flashed across her mind, and she pushed it away. Bonny was scum, but it was true that he had never violated her.

Would he this time? She wouldn't stick around to find out.

For the remainder of the ride, Anne didn't speak. They cleared a stockade—another barrier to any immediate attempts to escape—and then the coachman announced their arrival as the carriage stopped in front of a grand government estate. Palm fronds framed the entrance. Anne fought her way out of the carriage and stormed inside.

What devilry had landed him this new situation?

"Rest will do you good," Bonny said, his tone softening. He pointed to a door. "That's your room. By dinner, I hope you will be ready to apologize."

She spun on him, her boots scuffing the tiled entry. "Oh, and what of *your* apology?" she retorted. "For threatening to get my friends hanged for piracy, abandoning me with no means, and kidnapping me in front of a gawking crowd today?" Anne spat, marched into her room, and slammed the door behind her.

"Good day, Mrs. Bonny."

Anne startled at seeing a middle-aged maid holding a platter of tea. A new dress lay on the canopy bed. Flowers sat in a vase on the mahogany bureau.

Gifts?

From Bonny?

Bloody hell, why? Again, she wondered how he came by this money. But she knew. The traitor. How many people had he turned in by now? The rented estate and guards signaled he was under the thumb of Governor Rogers.

"That won't be necessary," Anne said. "I require privacy. Don't disturb me until supper." They were the words she imagined a noblewoman, accustomed to being waited upon, might say.

The stout woman stood there, unmoving. "Mr. Bonny said you're not to be left alone. He also said—"

"I have to piss. I don't give a damn what he said!"

Anne pitied the woman, who retreated in a hurry. The second the door clicked behind her, Anne looked around. She rifled through every drawer of the ebony-edged trousseau. Not a coin or jeweled necklace in sight. Nothing that could be of use to her.

She gritted her teeth and reached for the knife under her skirts. Her eyes flicked to the window. A dense woodland of ferns and mossy branches loomed ahead.

Punching the hilt of the knife into the window, the panes gave way, shards of glass falling into the hedge outside. A fragment nicked her finger, but she didn't stop her work to suck off the blood.

Once there was enough room to crawl through, Anne lowered herself onto the dirt below and pushed her way into the forest. A twig sliced her cheek, and her courage hitched.

Pretend, she breathed. *This is emerald heather and green grass along the River Bandon.*

She ran, knife raised, like her life depended on it.

CHAPTER 37

Huxley frowned when Mary returned hours after her abrupt departure. "Take these to the guests at the far-right table," he directed, handing her two bowls of conch stew. The broth was noticeably thin on vegetables. "Not like you to abandon your post."

"Not like you to wait for an earful of gossip," Mary said. She delivered the bowls, then returned to the blazing hot kitchen. She felt dizzy. She must have run too hard in the heat. If she could just sit down . . .

"Fine," Huxley relented with an exaggerated sigh. "What happened?"

She told the cook about the incident at the dock, including what she'd overheard. "Bonny lives near the middle of the island. Right under the nose of the governor. Bonny must work for Rogers now. The carriage went in that direction."

"The prick."

She knew Huxley was referring to the new governor, but Mary felt the word was equally fitting for Bonny.

"Will Rackham and his crew make their way here tonight?"

"Unclear." Mary thought that was beside the point. She wasn't sure Rackham would be in the mood for merriment for a long time. And she rather hoped not to see him drunk on rage *and* wine.

"More rum?" came a singsong request from a stranger leaning into the kitchen.

"Here," Mary said, handing him a squat glass bottle. When the man had left, she leveled a stare at Huxley. "What are we to do about Anne?"

"We?" he scoffed, filling more pewter bowls with the thin broth. "That little miss made her choices. Gave 'er a place to sleep, good food to eat." He gestured toward the hearth and cast-iron cauldron. "I don't see what there is for me or you to do."

Huxley wasn't wrong. But was he right?

Disappointment settled into her gut as she delivered the meal to the dining room. Between the barking orders and the riotous laughs, her head thrummed. The hearth burned too hot, the tobacco from the pipes smelled too strong. She willed her brain to think, or maybe not to think. To return to that deep, inner well of calm and knowing that used to guide her so long ago.

Stepping into the night air, Mary paused outside the threshold of the Jubilee.

A quiet evening, a startling contrast to the bustling tavern. The stillness soothed her after such an unsettling day. Wind brought in a fishy smell from the sea. The summer stars gleamed as if newly polished. She could read these constellations like the pages of one of Björn's books. She'd done so as a navigator for Captain Southwick and again, later, for the rogue crew that had interrupted her passage to America.

Pausing to study Draco's curve and the luminous shape of Aquila bejeweling the Summer Triangle, Mary shifted her weight and felt a small thump of awe in her chest. She missed the weight of a ring dial and navigational divider in her hand—of being a person with a heading and clear goal. Of late, she'd resorted to mindless work, saving coin for her next, unknown step. Would ambition ever rise in her again? She missed the texture of a mottled map, a sense of certainty and purpose. How had she ever gotten so lost? So far from home?

Ma's face as the ship pulled away from the dock.

The pit of helplessness as Mary was drawn out to the open sea.

I've never had a home.

No, that isn't true. You know that isn't true.

She'd had a home in Björn. It had been three years since his death, three years since the baron had stolen her home and declared her "unnatural and unworthy" of connection to the Van Acker family. Mary summoned Björn's image: His squint in the sun atop a horse and that furrow in his brow while writing letters by a crackling fire. His hands massaging her neck after a hard day of work at the inn they'd built together. The tops of carrots in the garden shooting up in the spring. That specific, startling green during the long, summer days in the glorious, tucked-away town of Breda. The sheen of the oak floor at the Three Horse-Shoes and the rickety third stair that they always meant to fix. Henry stopping in town for a drink every New Year, dressed in his finest, drinking to their mutual survival and the end of a miserable war. There he was, just *there*—among their other friends and patrons— raising a glass to Mary and Björn's health.

Björn's health. Never the same after the war. The shot he took for her.

Mary found her footing again, starting toward the west end of town, where she and Thomas kept a single room. Maybe it wasn't so surprising, Mary being here—she was the daughter of a pirate, after all. She wished she'd asked Ma more questions. Had her father ever walked these sand-covered streets or sailed into this aquamarine harbor?

Did he also live with regrets?

A rustle in the bushes stopped Mary in her tracks. She whipped around, then drew the flintlock pistol she kept in her jacket pocket. Her ears pricked.

The rustle continued. And it wasn't the wind or a lizard.

Mary felt her pulse rise in her throat. She knew that running was the surest way out of this—she outran most men, always could. But curiosity gripped her. Was it a hutia? Thomas wouldn't say no to some fresh meat, even a small rodent. It wouldn't be the first time she landed a clean shot in the dark of night.

"Who goes there?" she said, pistol raised. She tested the bush by kicking at a frond.

Then, out spilled a woman brandishing a tiny knife. "Read, is that you?"

"Anne?" Mary lowered her weapon. "What the Devil are you doing out here?"

"Escaping!" Anne's knife fell to the ground and she flung her arms around Mary. Sticks and leaves covered her dress. Mary froze, baffled. "Lord, I worried you might be a stranger come to drag me back to Bonny. There's no time to explain. Please, can you let me sneak into the tavern? Is the bar cleared out? I need a place to hide until morning."

Mary pocketed her pistol. "At the one place where the whole world will be looking for you?" Even though Mary couldn't see Anne's face, she could feel the vibrating hum of fear and exhilaration and nerves. What had it taken to get away from Bonny? And what might he do if he caught her again?

"The second most suspicious place, maybe," Anne fumbled. "The first place would be the *Ranger*. I already scanned the docks from a hill above. There are soldiers posted all along the harbor."

There was no way for Anne to slip off this island undetected. Not with the governor's involvement. But how could Mary say this aloud?

With staggering clarity, Mary finally saw what her soft spot for this young woman was all about. It was her blind hope and youth. The way she, too, had been abandoned. In worrying after Anne, she was reaching back in time to be the wiser guide she'd always wanted for herself.

Huxley was right. This wasn't her problem. And yet . . .

Don't do anything impulsive or draw attention to yourself.

A second passed, then another. "Come with me," Mary said decidedly, pulling off her jacket and tossing it over Anne. "We have to move. *Now*."

"Where?" Anne picked up the knife she'd dropped. Heaven help her. She needed to learn to use that little prop.

"I share a room with one of Rackham's former crewmen on the other side of town." Mary couldn't bring herself to call Thomas a lover, to herself or to Anne—whatever Anne would make of the situation. "He'll be shocked and not so generous as I, but he can keep a secret."

Anne stiffened. "You're suggesting that I spend the night with two men?"

Mary sighed. She'd been so worried about her own secrets that she hadn't considered Anne's actual concerns. "Anne, no harm will come to you—I promise."

She gave a curt nod of understanding, then they were off.

Anne couldn't stay at the Jubilee, and she also couldn't escape Nassau by running—not after what Mary witnessed on the docks. But all that bad news could wait until tomorrow.

CHAPTER 38

Spanish Town, Jamaica
February 1721

"You took Miss Bonny back with you, then? To share sleeping accommodations with you and your husband?"

Mary stared at the ceiling as she lay on her back, her blanket wadded up into a pillow. How did Anne fare in these conditions? Better than herself, Mary hoped. Today, Mary could clearly make out the texture of the stone ceiling. She saw shapes in the contours the way she used to see wild horses in the clouds during long days at sea.

The fever had lifted for the moment. For once, her white shirt and trousers were not soaked through with sweat. A blessing.

Her hands rested on her stomach.

"Thomas was never my husband," she said, ignoring whatever else this strange captain implied.

"The court said Thomas Brown was your common-law husband."

Mary turned her head to consider Captain Johnson. Such a curious gentleman. He looked rather ridiculous, particularly from this angle: a man of his breadth, teetering on the edge of a rough-hewn stool sized for a child with a writing desk on his lap. But she never minded his questions. It passed the time.

And her baby needed time.

"The court said many things," Mary said, returning her gaze to the ceiling. "I only ever had one husband. And it was not Thomas." For all Thomas had meant to her—and for all his good merits—her affection toward him had been like the comfort of candlelight in a pit of darkness. Björn, in contrast, lit her world ablaze like a summer solstice sun. For ten precious years, she crackled with aliveness that could challenge the pagan gods. She didn't fear death, for she'd lived each second of her days with Björn—whether they were traveling through the countryside outside of Breda, reading books aloud as they huddled under a blanket beside the hearth, or waiting on customers and old friends at the Three Horse-Shoes. Even washing the tavern's bedsheets together, Björn splashing her with a fresh bucket, held an unspeakable joy that bordered on sacred. It never mattered what they did, so long as they were together. Björn did not flinch as death stalked him in the shape of a wound that refused to heal. It was not the first time Mary had seen, up close, a man truly measured when he stood face-to-face with his end. Most others were found wanting.

If it was her time, Mary would not cower either. But she would fight; for herself and for the life growing inside her.

"Where is your husband now?"

Mary closed her eyes. "Gone."

"Gone where?"

"To wherever the best of souls go."

"My condolences," the captain said, mopping his brow with his kerchief. "Forgive my interruptions. You were saying . . . ?"

CHAPTER 39

New Providence, Nassau
July 1720

"Morning," Mary said, handing Anne a cup of bush tea.

Anne nodded in thanks and took it.

Mary wouldn't stoop to call the morning "good," not after she and Thomas had taken the cot, leaving their guest on the cold floor with their only spare blanket. "Did you sleep all right?"

"Yes, thank you," Anne said, staring into the pale tea. She had an angry slash across her cheek and similar cuts covering her exposed skin from trekking through the woodlands.

It was clear that neither of them had slept. Mary had tossed until dawn. Before the sun broke the horizon, Thomas had already risen—none of his usual whistling—heading to the docks to attend to his nets. Mary anticipated she'd get an earful from Thomas about not exercising discretion about her identity, an identity that brought in more coin than she could ever make as a barmaid. This was *her* plan, after all. He might be more worried about blowing their guise than harboring a risky runaway. Not that they needed the governor sniffing around.

What did Anne make of two men sharing a single bed? All

forms of relationships existed in New Providence, but this scrappy young woman who still smelled of high society likely didn't know better.

Am I . . . justifying myself? Worried about what Anne would think? Mary had nothing to justify. She had exactly three reasons for being with Thomas. First, he was one of four people on this island who knew the truth of who she was and, of those four, he was the only man who was unwed and didn't have a head of gray hair. Second, by pooling their modest incomes, they could afford to share a single room rather than Mary having to rent a bed in a dormitory or inn and risk revealing her identity. Third, she fancied him—even if he acted, at times, like a self-serving child. He could whistle better than a nightingale, smell a storm hours before it arrived, and—most of all—he was a friend. It didn't hurt that he was handsome and generous with his physical affection; he made for a fine companion. He, too, had a history that haunted him and knew when to stop asking questions.

Mary dared anyone to judge her for dulling the stab of loneliness.

Anne brought the saucer to her lips. Her face scrunched at the bitterness as she swallowed. "I'm grateful—for everything. I didn't mean to drag you into this."

Mary sat on the floor across from Anne, surveying her puffy eyes. Her hair looked messier than usual, with leaves poking through the strands.

"Ready to talk?"

Anne looked up, and something like surprise passed across her face.

Mary sipped at her own tea. "What happened?"

Anne leaned against the wall and closed her eyes. "I've told you about James Bonny."

"Yes," Mary said. She knew what Anne herself had mentioned and then some—as was the custom in Nassau.

Her fingers clinked against the chipped teacup. Anne opened

her mouth, then closed it again. "I was . . . in trouble when I married him. Desperate. We made a kind of agreement."

Anne paused as tears welled behind her eyes.

Mary had never seen her struggle for words. "I've made a lifetime's worth of mistakes in an existence that presented few real choices," Mary offered. Not realizing Ma was sending her away in time. Not asking Ma enough questions that would have helped Mary find her again. Lying about who she was for so long. Not responding fast enough to the shot that struck Björn. Not putting away money before losing the inn. The thousands of errors she'd made in her unending grief that led her to share this room with a man she didn't love while facing a future that didn't matter anymore.

"I don't know where to begin," Anne said, rubbing her temple. "This is a disaster."

To deny the truth of that statement would be foolish. But Mary couldn't help Anne if she didn't know the full extent of her situation. Mary offered a small smile. "I'm listening."

So Mary listened. For an hour, they did not move. Mary gritted her teeth as Anne wrestled with language for what to call Nathaniel's assault. Mary wanted to hug her, but instead of reaching out, she held back, holding her heart in as she always did. It wouldn't be appropriate or comforting, Mary reasoned. Anne continued to talk as the bush tea grew cold.

"That's not all," Anne added. "I'm with child again."

Mary closed her eyes and sucked in a breath. "Does Rackham know?"

"Not yet. I'm only two months along and don't want him dumping me off in Cuba for a second time. I feel perfectly well. I want to show him I'm more than capable of serving on the crew despite my condition." Her chest fell. "Not that 'resting' on land did much good for the first pregnancy."

"He made you stay on shore?"

"He has a kind of family in Havana. Jack's protective of me. And I was, to his credit, quite ill."

Mary had a lot of questions about Rackham's behavior, but those questions could wait. "And you had the sense to *not* tell Bonny about this new development?"

Anne frowned as if wrongly scolded. "It didn't come up."

Mary held up her hands. "I only wanted to make sure."

Anne stood to stretch when the door flung open. In barged Thomas. His crazed stare latched onto Anne, then Mary.

"Thomas—"

He dropped a net filled with fish at the threshold. They wriggled and water pooled on the ground outside. The smell, oh Lord, the smell—

Thomas slammed the door. "Bonny is searching the town," he said, breathless. "Questioning everyone with known connections to his wife."

Anne stiffened. "I am *not* his wife."

"Tell that to the governor." He rolled his eyes and turned to Mary. "Bonny knows she lived at the Jubilee. He's hunting down everyone who worked there. And a certain cook thinks you might have information."

"Huxley," Mary sighed. Her stomach twisted. The lingering stench of the fish. The sour, awful—

Breathe through your mouth. "We need to move Anne," Mary said.

"Where?" Thomas panted.

Mary had to sit down. There was no time. She sorted through the limited options, lowering a bucket into the mental well of stillness she thought had dried up for good. "Your rowboat," she said at last. "Anne might paddle to the other side of the island. Catch a sloop headed to Barbados."

"I'm not leaving Jack," Anne fired. "I have no reason to run."

"Fine," Mary said. It was fool-headed. But Mary had done more foolish things for love. She clutched her abdomen.

"Are you feeling all right?" Anne said as Thomas moved toward her.

No time.

Avoid risk at all cost.

Risk. It was already at her door, in the room.

"I'll feel better after I eat something. Disguise Anne. Get her to the rowboat." Acid rose and she held it back. "Anchor for the day. Let Bonny come knocking. We'll fetch her after dark. I have"— she swallowed—an idea."

Mary dry-heaved, and Thomas caught her with both strong arms. "Mary?" He searched her eyes. His dark tresses and hard facial features appeared blurry.

Bile coated Mary's throat.

Anne whirled on her. "*Mary?*" she said, the pieces starting to click into place as she studied Mary's visage, then body.

Thomas cursed, realizing his mistake. Mary lunged for the water basin, felt her insides roil, then vomited with enough violence to double her over.

Thomas and Anne were kneeling at her side in an instant. Anne held back her hair as the insides of Mary's stomach rose again.

"Do you have bread? Anything?" Anne snapped at Thomas.

The room spun. Thomas scurried away, then returned with a bit of crust. "She's been like this for weeks now. Always tired. Lightheaded. Queasy."

"It gets better when I—" Mary bent forward again, knocking the bread crust out of the way. Every muscle in her lower back strained.

"Read," Anne said with trepidation. "Are you . . . ?"

"A woman?" she scoffed with a glare at Thomas—his handsome features pale with fear—before wiping her mouth. *A fraud? A liar? A washed-up piece of flotsam from the fragments of a beautiful, shattered life?*

Anne placed her cold inner wrist against Mary's forehead. "With child?"

Mary laughed.

Impossible. Cruel to suggest.

Mary meant to say all of that before burying her head in the basin again.

CHAPTER 40

"Listen well," Thomas said after Anne climbed into his cart. She lay flat, covering herself with the pungent fishnets. "You must tell no one of Mary's true identity. You hear?"

Anne could see a snatch of blue sky through the heap of nets. Did he honestly think she'd do such a disservice to the person who'd helped her—baffling as this new revelation was? "Understood." She wasn't nearly as sensitive to smell as Mary, but still, she breathed through her mouth.

"Good," he said. Anne detected a shake in his voice. She heard him heave the cart up and begin to pull.

"No donkey?" Anne whispered.

"No money. You can thank your Captain Rackham for that."

What the Devil did that mean? Anne glowered, even though he could not see her face.

"When I say 'lovely morning,' that means someone is on the road. It's your cue to shut it. Understood?"

"You seem to think there is a great deal I don't understand!" Anne shot. She regretted her biting words immediately. He and Mary—for apparently that was Read's real name—were risking everything.

"Well, pardon me! I'm not the one covered in fishnets wreaking havoc on all the inhabitants of New Providence."

Anne shifted. "I'm thankful," she said. "And sorry," she added. She felt like a louse for endangering them in this way.

The wheels creaked, and for a moment, Anne wondered if Thomas heard her.

"My apologies," he said in a tone Anne had not heard from him yet—all the bravado gone. "I know it's not your fault. There is a lot on my mind. A lot that could go wrong."

"And you're troubled by Mary's condition?"

"Aye," he grunted. "But what you said isn't possible. I fear you've upset her. Mary is barren—a point that has been most distressing in her past. It's best not to give her false hope."

The cart moved over a bump and Thomas yelled out, "Lovely morning!"

Anne kept still until his whistling—beautiful whistling, she noted—returned to speech.

"Another five minutes and we'll be to the boat. It's all I have in the world. Can we trust you with the plan?"

"Yes," Anne said, revisiting it in her head. Anne would spend the day in hiding, waiting for Mary to come for her that night. Mary would welcome Bonny when he came to the house—learn what she could, see if she might negotiate an agreement. Thomas had the job of notifying Rackham.

Anne wished she had Thomas's task instead of hiding under this pile of slimy mesh. But she knew this was the only viable plan. "You know Jack?" she asked.

"Aye," Thomas said, puffing. "I was part of his original crew when he took over command from Charles Vane."

"You were a pirate?"

"You'd be hard-pressed to find someone in these parts who wasn't part of 'The Flying Gang.' Most still are."

Jack had told her about his time sailing under Captain Vane. The day he'd called Vane out for his cowardice. How the crew rallied and ousted Vane, capturing a French man-of-war, calling for Rackham to serve as captain—a position he held with distinction and benevolence until taking the king's pardon. "You resent him, for putting an end to the pirating?"

Thomas chuckled. "I took up King Georgie's amnesty like the rest of 'em. But Rackham kicked me out of his crew before that."

"What for?"

"Idleness. Gambling. Excessive drinking."

"And?" Anne said. Jack kept a tight ship, but he was no stranger to fun. Especially if it involved rum.

"Stealing a few pieces of silver from the hold."

This Anne was not expecting. According to the Articles that governed pirates—strict rules that afforded every crew member an equal vote, compensation for any injury, a fair share of the treasure, and more—she knew any man caught stealing should be shot or marooned.

"He was good to let me go rather than make me governor of my own island. Charles Vane, that sick bastard, would never have done the same," Thomas said, following her line of thinking. "Though punishment found me anyway. That onetime mistake has its hooks in my reputation. It's hard to find work." The cart picked up speed as they descended a hill. "Maybe this makes me even with Rackham, my helping you. All the same, I'm not looking forward to facing him aboard the *Ranger* again."

Thomas stopped and lowered the cart. The sea flooded Anne's nostrils and she heard water lap the white shore. The crunch of boots announced that Thomas had returned with the rowboat. She saw him look in all directions through the mesh. Then he scooped her and the nets up like a sack of flour and placed her in the bottom of the vessel. The rowboat wobbled under her weight.

"I'll tie it off so you don't drift," Thomas said. He hesitated, then cleared his throat. "Please don't stray from the plan. I really can't afford to lose the boat."

Anne had no intention of betraying his trust. However uncomfortable a day of waiting idly in this condition sounded, it was nothing compared to a day with Bonny. "Find Jack," she said. "I'll be here, waiting for Mary."

Whoever the hell Mary Read was.

After waiting in the rowboat until midnight, Anne startled awake when the rope jerked. Her eyes flung open in the darkness, the stars visible through the net. She felt around for her knife, then remembered the plan. "Read?"

"Shh," came a familiar yet different voice. Mary, it seemed, used a different register for speaking as a woman.

Anne suppressed the urge to sit up, to stretch out her aching spine, to demand answers. The boat rocked, and Mary stepped inside. She picked up an oar, and Anne went to reach for the other.

"Not yet," Mary said, clutching the second oar and using them both to row out. The minutes crawled by. Anne held her breath until, at last, Mary dropped the paddles. "That should be far enough."

Anne flung off the nets and sat across from Mary. "Is the smell . . . ?

Mary waved the concern away, halting that direction of conversation.

"I'm sorry," Anne said. She'd had all day to think about the danger she'd put Mary and Thomas in. Mary was also missing the night shift at the Jubilee. "You shouldn't be out here."

"Nor should you. But here we are."

Anne braced against the chill in the night breeze. "And where exactly is that?"

Mary took a moment before responding. "What motivates Bonny?"

"Spite," Anne spat. A wave caused the boat to rise and fall.

"Think deeper, Anne. Resentment blinds you. You know him. You know him better than anyone."

Anne bit the inside of her cheek. She did not, under any circumstances, want to admit that she knew—let alone understood—that man. But when Mary said nothing, Anne saw the question was in earnest. She exhaled. "Money."

"Yes."

Anne furrowed her brow and scoured her memories. "Recognition?"

Mary nodded.

Anne pressed her temple, remembering their days aboard the *Swallow* and how possessed he could be about the fortune he felt entitled to—an entitlement he applied to her. "And ownership," Anne concluded.

Mary made a noise of acknowledgment. "That was my sense, too. Though to be frank, I think he does have some feelings for you."

Anne's gut twisted. "He came, then?"

"Indeed."

She sat up straighter and cursed. "What happened?"

"We talked," Mary said with a shrug. "That is, once he stopped his hollering. I asked him what he wanted. He said you. I asked why. He said it didn't matter why. It went on like that for a while."

Anne balled her fists and suppressed a scream. "I divorced him."

"So I said. He remains unconvinced."

"It doesn't bloody well matter if he's convinced."

"While I tend to agree, that isn't going to give you freedom in the eyes of English law."

"To hell with the law." Anne could have laughed. She was a papist in Ireland, the bastard daughter of a lawyer run out of town. All her life she'd seen how laws came and went, crushing people under their heels whenever convenient.

"I've been burned by that hellfire myself," Mary said. "My . . . discretion about my sex helps me avoid that particular purgatory again." She paused. "I lost everything when—" Her voice quieted. "It doesn't matter right now. What *does* matter is that you are a woman and you are considered Bonny's rightful property. You can't argue against his ideals or scream your dissent against the law. You have to find another way, another jab at his motivations."

Anne groaned and buried her face in her hands.

"Think, Anne. What does Bonny want that is stronger than his feeling of ownership? Perhaps even over his affection for you?"

Affection was laughable. But the answer rose quickly. "Wealth." Yes, that was it. "If Bonny had enough money to stop scheming, the dog might drop the bone."

"Let's hope you're right. I proposed another meeting with Bonny. Between him and Rackham. At the docks yesterday, Rackham all but offered up gold. I heard him. 'Name your price' was what he said."

Anne squirmed with discomfort. Did Jack know, even before she did, what it would take to stop James Bonny's pursuit? She did not want to know how much her soul was worth, like appraising a milking cow or a horse. Her gut clenched with disgust. She despised everything about this plan, but she was in little position to protest.

Mary moved to pick up the oars again, and Anne reached out to stop her. "Wait."

The air stilled as waves nudged the boat.

"Who are you?" Anne asked.

Mary exhaled and looked up, as if studying the constellations. "You don't want to know who I am."

Anne felt anger scorch her cheeks. "Of course I do! You're risking your neck to help me. I've told you everything about my life—including the worst thing that has ever happened to me." Her voice caught. It was the high tide of emotion. It was the idea of Rackham and Bonny haggling over her. It was the whole of it. "I know you don't owe me anything—especially after all of this. But I trust you. Can you trust me?"

Mary stared ahead, considering.

"Don't answer if you'd rather not, but I'll say it in case in case you do: When was the last time you bled?" Anne asked.

Mary exhaled. "I don't keep track. It comes and goes without consistency. Always has. What you are suggesting is—"

"Impossible. Thomas said as much. But why?" She placed a hand on Mary's.

Mary squeezed, then pulled away and looked off at the black ocean. After a long moment, she finally spoke. "I was married once. To a good man named Björn. All we wanted was a child. I ached to be a mother more than I longed for anything in my life. And there was no shortage of trying, I assure you." Anne thought she heard a smile behind Mary's words. "But that hope was never realized. Month after month, disappointment after disappointment. Until eventually, God also snatched the love of my life from the warmth of my arms. I took it as a sign. So did his resentful father. My questionable past, and never producing a child, earned me nothing in the end."

"A sign?"

"That maybe I'd sinned. That I wasn't a real woman after all, that my choices had turned me into a monster. I met my husband in the army. It's a long story. But I've spent all except those precious wedded years of my life pretending to be Mark Read, the man you met. I've been a sailor and a soldier. A barmaid in Breda and now a barkeep here in Nassau. When Björn died, and his father made sure I lost the inn we'd built together, I tried to return to the army. They turned me away on grounds of an "unfit mind," a condition recorded upon my release in the cavalry. Desperate, I booked passage to America, boarding as Mary Read—a woman. During that strange summer, circumstances . . . changed. I became a navigator on the ship."

"Which landed you here."

"Which landed me here," Mary repeated. "Thomas was on that merchant vessel. This was after Rackham banished him from his own crew. Thomas and a handful of others knew me—know me—as a woman. I didn't want to return to a life of lies when I set passage west, so I traveled under my true name. The ship's leadership was so vile, so cruel, that the whole crew revolted before we reached America. Voted to turn pirate. They commandeered the ship with big promises of grand dreams and riches and fairness and equality. They didn't believe me when I told them I was a trained navigator." She huffed. "But they saw my merits soon enough. And to their credit, they took me on while knowing I was a woman. That told me a lot about them. I was vulnerable. Lonely. Unmoored. And in the pit of my heart? I leapt at their ideals, however unlikely they seemed in practicality. I sailed with them just long enough to make passage here. Thomas and I became friends and decided to break with the pirates and live in this free haven until we each came up with a better plan. One thing led to another."

Anne fought to keep her jaw closed. What might her own life have looked like if she'd continued to dress as a boy after that brief stint as a child? "You've fought in wars?"

"Battles, yes."

"And sailed under merchants and pirates alike?"

"Yes. Since I was a child."

Anne leaned forward and the boat shimmied. "Jesus, Mary, and Joseph! All of that? And you think somehow you are a sinner rather than being the most remarkable woman I've ever heard of?"

Mary gripped the oars. "The tide is taking us out. We should return. Thomas found you another place to stay for the night."

Anne snatched the oar away. "You've outsmarted them all!"

Mary pulled some kind of maneuver, knocking the paddle out of Anne's hand and putting it back into her own again with ease. "I've *survived*. There is a difference. I've killed and deceived, lived half lives and run. And I've lost everything—everyone that ever mattered."

Anne backed down at the rare rawness in Mary's tone, but the wonder still flooded her veins and left her dizzy and brazen. "Not everyone. Not this child."

When Mary answered with silence, Anne dared to continue. "You don't have to believe me. Not yet. And it must hurt like the Devil to know it's not Björn's." Anne's fingers rested on her own stomach. Not feeling ill, she often forgot she was carrying a baby. Though she had never felt that palpable desire for children the way Mary described, she could recognize it clearly. "I can't pretend to fathom all of your pain. But what if what I say is true?

What if you aren't being punished, as you seem to believe? Terrible things happen. Wearing dresses doesn't mitigate disaster, as you have observed."

Mary took long, slow breaths as she rowed to the fishing dock. Anne willed her to speak again, to say anything, but it was clear that Mary had no more she wished to share that night.

They tied off the rowboat, and Mary threw her a cloak. "Put this on. You'll stay nearby with a fisherman until tomorrow. Had to pay him a fee to keep quiet. Someone will come for you, but only after we devise a meeting between Bonny and Rackham and come to an agreement."

A pang of longing for Jack walloped her, but she nodded with understanding. How vile, to think of the two men talking together. But without another word, Anne and Mary walked the dark, sand-covered paths. Anne's boots felt heavy with exhaustion. Questions pummeled her skull. She warred with herself, humiliated to be so dependent on these people risking so much, worried she'd offended Mary again, and desperate to repay her kindness. Nothing else moved except for palms in the whistling wind from the open ocean.

CHAPTER 41

The meeting time was set. The Jubilee at six. Better to convene in public than in a back-alley duel, Mary figured. Besides, their private business was about as public as waving a flag to the whole of Nassau.

"I don't want any guts or brains spilled on these new tables, you hear, Read?" Huxley barked as he puttered around and stirred the bubbling contents of the cast-iron pot with more energy than Mary had ever known him to show. He snatched a bottle of rum, paused, then took a swig before handing it over to Mary to deliver to the anticipated guests.

"It won't come to that," she said. For a moment, she contemplated poisoning Bonny's drink. Not that she would. She had sworn off killing after the war, and this wasn't her mess to clean up.

Fewer risks, she berated herself for the hundredth time in the past two days. *Stop intervening and get out fast.* Her stomach swirled with mild nausea from the meaty fumes coming from the kitchen, but she tried to ignore it. The sooner all this was behind her—with Anne and Rackham sailing into the sunset and away from her quiet life—the better.

Bonny arrived first, flanked with three other men not in uniform. "Rackham better show," he growled. He slunk into a seat and flung an arm over the neighboring chair.

"He will," Mary answered, straightening her posture to exude strength. She knew better than to ask the men to hand off their weapons. There was always a hidden dagger somewhere. It would only waste time to ask.

Bonny tossed Mary a coin, the payment for organizing a meeting after he accepted that she either did not know, or would not tell him, where Anne was hiding. She passed the coin to Thomas, who pocketed it with more haste than needed. A few onlookers eyed the scene while sipping their ale from a safe distance.

The door flew open, and in stormed Rackham. Alone. He balled his fists, then relaxed them. Huxley offered all his usual pleasantries and tried to put him at ease.

He needn't have bothered. Rackham didn't need directions to take the seat facing Bonny. Rackham glared hard enough to shatter glass. He leaned his elbows on the round oak table, his jaw glowing red in the hearth light.

"Settle this," Mary said, infusing her voice with a confidence that she didn't feel at the moment, the self-assuredness that projected male authority. She hadn't been at ease since talking with Anne the night before in the rowboat. "For the sake of all of us in New Providence." She shoved a bottle toward Bonny. "*You* know better than to bring Governor Rogers into this part of town—if you value your life at all," she said. Then she pushed a decanter of Meridian toward Rackham. "And *you*. *You* have a record to keep clean and the funds to put this right."

The vein in Rackham's throat twitched. "There's nothing to make right. She divorced this blunderbuss well before meeting me."

Bonny slammed his palm against the table. "Not that 'Brehon law' backwater nonsense again. It doesn't hold here or anywhere else. You've been whoring around with my wife in plain sight!"

Rackham sprang, and Mary slammed her hand against the table. "Sort this out," she said with a deafening whisper. "If you want Anne to go free."

Rackham settled into his chair as a crooked smile stretched over Bonny's face.

"No sense in arguing about whether or not Anne was or is married—it's an impasse," Mary continued. "What matters now is whether or not she is still married by the end of the week. And that depends entirely on you." It shouldn't, Mary noted in the back of her mind. Anne should have a say. Mary may have lost Björn to the grips of death and had the Three Horse-Shoes taken from under her when Björn's property went to his family instead of his widow, but she had never felt like a pawn on a chessboard when it came to her heart. She at least imagined she had some control over her life since the day she left Southwick's crew. "James Bonny. Under what conditions would you grant Anne a divorce?"

Bonny's lip curled. "The governor doesn't believe in divorce."

"I'm not asking what that tyrant believes." The other guests muttered at the mention of Governor Rogers. "I'm asking what it would take for *you* to give up Anne as your wife."

As Bonny scratched his patchy beard, Rackham cursed and took a decisive, furious gulp of wine. He slammed it on the table, and liquid sloshed over the sides.

"A man's property has value, does it not?" Bonny said at last. "To say nothing of the trouble it's cost 'im. Anne has wreaked havoc on me, and on my reputation."

"And what a fine, fine reputation that is!" Rackham growled, then turned to Mary. "How much longer do I have to endure this drivel? Anne should be sainted for staying with him as long as she did."

Mary threw him a look so severe it silenced him.

"As I was saying before I was rudely interrupted by this es-teemed . . . gentleman," Bonny droned. "Not only do these dam-ages have to be taken into account, but there is also the matter of the debt she pledged before our marriage. A dowry I never re-ceived."

Rackham stood. "You lying, sniveling scum. She owes you *noth-ing* and you know it."

Bonny rose and leaned into his opponent. "She lies," he breathed. A strand of oily hair fell into his face.

"I could crush you with a single blow like a cockroach," Rackham snarled. "That might make things easier."

"But hardly legal," Bonny taunted. "And you so dearly want to avoid the noose a second time, no doubt."

Before someone threw a punch, Mary stepped between them and calmly pulled out her pistol as a warning. The two backed down, and she lowered her gun. Her pulse hammered as she fought for balance. Sweat beaded on her forehead. She felt like she'd swallowed an entire swamp. The room spun, but she blinked to force the spell aside. "Your price, Bonny. We all grow impatient."

Bonny puffed his chest. He looked around at what Mary could only assume he mistook as admirers. "I have a number in mind. But to make this a little more lawful—being the only one here who thinks that matters—we have to go about it in a proper way. An uncommon method but, nonetheless, a vetted tradition."

All attention snapped on Bonny. His gray eyes lit anew, as if relishing the dramatic pause and power.

"Go on . . ." Mary said. Her stomach scized. She tasted bile. This development she hadn't foreseen. Why couldn't he take the payment and run?

"Tomorrow in the main square, I propose a wife sale."

A collective gasp came from around the room as Bonny spun on Rackham, whose jaw hung open in horror.

No. Mary gagged. Her hand clamped over her mouth.

"Read?" she heard Thomas whisper.

"Pay me my sum," Bonny continued, "and you—or anyone else—can buy her through a proper sale."

No, no, no . . .

Without another warning, up came the contents of Mary's stomach—all over James Bonny.

"What happened?" Thomas asked the moment they returned home.

Mary set aside her pistol and tugged off her shirt. Her breasts felt sore. She sat on the bed and unwound the tight wrap over her chest while avoiding Thomas's gaze. She did not like the worried way he looked at her since Anne had insinuated the impossible.

An impossibility that was feeling more and more possible.

Thomas sat on the edge of the cot and took her hand.

"It's just not like you," he said gently. "What's going on?"

Mary coiled the fabric of the brace and tossed it on top of a trunk. "Must have eaten some bad meat. I admit I found it satisfying, taking Bonny's arrogance down a notch before he ran out."

"People were shocked."

"It's hardly surprising to find vomit in a tavern. I've cleaned up my share of it."

"Not surprising? When everyone knows you well as the only person in Nassau who doesn't drink?" He paused. "It's not just that either," Thomas said. He drummed a thumb against his leg. "All of this—it's so out of character. Taking in a stranger. Compromising our position—your job, our . . . arrangement."

Mary leaned forward and buried her head in her hands. She'd always been clear with Thomas about her feelings. She cared for him and valued his friendship, but she knew what love was. She'd drunken deeply from that infinite well. Mary would not disgrace its sweetness by calling something else by the same name. Thomas, in turn, took what she could give. They had a mutual understanding and basic respect. Sharing expenses helped them both get by. She overlooked his history as a thief. And the comfort of a warm body in the depth of night kept the ghosts away. In those moments of lust, throwing down her many cares and pent up fears, a storm burst in her. She could almost pretend she was still alive then. That there was something left of her body, even if her soul had gone with Björn.

Thomas was not Björn, and he knew it. But he gave her a lot, and she did not want to lose him.

"You are usually so careful. So cautious."

"I know," Mary said, wincing at the thought of having to tell

Anne about the wife sale. This was about Anne, and it also wasn't about Anne. "I just couldn't step aside this time. It wasn't right." At last she found his dark eyes. "I'm sorry."

He stilled for a moment, then placed his head on her shoulder. She put her arms around him. The single bed in that single plain room felt like a raft in a big, bitter sea.

"I imagine it wasn't pleasant, approaching Rackham," Mary said.

"I can't say it was a pleasure." She felt him laugh. "But at least we've earned a few coins by arranging this. Maybe we can make a business of meddling in our neighbors' affairs?"

Thomas nuzzled into her, and they tumbled onto their backs. She thought he might start kissing her, but instead, he leveled a look at her that made her uneasy, that strange look like she might be fragile or something worse. "Is it . . . possible? What Anne suggested?"

Mary shook her head as if to push away the truth settling in her veins.

But could it be true?

A child?

Her child?

"I don't know anymore," she said. A wave of lightness rose in her chest.

"Is there a way to know?" he asked. "Something that can be done? It's hard to imagine how we'd manage it. This would change everything."

Mary breathed. She heard his fretting, his fear. An oceanic pain swelled in her heart, and she rose.

It should be Björn's, too.

"Mary?"

"Which one of us is going to fetch Anne and tell her what awaits her?" Mary said. "That is the only question we can answer for certain tonight."

CHAPTER 42

Anne held her chin high, higher than a solstice sun. But under her skirt, her knees shook. "Everyone is looking at me," she whispered to Mary as they walked toward the main square.

To the place where she would face James Bonny again, along with the rest of New Providence if this crowd was any indication.

"Ignore them," Mary said. "This ritual thrives on humiliation. They expect you to break. Don't give them what they want."

Anne swallowed. At least Jack would be there. Then again, maybe she didn't want him there. He might mistake her cuts and bruises from the woodland as a beating. She dreaded him seeing her like this—trembling, pathetic, still smelling like a fishmonger's bin. But damn, she also needed him to "buy" her.

"This way," Mary said, lending Anne her arm as the press of bodies thickened.

Anne quickened her steps, going over what Mary had explained. Though Anne—a lawyer's daughter—had never seen or heard of such an abominable practice, Mary had. Among the poor folk in England, anyone could procure a permanent, socially accepted separation from a wife by putting her on the market and auctioning her off to the highest bidder. There was, Mary said, almost always only one bidder—the wife's lover. Sometimes all parties involved laughed the whole way to and from the wife sale, a happy parting of ways that circumvented the fees and hassle of divorce—the sum already decided ahead of the sale, and the possibility of being sued by a former husband closed for good. A joke of a ritual that got everyone what they wanted. But not always.

Anne's situation was, of course, a case of revenge.

When they reached the noisy square, Anne lit up with emotion when she saw Jack. He caught her eye and relief flooded his features. She moved toward him.

"Wait," Mary said, throwing out an arm to stop her. "I'm sorry, Anne. You really won't like this part."

Anne whipped her head around just in time to see Bonny. He wore a fine waistcoat and his greasy hair was tied back in a ribbon. And in his hand, he held a rope.

"A wife sale models a cattle auction," Mary said, turning Anne around and bracing her by the shoulders. "Sometimes exactly."

Anne felt her cheeks glow scarlet with rage. "I will not bloody—"

"Oh yes, you will," Bonny said, stepping toward her. "My dear, darling wife." He brushed the slash on her cheek. "Did you have a nice time in the woods?"

She snarled.

He held out the halter rope and Anne cursed.

Mary pulled her aside and said in a cutting whisper, "Do *not* give them what they want, Anne. Remember?"

Anne seethed, chest heaving. For a moment, she felt like that powerless little girl frozen in front of her grandparents' estate. She reached into her bones and tried to summon the strength of Queen Maeve, Grace O'Malley, Joan of Arc, Mam, Ellen—anyone. But she struggled to imagine any of them stooping so low as to be sold like a common heifer.

Anne twisted her sneer into a smile as Bonny tied a rope around her waist. With a yank, he tugged her to the middle of the square. Her steps trailed through sand, dirt, and clumps of cattle manure. People cheered or booed. Anne craned to find Jack in the crowd. He gave her a sympathetic nod. His gaze shifted to Bonny, and it seethed pure murder. Lord how she loved him for it—that reckless, wonderful, beautiful man.

When they reached the middle of the market, Anne turned to face the crowd. Sweet Jesus, there had to be a hundred people watching this spectacle.

"I hereby place my wife, Anne Bonny—formerly Anne Cormac—for sale." Bonny circled her, as if scrutinizing Anne from every angle. "She weighs about ten stone," he said. "Some slight damage to her skin, but that will heal. A fine color of hair, as you can plainly see. Anne, my dear, please uncover your lovely tresses and show your beauty."

Anne scowled. He tore the cloak from off her head and the onlookers whooped with false delight.

"But," Bonny crowed, "I would be remiss if I didn't name some of Anne's less desirable qualities." He shot her a smug look, then continued to pace. "Anne is a born serpent, and frolicsome and tempestuous as a mad dog, a roaring lion, a loaded pistol, and cholera combined." People laughed. "Oh. And she is also a filthy, wanton slut."

To this, the laughing turned deafening. Her ears rang with the sound. Pressure formed behind her eyes but she would not, could not, let her emotion come to the surface.

Act, her whole body screamed. *Move. Run. Fight.*

Instead, she dug her fingernails into her palms.

"However, Anne has reasonable market value. I should also note that my wife can cook a half-decent stew, milk a goat"—he squeezed her arm—"sing well enough, and serve as an adequate drinking companion. I, therefore, offer here all her perfections and imperfections, for the sum of no less than a thousand pounds."

Anne whirled on him. "A thousand pounds? Have you lost your mind?"

The sound of hooves thundered down the street. Everyone turned to stare, a few darting out of the way of the horses.

Anne watched Bonny's smirk fade, then turned to face the commotion.

"What is the meaning of this?" roared Governor Woodes Rogers from the back of his black horse. Behind him rode a dozen others in full uniform.

The spectators fled like scattered vultures scared off a carcass as the soldiers closed in. Jack fought through the chaos and found Anne. He stood between her and the governor.

"Mr. Bonny?" Rogers said, glaring down from his perch. "What evil is this?"

"Well, Governor," Bonny said, pulling at his cravat, "seeing as my wife is a harlot, and I'm owed a debt—"

"I told you quite clearly that I do not grant divorce."

A hush fell over the remaining parties, and Anne glanced around at the confusion. Even Mary had a pinched look of concern. Mary and Thomas had told her that this was a common practice. They told her that if she endured this humiliation well, she would walk free. Anne untied the rope around her waist and flung it to the ground.

"But a wife sale—"

"I know very well what a wife sale is!" Rogers barked. He dismounted, the ringlets of his powdered wig jostling. "A peasant practice that is not respected by honorable men or God Almighty."

"I understand, Governor," Bonny said with a deep bow. His groveling made Anne want to kick him in the bollocks.

"You," Governor Rogers said, standing close enough that Anne could smell his foul breath and see the gnarled musket-ball scar and missing teeth on the left side of his once-shattered jaw. "Have you not caused enough commotion for one day? Had to do it again within the week?"

"This had nothing to do with her!" Jack said, stepping in. "Look at her welts. No doubt from *that* scoundrel." His voice shook with fury.

The governor shifted his catlike interest from Anne to Jack. Her insides twisted. Jack had been so careful, so painstakingly careful, to avoid catching Rogers's notice since taking the king's pardon and forsaking piracy.

This was all her fault.

Bloody hell. This was *not* all her fault. Damn James Bonny for making her doubt herself.

"Lieutenant," Governor Rogers called to a man behind him. "This woman has disturbed the public order. Would you be so kind as to retrieve the cat-o'-nine tails?" Anne watched as the soldier retrieved a whip. She felt the air abandon her lungs.

Governor Rogers gripped the flogger in his hand, studying it. Anne's whole body crumpled inward.

"Governor, please," Jack said, stepping forward. "I'll take the lashes. She had nothing to do with this spectacle. This was all Bonny. This was all arranged."

Anne trembled like a blade of seagrass. "No." She wouldn't let him do this. She wouldn't let him take this blow for her. Not with a flogger like that—a weapon meant to tear flesh, to mangle skin, to end the lives of even the strongest men.

Then her mind tore from Jack to the unseen life stirring inside her.

A life that, this time, she would do anything to keep.

The corner of the governor's thin lips curled. "Oh, I had something else in mind, Rackham." He held up the leather whip, as if brandishing the coiled handle in the light. "As a captain and renowned, honest *sailor*," he emphasized, "I imagine you are quite familiar with a cat-o'-nine tails."

Jack paled. "I am."

Bonny shifted his weight, clearly worried about what this meant for him. But the governor relieved any of the bilge rat's fears by handing Bonny the whip. "Ten lashes, followed by a stint in jail, might help the message sink in."

Jack lunged, knocking Bonny to the ground and wrestling the cat-o'-nine tails from his grip and flinging it to the ground. The remaining people watching—were there still people?—sucked in a collective breath.

Bonny found his footing and shook the sand off his waistcoat, revenge coiling like a viper in his pupils. But the governor held up a rapier to signal them to stop. "I've changed my mind."

Anne caught herself from collapsing in terror, snagging on hope despite the sharp blade. She inhaled sharply, struggling for balance.

Then Rogers bent over, picking up the leather whip from the sandy street, and handed it to Jack. "Far better, and more effective, if you do it."

The color drained from Jack's face, and Bonny let out a hoarse, wicked cackle.

Act! Every nerve in her screamed again. *Go boldly.*

Jack. The baby.

Her life.

Her freedom to fight another way.

"I'll reform!" Anne shouted, the words ripping from her like a tempest.

All parties turned to gawk. Anne threw herself at the boots of her miserable former husband. She placed her knife down. "I will be a good wife!" she lied through real, terrible tears. "I will be a good wife and repent of my wayward behaviors." She pushed herself to her knees and shuffled to kneel in front of Rogers.

"Bon . . ." Jack said, barely louder than a whisper.

She caught his gaze and held it, then resumed her dramatics. "Please," she begged, wiping at her eyes and prostrating before the governor. "You won't have trouble with me again. I swear it. Send me home with my husband." *Not a jail cell. Anything but that.*

"You swear it?" Rogers said, his rapier now lowered near her shoulder.

"On my life," Anne pledged.

CHAPTER 43

"Why didn't you run?"

"I already told you," Mary said with steady calmness as she and Thomas made their way toward the *Ranger* in the velvet night. The fresh air offered a welcomed respite from the nausea that had been unrelenting since the despicable scene in the square.

Because it wasn't right, how they treated Anne.

Because I can't stand by and stay silent.

Because I'm sick of running.

"It's not too late to stop. To turn around," Thomas said.

"We can't miss the meeting."

"Oh, yes we can."

Mary halted in her tracks. Thomas stepped in front of her and held her shoulders. "Please, Mary. Think about this. Our risky position. You've drawn more attention to yourself, and us, in a week than in the last three years we've been on this island. People are watching. They talk."

"I know," Mary said, reaching out a hand and tenderly touching the stubble of his cheek. "But running away from Governor Rogers today wouldn't have solved anything." Neither would running from the remaining days of her life.

Thomas sighed with heaviness.

"I know you're afraid," Mary said with compassion. "I am, too. But Thomas, I've spent too many years in the shadows of fear. And if it's true . . ." She took his hand and moved it to her stomach. "If it's true that I'm with child, it changes everything."

He turned away. She didn't have to see his expression in the dark to picture the lines of worry etched across his brow. Thomas could have his own feelings, but she must be allowed to have hers. The more it seemed possible, the more a billow of hope rose in her heart—something she hadn't felt since Björn.

Björn would not want her to wallow in grief. To continue living a half life when it was he who'd escorted her out of the land of secrets into an expanse of brilliant light.

"With effort, I pass as a man now," Mary said. "We scrape together the rent. But what happens when I cannot bind my breasts any longer? When my stomach swells and I can't do what other women do—layering skirts and aprons to hide their bellies? When Rogers with all of his morals hears of this disturbing change? We can't even afford the passage off this island."

He squared his shoulders, but she could tell she had his ear. "Captain Rackham will take you again," Mary said, "or he won't. But by the end of the night, we'll know." She brushed her fingers against his. "Whatever he decides does not define you. No one can brand you a thief forever. People change. The truth is in your heart alone."

The salty breeze rustled her hair and he squeezed her wrist. "And if Rackham is only willing to take one of us?"

"If it comes to that, we'll forge another plan. But no sense in fretting until we know for sure."

They gripped hands with renewed strength, then continued toward the docks.

The dozen faces crammed into the captain's quarters of the *Ranger* glowed in the flickering lantern light, their frowns and displeasure vivid. Mary and Thomas stood at the back of the gathering, behind the map table.

"What now, Captain?"

Rackham, with a bottle in hand, paced across the rug on the floorboard. He wore a yellow calico shirt that had seen cleaner days. He smelled of rum, and his eyes blazed red with drink. "We arm ourselves and get her back by any means necessary," he growled.

Mary scanned the cramped room and saw that the listeners were not pleased with this answer.

"Rackham," she said, speaking like a confident man, "with all due respect, Anne has proven herself capable of getting away on her own."

He paused and his gaze hardened. "She's unarmed."

Did men only think of power in terms of weapons? It continually amazed her. "She gave a convincing act. I suspect Anne would have kept it up all the way to wherever she's staying. They may loosen their security. She'll slip away at the first opportunity."

Rackham flexed his jaw. "And if not?"

"And if not, then we make new plans. But right now, we have to create a plan worthy of Anne's escape."

A grunt of agreement rose from the motley crew.

"I won't stomach a New Providence run by Governor Rogers," one man said. He was old enough to be a grandfather, with brown skin leathered by the sun. "I'd rather see 'er shrinking away forever on the horizon or swallowed up in flames than in the hands of the king's puppet."

"Aye! I'm with old Fenwick," another piped up. "Rogers's stunt in the square today is 'bout more than just a lass. Nassau has fallen. Freedom to govern ourselves has fallen."

"Who among us will be hauled off next?"

"Nothing to stop him from tossing anyone aside or up the gallows at his pleasure!" roared another, punching the air with a pale fist.

Mary caught Thomas's eye; he still hadn't said a word since the secret meeting began. "If everyone is already suspect and in danger," she said, "why don't we give the good governor what he

wants and all go back 'on the account'? Take up the Articles of
Agreement again and turn pirate? That is what this meeting is
really about, is it not?"

All eyes looked at her. But none, she observed, showed displeasure or surprise.

"Read is right," Rackham said. "Everyone here has served under the Articles. We made more coin. Worked together. Trusted
each other." At this, Thomas looked away, but Rackham did not
notice.

Mary's pulse skipped. Six months, maybe even less, under a
lauded captain like Rackham might get her enough savings to settle in a quiet town, one she'd never have to leave. To raise a child
in the way Ma would have done if they'd had the means. Thomas
could come along if he wanted to, or not—he had to make his own
choices. But a child deserved solid ground beneath its feet. Finally, at long last, Mary felt a bearing in her heart. A navigational
point to guide her energies.

She'd make herself indispensable before they discovered her
secret and condition.

"That would stick it to Rogers!" someone yelled out, raising a
bottle. "Rub his nose in his own filth."

"The people might rise again—see he ain't so high and mighty."

"The *Ranger* is too well known," someone offered up, a large
man with a dark, shaved head. "It would be impossible to avoid
detection."

"Aye, Corner," Rackham said with sorrow. "That thinking
makes you a loyal quartermaster. We'll have to leave the *Ranger*
behind, same as we did the *Kingston* a few years back. But"—he
paused—"I have my sights on another sloop."

"Better be fast."

"Oh, that it is. But before I divulge more, I have to know: is
everyone here willing and able to serve in this brotherhood? Of
breaking their pardon with the king? You wouldn't have come
here tonight if it was a risk you wanted to avoid—that much is
evident. But all the same, anyone can leave now. By staying, you

swear your loyalty to this new crew and agree to help draft the Articles we will collectively abide by."

Mary surveyed the sailors. Mostly young. Desperate. Tar-stained fingers. Threadbare clothes covered in patches. Radicals, no doubt. Down on their luck, high on their ideals and sense of rightness. Were they capable? Experienced? Rackham clearly hadn't the time or luxury to be picky. No one protested or raised a hand. No one left the room.

"That's a promise, then. We'll do everything according to the Articles—by voting—starting with our next move," Rackham said. He threw a map down on the table and stretched it out for all to see. "See this cove outside of Nassau Harbor?"

A murmur of acknowledgment as they leaned to look.

Madness.

"Isn't that," Corner began with a hitch in his voice, "where Captain Ham keeps the *William*?"

CHAPTER 44

New Providence, Nassau
August 22, 1720

A deluge blinded Anne's vision, rain pelting her cheeks as she fled into the night. She slipped around street corners amid the storm, feigning confidence despite the chaos of drunken card games between seafarers under pavilions.

Her pulse hammered and she tightened the scarf shielding her face. A week had passed since the wife sale, and she missed the knife she'd abandoned in the square every day. She had studied the path to Bonny's estate, but it was harder to recognize side streets in the soggy darkness. And to think she'd once believed the Jubilee was in the rough area of Nassau. The stench of Mary's part of town made Anne's nostrils flare. The rain did little to alleviate it. Her boots were soaked through. Lord, she had been walking for hours.

Bonny might already be looking. This flight was, she knew, her final chance. She would either escape with her life or forfeit it.

Thunder rumbled overhead. She'd made a wager—Mary or Rackham—and Anne bet on what she hoped was the less obvious option to anyone hunting her down.

A mutt yapped at her heels, and Anne nearly knocked over an umbrella covering a gambling table.

"Watch it, will ya?" A man swatted at her before righting a candle that had fallen over.

She raised her hands in silent apology, her eyes not leaving the dog.

This is not Ireland.

I am no longer a helpless child.

At last, Anne reached Mary's familiar door. Mary pulled her inside.

"Thomas," Mary said with a calm yet firm tone using her resonant female voice. "She's here."

Thomas dropped the fishnet he was mending and glanced up. Seeing Anne, he stood in a hurry.

"Go," Mary said. "Tell Rackham. Gather the others."

Thomas sprang to leave without a word.

"What others? What the Devil is happening?" Anne asked. She surveyed the room, even more bare than before. "Are you . . . packing?"

Mary flung a cutlass into the single trunk and gave Anne one of Thomas's coats to wear. "We knew we'd need to move fast."

We?

"I've been gathering arms. I'll explain on the way; there isn't time," Mary said. She closed the lid of the ironbound sea chest. "Help me? Drag this to the door. The two of us will carry it out."

"What about Thomas's fishing net?"

"Leave it."

Thunder boomed outside as Mary took an armful of weapons out from under the bed—a sawed-off musket, a pistol, several cast-iron grenades, and a dirk.

The sight left Anne queasy. She swallowed. "Tell me we aren't staging a revolt." She'd just escaped Bonny—she had little interest in going back to fight him.

"Not exactly," Mary said, tucking the pistol into her belt and throwing the musket strap over her back. "Rackham said you're a fine hand on a ship. We'll need it." Mary held out a small blade for Anne to take.

"You found my knife?" she breathed, hesitating.

"I'll teach you how to use this one day. But with any luck, you won't have to use it tonight."

A heartbeat passed, then another, before Anne took the dagger. Then they fled into the torrential rain.

When Jack threw his arms around Anne, squeezing her like a vise, she inhaled his scent—rain and rum and cedar—and every muscle in her body relaxed.

Safe.

At last, she felt she'd be all right.

"Bon," he breathed, picking her up and spinning her on the dark shore. He kissed her, hard, desperately, and she leaned into his heat, knocking off his tricorn. Then he ripped away, looking her over as his hair dripped, and ran a finger along her jaw. "Did that bastard hurt you? I'll kill him. I'll slit his scheming throat."

Anne shook her head and hid the shiver that shot down her spine. She did not want to recount her revolting week of pretending to be a grateful, repentant wife. Jack didn't need to hear it. All that mattered now was that they were together. "I'm fine," she said, touching his chest. "I'm here." His strong embrace instantly singed her senses. She could have taken him right there and then on the beach.

Someone cleared their throat, and Anne turned to see the crew Mary had described.

"Earl's returned from scouting," said Richard Corner, Jack's quartermaster. Despite his enormous size, he had a friendly face—the kind one might expect from a priest.

"How many aboard the *William?*" Jack said, retrieving his hat.

"Two, Captain. Seems to be stocked for the privateer's journey, as we predicted."

"And at Fort Nassau?"

"Half the men at their stations with twenty-eight cannons and a guard ship. But with this wretched weather, we might slip past unscathed."

"Everyone is in position?" Rackham said.

"Aye. We're ready."

Anne searched the faces in the fog as the breakers crashed. She recognized half of the crew from men who'd served under Jack during her year on the ship.

Then she spotted Thomas's rowboat pulled up onto the sand.

Was he back in Jack's good graces?

Mary sprang open the trunk they'd carried to the shore. "Gather your weapons. Remember, intimidation is your sharpest blade." She handed out arms and cartridges of gunpowder. Thomas pulled the fishing vessel toward the sea. The swells threatened to knock him over. A bolt of lightning lashed overhead.

"Seems like a bad night to steal a ship," Anne said.

"That's why it's the perfect night, Bon," Jack said, flashing his winning smile. "You chose your escape well. Now, after you, my lady." He offered her a hand and helped her into the boat. Her fingers tingled at his touch. Lord, she ached to get him alone.

When the last of the crew were aboard, Thomas pushed off as the leaders paddled with all they were worth. The waves slammed into them, sending ocean spilling over the sides. Anne gasped and blinked against the rain, her heart thumping like an angry fist against her ribs as the silhouette of the ship emerged from the fog.

"Ladders are on the starboard side," said Earl, the spindly young scout.

They dug the oars against the violent current and angled for the *William* in perfect silence. The sloop sat high above the waterline. At one point, Mary leaned over the side—to vomit, Anne presumed. Thomas didn't look up from his rowing. Was Mary well enough for this plan?

When the rowboat knocked into the hull, Thomas stood and

latched a boarding pike to the ladder, drawing them in and tying off.

Thomas held the boat steady as one, then two crew members scrambled up the ladder. The rest did the same, followed by Mary and Thomas. Then, Jack swept Anne up with one arm, surveying her face and the knife tucked into her belt. He kissed her wet forehead before sending her up. "I'll never let anything bad happen to you again," he whispered.

Her throat squeezed and her stomach fluttered. "I know. Besides, I'm not done with you." She kissed him fiercely before climbing up the ladder ahead of Jack, his body pressed close behind her as the fishing vessel below shrank from view.

Flinging themselves onto the upper deck, Anne found her footing and drew her knife. She flicked her gaze to each member of the silent crew. They'd boarded undetected—a step toward victory. The scout signaled to a hatch near the mainmast, below which the sailors manning the *William* must be stationed. Her pulse hammered as they crept along the damp planks, the ship bucking under the swells, threatening to knock her over.

Jack's hand found hers. She caught his eye, and courage welled within her once more.

Mary, Thomas, and another crewmate moved right, steel raised. In her other hand, Mary also held a flintlock pistol.

Surrounding the hatch, everyone looked at Rackham. He pressed a finger to his lips before pulling a bottle of wine from his coat.

Now? Really, Jack? At a time like this?

Then, George Featherstone—Jack's sailing master—threw open the hatch as Jack shattered the bottle on the deck, loud enough to draw notice.

"Did you hear that?" came a voice from below.

Silence. Anne's crewmates withdrew to the shadows, weapons ready. She felt her knees shake and she clutched her knife tighter.

"Wind blew open the hatch."

Stop shaking, she told herself. *Don't show your fear.*

"Better check," came another voice. "Could be something amiss with the rigging."

His companion let out an exaggerated sigh. The seconds dragged like minutes as boots clomped up each step. Anne closed her eyes, then forced them open. Her heart sounded like cannon fire in her ears. She braced herself.

When the sailor emerged, Featherstone tackled him to the floor as another stuffed a gag in his mouth. Thomas bound his hands.

"Disarm him," Rackham mouthed. Anne helped the others search the man's waistcoat. His feet banged against the deck in protest as he tried to yell through his gag.

"Everything all right, Fletcher?"

The sailor squirmed all the harder at his name, rain pelting the main deck around him like grapeshot, until the second set of boots made their way up the ladder.

The second man didn't have time to use his raised musket before Richard Corner pushed him down and snatched the weapon from his grip. He crashed onto his stomach. The others held back his arms and pinned him down, tying his wrists.

"Sorry about that," Corner muttered.

"Who are you?" the bearded sailor bellowed, eyes wild as he took in the sight of his thrashing companion on the deck beside him. "How dare you board this vessel without permission!"

Jack stepped forward. "Sorry to disturb you, fellow seafarers. We mean you no harm, but we are in need of this ship."

The man barked out a laugh. "Are you deranged? Do you have any idea who commands this sloop?"

"Aye, I do," Jack said. "And, much as I admire Captain Ham and his mission to hunt down sea rogues, urgency demands sacrifices."

The sailor scoffed as half the crew dispersed to check the inventory and the other half saw to the rigging. The wooden yards knocked against the mast. Reefing the mainsail was necessary if they didn't want to capsize. Featherstone and Corner, the largest of the crew, stood guard over their captives.

"Fully stocked hold, Captain," Howell reported—the biggest drunkard in their crew. Anne never did like him. "Provisions to last a month. Some great wine selections, too!"

"We're ready to sail," Earl said, elbowing Howell in the ribs.

Jack turned to the captives. "Seems we will be on our way now. Once we put enough distance between the *William* and shore, my men will escort you to your escape vessel—a nice little rowboat."

The bearded one without a gag leaned forward. He studied Anne's face and hair, then sneered at Jack. "I know you. I know what you are."

Anne's grip tightened on her knife.

"A pleasure to meet you, despite these regrettable conditions," Jack said, ignoring the threat as the crew returned to their positions.

"We should just kill 'em," Howell growled, his missing front tooth on full display. "They'll turn us in the second they can."

"We don't kill unarmed men," Mary snapped with conviction. Jesus, Mary, and Joseph, she could be scary. And to think, only Anne and Thomas knew the half of it.

Jack raised his tricorn, bidding the sailors adieu. While the rest of the crew sprang into position, Anne stayed at Jack's side.

"I suppose there is no return now." She looked up at him, his smiling eyes, the rain caught in his lashes.

"Nothing to return *to*, Bon," he said, pulling her in, his lips finding hers. She tasted the sweetness of his mouth. His ragged breath sent her blood aflame as he whispered, "The horizon is ours now." He nipped her earlobe before darting for the helm, where Mary and Featherstone were busy shouting coordinates and directives.

Anne panted, relishing the warmth returning to her numbed toes. Even in a downpour, that man could light a fire in her with a single strike of flint and steel. She tucked her knife into her belt. Her fingers lingered there for a moment, on her stomach.

I'll tell him. When the time is right.

She shook herself alert and sprinted for the ropes, the halyard line with a white pennant flag knocking against the mainmast. Her drenched hem slapped against her legs. The wind whipped at her hair and the shrouds as the reefed sails caught the full strength of the squall.

CHAPTER 45

Rackham had no problem counting the votes of his small crew of twelve.

The votes were unanimous, all hands raised as everyone stood on the sleek oak main deck in the blinding sunlight. Mary sat with her spine against the rail. She felt light, the queasy nerves she'd tried to hide abated, especially now that they were safe in the calm, open sea.

"Shipmates!" Rackham bellowed, raising a squat bottle that glinted in the late August sun. "Your vote settles it. As captain, I therefore rechristen this sloop—all twelve tons of her, four long ranges and two swivels, as well as a *shapely* hull—for our own purposes." He paused for dramatic effect and laughed, then popped the cork. "Welcome to the *Revenge*, the fastest ship in the Caribbean!"

A deafening cheer rang out as the crew clinked their pewter mugs around the single mast of the sloop. The *Revenge* was longer than the *Ranger*, but with her slender build and shallow draft, they could sneak into almost any cove or beach, leaving the navy's men-of-war or heavy two-mast vessels and schooners in their wake as they reached speeds of fifteen knots or more.

Mary smiled when she saw Thomas grinning in the thick of the fun, whistling a song of celebration and brushing shoulders with the men who esteemed him again. She hoped this might heal his wounded pride. Who might Thomas be if he could forgive himself?

A father?

A wave of sorrow swelled in her heart. He was not Björn and never would be. Thomas was his own person. It was hard to imagine him taking responsibility or looking out for more than his own hide. But maybe she hadn't imagined it hard enough. He had, after all, stepped up to help Anne despite the risks.

Thomas, whistling a lullaby to a child in that rich, melodic voice. His strong arms cradling an infant instead of a fishnet.

She closed her eyes, resting her palms on the knees of her canvas breeches, and tried to picture the life growing inside her.

Hello, there, she tried.

I'm so pleased to finally meet you.

Pressure built behind her eyes, and she inhaled sharply, blinking the sudden emotion away. What was she doing? She worried that thinking of it, talking to it, might somehow snatch the dream away. She drew her attention to the taut sail of the single mast. Yes, focus there. Clever, really, for Rackham to steal this ship of all ships—a vessel careened and scrubbed of barnacles only days prior. Even without that added advantage, the *William*—or, rather, the *Revenge*—could fly compared to a merchant ship. The shallow draft made them swift but also savvy. They could pull into any harbor, escape any predator.

Steal back the fighting chance I lost after Björn.

A chance, Mary recognized, as the one her own mother had sacrificed everything to give her. By God, where was Ma now? Despite Mary's searching, she and Björn never found her. And yet, Mary still hoped.

"Cheers," Anne said, pulling Mary from her thoughts. She handed Mary a decanter.

"I don't drink."

"I know. It's water."

Mary eyed Anne with surprise, then accepted it with gratitude. Anne took the seat next to her on the deck and spread out her indigo skirt while stretching her legs. "How are you feeling today?"

"Well, for once." Salt breeze, fresh air, a sense of expanse and openness. Routines she knew so well she could manage them in her sleep. She'd always felt at ease with herself aboard a ship with a compass in her grip. Maybe it was having a pirate for a father. Maybe it was the fondness she felt for Captain Southwick and his kindness after losing Ma.

Or, maybe it was her, pure and simple.

"No one else knows?"

Mary shook her head, understanding that Anne referred to the pregnancy, and in turn, her sex. She tucked a stray black hair into her shoulder-length braid.

"How much longer will that last?"

Mary exhaled. She did not have an answer.

"You can trust this crew."

"Yes, I believe so." Without trust, any crew like theirs was doomed from the outset. They already had one woman aboard the ship without complaint or superstitious drivel, though Anne only had minor responsibilities and got saddled with meal prep at every opportunity. Maybe they'd suffer another female after recovering from the shock. Then again, Mary had no interest in being thrown on meal duty. She repressed a gag, imagining the cramped quarters and pungent fumes of the galley.

"You can trust me," Anne said, swirling the contents of her mug.

The corner of Mary's lip tugged up. This again. "I know."

They exchanged a look that made Anne smile. Her eyes crinkled, and she drew the dagger from her belt. "You said you would teach me how to use this."

"I did," Mary said, taking a swig of water.

"Will you?"

Mary wiped her mouth. "Rackham hasn't taught you how to wield a blade?" If such a little dirk could be called a blade.

"No." Anne cursed and her chest fell. "He doesn't think it necessary. He says he is the only protection I need."

Mary suppressed a scoff of annoyance. "A lot of help that was with Bonny."

Anne shrugged.

"Have you told Rackham?"

"Not yet," Anne said, glancing at the pack of men to ensure no one would overhear.

"Then that makes two secrets between us," Mary said, taking the blade from Anne. She balanced it on one finger, then tossed it in the air, catching it by the handle—an old trick Captain Southwick had taught her. It was one Henry had especially appreciated. She wondered where Henry Danby was now. Every day she regretted the fact that she wasn't able to find where he was stationed after losing the inn.

She shook her head. That life was over. Why did it always insist on springing up unannounced? "And will Rackham approve of my teaching you?"

Anne's mouth twisted. "I get a say, do I not?"

"It's your life. I think you do." Mary shuddered to think what would have happened to her in the army if she'd been treated as a fragile woman.

"Then I say we begin," Anne said. "If you aren't too ill, of course. I feel well enough this time around, but bloody hell, I remember what it was like when I didn't." She grimaced.

They looked up in time to see Rackham glance their way, shifting his gaze between them. His radiant grin wavering for a heartbeat before he raised a second bottle. "Come, Bon! Join us. Sing us a song. One of the Irish ballads."

Summoned to his side, Anne moved to join the noise and festivities. Howell was already sloshed, flat on his back, while Thomas and Featherstone debated the worth of the hold's contents. Earl retrieved his fiddle, and Fenwick—also known as "Old Dad the

Cooper"—tapped his foot to the folk tune despite being three times older than most of the crew.

Mary remained seated. She studied the blade Anne had handed her and ran a thumb across the steel edge. Anne's knife was small, but sharp.

CHAPTER 46

Anne circled the narrow deck near the helm. She hated the way her skirt swished around her ankles when she moved. She envied Mary's canvas trousers.

"If I struck you from the left?" Mary said, slicing a hand toward Anne's arm.

"Then dodge and stab."

"From what angle?"

Anne paused and lowered her knife. "What do you mean?"

Mary tapped her chin. "Brown!" she called up to Thomas, who was working overhead as a topman. "Can you come down here for a moment?"

It was odd hearing Mary call Thomas by his last name. But the rest of the crew called him "Brown," and Mary refused to give away her position. He was twenty feet in the air and finished trimming the mainsail before descending. Feet clapping the main deck, he approached Anne and Mary.

"I'm demonstrating short-range blows."

"I see that," Thomas said, eyes shifting to the dirk in Anne's grip.

A roar of laughs emerged from the port side. "Take care, Brown!"

"Would hate to see you bested by a woman."

Anne's face flushed. She didn't see what was so humorous about this. Maybe she—the de facto sailmaker on the crew—should return to patching the rat-eaten canvas or to weatherproofing the leech line that sorely needed it. Thomas pursed his lips, his dark eyes pleading for this to be over already.

"Stand here," Mary said, moving him in front of Anne.

"Sorry," Anne mouthed.

"It takes an enormous amount of effort to stab someone. I recommend running and avoiding a knife attack, if you can. This isn't a duel or a cross of swords. It's a fight to the death, reserved for desperate circumstances. To be effective with a knife, you have to know where to push the blade."

From the corner of Anne's mind, she saw herself standing in the drawing room. The door being pushed open. Nathaniel leering, his lips tearing into hers. Her protests. His force.

The paper knife.

Her pathetic use of it.

You got away, Anne chided herself. *That was all you needed.*

Anne swallowed. "Show me."

"You have to avoid bone," Mary said. She surveyed Anne. "Muscle can be that dense, too. Rely on accuracy over brute strength. It's just as deadly."

Anne saw the red pooling from Nathaniel's abdomen. The crimson stamping her hands.

Good Lord, she didn't want to kill anyone.

She also didn't want anyone to kill her. Nathaniel, and others like him, were out there. And so was James Bonny.

Mary pointed at Thomas's tanned neck. He rolled his eyes. "Go for the jugular," she said. "See this vein?"

Anne nodded.

"The throat is tough. You won't get through the cartilage with a dull edge." She repositioned her hand. "Use the blade to stab your opponent's Adam's apple, angling toward the back of the neck, then retreat. No cutting."

"No cutting or slashing. Got it," Anne repeated.

"Yes, please none of that," Thomas mumbled.

Mary smiled. Anne noticed she smiled more and more now that they were out of Nassau—her face more relaxed. "Can you put your arms out, Brown? Yes, like that." She pointed. "The ribs are risky, as the steel is likely to hit bone. But if you angle here, with the blade flat, you might strike the liver of your attacker."

Anne must have blanched, because Mary paused. "It's unpleasant business, Anne, causing someone to bleed out. Like I said, run if you can. But if you strike, don't hesitate. You can't afford it."

"I understand." Jesus, Mary, and Joseph, she understood.

"Another lethal move . . ." Mary said before jabbing Thomas in the armpit.

He recoiled. "What was that for?"

"Had to keep you humble," Mary said before patting him on the shoulder. Then, in a whisper, "Better not let the rest of them know you're ticklish."

Thomas huffed and tried to leave, but Mary held onto his elbow. She spun on Anne. "No one is ever expecting the armpit, so few people defend it. But that close to the heart?" Mary tsked. She grabbed the knife. "It's best if your opponent isn't wearing a thick coat or armor—but we are, fortunately, in the Caribbean." She demonstrated what to do over Thomas's white shirt. "Thrust up, with the blade parallel to your face." When no one else was watching, Mary tickled Thomas one last time, and he squirmed away. It was a risk, this playful behavior. Anne wondered if she missed Thomas's affections.

"I'm done," he said with a wave before sulking off to resume his position.

"Thanks, Thomas!" Anne shouted after him.

Mary returned the blade, and Anne felt its weight in her palms.

"Now, you try—"

"Ship on the horizon!" Featherstone shouted from the wheel. "Port side."

All attention snapped to the shipmaster. From the captain's quarters, Jack flung open the door and ran toward the sighting. He gripped a brass spyglass in his hand.

Mary bolted, leaving Anne standing alone with her knife. She scurried after the party and squinted at the blurry dot causing all the commotion.

"What is it?" Jack asked, tossing Featherstone the spyglass.

"Hard to make it out."

"Corner? What say you?" Jack said, turning to his quartermaster as Featherstone passed Corner the instrument.

Corner, standing a solid foot above the rest of them, clicked his tongue. "Could be a merchant vessel. A nice prize."

Anne felt her stomach squeeze. She'd engaged in illegal activities with the *Swallow*'s crew. But nothing like this. Would this be her first time participating in an attack?

Mary held out a hand, and Corner placed the spyglass in her grip. "It's a pink," Mary said. "Square-rigging, two masts, and a narrow stern. Likely fishermen or modest merchants."

After a silence, Jack faced the full crew. He straightened and put on the captain's face that Anne had seen a thousand times: severe, flexed jaw, amplified voice. She preferred the soft expressions he wore when it was just the two of them in the captain's quarters. The sweetness of his sleepy countenance when he awoke, nuzzling into her until she laughed and he threw her on top of him, her legs straddling his hips. The restless sea of white sheets.

Her skin flushed with hunger. *Focus, Anne.* If she ever wanted the crew to take her more seriously, she needed to work hard—no, she *did* work hard. But she would need to work even harder than the rest of them.

"If it's a small vessel, I vote we give chase. If not, we clear these waters at first opportunity."

"What do you mean, Captain?" Earl, eager to prove himself, interjected. "What of the biggest prizes?"

Anne could see a vein ticking in Jack's throat. "Corner and I have discussed our options. We need to keep our heads down, especially after our illustrious escape. Taking smaller ships for the time being will be in our favor."

Anne thought she heard a sigh of nostalgia from Howell at her right. He reeked of alcohol, though she preferred that smell to his rank breath and the scowl he wore when sober.

"No vote?" Mary asked. "Wouldn't a quick succession of wind-falls allow us to go into hiding sooner?"

"That's the captain's call," Featherstone growled.

"No, Read is right," Jack said. "We can vote. But I assure you all, my strategy is best. We can't rendezvous in a big way in these waters. We need to keep northwest of Jamaica. Small ships pass through frequently. There will be prey aplenty."

They held a vote about whether or not to pursue the pink in question. Anne's nerves held her back; she'd only raise her hand if a tie required it.

A clear majority was in favor of pursuit.

Anne swallowed and felt her knife at her side. She knew what that meant, and she wished she had a few more lessons from Mary before this day arrived. She had a child to protect now in addition to her own hide.

"We make chase, then," Jack said. "Everyone, to your positions."

They flew into action without further directives, half the crew racing belowdecks to put out the oars. Anne sprinted for the mainmast to help furl the sail as Corner ordered them to tack. The *Revenge* swung, pivoting with a needlelike bowsprit aimed at the pink on the horizon like a rapier. They gained the advantage, closing in.

"Run up the Jolly Roger!" Jack shouted to Fenwick, whose wrinkled hands fumbled to bring down the white pennant and switch flags. "They'll know they're outmatched," Jack added. "Give them a chance to surrender."

The black flag rose. Anne held her head high and let the wind rip at her hair. Her courage flapped like a trapped bird in her rib cage. She imagined Queen Maeve battling Furbaide. Queen Maeve would never have turned down a fight, even if it meant the end of her. Mam made that clear.

Bloody hell, Queen Maeve was probably a myth. Mam swore it was true, but it was just a foolish bedtime story.

This, however, was real—very, very real.

"Fire a warning shot over the bow," Jack shouted when they got within cannon range.

Earl sprang for the nine-iron cannon, manned by four other gunners, and Anne ran after him. She handed Earl a cartridge of powder, which he stuffed into the muzzle. On the next upswell, he lowered the smoking slow match to the touchhole. Everyone dove out of the way before the kickback.

A deafening blast made Anne's bones rattle and inner ear ring. Her nostrils flared with the acrid scent. Black powder dusted her dress.

The crew stared at the pink's slack sails, unmoving, like a deer shot through the heart.

"Lower your damn sails," Jack said. "Surrender quick." It would be a grace to both sides.

"We're heading for their broadside," Corner said.

"Ready the boarding pikes," Jack said as he darted between the crew manning the lines. "Bon," he said, his voice half as loud. "Come with me."

She left Featherstone and Earl to take in the line and followed Jack to the hatch. He flung it open. "All hands on deck!" he bellowed to the others manning the oars. "Arm yourselves to the teeth."

He turned to Anne, his brown eyes blazing with intent. "You'll stay below."

Anne gawked. "I'll *what?*"

"Stay safe," he said, placing a hand on hers.

She snatched it away. "I'm part of this crew." The Articles demanded equality. How could they respect her as an equal if she abandoned them? If anything happened while she hid like a coward?

"A worthy part, to be sure. My favorite part. But unsuited for battle."

Whose fault is that? "I understand the risks." But even as she said it, she thought of her quivering fingers on the knife. Her baby. The terror in her heart.

All the same, if others were risking their lives, she must as well. Mary certainly would. Last she saw, Mary and Corner were leading the charge.

"I swore I'd protect you!" Jack said, tucking a strand of her hair behind her ear. "Do you know what might happen if someone snatched you? If they used you as leverage? What a bunch of scared sailors do to females in their possession?"

"Making contact in thirty seconds, Rackham!" Corner yelled. "Boarding party is ready."

Jack turned, desperate. "Bon, please. You must do this." He clutched her head in his hands. "For me."

She scowled but said no more. She was a worthless liability. As the others poured out the hatch to stage the attack, Jack all but threw Anne down the ladder. She froze. Mother of God, she froze, hands white-knuckling the rungs.

Act.

But what of the child in her womb? The danger her inexperience posed to the crew?

"Stay out of sight," Jack ordered before slamming the hatch closed, leaving her in darkness.

CHAPTER 47

As the crew surveyed the loot they brought back to the *Revenge*, Mary's heart sank like a sounding weight.

So little. So pathetically little in the hold.

Howell tipped his flask and gurgled the contents as Fenwick rested his bad knee.

"All that, and only a pile of wool and linen to show for it?" said Earl with a hard frown. Mary suspected it was the scout's first time waging battle.

She glanced around the dim hold, the stench from the bilge water beneath them. Thomas massaged his right arm, strained but not injured—she'd made sure of it. He, like most of the crew, was more of a sailor than a soldier; she'd kept him within her sight during the entire siege. Anne sat off to the side with her lips pressed tight. She hadn't spoken a word since the raid.

Howell belched.

"Well done, Read," Corner said, clapping Mary on the back with enough force to leave a bruise. "We led them well." His bluster did not match the mood.

"Aye, well done, Read," Rackham said, billowing up the crew alongside his quartermaster. "Next time, we'll seize more. But this is a fine start."

Mary didn't know what sort of "fine start" Rackham had in mind. But for her, it required more than a few bolts of rat-eaten cloth that would fetch a few coins apiece. She'd pitied the crew on the pink. They'd surrendered immediately, as anticipated, and no physical harm came to them. But this pile of goods would mean more to them.

Her stomach sloshed like a swamp.

Mary rose abruptly. "Need some air," she said, making her way for the ladder. As she climbed from the hold to the lower deck to the main deck, she studied each stair in front of her, focusing on anything but the bile rising in her throat. When she was out of earshot and in the open air, she ran, emptying her guts over the side of the *Revenge*.

"Are you all right?"

Mary spun around. "It's you." She heaved again. "You scared me."

Anne grimaced. "You're sick."

Mary pressed her forehead against the cold rail and unfastened the heavy brace of pistols and the cutlass at her side. They clinked against the cedar boards. She was sick. Every other hour she was sick. Part of her wanted to tear her hair out and throw herself over the side of the sloop to end the agony. The other part knew that this nausea meant that her baby was real. Somehow, in some awful way, this feeling—the illness—brought her comfort. It meant she wasn't dreaming.

She didn't expect Anne to understand. Then again, maybe she didn't have to explain.

"I'm sorry," Anne said. "It isn't easy."

"No." But what had ever been?

"Were you scared?"

Mary rubbed her throbbing forehead. "Yes."

"But you led them."

"I'm no stranger to fear."

Anne held out a waterskin. The compassionate gesture stirred something gentle inside Mary. She accepted and drank the water in slow, tentative sips. "And you," Mary said, returning it, "are angry."

Anne's cheeks reddened as if on command, making her freckles more visible. Did Anne have no experience hiding her emotions? What must that have been like?

"I felt like a mouse being stuffed below deck," Anne said, "wondering who would come back dead or alive. But the Articles say a captain's orders during a raid are beyond challenge."

"True. But it's not just that. Rackham did what he thought was best for you and the mission. You're angry. You're always angry."

Anne's eyes narrowed. "No, I'm not."

"Yes, you are," Mary pushed. "And you fear your anger."

The conversation died when the sound of boots pounded against the main deck, a group gathering around the raised platform of the helm. Meeting adjourned, apparently. All contents tallied and accounted for.

Mary glanced up. Rackham approached, his attention rapt on Anne and her flattering indigo dress. That crinkle in his forehead, the intensity of gaze—so eager to make things right. Anne seemed less impressed. She didn't return his look.

"Captain Rackham," Mary said, squaring her shoulders. She hoped she appeared stronger than she felt. "As you well know, a small crew requires everyone aboard to be equipped for a raid. According to the Articles, all of us must be armed and ready to strike at any given moment."

"That code is for pirates."

"Which Anne is." They all were.

His mouth twisted. Mary played to his pride. "I commend your quick thinking, protecting our liabilities today. But what of the next time?"

Anne cursed and balled her fists. "I can fight."

"No, you can't," Mary and Rackham said at the same time. And Mary knew that Anne knew they were right.

Rackham sighed and adjusted his tricorn. His eyes pled with Anne. "I can't lose you, Bon. Your safety is everything to me."

If this was how Rackham behaved now, Mary had no trouble picturing how he would act when he found out about his child.

Little wonder he'd forced Anne ashore against her wishes during the first pregnancy. How much longer could Anne hide this one? She had to be three months along by now. Mary wondered how long Anne, and herself for that matter, could hide their conditions under layers and loose-fitting clothes. Anne was small, but surely Rackham would soon notice changes in the woman he shared a bed with.

"And who'll keep me safe if someone comes aboard while you're off pillaging? If a ball goes through your chest?"

At the image of a shot tearing through flesh, Mary winced.

"Bon . . . I'm sorry. I only meant—"

His fussing threatened to make the bile rise again. Coddling and favoritism were luxuries Björn and all of her superiors had never afforded her—stances that would've gotten her slaughtered.

"Rackham," Mary interrupted. "Anne is capable of dying like the rest of us mere mortals. If you love her, you'll prepare her for the worst, should the worst ever come. Will you be seeing to the rest of Anne's training, or shall I?"

After a dramatic sigh and slight hesitation, he gave a solemn nod. "I will."

CHAPTER 48

Mary lay on her back and looked up at the first pinpricks emerging in the greenish tinge of dusk. The off-watch crew lounged on the quarterdeck after devouring a feast of fresh pork—courtesy of a sloop they'd boarded the day prior. She counted her blessings that she'd kept the food down. Her queasiness had dimmed over the past week. While she worried what that might mean, no bleeding came. Not yet. Anne told her to put it out of mind, that this was common and not a terrible omen.

Mary breathed in. Fall now reigned, its constellations moving like a chariot across the sky. Last night, she'd spotted the ram, Aries. Also the *W* of Cassiopeia. Her heart squeezed. She smiled to remember pointing out the latter constellation for Björn, the way he beamed and said that this shape was also a letter. How she burst with a flurry of explanations, drawing his attention to her favorite clusters of stars from her navigational training, pointing them out one by one. Björn's undiluted excitement as she made connections between past and present.

What would he make of this *present?* Mary thought, listening to the sound of blades clinking near the bow.

Her attention drifted to the commotion. For three weeks, Rackham had held true to his word. Mary watched as he trained Anne in the mornings and early evenings, like now. In those three weeks, the crew had intercepted seven other small vessels—mostly fishing boats near Harbour Island. The *Revenge*'s hold swelled with more odds and ends. On the last raid, they'd taken a pile of fraying fishing nets and the coats off the backs of the sailors—despicable. But provisions that mattered? Food? Valuables that would fetch a large and swift profit at the nearest dock? Those were in short supply. They still didn't have a single gold coin or handful of silver aboard. Yesterday, the crew voted to begin rationing and head southeast with due haste for the French side of Hispaniola. The pork feast had kicked off the gradual fast. Howell, reduced to one glass of ale per day, snarled at everyone. He vocalized what everyone began to feel. Morale soured, even as Rackham and Corner stuck to their mission.

The clang of cutlasses continued. Mary heard Anne curse.

"Well done, Bon," Rackham said. "Again."

Mary stood and approached the scene, where Thomas and Corner also observed the training as the night watch kept an eye on the lines. Sweat drenched Anne's hair and the red kerchief around her neck. She swung the cutlass, her face aglow with the reflected remnants of the sunset. Rackham blocked, making her curse like the Devil.

"Our weapons are turning into decorations, no matter how many times I visit the grindstone to quell my boredom," Thomas said. "We'd all do well to practice."

And bathe, Mary thought, overwhelmed by their sour clothes. But yes, practice was also in order.

"A fine idea, Brown," Corner said, drawing his rapier. "Shall we?"

Thomas hesitated, and Mary held back a chuckle. Corner, gentle though he may be, was not a giant anyone wanted to slay. Not that anyone could.

She nodded at Thomas. A worthy foe, a worthy exercise.

With the two of them joining the throng, Mary shifted her attention to Anne. Her bared teeth. The way she heaved from exhaustion. Her form.

What on God's green earth was she doing with her footing?

"Rackham, may I?" Mary said, cutting in.

Anne wiped sweat from her brow and Rackham glared. It was a look he often wore after Mary offered a suggestion or when she and Anne engaged in conversation.

Fool. His efforts would be better spent on devising a better strategy to fill the hold. "She doesn't have the advantage of your upper body strength," Mary said before directing her words at Anne. "You need to use your legs."

Anne panted so hard that Mary feared she would collapse. But to her credit, she didn't protest. "Show me."

Rackham, backlit by the fading sunset, let out a noise of annoyance and stepped aside.

Mary drew her cutlass. "Study my feet."

Anne watched as Mary stepped right over left, left over right. Then she made Anne do the same. "When you move to strike, surge using your legs. Lead with that power."

Anne laughed, squatting lower. "I look ridiculous."

"Battle is ridiculous."

They circled, a blur of steel. Anne had improved immensely over the past month—Mary had to at least give credit to Rackham for that.

"You have to learn to channel your anger," Mary whispered. "Direct it at an opponent, a goal. Move your anger from your head into your bones."

Anne swung and missed. "You're distracting me on purpose."

"It's like fear. You have to move *through* it."

"She's tired," Rackham interrupted. "Let's be done. It's growing dark."

Without thinking, Mary whipped her blade around, facing him. Out of instinct, he raised his own cutlass and blocked. The metal sang.

The crew walloped with delight. Thomas and Corner lowered their weapons to watch.

"This I have to see," Earl said with a trill.

"Let's have it, Captain! Give us a proper demonstration," said Corner.

Rackham rolled his eyes, then lunged. Mary dodged, then cut left. Her balance felt different after carrying this child for three months, but she still had sturdy footing. Rackham parried. She exhaled, feeling her opponent escalate as she settled into that deep place within herself.

He didn't stand a chance.

He attacked from overhead, and she absorbed the force of his blow with a parry. He tried again, and she threw her arm outward, blocking the diagonal cut. She thrust left; her feet moved the way they had a thousand times before.

Rackham bellowed. He swung with all his might, and she saw her opening. She thrust up using her legs as a springboard, whipped her wrist, and sent the cutlass flying from his hand.

The crowd behind him cheered, but his eyes narrowed to daggers.

"Come, Jack," Anne said, looping her arm through his—all adoration. Mary saw it for what it was: appeasing his wounded pride, staving off a foul mood. "Let's have a song. Earl? Your fiddle?"

Mary lowered her blade and tucked it into her belt alongside her pistol. She really did prefer the pistol, particularly this new one—a breech-loading flintlock with lavish silver markings and an anguished face stamping the butt cap.

Thomas lingered behind the others. "What were you thinking?" he shot.

She frowned. "What do you mean?"

He inched closer to her, closer than he'd been in weeks. He'd even moved his hammock to the other end of the sleeping berth and called it a precaution. "You challenged the captain."

Mary raised a brow. "Maybe someone should. We've been preying on poor fishermen instead of ships worth our time for weeks.

Time I don't have." She felt her pulse rise and willed herself to calm, to steady.

Thomas stepped in front of her. "We have to stay patient. We can't risk another blow to our reputation."

Our reputation? She studied him—so stiff, so severe, so different now that he'd regained his status among his peers. How the tides had turned. Now, she was a liability. Their child, an inconvenience.

Mary curled her toes in her boots and swallowed the bitter realization. A chasm of loneliness gaped open in the pit of her chest.

"You have to exercise more caution," Thomas said.

Mary said nothing, hearing the fear behind his words. Caution. Care. Vigilance. She had a lifetime of training in these, avoiding risk at all cost—not weighing the counter costs of hiding.

And a child was not a thing she could hide much longer.

She brushed the back of Thomas's hand with hers for a moment, remembering the warm feel of him, then walked away to join the others.

CHAPTER 49

By dinner the next evening, Rackham had regained his composure and confidence with the help of Anne's fawning. Mary surveyed him with disinterest as he downed four cups of punch. The entire crew bypassed the alcohol rations, Mary noted, and no one dared or desired to protest.

She took a spoonful of mackerel stew and swallowed. Salty. Oily. The beans a bit crunchy and undercooked. She felt a bone with her tongue and picked it out. Dunking hardtack in the hot broth, Mary felt relieved she managed to keep meals down now.

Corner and Rackham were arm wrestling on the table in the brisk night. Howell, with a bottle in each hand, crowed like a rooster again—good as new.

As Mary raised her spoon, she froze.

What was that?

Her hand flew to her stomach. The unpleasant fluttering in her gut.

Oh no, she thought, dropping her spoon with a clatter.

I can't lose you.

Not you, too.

Anne caught Mary's attention. Her eyes mirrored the terror in Mary's face.

No.

Mary rose so fast she knocked aside her bowl. She darted away, feeling her throat constrict. She needed to get away. Privacy. She needed . . . What did she need? What was going on?

She paused at the hatch. The lower deck? Too exposed. She hurtled past the single mast and continued toward the stern, where the lantern light was low and she wouldn't be disturbed.

Then it came again. That strange onset of pressure, altogether new.

Crouching in the dark, Mary checked her undergarments. No blood that she could see. She felt her chest seize—from relief or terror, she couldn't assess. She inhaled, exhaled, then pulled her trousers up and sat with her back against the rail. She closed her eyes and prayed with all her feeble faith.

"What's wrong?"

Mary turned, and the heat behind her eyes morphed into tears. "What did it feel like to lose the baby?" she asked Anne.

Anne hurried forward and unclamped Mary's hands from her stomach. "Like a tidal wave of unbearable exhaustion. Illness— like the onset of ship's fever. Then cramps pummeling my lower back. Like the pains of monthly bleeding, but ten times worse."

Mary sucked in a breath. This didn't feel like that, she told herself.

"Hurry," Anne said, shouldering Mary up. "You could be seen here." She glanced around, then led Mary to the captain's quarters, shutting the door quietly behind them.

"What do you feel?" Anne said, rummaging for clean cloths and medications in the cabinet.

"I . . ." Mary began, shaking.

"Are you losing blood?"

"I don't think so. Not yet."

Anne's lines of worry eased and she stopped rifling through the trunks. "Take the bed."

Mary pulled a face. "I'm not taking the bed you share with Rackham."

"Take it! You order me around all the time. Do as I say for once."

Mary sat on the mattress, her whole body stiff. She refused to lie down.

"What happened?" Anne demanded, taking her hand.

Mary inhaled, long and steady. *What happened?*

"I felt something shift," she said at last. "An uneasy pressure in my abdomen."

"Like you have to pass wind?"

Mary reddened. "Not quite . . ."

"Like a fish flopped?"

Mary lifted her chin. "Actually . . ."

"A kind of quickening?"

"Yes," Mary said, whirling to search Anne's face—all traces of anxiety dispelled. "That. I felt that."

Anne beamed. "You're not losing the baby. Holy God above, and to think you felt it before me, when I'm a good month ahead of you." Anne gestured toward Mary's stomach. "May I?"

Mary hesitated, then drew up her linen shirt. Anne pressed a cold hand to the slight swell of Mary's stomach.

The door flung open, and in stormed Rackham.

Anne tore away as Rackham glared from her, to Mary, then back to Anne. "This is where you go behind my back?" he roared, stalking forward and knocking into the map table. He snatched Anne away, holding her by the arms. "Sneaking into my quarters to pleasure another man!"

Mary pulled down her shirt and stood. "Rackham."

He spun on her and drew his pistol. She sighed and did the same.

"Enough!" Anne said, throwing her arms between them. "Jack, *listen*. I can explain."

He reeked of alcohol, and the fury in his glazed eyes shone with something dangerous. "How could you?" he groveled, searching Anne's face. He ran a finger along her jaw, then gripped her shoulder. "After everything—"

"I'm with child," Mary shouted, lowering her pistol.

Anne and Rackham spun on her. It took him a few seconds to process this information before raking his eyes over her body. His hold on Anne's shoulder loosened.

Mary swallowed. *Definitely drawing attention to yourself.* This was not how she meant to leave the crew. Penniless.

"It's true," Anne said, reaching for Rackham. "I've been tending to her. She's been a friend to me, and I to her."

"Read is a . . . woman?" he said, mouth twisted, though the hardness of his features had softened. He rubbed his head, then laughed.

Anne and Mary smiled nervously.

"A woman," he repeated, his laugh ringing louder. "Anne, do you have any idea how mad you've made me? A common brute crazed with jealousy? And now you're telling me Read is a woman?"

Mary bit the inside of her cheek.

He swayed, then hugged Anne before kissing her with a world of relief. "You had me worried sick," he slurred.

"There is one more thing," Anne said, pushing him back and staring up into his face.

Mary closed her eyes. Anne sure had a curious sense of timing.

"I'm with child, too," she said.

CHAPTER 50

Spanish Town, Jamaica
March 1721

"How is she this morning?" Anne demanded when Johnson returned.

The cell door clicked behind him. He hesitated before responding. "Fighting."

Anne slumped on the cot and buried her head in her hands as the captain took his usual perch on the stool. The bulge of her stomach felt like a cannonball. It strained against Jack's shirt. Anne didn't have time. Sweet Jesus, they had no more time. The doctors, Johnson assured her, were doing everything they could.

But then what?

"My paper? The ink you promised?"

"I have it with me."

Anne glanced up. "Today?"

"Yes," he said, patting a second leather bag at his side. "A deal is a deal. A man of my word, remember?"

She could already feel her hands around the quill. The words burning inside her. The names, their locations. She fanned the flames of hope.

She'd have to wait for him to leave.

"Mary told me a rather peculiar story," Johnson said, clearing his throat. "It is quite delicate. I wondered if you might clarify what she meant—fevered as she is, not in her right mind."

Anne raised a brow. She reminded herself that she still needed Johnson.

There was one last favor she had not asked of him yet.

"Is it true," he said, his cheeks pink as a sunburn, "that you were rather intimate with your female comrade? That at one point, you touched her bare skin?"

She scoffed. "You can't be serious?" Of everything—out of all that they'd been through—*that* was what the blithering captain wanted to talk about?

"Did you love Mary Read?"

Why the bloody hell was he talking in past tense? "Of course I love Mary Read!" Anyone who ever knew Mary, truly knew her, loved her. "She is the closest companion I've ever had."

Steadier than Mam. More temperate than Da.

Kinder and wiser than Ellen—with the same dark, beautiful lashes.

Smarter than Jack. Stronger, too.

More interesting, more complicated, and braver than the hundreds of other sailors and pirates she had been acquainted with. Selfless. Thoughtful. Curious. The person she wanted at her side, whether with a cutlass raised against an attacker or with a gentle hand of reassurance.

Mary had saved her life in more ways than one. Anne wouldn't let her die in a cell. Not her, and not her child either. They'd come too far.

"But you do love her," Johnson repeated. "For the record."

"For the record, yes." In a thousand ways he, and maybe no man, could ever understand.

Johnson scratched down some notes, then paused. "Charles Vane was taken to the gallows. That's what detained me this week. I had to record his history."

Good. Unsurprising. Vane had pillaged long enough, murdered enough captives and brother sailors alike. If they all had to end up here, a demon and a coward like Vane at least deserved it.

Whatever her fate, she would not die like a coward.

"Did you know that Bonny sailed with him, after you captured the *William?*"

Anne balled her fists, the area around her nails raw and angry from chewing. She hadn't heard word of Bonny since fleeing Nassau.

"Vane, who knew Rackham better than most, jumped at this brief stint as a privateer before turning pirate again. Rumor has it that Bonny was hired to join him as a mercenary to hunt you. Governor Rogers has not confirmed this information with me—whether or not he ever granted Bonny or Vane an official letter of marque. No matter the details, Bonny seems to have disappeared. I thought, given what you shared with me, that you ought to know. They are still searching for Bonny—though the remains of the ship . . ."

It was him, Anne realized at once, staring at the stone wall. *It was he who put Governor Rogers up to it all.*

CHAPTER 51

Caribbean Sea
September 1720

"Read it aloud, Anne," Jack said, urging her on.

Anne stared at the paper in her hand, then out at the crew—sweaty and exhausted after a week of pillaging. They'd taken a merchant ship called the *Neptune*, led by Captain Spenlow. No gold or silver, but they'd snatched some modest goods and fifty rolls of tobacco—their biggest haul yet. They'd found the newspaper buried in a trunk a week after they'd hauled it aboard. Anne, Mary, and only a handful of others could read it.

But now, the parchment billowing in the east-west breeze as they made for the risky path north of Jamaica, Anne wished someone else—anyone else—could deliver this news.

"Go on," Howell shouted. "Get it over with!"

Mary—which everyone had started calling her once the shock wore off—gave Anne an encouraging nod. God Almighty. What a scene *that* reveal had been. No one spoke for a full minute after Mary shared her truth with the crew. Mary never disclosed that Thomas was the father. All wide eyes were fixed on Mary or the deck, but Anne watched Thomas. The vein in his neck ticked.

If Anne had stood nearer, she might have stomped on his foot to urge him to make himself known rather than letting Mary endure this alone.

"Well then," Corner had said, guiding the mood to humor. "A woman who bested Captain Rackham with a blade? I say we keep her."

"We're short enough hands," said Featherstone.

"But consider our luck—"

Earl cut Howell off from whatever the drunkard was going to say. "There's no one else I'd rather sail with," he said with a smile of admiration.

Jack led the crew in a vote to keep Mary on. She wore the occasional dress now, which Anne was more than willing to lend her. Mary looked radiant as she worked the lines with a newfound lightness, her identity no longer a hindrance to her mannerisms or choice of clothing.

Anne blinked, staring down at the damning ink in her hands. This, too, would be a scene—one less easy to overcome.

At last, she read the legal proclamation: "By his Excellency Woodes Rogers, Governor of New Providence. Whereas: John Rackham, George Featherstone, John Howell, etc. and two women, by name, Anne Bonny and Mary Read, did on the 22nd of August last combine together to enter on board, take, steal and run away with a certain sloop called the *William*, mounted with four great guns and two swivel ones, also ammunition, sails, rigging, anchor, cables, and a canoe, owned by and belonging to Captain John Ham, and with the said sloop did proceed to commit robbery and piracy. Wherefore these are to publish and make known to all persons whatsoever, that the said John Rackham and his said company are hereby proclaimed Pirates and Enemies to the Crown of Great Britain, and are to be so treated and deemed by all his majesty's subjects. Given at Nassau, this 5th of September, 1720."

Silence. The *Revenge* rose, then fell, before anyone dared to speak.

"I suppose we should have expected something like this," Corner muttered.

"It's signed by the governor," Anne confirmed, handing Jack the broadsheet. He passed it around for all to scrutinize.

"What does this mean?" Earl said.

"It means we're doomed," Thomas said, kicking an empty cask they'd been using to play backgammon. "The governor hunts us down, some of us listed out! I've never heard of such a thing."

Mary took the paper from Corner. "It lists *my* real name." Her dark hair fell in front of her face as she read. "How did the governor know I was a woman?"

Anne stood beside her and looked at her own name blazing in plain sight. "You always said people in Nassau talk."

Mary rubbed her temple. "So few people knew. I thought they were friends."

"Friends can be bought," Howell said, taking a swig of his flask, the sun reflecting off the metal.

Anne glanced at Jack, who removed his tricorn and tore a hand through his sun-bleached brown hair. What were they to do? What did it mean? Even Jack, with an illustrious history in this pirating business, had never had a target of this size on his back.

"Jack?" she asked, drawing near. The glint of fear she saw in his pupils shifted to something brazen, almost joyful.

"This is just what we want—their attention. People are watching, listening. We have to strike hard," he said. "Show them they can't scare us."

"Captain," said Fenwick.

Jack ignored him. "This is the *Revenge*! We can't quit, and we can't show our faces ashore. Not yet. We must—"

"Captain," Fenwick said, this time with more force. "There's a canoe off the port side." He tossed the spyglass to Jack, who peered through it.

"So there is," he said. "Corner, ready the crew to board."

"That's our next prize? A common canoe?" Mary said. She lev-

eled a look at Thomas. Anne imagined that Mary must be thinking of Thomas's abandoned fishing boat—his sole possession.
Sometimes Anne thought she could still smell the stink of those
nets.

Thomas did not catch Mary's eye. According to Mary, he'd kept
his distance since her reveal. Mary said it was complicated and
that it was up to Thomas to decide when to come forward to the
others. He "had a reputation to mind." That reasoning left a sour
taste on Anne's tongue. Why would Thomas remain silent? Even
his lovely whistling had stopped. Why wouldn't he be proud to be
with a woman like Mary? Jack, in contrast, made his affection for
Anne clear. After a week of late-night battles and drunken promises, she'd convinced him to let her remain aboard. To not dump
her with "relatives" in Cuba.

She took her victories where she could.

"We'll pass on nothing," Jack said as Corner gave directions to
the others. He turned to Mary. "Isn't that what you've been telling
me all along? Go for all the prizes?"

Anne crossed her arms. What kind of people were they rob-
bing?

Her stomach squirmed, seeing how Jack and Mary looked at
each other with distrust. Mary took the spyglass and looked for
herself. Her mouth hung open.

"Two men. But also a woman." Mary turned, eyes blazing.

"We have two of those, too," Jack said. "What's your point?"

"We can't board! Did you see the parasol? It's a grand lady, out
for—well, I don't know what—but she'll carry little of value. She'll
be nothing but trouble."

"Bring the boarding pikes," Corner said.

"Captain's orders," Featherstone growled. "We just took on
Spenlow's double-masted schooner last week without a single shot
fired. Show some respect."

Mary glanced over her shoulder, as if to say, *Are you seeing this?*
Anne shrugged. Perhaps Mary *had* slid down a few rungs in some

crew members' regard, as her friend kept insisting. They gripped their weapons and followed, tugging at the cords holding their own rowboat.

"He's a fool," Mary whispered as they lowered the vessel into the water. "This overconfidence could be the end of us."

Anne stared at the swells and touched the pistol at her side. Mary didn't trust Jack—she made that known. But Mary also didn't know him the way Anne did.

Staring at the back of Jack's tricorn while he shouted directives at the crew as they loaded into the ship's rowboat, she wondered at all the ways in which she knew him. And all the ways she maybe didn't.

"Varmints! Thieves!" the woman screeched as they brought her onto the *Revenge*. She flung herself to the left, then the right, until Corner set her in a chair taken from the captain's quarters.

"I'm sorry, miss," Corner said, removing his cap. "We mean you no harm."

"Murderers! Rovers!" she continued, clutching her bonnet to her tight ringlets as everyone faced her on the main deck.

Jack pushed his quartermaster aside. "What other valuables do you have? Where do you keep your gems? Hand them over, and we'll be on our way."

"Let me go!" the woman sobbed. "Return me to my companions. I have nothing. Nothing for you scoundrels. And I'll not unhand my virtue." At this, she began to wail.

Earl covered his ears and Thomas flushed with shame.

"I think she's going to faint," Howell said.

Anne stood shoulder to shoulder with Mary, taking in the horrible display. Jack turned around, scanning the provisions the crew had brought aboard. His golden-brown eyes landed on her and Mary, and he bade them to come closer.

Anne went to move, but Mary held out her arm. "Not sure that's a good idea, Captain," Mary said, keeping her voice low and holding her ground.

"Try," Corner said, bidding them to come to the front of the throng. "For all our sakes."

Inching forward, they planted themselves in front of the distressed woman.

"What's your name?" Anne asked.

Hearing a female voice, the captive wiped away her tears. Her green eyes grew to the size of moons as she took in Anne, then Mary beside her. "You? Why, you're women!"

Anne nodded and Mary huffed.

"My name is Dorothy. These pirates, they snatched you, too? We have to return to shore. They—"

"I'm afraid we can't do that, Dorothy."

Dorothy's black curls jostled, waiting for them to say more. When no explanations came, the woman blanched. "You're . . . with these mongrels?"

Mary snapped her attention to Jack. "Captain, a word?" She turned on her heel and stepped aside. Jack joined her, his arms crossed and jaw set. Anne couldn't make out their conversation, but their tone suggested that it was an argument.

Anne bit her cheek and returned to Dorothy. "No one here will violate you," she said, straining to hit a note of comfort. "We aren't those kind of pirates. But you must turn over all else of value you have."

Tears streamed down the woman's face and her lip curled with revulsion. Anne paused to consider Dorothy, her silk dress and slippers, a well-bred woman like the one Anne herself had been brought up to be. That was what Mam wanted—for herself and also for her daughter. Was this not the dream Anne had cast away?

The boom knocked against the sail, and Anne held that moment in her mind: the terrified woman in front of her—the kind of woman Anne should have been—staring in horror at the woman Anne had become.

But she wouldn't trade places. Not for a second.

"We found a few valuables and provisions among her effects," Thomas said, nudging his toe at the lace parasol. "A necklace.

Some fishing gear and tackle." He tapped his fingers against his leg. "Can we let her go and be done with this?"

Jack had his back to them and took a moment to respond. "Aye," he said.

"Her dress?" Howell asked. "Fine silk, I'd wager."

Dorothy screamed, and Anne shot daggers at Howell. "She keeps the damn dress."

Everyone agreed. After a dramatic departure, Corner saw Dorothy to her canoe as the others picked up anchor to make due haste. Anne watched as Dorothy and her two male companions paddled like the Devil toward the beach of Ocho Rios.

She couldn't shake Dorothy's disgust.

Mary appeared at Anne's side, her countenance shadowed.

"What did you tell Jack?"

"That we needed to kill her."

Her blood chilled. Anne spun with disbelief, her mouth agape. "Kill her? An innocent, unarmed woman?"

Mary paled, but she did not take back her words. "Rackham put us in an impossible position. He's taking terrible risks, and we're too close to Jamaica for mistakes." She closed her eyes. "When was the last time he held a vote about our strategy? He was careless with capturing the *Neptune* and bringing Captain Spenlow aboard as a captive for days. And why? Because Rackham had to play with his food? So a handful of sailors could defect and join us? Because Rackham couldn't decide if he wanted Spenlow's schooner to form a flotilla, only to set Spenlow and the *Neptune* loose? Spenlow saw *us*, Anne, and so did Dorothy." She leaned forward on her elbows as the canoe grew to a speck on the horizon. "This high-and-mighty damsel in distress with a tale of woe knows where we are, what we are—and now, who we are. We're the only ship in the Caribbean with two pirate women aboard."

CHAPTER 52

Mary lay awake as her hammock swayed with the rhythmic rocking of the ship. Her hands rested on the small swell of her stomach as she inhaled the damp smell of cedar and listened to the sound of the ballast. Mary waited all day for this time of night—the chance to be alone with her better thoughts, and her baby, without prying eyes on her or weapons tied to her hip.

She wiggled her toes with joy—a joy that was *hers*, a feeling that had returned after years of winter. How sweet it tasted, this spring of unexpected happiness. She tapped her fingers to her belly, wondering if the baby could feel her playing, hear her tap out a tune as if on a grand pianoforte—all those seafaring songs Ma used to sing at the docks on frigid mornings while selling bread, her breath visible in the crisp dawn.

What Mary wouldn't do, what she wouldn't give, to raise this wondrous gift in a safe place of their own—a home filled with love. Mary still felt that quickening inside her, that subtle flop. She recalled the night when the captain walked in on her and Anne.

Rackham. Her fingers stilled, then flexed. She couldn't stand by and let him drive the crew toward disaster. She wouldn't let him ruin her chances for a better life.

Howell and Fenwick took turns snoring somewhere down the berth, and Anne tossed and turned in the hammock to her left.

It was Anne's first time not sleeping in the captain's quarters. She'd entered the sleeping berth long after the others, her eyes rimmed and puffy. She'd slipped into a hammock without a word to anyone, avoiding Mary's gaze, then blew out the candle.

Anne rustled, then exhaled with exasperation.

Mary looked over the rim of her own hammock. "Trouble sleeping?" she whispered in the dark.

The rustling stopped, but Anne didn't answer. Mary closed her eyes, unfazed. She understood the need for privacy. If Anne wasn't ready to talk about whatever argument she'd had with Rackham, Mary would be the last to force her.

"It's that woman, Dorothy, that we interrogated today. I can't stop thinking about her."

"Ah," Mary said. Anne had said very little to Mary since Rackham had foolishly seized the lady. The liability hung in the air, and Mary had made her concerns known to all—much to Rackham's displeasure. But Mary did not apologize for recommending that they kill the woman, however vile the thought. Anne must have known that Mary had killed before as a soldier. But perhaps the full truth had not settled in until now.

Snuffing out a beating, human heart. It was the very thing Mary vowed she would never do again after she and Björn broke away to start a new life.

Male. Female. Unarmed victims deserved better. But she did not, Mary admitted, give preference to the life of a woman over a man. All life was precious and fleeting. Why did a fine dress and a delicate disposition privilege Dorothy's life over others? She failed to understand.

"What does it mean to be a woman?" Mary asked.

Anne snorted. Mary worried it might wake up the others, but Howell went on snoring.

"I'm serious," Mary said, hands resting on her stomach again. "I've spent more days pretending to be a man than not, and yet,

I was born a woman. And when others find that out, it changes everything. But nothing about who I actually am has changed."

"Bloody hell. Not like you to be the talkative one."

Mary smiled, and the words kept tumbling out. "Is being a woman a behavior? The ability to bear children?" Mary shook her head. "That's not right. Because even when I couldn't, I was still a woman—still unfit for the path I've trod according to a great many others." People like Björn's father, who needed no other evidence to cut her out after Björn passed.

Anne said nothing for a moment. "No, surely being a woman means you have a natural ability to scour chamber pots or serve extra shifts cooking in the galley."

They laughed under their breaths, a bitter yet relieving feeling that knocked something loose in Mary's chest. Since her reveal, she *had* been relegated to more menial tasks, *had* been less esteemed by some of her male peers—and this after proving herself in a dozen raids. Sure, half of the crew—Corner, Featherstone, and other men worth their salt—still respected her hard-earned skills, never forgetting that she'd recently bested their own captain. But the other shipmates? She caught them staring at times, something unnerving in their gaze, as if they found her strange. Unnatural. A monster they were pleased to have on their side, but a monster all the same.

How wondrous and strange and beautiful, to have someone to talk with about this dimension for which she'd never had words. It was as easy as breathing. Was this what she'd missed all those years without female companionship?

"Perhaps being a woman is a kind of stance or expected conduct in the world," Anne said. "I haven't told a soul, but"—her voice lowered—"the other week, I walked in on Earl in the hold. He'd draped himself in a bolt of red linen, donning it like a ball gown."

Earl? Mary puzzled over this information. At least someone seemed to have found a use for the fabric they'd stolen. Did this new knowledge fundamentally change how she saw or esteemed

Earl as a crewmate—as a talented scout and a hardworking sailor? No. Should it? "What has it meant for you?" Mary asked. "This business of being a woman?"

Anne sighed. "Being a burden—not a son. I told you of my own disguises as a child, my parents' notion to pass me off as an heir." She paused. "To be a woman is to be a liability. Dependent. Vulnerable. Trapped. Blamed. Hunted." Then she sighed. "No, that's not right—not the better part, anyway. But to give it language somehow feels . . . small. Limiting. And whoever I am—whatever it means that I was born a female and go about the world as such— I resist being caged, confined and cornered, fixed into a time and place, stuck in a certain way or position. Determined. I'm as much in flux as the shifting tides, as a ship aching to make way."

"If this is fundamentally female, as you are suggesting," Mary said, burning with a truth she recognized—whether or not it was specific to women and not the whole of humankind, "then why are women not welcomed aboard ships? If men call the ocean female, and refer to their beloved sloops and pinks and brigs and even their tiny fishing boats as female, why don't women make up the majority of the crews?"

"My mam used to tell me old stories. Didn't yours? Tales of sirens. The old pagan legends?"

"No," Mary said, the word like a vise around her heart. Ma only had her secrets and her songs.

"The Greeks saw the sea as female. The Cretans worshiped a gorgeous goddess of fertility who also granted protection to sailors."

Mary didn't know who the Cretans were, but she'd spent many nights at sea. She had poured out thousands of prayers while lying next to Björn, and they had done nothing for her fertility.

"Then there were the sirens, who ate up the hearts of poor, defenseless sailors. Mermaids, as you're no doubt familiar with— seducing men and luring them to their demise by using their appetites and fantasies against them."

Mary knitted her brow. "You're suggesting that it isn't women's competency that prevents them from joining crews, but rather men's fear of them?"

"Yes. Some rubbish like that. It threatens a man's strength. His way of being in the world. The natural order of things."

At this, Mary sat upright. It came to her in a flood of revelation. The way forward. A way to change their fortunes. "I have an idea," she said, fighting the urge to shout it to the entire crew.

CHAPTER 53

"You're sure about this?" Anne asked. Her nerves quivered. She couldn't bear to see Jack again after their harsh words the night before. But this was more important.

"If what you say is true, then yes," Mary said.

"You'll say it was all your idea?"

"As you insist. Though I still think you should take some credit."

Mary knocked on the door to the captain's quarters. It swung open, and inside sat Jack, Corner, and Featherstone hunched over the map table.

Anne caught Jack's eyes. Those dark circles. The glaze from drink. He appeared to have slept about as much as she had.

I'm sorry, that look said.

I am, too, said hers, though her instincts wavered. Had she done something so wrong in voicing her concerns? In being angry about taking Dorothy aboard?

In not wanting to lie with him, after all of that?

But that look of remorse undid her, stitch by stitch. She yearned to touch him. To burn in his heat and make everything all right. To get him alone. To put the hurt behind them and bury it. To forget about the present crisis and predicaments.

"I have a proposition, a way to utilize the full strength of our small crew to take on larger prizes," Mary said.

Jack tore his attention from Anne to Mary, resting his chin on his fist with obvious annoyance. Featherstone tapped the table.

"What do you have in mind?" Corner said with his usual cheer, sitting taller.

"This week, we exposed our position and the uniqueness of our crew."

"Aye," Jack said. "As you made everyone aware of yesterday."

Mary squared her shoulders. "But what if, rather than ignoring this liability, we used it as a weapon?"

This caught their curiosity. The men listened as Mary explained more or less the plan Anne had described the evening before. The nonsense about sirens and mermaids and murder ladies.

"The Cretions?" Jack probed.

"Cretans," Anne corrected. "But where these beliefs come from doesn't matter. Whatever their origins, we can all agree that men fear women aboard ships." She studied the bookcase, the instruments and hourglass on the shelf. The bottles littering the floor. "Half of you protested my joining Rackham when I first came aboard the *Ranger*. Did you not? Superstitions. Strong beliefs. A vocal resistance that my being there 'wasn't right' and 'wasn't natural.'"

Jack took her hand. "It doesn't matter what they thought."

Anne squeezed Jack's fingers. "I know. And I proved myself. But there is a reason why we don't meet other crews with women beyond the occasional cook or caretaker."

"What about a siege led by a pair of defiant women?" Mary beamed, then turned back to the ship's leadership. "What would be scarier to opponents than storming their decks like that?"

Corner laughed, then cleared his throat and scratched his shaved head when he saw this was not a joke.

"For our next prize that is actually worthy of capture, I propose you send the two of us to the front. We'll wear trousers and let our shirts hang open, our breasts bare and visible. We'll scream and holler like the rowdiest of rogues, but we'll wear our hair down like gentle maidens. We'll be warriors, and we'll be women, a sight of sirens, mermaids, and corrupted female power alike, and while they're gaping in shock and horror, shaking in their boots and fearing for their souls, we'll take the ship before anyone has a chance to raise a blade against us."

Anne quite liked the plan. Could Jack listen long enough to agree?

"I've never heard of such a strategy," Corner said, searching the others. "But it could work. What do you think, Captain?"

Anne watched as the words sank into Jack's mind, his hand combing through his hair.

"Why not?" he said, glancing up at Anne. His eyes crinkled. "We'll try it. My only modification is insisting that the full crew flank the women for protection. I won't put the mother of my child in any real harm's way." He opened up a fresh bottle of ale. "Now, if you'll excuse us," he said, resting his golden gaze on Anne's lips as he took a swig. "Anne and I have some private matters to discuss."

Within the day, while traveling west alongside Point Fortaleza and scaling the coast of Dry Harbour Bay, Anne heard the words she'd been anticipating in the marrow of her bones.

"Merchant ship straight ahead!" Fenwick called out, running as fast as his bowlegs could carry him to hand Jack the spyglass.

"Make chase," Jack ordered, and the whole crew sprang into action.

Anne took the spyglass to study their victim. The white letters on the side spelled out *Mary and Sarah*. A large sloop like theirs. One mast, with a jib and mainsail, and fractional rigged. It moved slowly. Weighed down with something of value, she bloody well hoped.

This better be worth it.

"To your positions!" Corner shouted, rallying the sailors to grab the oars as the shipmaster saw to the lines. "Let's move, let's move." The *Revenge* sprang forward with a lurch, nearly knocking Anne to her knees. The sails caught the wind and the liquid blue flew beneath them as the oars carried the sloop forward, hurtling toward their target.

The Jolly Roger flew above, snapping like teeth.

Anne swallowed, turning to Mary for reassurance. Mary didn't notice. Instead, she checked her cutlass, appraising it from point to hilt before turning her attention to the three Queen Anne pistols she'd strapped to her waist.

Anne shifted under the weight of her own pistols, strapped in a harness at her side. At four months, she was beginning to show, even under her borrowed canvas breeches. Her cutlass hung beside her leg, and she'd fastened her dagger to her thigh.

"Boarding pikes out!" Corner called to the crew with a trill—no doubt curious to see what would happen next.

Jack flashed a forced smile, then looked at Anne. "Ready?"

Her stomach somersaulted. She liked and also didn't like his intense stare as she loosened the front laces of her shirt—*his* calico shirt—to reveal her swollen belly and enlarged breasts. Her thighs felt sore from a rough morning of lovemaking—rougher than she cared for. She worried there might be a visible bite mark on her neck. What might the others think?

Who was she kidding? Rackham couldn't keep his hands off her and hadn't since she'd first joined his crew. They took no notice anymore. This wasn't about them. What did *she* think?

You're angry.

You're always angry.

Mary's words. But hadn't Ellen also said as much? She brushed the thought away.

"Anyone here caught ogling Bon need not worry about returning aboard," Jack yelled. "Understood?"

Everyone shouted in acknowledgment as Anne finished opening her shirt laces. She hunched, suddenly feeling shy, and clutched her cutlass in one hand, a flintlock pistol in the other. Her hair whipped all around her, red veins flying in the corners of her vision. A damn nuisance. How was she supposed to see? She preferred it tied back.

Anne stepped forward to join Mary, who'd loosened her own shirt and was staring straight ahead. Anne scanned behind them for Thomas, who stood a way back, then looked again at Mary. The paleness of her chest, the slight bulge of her growing belly.

Mary set her jaw, her eye on the prey. Beautiful. Fierce. That chilling calm.

Does Mary really not need Thomas?

Do I need Jack?

Shouts from the sailors broke Anne's trance, and she braced herself. Her blood hummed, a bonfire raging.

Act. Her own words.

Learn to channel your anger. Mary's words. *It's like fear. You have to move* through *it.*

"Now!" Corner roared as Jack fired a warning shot.

The crew closed the gap with boarding pikes. Mary surged forward, cutlass raised as she flung herself onto the merchant's deck with a wild, animal scream. Anne leapt next, shrieking like she hadn't since she was a child—hard enough to strain her throat, hard enough to shatter glass. She swung her blade, cursing and slicing at the air, as the sailors' eyes bulged in horror and their jaws dropped in disbelief.

Anne swung and slashed at the space between them. Mary at her right. A roar, a swell of bellows from the men behind her, beside her. Jack somewhere in that sound. She lunged and raised her blade. Drew strength from this rush. The raw energy of a battle cry. Her lungs singing, vibrating, ribs cracked open. Eve redeemed, freed. Anne was a siren, thirsting for revenge, a mermaid wreathed in seaweed, snatching her own life from the depths, from all who once stood in her path. She was power, unapologetic. A warrior. A woman. A myth and a fact—for herself and for all those voiceless others. A force to make the whole earth shake.

A musket dropped on the deck planks, then a clatter of swords. Anne heaved, her whole body shaking. She snarled like a wolf at the sailors stepping back, running away from her and retreating toward their rowboats. She felt the wind ripple her naked skin into gooseflesh.

Move your anger from your head into your bones.

"We're English pirates," Featherstone called out. "We'll not harm a single one of you if you turn over your schooner."

The schooner's captain, Dillon, surrendered. The ship was theirs in a matter of minutes.

CHAPTER 54

The victorious crew camped on a remote shore, gathered around a fire dug into the smooth sand. Mary listened to the damp wood hiss, sending plumes of smoke like an offering to the watchful, unblinking stars above. Corner had hunted down a wild boar, and its skin crackled over the flame as he turned it over a spit alongside a row of fish he'd seasoned with lime juice. The aroma wafted in the breeze.

"When do we eat?" Howell groaned, giving voice to Mary's own torment at being hit with the savory smell of fresh meat. Now that she could stomach food, it was all she ever wanted.

"Another hour or two, if you're not passed out by then," Corner said.

The *Revenge* had laid anchor alongside the *Mary and Sarah*, whose captain and sailors—unharmed, as promised—were held captive in the brig. Unpleasant business, but at least this would keep them silent until Rackham decided what to do with this prize. Did he mean to add this merchant ship to their own and form a flotilla? Or keep the captain and crew prisoner until they could get far enough away to set them free without repercussions? If Mary was honest with herself, she didn't know what to make of Rackham's sloppy strategy anymore. He'd been sharing drinks with Captain Dillon last she spotted him.

She huffed. At least she and Anne had fought well today.

Mary rested against the trunk of a palm tree and watched her companions in the flickering light. They'd been celebrating—drinking—since taking the *Mary and Sarah* that afternoon. Earl played his fiddle, his nimble fingers flying and the bow ripping across the strings as others clapped and sang like howling dogs, their words slurring. A few others gambled on an overturned cask. To avoid fights and injury, the Articles didn't allow for cards aboard the ship. But ashore? Anything could happen.

The shadows cast by the jungle behind Mary felt alive, oppressive. But she refused to give into fear after their feat today. Unlike their other small victories, the *Mary and Sarah* held three hundred British pounds. If the crew continued at this rate under the new strategy, the pirates could retire quickly. Mary could manage a few more raids, then she'd say her goodbyes and part with the crew—with more coin than she could carry in her pockets. And she knew, even now, that she would leave alone.

Her fingers felt the round of her abdomen. She had everything she needed.

Mary looked for Thomas in the circle of faces around the bonfire. His silence spoke for itself. Mary didn't need to discuss her plans with him, but she would all the same. Maybe tonight would be the night to do so.

Where was he?

Mary's thoughts were interrupted by Anne taking a seat beside her. Anne's presence warmed her, but a wave of guilt quelled it. She needed to tell Anne too, and soon.

"You look well in trousers," Mary said.

"I'd forgotten what it was like—wearing breeches like I did as a child. I admit they are more comfortable than a dress," Anne said, running her hands through the sand. "Though they have less airflow. A skirt has its merits."

"That it does," Mary said. Now that she wasn't constrained by what she could and could not wear, it was easy to see the benefits of both. She hoped to never bind her breasts again.

Anne threw herself flat on her back, causing grains of sand to fly. "Do you ever miss home?"

"Home?" Mary had grown used to Anne's spontaneous, intrusive questions—about her life in England, her parents, serving as a cabin boy under Southwick, learning to ride a horse, fighting in the war. She'd even grown to welcome them. "I suppose I've never really had one." No, that wasn't true. "I miss Björn. The Three Horse-Shoes. Those ten years. Can memories be a home?"

"I don't see why not." Anne teased out a knot in her hair. "How was it between you two?"

"I've told you many times." Mary suspected this question was not about her, but about Anne.

"But did you ever shout and argue?"

Mary shifted her weight, her eyes following the flames of the fire. "No. But disagree? Yes." She snorted. "I remember once, Björn finally invited his father, Lord Van Acker, to visit us one Christmas. He was a nobleman who made disparaging comments about my lineage and the life Björn and I had chosen with the inn—a sentiment I ignored. But Björn grew defensive. Lord, the *fight* over the dinner table that followed. The baron stormed out to his carriage in the snow, leaving his coat behind. And as I stared at the table, at the uneaten feast and roasted pheasant"—her stomach growled as she recalled the image—"Björn had the nerve to look proud. Like he'd done that for *me* and not for himself. We were furious at each other for a few days, but it worked itself out. Björn respected me, and I respected him. He saw me as his equal in heart and mind. We could talk through anything. Somehow in tying ourselves together, we also set each other free."

Anne didn't say anything for a minute, and Mary thought that might be the end of the line of questioning. It had been a long day for both of them. But then Anne said, "I'm sorry you never found your Ma."

Thumbing the hem of her shirt, Mary closed her eyes and settled into that deep place within herself—a pool of grief, but also
stillness. Joy, too. "Thank you," Mary said, letting a pinch of pain
within her rise, then float away like smoke. "With this child, I admit that Ma feels closer than ever. She gave me more than I lost.
She gave me everything." A chance. A radiant example of love,
however complicated.

Mary turned to look at Anne, her face barely visible in the red
glow of the distant fire. What did that face say? "I'm sorry you lost
your mother, too."

Anne pushed away a stray hair. "Mam wasn't perfect, but she
knew how things were—things I never got around to asking her.
Now I'm supposed to be a mother, and I don't know the first thing
about what to do. Or who will help me figure it out."

You'll have me, Mary thought. But the words never left her lips.
Would Anne come along? No. She'd never leave Rackham, and
Mary wouldn't ask that of her.

Anne laughed. "Jesus, Mary, and Joseph, what kind of mam am
I going to be? I'm a holy terror without sleep. I detest the sound of
crying children. And I find dogs far more agreeable than babies."

"Those things don't disqualify you for the task. I think you
know that."

"Maybe. But they are, alas, 'things.' Oh—and I'm also a bloody
pirate."

"What of bravery? Kindness? Intelligence? An ability to listen?" Mary prodded. "I daresay you'll make a fine mother because
you're a fine person."

A commotion from the fire drew their attention back to their
crewmates. Someone threw a punch, and Mary stood.

"Thomas?"

Rackham and Daniel York—one of the new men recruited from
Spenlow's captured schooner—threw Thomas onto the ground.

"Filthy, disgusting thief!" York shrieked.

No. Mary sprinted forward, leaving Anne.

Not again.

"You lie!" Thomas roared, standing and raising a fist. Rackham pulled him back, and someone else held York from behind.

"I saw ye. Pawing at my coin purse! Snooping in the hold!"

"Lies!" Thomas bellowed again, swinging his arms like a windmill. "Don't listen to him, Captain. He's mad in the head—has no idea what he saw."

"Then what did he see, Brown?" Rackham said, arms folded.

Mary shook when she saw the terror in Thomas's dark eyes. *Please tell the truth.*

"I found this," Thomas said, pulling a crumpled paper from his pocket. "I . . . wanted to be sure we did a thorough search of all the documents on the *Mary and Sarah*. Didn't want to wait a week like last time to know we're being hunted like turkeys."

Rackham took the broadsheet and smoothed it out, holding it up to the fire to examine. His eyes grew. "You can't read."

"No, Captain. But I recognize the legal look of a proclamation when I see it. They were posted all over Nassau."

All eyes stared at Rackham. After an agonizing minute, he threw the paper into the fire.

"Captain!"

"It's nothing to worry ourselves over. I find Brown innocent. Everyone, go about your evening. Earl—what happened to the music? And Corner, let's carve the boar."

York scoffed. "And what of the violation of my possessions?"

"Check them," Thomas said. "You'll find nothing unaccounted for."

At the captain's demand, Earl resumed playing his fiddle. Growing bored with the spiraling argument, the other men returned to their drinks and games. Rackham joined them, raising a pewter mug as Corner took a knife to the sizzling meat. But Mary's appetite had vanished. She watched Thomas like a sparrow hawk, waiting for a moment to pull him aside.

"I know what I saw. I summon ye to a duel," York hissed at Thomas. "Tomorrow. Noon. Before we set sail." He flung a handful of sand into Thomas's face, then stormed off.

Thomas shrank to the side, stumbling and clutching his eyes until he left the glow of the fire. Mary followed, the sound of the breakers against the shore as her mind whirred.

"Is it true?"

"That there's a second proclamation? Aye."

Mary handed him her water flask to flush out the sand in his eyes. He hissed in pain.

"Did you try to steal from York?"

Thomas fell to his knees, letting out a sob of anguish. "I can't do it anymore, Mary. I can't continue another day on this miserable ship. The raids. The waiting to be caught. The nightmares—Governor Rogers leering over me with a noose." He convulsed, and Mary bit her lip, unsure of what to do, until at last she sank into the sand and placed an arm around his shuddering frame.

"Why didn't you tell me?" she said, steadying her voice. "Why have you avoided me at every turn?"

"I wasn't sure what they'd think," he said. "You aren't like other women. I didn't want to endanger us both. Damnation, Mary. I was scared. I was a fool."

Mary's chest fell. "You thought you might get ahead, nab some coin, and be on your way, then?"

Thomas nodded, then broke down again.

"Without me?" *Without our child.*

He didn't answer. He didn't have to.

"I wasn't thinking. I'm sorry, Mary. But I can't duel with York! You know I can't shoot straight. And my sight?" He spat with scorn. "From that far away?"

"I know," Mary said, feeling her throat burn. The closeness she and Thomas had once shared was gone. But death had snatched her own father. Her child would not face the same despair, no matter the man's character. Not if she could help it. Death she could not bridge, but the possibility of change? That her child, or Thomas, might seek each other out in the future? With a flare of white-hot realization, she knew what she had to do: one last favor for this man she once held dear. "I'll speak to York. See if I might talk him down."

Thomas pulled his elbows in and rocked. The pressure built behind Mary's eyes.

"But you have to be ready, Thomas. It's time you learned courage."

You are more than this, she thought.

Knew.

She placed a sturdy hand on his shoulder, then stood, brushing the grains of sand from her trousers. She gulped down her springtide of emotions and walked away, forcing herself not to look back.

CHAPTER 55

When Anne entered the captain's quarters, her grasp lingered on the brass door handle.

Jack approached her, draping his hands over her hips, his teeth finding her neck. "You were wonderful today. Delicious, too." He smelled like a tavern.

She turned, stopping him with a palm to his bare chest. "What did that paper say?"

"What paper?" He teased. His fingers slid up her torso to the crossing laces of the calico shirt she still wore. His shirt.

She stilled his fingers. "The one you burned in front of everyone?"

"Really, Bon?" he said, loosening the lowest lace below her sternum. The hardness in his trousers pushed into her. "Can't it wait? Have mercy. I'm burning for you—the most gorgeous woman in the Caribbean."

She took a step away, staring at his red, glazed eyes. His beautiful face and angular jaw. "The crew has trepidations."

"The whole crew? Or a certain female friend?"

Anne frowned.

"Fine," he said, throwing up his hands. "Not sure what's put you in a foul mood." He knocked into the table and cursed. "It was a proclamation from Sir Nicholas Lawes."

Anne spun on him. *Another* warrant? This time from the governor of Jamaica? God have mercy. They were getting hemmed in on all sides. "How could you keep this from us?" she spat. "We have a right to know."

"We made the impression we hoped for," he beamed, a glint kindling in his pupil. "The *Revenge* is earning her name, a ship so fast they're chasing their tails."

He leaned in to kiss her, and she tilted her head away, stunned. "Not now, Jack."

He tried again, not hearing.

"I said no."

The mirth leached from his features, his usual warmth shifting slowly into an unreadable coldness. The gold of his brown eyes hardened into stone. "It's always 'no' with you these days, isn't it? No time to think or consider. Just an immediate 'no, no, no.'"

Anne crossed her arms as if stabbed. "That's not true."

"You said 'no' to returning to Cuba, where you and our baby could be kept safe—you're welcome!"

"Jack, I didn't mean—"

"You said 'no' to staying in the hold during raids, 'no' to my orders as captain. You made me look ridiculous in front of the crew. And now this? Abandoning me, doubting me when I need you most? You used to love me." He flung out an arm, the contents on the table knocking to the floor. The hourglass shattered, sand flooding onto the rug.

"I do love you, Jack." A scared little girl inside her froze, a piece of her she'd long buried. "Of course I love you."

Make him happy.

Make the cruel words stop, his smile return, the world upright again.

He stepped toward her, alcohol on his breath, a finger running over her neck. "You no longer welcome my affections. What's happened to the fire of a woman I used to know? Her sense of risk, fun, adventure?"

His words stung like a slap. "That isn't fair, Jack."

"How can you be so cold? You've become unfeeling and selfish. I hear a lot about you and your many concerns these days, but what about my needs? Be generous. Think of how I might feel. I've been waiting all day to get you alone."

"I do think of you," she ground out. Her gaze flicked to the door. She should leave. Let him tantrum alone. She'd seen this before and knew what would happen if she stayed.

Her feet didn't move. Why couldn't she move?

This was Jack. Her partner, her country, the father of her unborn child. He was her joy, her delight. Without that glow, his adoration and the shelter of his effusive love, she shriveled. Became unrecognizable to herself.

"All I want is your happiness," he continued, face fevered. "To give you pleasure. I love you, Bon."

"You're drunk."

"You're pulling away!" He gripped her wrist, and a shiver of apprehension rose in her gut.

She knew the movement Mary had taught her, how to get free of his hold.

Still, she didn't move.

Wouldn't move. Couldn't.

His mouth pressed into hers, his fingers gripping the hair at the base of her skull. He moaned, then dropped his clutch on her wrist to remove the rest of her calico shirt.

No.

Did she whisper it?

Scream it?

Did the word ever leave her lips?

He ripped off her shirt, then fumbled with the belt of her trousers. She stiffened as if paralyzed. Growling in frustration, he picked up her inert form and carried her to the bed.

CHAPTER 56

"Where is he?" York sneered when Mary approached, the sun beating down from its watchful position at exactly ten in the morning.

Mary said nothing, feeling the weight of the flintlock pistol in her brace. She dug her heels into the soft sand and reached for the well of deadly calm within her.

York scanned the empty beach behind her, then scowled. "Ye changed the time by two hours, and now the bilge rat has the guts to be late?"

"I'm his second," Mary said.

"We agreed. No seconds." He glowered, deep lines grooved into his wiry brow.

"If he fails to show, you'll be glad I'm here. A position filled. Your word confirmed and honor cleared."

York snorted, sucking something juicy through his nose, then spit. "I'll not be killing a woman."

No, Mary thought. *You won't.* "This isn't a gentleman's duel," Mary said. "No rules apply." Apparently he'd not taken note of her belly.

"The capt'n wouldn't like this."

York did not, Mary observed, say anything about not liking it himself. "The captain wouldn't approve of you dismissing his judgment and initiating a duel in any case. Not while you're on duty under the Articles." She had no way of knowing if hotheaded Rackham truly would have disapproved. But even if he did, men did not withdraw from such a challenge—even dishonorable ones. Even Thomas. And while Thomas may have deserved such an end, she would not send him here to die.

York stiffened. Mary tried not to study his face. To think about where he came by such a hardened look, the people who'd no doubt loved him, and how he got here—on this stretch of shore— where the fifty-something years of his life would come to an abrupt end.

And it would end. If she'd had a shadow of a doubt, she wouldn't risk her child.

He paced, his movements twitchy, and Mary stared at the rolling surf. She said nothing for several minutes.

He could forfeit. Put this manly honor nonsense aside.

Save his own hide.

"My patience grows thin," York said. "We start."

"Agreed," Mary said. "Before any of the crewmates who are hunting down provisions find us."

York shook out his shoulders. He was jittery, puffing out his chest and bracing himself the way she'd seen a thousand inexperienced soldiers do before a battle. "If I can't kill the rat, at least I can kill his loyal whore."

Mary almost laughed. But it was a cruel thing to mock a creature that didn't know it was about to die. His fingers trembled as they gripped his pistol.

"Ten paces each."

"Aye," he said, taking a swig from a silver flask.

They stood back to back.

"One . . . two . . ."

She breathed, reaching into her calm. She could almost feel

Björn, hear him marvel at her opponent's stupidity, his words a warning in the breeze. *Do you have any idea who you're dealing with? Have you seen my wife shoot?*

"Eight . . . nine . . ."

Only a fool would underestimate her.

"Ten."

Mary whipped around in a flash, meeting York's eyes, her pistol firing before he had a chance to steady his shaky aim.

Then the scream. The unmistakable sound of the shot meeting its intended mark before York crumpled.

Silence.

Mary inhaled the acrid burn of gunpowder and fresh blood. Smells she'd vowed to give up. The life of hiding, of killing, that she'd put behind her the night she rode to the chapel to meet Björn.

She fell to her knees, unscathed yet wounded. She slowly opened her eyes and studied the weapon in her hand. She hefted the weight of it in her fingers, and her throat tightened.

What are you doing here, Mary? she felt Björn say, the feeling of his voice like a caress. *Is this what you want? What you need?*

It wasn't just York who'd underestimated her. She'd underestimated herself, her ability to go on without Björn.

"What has become of me?" she said aloud.

For a long moment, Mary didn't move. She willed Björn to linger with her, to point her in a better direction. But she was the trained navigator. She was the one left here, alive, with a heartbeat pumping life into another.

Mary stilled, hoping to hear Björn's words emerge again in her mind. Was she mad with grief at last, shipwrecked on the shores of memory? All she heard was the crash of the sea.

"Stay with me," she whispered into the space between them.

The wind whipped at her dark braided hair until at last, without another glance at York's body, she stood and turned away, walking along the beach, toward the *Revenge* readying to make way, toward a future she would no longer leave up to chance.

Not to apathy. Not to fear. And especially not to the reckless whims of Calico Jack Rackham.

Mary returned half an hour later to the noise and commotion of the late morning. The crew was busy hauling fresh water, chopped firewood, and other supplies aboard the *Revenge*. The *Mary and Sarah* bobbed, anchored at its side.

The unblinking sun continued its trek across the sky. The tide rose. The world moved on as if nothing had happened. But something did happen, and Mary felt the undeniable shift. Fingers cradling her stomach, she made for the boarding ladder of the Revenge, then paused. How would she answer for the missing crew member?

She spotted a rowboat hitched to the side of the *Revenge*. Scanning to see if anyone was watching, she untied it, then tipped it onto its side, filling the transport vessel with stones and water until it sank out of sight.

Whipping around, smoothing out her damp clothes, Mary ascended the ladder to find the rest of York's effects. Guilt slithered down her spine as she rifled through his berth—the coins fussed over the night before long gone, likely still on his person. Then she slipped his single linen bag through a gunport and turned around to search for Thomas.

She found him loading his pistol near the bow, fingers quivering as he stuffed the gunpowder with a ramrod.

"Thomas."

He glanced up, deep circles forming moons under his eyes. He'd not slept a wink.

She placed a hand on his shoulder, not caring who saw. He inhaled a shaky breath.

"It's done," she whispered.

His eyes snapped open. "What do—"

"I took care of it. York is gone." Friendless brute that he was, they'd likely be halfway to Port Royal by the time anyone noticed his absence. They'd assume he'd abandoned ship in protest.

The ramrod hit the deck with a clank. Thomas stood, wiping his sweaty palms on his trousers.

"What of my honor?" he said, staring at his feet. "The crew, what will they think?"

Mary winced. This was what he thought of first? Where were the thanks for saving his life?

"I'll be scorned. Branded a coward, letting a woman fight my fights."

Her throat burned as if she'd swallowed seawater. But she hadn't done it for him, she reminded herself, thinking of the child inside her.

"Who knows? Who saw?"

"The only people still alive who knew about the duel are standing here in this conversation." She jabbed him in the heart. "You brand yourself with your short-sightedness."

"Weigh anchor!" Corner shouted as their crewmates sprang to their positions. The sails flapped, canvas catching the wind.

Mary left Thomas without a further word. What more was there to say? A pressure mounted in her head, leaving her dizzy from this fresh gash of sorrow. She moved around the deck, searching for Anne. *Find Anne.* Find her last friend left.

After ten minutes of scanning Anne's usual haunts, she found Earl and Howell laughing as they brought in a line.

"Have you seen Anne?" she asked.

"Not since last night," Earl said, brow glistening as he heaved the rope.

The *Revenge* lurched, and everyone fumbled for balance except for Mary.

Was Anne still ashore? Her mouth soured. Mary scanned the horizon, the empty beach, the section of the island where she'd left York to rot.

She searched again, this time with more deliberation. She started in the foul-smelling hold, making her way through the berth, then across the rest of the lower deck, until at last, she found her.

Anne stood in the galley, bent over a large iron pot while stirring its steaming contents. The aroma of peas overwhelmed the room.

"I have to tell you something," Mary said, the words tumbling out as she hurtled toward her friend. Then she stopped dead. "Anne?"

Anne turned away, her cheeks drained of color, the spoon shaking in her grasp.

"Anne," Mary said, softer, taking her by the shoulders. She searched for a new bruise, but there was none. "What's wrong?"

"Nothing," Anne said, staring past her.

Mary did not let go of her hold. Her veins constricted. Mary knew the sacredness of privacy, the loneliness of grief. The war between wanting to intervene and knowing when to stand back and avoid risking offense or notice.

Now was not the time to retreat. "I see that something happened."

Anne blinked, as if unseeing. "I . . . don't know."

"I'm listening," Mary said. "And not a word of judgment from me, whatever it is. I was about to tell you what atrocities I've been up to this very morning."

Anne's eyes crinkled, then filled with emotion. She collapsed with a sudden, horrible sob into Mary's chest. Mary stiffened, shocked, then wrapped her arms around Anne.

"Tell me," Mary said, feeling her own eyes burn with tears.

And Anne did. Fumbling with language. Struggling with words. Gaps. Self-flagellation and a dozen justifications for Rackham. But it didn't matter. The truth was there and as clear to Mary as true north. Apparently, this was a pattern when Rackham got drunk.

"Why didn't I act?" Anne said. "Why didn't I just leave? The door was right there."

Mary helped Anne take a seat by the warmth of the stove. The sight of Anne's rumpled hair, her hollow eyes, made Mary want to kill another man in cold blood that day.

But she knew that would give Anne no relief. Mary's feelings toward Rackham were her own.

Anne buried her face in her hands. "Curse my own stupidity! My own weakness. Haven't I learned? I saw Da's drunken tirades for what they were." She paused to catch her breath. "I stabbed Nathaniel Fulworth. I escaped James Bonny—twice! I wouldn't let those devils violate me. But Jack?" Her voice trailed off. "I love Jack. And I know he damn well loves me. How could he fail to see that he was making love to a corpse? How does he see right through me—past me?" She swore again. "Why didn't he stop?"

"He may love you," Mary said. "But that—what he did to you—wasn't love, Anne."

Anne shrugged, wiping her nose with her sleeve. "I could have stopped him. Said something. I didn't—I never do. I froze like a fool."

Mary took Anne's hands. "Look at me." Anne exhaled, then returned her look. "That wasn't love," Mary repeated. "And it wasn't your fault."

"I guess I don't have a pissing clue what love is anymore," Anne scoffed, straining to find a bit of humor. It didn't work. She tore at her hair and wept with renewed bitterness.

Mary moved to sit beside her friend. She tried to pull her knees to her chest, but the bump—the baby—made the gesture impossible. She crossed her legs instead, then massaged her throbbing temple to think.

I can't leave without Anne. Not now.

But Mary had no right to ask. Or did she? Anne's choice to retreat into denial or break away balanced on a knife's edge. It was Anne's decision, ultimately. Nothing to be pushed. And yet, if there was even the smallest chance that Anne would leave with her, Mary would ask.

They sat together in the unease. Witnesses. Survivors in their own ways.

"It feels as if a cannonball has crashed through every deck of my soul," Anne whimpered. "I don't know who I am or what I know anymore. Are all men this way, beneath it all? Is this just the way—"

"No," Mary said, cutting her off with force. "No, Anne. I swear it on my life, and Björn's." She caught herself, calming her tone. "I'll add Henry Danby to the list. Captain Southwick. Your tutor, Monsieur Perrin. Your friends on the *Swallow*, and half the crew aboard this ship." She found Anne's watchful eyes, that pooling skepticism. "And if you can't believe it now, borrow my conviction. There is a bigger life, and bigger loves, ahead of you. If that is what you want. If that is what you choose."

"Ah, yes," Anne huffed, touching her stomach. "I have to figure out how to love this sorry baby that ended up with me for a mam. And him for a father."

"I wasn't referring to the baby," Mary said, taking hold of Anne's fingers and moving them to her heart. "I meant yourself."

Anne stilled, closing her eyes and feeling her own pulse. She bit her trembling lip and didn't speak for a full minute.

The pot boiled over, and Mary sprang to attend to it.

"I'm leaving Jack," Anne said from behind her. "I had to say it aloud before I change my mind."

Mary exhaled, the steam from the pot coating her skin. "Then we'll go together," Mary said, staring into the bubbling broth, courage rising as she stirred. Salt stung her eyes. "We'll go as sisters. War widows. It doesn't matter what we tell people. I can find work as a shipwright. A merchant or a stablehand—I'm good with horses and like them better than most people. With your swift needle skills and nimble fingers, you can mend sails at any port and complete the task twice as fast as any man. It wouldn't be a fortune, but enough to support yourself and a child. Or you could work as a tutor, a teacher or a governess—making use of your fancy upbringing. Your fine wit. You're clever, Anne. Discreet and efficient and capable."

Mary could pretend to be a man if she had to, a husband— if they got desperate. Her blood chilled at the thought. No, she wouldn't pretend. She wouldn't hide who she was any longer. Never again. "We'll find a way—we'll look after each other. And the babies."

"When do we leave?" Anne said, voice lowered.

They could take the ship's second rowboat and be gone that same day. But how far could they get? In what direction and with what provisions?

"The next time we make port. Or get close enough. It'll give us time to prepare."

As Mary stirred the pot, she craned to see Anne's subtle nod of approval.

CHAPTER 57

Spanish Town, Jamaica,
March 1721

We'll look after each other.
And the babies.

Anne punched a fist into her cot, letting out a scream that echoed through the dark corridor of the garrison. She stood and cursed, slamming her sweaty palm into the stone wall, the hit vibrating through her elbow to her toes. She steadied herself, bracing for calm through bared teeth, the other hand holding the bulge of her enormous stomach. The weight had shifted lower, sitting like a boulder on her bladder. Any second now, this would end and the child would arrive. Her lower back ached with anticipation.

I've failed you, Mary.

The letters, still unwritten, were laid out on the floor, visible in the dim light. The paper. The ink.

"I've failed," Anne wheezed. Why couldn't she go to Mary now in her time of need—be there as Mary had been there for her so many times before? Who insisted on keeping them apart like this, in isolation, when the men from their crew had been allowed to share a cell?

Why didn't we leave when we had the chance?

Anne paced the straw-covered floor with her swollen bare feet, fury galloping through her veins. She looked everywhere but at the blank paper and writing materials Captain Johnson had left that morning. She'd spent the past two of her four months in jail toying with him while he extracted what he wanted from her. She'd spent countless silent moments thinking about getting her hands on the tools she needed—what to say, how and why to say it.

But now that she had the chance to write it all down, her whole body trembled with fear. She had limited ink. Could she say the right thing? Make a case to the right people?

Could she trust herself?

And even if she could, could she trust Captain Johnson to do her one final favor?

Anne threw her head back and howled. It didn't matter if she shrieked or stayed silent as a ship mouse—no one came. No one ever came.

Was she too late?

You're clever, Anne. Discreet and efficient and capable.

Ellen had said so too: *more clever than you give yourself credit for. Stop underestimating yourself—it's irritating.*

Anne's jaw tightened with resolve, and a vein in her throat twitched. She was raised for this, was she not? Stuffed into a chair, made to study laws, politics, and arguments ever since she was a child in Ireland? She was a bloody lawyer's daughter.

She snapped her gaze back to the piles of paper, then knelt in front of them, resting her hands on the ball of her stomach. She pictured the faces of the recipients.

Ellen Fulworth, she thought, putting aside a stack of pages. She had no idea where Ellen was, but she must be somewhere in the Caribbean. Maybe someone in power here could trace down Mr. Fulworth.

Captain Eford. That is, if he hadn't taken Bonny's betrayal as a sign to abandon the Tropics, change his name, and retire somewhere near his grown children.

Jack's "family" in Cuba. She knew where they could be found in Havana. She also knew they were experts in all matters related to piracy.

Henry Danby. Good luck finding him. But Mary said he was campaigning. Perhaps the English army knew where he was?

Bartholomew Roberts, she noted with a touch of whimsy. Rumor said that this dreaded captain was actually a woman. If so, perhaps she'd intervene on their behalf? Mary would shoot every shot she had, so Anne would too.

Another pile. More names. More chances.

Da? She cringed with revulsion. Then she remembered Mary's child as well as her own. She would swallow her pride and the values she held dear—just this once. *Him, too.*

And if him, then why not the Devil himself?

She breathed through her mouth, cooling off her temper. Might as well start with her foulest, most delicate plea of all, before she could stop herself. Governor Woodes Rogers was a lost cause. She was thinking of someone else, a wizened face from the courtroom.

She snatched the wooden stool to use as a hard surface to write on, then dipped her quill into the inkpot and began to write:

To His Excellency and Governor of Jamaica, Sir Nicholas Lawes . . .

CHAPTER 58

Caribbean Sea
October 31, 1720

"Bested the famous Jean Bondavais!" Howell bragged, passing around his silver flask. "How 'bout that?"

"Aye, we did!"

"Ran like a sniveling whelp," said Corner, his cheery cheeks flushed with sun and drink. "Wonderful work today, brothers. You too, Anne and Mary."

Anne's hands still stank of powder from running ammunition to the gunners. Everyone had recognized Bondavais's ship and colors—a famed privateer hired to rid the sea of pirates. The *Revenge*'s swivel cannons and fast thinking on the part of the whole crew had staved off his attack.

But what was next? How many more raids until they anchored in or near a port?

Anne stared at her splayed fingers in the brightness of the warm October afternoon, the grit of black dust between her nails, then a shadow passed over them.

"Bon?"

Jack took her hand, and she shrank. He'd said little since Anne had confronted him about his behavior the prior week. He failed to apologize. Instead, he mounted a stronger defense of his "affections." His advances had only become more frequent, more desperate, when she stopped coming to his bed at night.

He placed a hand on her hip, and she turned away.

"Have it your way. *Again.*" The edge returned to his voice as he shouldered past her to join the celebration, a bottle in his grip. The sting of his disappointment left her rattled, disoriented—like a slap. Even when she wished it wouldn't and knew better.

"You all right?" Mary said—quietly, suddenly, at her side.

"Yes," Anne said. Her mouth dried at the prospect of telling Jack her plan to part ways with him and the crew. His blinding anger. She would have to tell him soon. The moment they were within a rowboat's distance to Kingston Port, they'd be gone.

Maybe she shouldn't tell him at all. But in the pit of her heart, hope burned like an ember—that Jack would say he was sorry. That he'd try another tactic, not only in their battles at sea but also in their private conversations.

That she wouldn't have to lose him, too.

"We passed Trelawny Parish. Did you see the church steeple?" Mary asked.

Anne nodded, adjusting the red kerchief around her neck. They were continuing on, curving around the eastern point of Jamaica with due speed. The bright blue of the clear water seared her pupils. The white beaches stretched on for miles and miles without interruption—a tropical paradise.

"What's that there?" Earl shouted from behind.

Half the crew moved to the rail, tenting their eyes to see.

"A small little thing," Corner said.

"Get closer," Jack ordered. The sails shifted, the canvas greeting a new direction.

Anne sighed, feeling the hilt of her cutlass. *Here we go again.*

* * *

It was a single pirogue. The swift rowboat held not a single shilling, but nine men—mostly English—who claimed they were out "turtling."

Dubious, given their shifty gazes and the pirate weapons they bore. But maybe they really were gathering turtles to sell to passing ships. Turtles needed little to survive and were invaluable to sailors in need of fresh meat on a long journey. Anne had always adored watching turtles swim with such grace in the crystal-clear bays of the Caribbean. She never cared for the taste. But at a certain point, taste was of the least of concerns. And respect for a beautiful creature? A luxury.

Whatever they were doing—whoever they claimed to be—why the hell were they being escorted like kings onto the *Revenge*?

"Lads," Jack said, showing the men to the upper deck with a slight swagger, "Meet our new friends."

Anne saw the marked annoyance on Mary's raised brow.

"Friends?" Anne asked.

"Potential recruits," Corner whispered to Anne, loud enough for Mary to hear. "Shipmates!" he then shouted. "Make our guests feel welcome."

Everyone off duty shook hands with the men. Anne knew Jack was eager for a larger crew, especially with the *Mary and Sarah* now in their possession. But what of trust, the most important component of any crew?

This desperate approach, taking sailors before they'd proved themselves on an opponent's ship, was how he was going about it?

"This here is Thomas Baker, John Eaton, and Edward Warner. That large fellow there is Thomas Quick." Jack bowed, waving his hat toward Quick with humor. "He looks like a man who can lead a raid." Jack pushed a bottle of rum into his hands. "Come! Let's retire for the day and properly meet these new gentlemen."

"We need to clear these waters," Mary said with a quiet firmness, her shoulders squared.

Jack scowled. "What we need, I assure you, is my top priority as captain. And what we need is recruits, Read."

He rejoined the pouring of drinks, but Mary spoke again. "This shore is too exposed. *Captain.*"

"Jack, please listen," Anne said. She felt her throat constrict with panic.

His jaw hardened, and no one else spoke. He didn't humor Anne by turning around. Instead, he smiled and poured a glass of rum, handing it to one of the newcomers. "Corner," he said to his quartermaster, "find us a place to anchor. We have much to discuss tonight."

A mosquito buzzed in Anne's ear, and she swatted it away. "We'll die of swamp fever before we reach the port."

"Clever, Rackham," Mary said, sitting beside her on the stern as they watched the blood-orange streaks of the setting sun over Negril's Bay. "A swamp might be an ideal hideout, were it not for the woods behind us." She pointed to the silhouette of land. "Those hills and trees block the westerlies. It'll take hours to catch enough wind to get out of here tomorrow morning."

Anne leaned back on her palms, glancing over her shoulder to see the men, deep into their cups, halfway down the main deck. Their faces appeared harsh in the lantern glow, the haze of pipe smoke blurring their features as they dunked goblet after goblet into the bowl of punch. They were engaging in some kind of drinking contest, the original crew against the turtlers. Earl played his fiddle, the deep voices of singers dissolving into yowls, more slurred as the evening wore on.

"I don't know that we are going anywhere in the morning if they don't stop drinking," Anne said, turning back as the orb of the sun began to sink into the sea. "They've been at it since noon."

"'Discussing,' you mean?" Mary said with a rueful laugh.

Anne smiled with unease. Mary kept fidgeting with her pistol. Creases marked her forehead. It was rare for Mary to be visibly worried.

"We have the coin we need?" Anne asked, shooing away another mosquito.

Mary rested her hands on her belly. She, like Anne, wore the trousers they'd put on for the earlier raid. "Just enough. I've set aside the pounds. They are still in the hold—findable, if anyone senses that something is amiss and decides to count. But ready for a quick escape."

"I've stashed a week's worth of hardtack and some dried beans," Anne said. "I hid them in the captain's quarters instead of my berth in case Jack prowls through my effects." His own cabin was the last place he'd find her.

Mary slapped the mosquito that had landed on her thigh. "These bugs are menaces. I'm calling it a night." She stood, stretching her legs in the green fade of dusk. "Can't get enough sleep these days anyway."

Anne nodded, understanding. Good hell, it took a lot to grow a little human.

Just as Mary was about to leave, Anne threw out an arm. "Do you see that?"

Mary whipped around. She didn't speak for three terrible seconds. "We're trapped," she breathed, stumbling back and sprinting for the men.

Trapped?

Anne's stomach hit the floorboards as she scrambled up, racing after Mary.

"Ships on the horizon!" Mary bellowed. "They waited until nightfall to attack."

The men blinked, taking a moment to respond, for the laughter to stop. The music died as Earl's bow fell from the strings.

"Two of them," Anne spat out. She found Jack's eye. "Mounted with dozens of guns."

We're under attack.

A gasp escaped from Howell while the others stood—or tried to stand.

Corner rose first, followed by Jack and the others. They passed around the spyglass, but it was too late, too dark. The ships drew nearer.

"Damn privateer! It's Jean Bondavais again," Featherstone cursed, kicking the table. He stumbled for balance, nearly falling out of his chair. A bark of muttering.

"We have to surrender."

The rising chaos ground to a halt as all eyes looked at Mary.

"Surrender, Captain Rackham," Mary said with slicing clarity. "We don't stand a chance—not in this position. And if we go quietly, we might be shown mercy. We'll need it."

Surrender? Anne's pulse rose like high tide. She knew the rules: a quick forfeit without waging resistance meant grace. Sparing lives and entering negotiations. They'd followed this principle a dozen times while pillaging others.

And if not . . .

Anne stared at the others. Waiting for someone, anyone, to act.

"Weigh anchor! Ready the swivel cannons," Jack yelled to Corner. "That's an order."

The men ran, or rather stumbled, into position. Half couldn't stand. Howell fell flat on his face and Thomas appeared green as he clutched his own gut.

Jesus, Mary, and Joseph. Was anyone in a condition to fight?

Mary grabbed Anne by the elbow. "Get to the armory. Grab extra weapons," she said. Anne did as she instructed as Mary chased after Jack.

"If we fire, there'll be no turning back, Rackham," Mary said.

Anne forced herself to keep moving, to not hear Mary's pleading voice crack.

No turning back.

She gathered her courage, boots pounding down the ladder as she moved through the armory.

An ear-shattering boom sounded overhead, sending Anne to her knees.

Jack had fired the first cannon. She cursed, lunging forward, searching through the spare weapons stacked beside the grindstone. A sawed-off musket. A long-abandoned pistol. An armful of cutlasses and three grenades. She flung open the lid of the storage keg and shoveled black gunpowder into silk cartridge bags before stuffing them into her pockets.

Another *boom* from above flung her into the cask, leaving her shaking.

She took everything, absolutely everything, she could carry.

On the main deck, Anne sprinted through the madness and clouds of smoke. She found Mary at the swivel cannons. Clearly, not a single one of the balls had met its target. Two of the recruits openly cried, curled up against the wall. No one had bothered with the long nines.

Mary had a set chin, that look of battle in the glint of her eyes. Her protests had vanished, accepting the new, bleak conditions. She took the extra weapons from Anne's arms, distributing them to anyone able to stand. She ran fore and aft, desperately trying to rally the men.

No turning back, that steely gaze said. All thanks to their captain. *Jack*.

Anne spotted him, and her heart lurched. He gripped the rail, glazed eyes bulging as he steadied himself and leered at the nearing ships. He was so beautiful, even now. After everything.

Damn him.

A shout from the closest ship sounded in their ears. "Strike immediately to the King of England's colors!"

No one spoke, and Thomas vomited on the deck planks.

"We will 'strike' no strikes!" Jack bellowed back, refusing to retreat. He gestured for Howell to light another swivel, but Howell couldn't move his fingers fast enough to light the slow match.

"Fire another warning shot," Jack roared at the crew. Another man crawled forward, attempting to clutch the flint and steel.

Anne pushed him out of the way, then struck, lighting the slow match fuse and lowering it to the cannon's touchhole. She dove onto her side to protect her stomach and covered her ears as the *crack* sang out. She felt the reverberations through her teeth.

Pulling herself up using the rail, she saw one of the sloops turn, its gunports open.

She closed her eyes, unable to watch.

A deafening crash ripped through the bulwark, tossing her several feet. She braced her fall with her elbows, still protecting her belly. Screams turned to wails. She heard someone fall overboard, their cry swallowed up in the sea.

"To the hold!" Jack yelled, his voice suddenly shaky. "Everyone, to the hold!"

"The hold?" Anne shouted, her voice hoarse. "I've already emptied the weapons from the armory."

"To the hold! Take cover!" He staggered past without seeing her, then clumsily hurtled toward the hatch.

He was . . . hiding?

As men scrambled for the hatch, falling over each other in a drunken stupor, Anne couldn't breathe.

A hand pulled her from the wreckage. "Anne, are you hurt?"

She pressed her eyes closed, wishing it was Jack. But grateful—so grateful—that it was Mary instead.

"Jack ordered—"

"I know," Mary said, pulling Anne to her feet. A new slash cut across Mary's cheek. Her mahogany eyes grew, seeing something from behind. "Incoming!" She threw Anne back down again, the two women taking cover.

The whistle tore through the broadside. The sound of shredding wood, the ship screaming in protest as deadly splinters flew. More shrieks from the men.

Through the smoke, Anne saw a line of longboats making their way for the *Revenge*. They paddled hard under the crescent moon. Her eyes burned, but she couldn't—wouldn't—blink.

"If Rackham chose to take a stand, then he bloody well better take a stand," Mary growled, boots hammering as she raced after the retreating crew.

Had Anne ever heard her swear? She shook her head, chasing

after Mary and catching up with her just in time to see her throw open the hatch.

"Is there a man left among you?" she yelled below. "Come out here and fight!"

Behind her, Anne heard the sound of boarding pikes making contact. Feet on the ladders and the shout of orders. She gaped into the hold, at the bile on the top step. She heard the crew wallowing in terror, but no one emerged.

"Jack!" Anne yelled, the word—his name on her tongue—splintering. "Please, Jack. They're boarding. They're here."

"Bon?" he slurred. "Bon, get down here!"

Mary took aim with her pistol, firing into the dark. The lock on the door burst open, along with the renewed sound of the crew.

"Fight like the men you pretend to be!" Mary shouted. "This sniveling won't save you now."

Over her shoulder, Anne heard the invaders storming the main deck. They had no more time . . .

Mary stood, stretching her neck. She pulled out her braid, letting her hair loose just below her shoulders. She grabbed a fresh pistol, then unsheathed her cutlass. It was a battle stance Anne had come to know well.

Anne's fingers shook as she untied the ribbon from her tresses and removed her own weapons from the belt on her waist.

"I'd rather die as a soldier than be skewered like a suckling pig as I grovel on my knees," Mary said with chilly calm.

"Or hang at the end of a rope," Anne said, swallowing. She knew, oh she knew how this story ended. Queen Maeve. Grace O'Malley. Joan of Arc. Their gruesome ends.

No turning back. They'd meet their death head-on. The gory, merciless death Jack had invited in like an expected houseguest.

Her eyes burned, thinking of the child she'd never meet. It was never supposed to be like this. Nothing like this. The wings of her erratic heart flapped against her ribs. She gripped her pistol.

The voices of strange men neared. Then, with a nod of shared understanding, Mary and Anne tore open their shirts and hurtled forward, blades raised.

A pair of hands pushed Anne down as another tied her hands behind her back.

She stared through the strands of her hair at the ruined main deck of the *Revenge*. Her whole body heaved. Someone flung Mary down beside her, disarming her of her remaining weapons and binding her hands. Anne caught her eye, rage simmering in her pupils, battle still pumping through her veins. They'd fought like fiends out of hell, the furious clanking of steel until they were totally surrounded and tackled to the ground.

"What do we do with them, Captain Barnet?" one of their captors said. It was the first anyone had spoken in several minutes.

Barnet? Another famed privateer. Mother of God, him too? Everyone worth half their salt had heard of Jonathan Barnet. A merciless bastard.

Anne lifted her chin, observing the men's faces. They couldn't tear their attention away. Mouths hung open. Some with revulsion. A few with pity.

But others?

Unmistakable awe.

"While Captain Bondavais empties the *Mary and Sarah*, we'll finish flushing out the hold."

To her right, Anne watched as a dozen men ushered her crew off the *Revenge*. Most were so drunk they had to be dragged. Few put up a struggle. Howell openly wailed. Thomas didn't take his eyes from his boots.

Anne's chest tightened as three men pulled Jack through the hatch. He threw his large shoulders into them, despairing sounds bubbling from his throat. The captors shoved him toward the gangplank.

His wild eyes found Anne's, the brown of them glazed almost beyond recognition.

She gritted her teeth, wishing it could stop the tears.

You betrayed me.

Your foolishness betrayed us all.

Barnet's men brought Anne and Mary to their feet, and someone closed the front of their shirts, his cheeks crimson as he did so. He took the dirk from the sheath on Anne's thigh, her final weapon. Her bound hands squirmed, aching to take it back. She'd miss that little dagger.

Captain Barnet then stepped in front of them, his blue waistcoat trim and stiff. He surveyed Anne, then Mary, with something that almost resembled approval.

"Take them back to my ship. Treat them with care."

"Captain?"

Barnet paused, his polished boots blacker than gunpowder, the aftermath still scorching the air.

"These women tried to kill us, sir. They're lethal."

Anne clamped her mouth tighter, suppressing an unexpected smile.

Barnet straightened. "I didn't say to behave as imbeciles. I said to treat them with care. And well, if you can manage that. We make for Port Royal to collect our reward. There, I assure you, Major Richard James and the local militia will see that their crimes are taken up with the Admiralty Court with due haste."

CHAPTER 59

Spanish Town, Jamaica
November 1720

Of all the stories Mam had told Anne about her days in prison, she'd never described the smell.

"In you go," the guard said, stepping inside as he led her by the elbow. The cell door swung closed, the air abandoning her lungs.

Thick stone walls. A single cot. A three-legged stool. Anne gagged, avoiding a glance at the chamber pot she only hoped she'd find clean. The odor of the room didn't promise anything.

She kicked at the straw. Old but not damp.

"You'll get slop once in the morning, once at night. Water, too."

"Practically a feast," Anne said, swallowing down bile. "How hospitable Jamaica is." The burly guard did not acknowledge her humor. But so long as her words had barbs, she wouldn't collapse into complete rubble. Not yet. Not while any of these devils watched. Her stomach ached as if the baby—five months along—was already protesting.

Sorry, my little one.

"Hands up," the guard ordered. Anne hesitated. If she'd had her knife, she might stand a chance. Spring for the door—assuming it wasn't locked yet. Puncture the liver of the other guard outside the door through the ribs, just as Mary had taught her.

Mary. Her throat tightened. Torn away from her and thrown into some other corner of the garrison. The men were taken to the other end to await their immediate trial.

Anne raised her wrists, the irons clinking. Then the guard took a small key and unlocked one. "You'll not be needing these," he said.

She let the cuff drop and the weight fall, then rubbed the welts on her wrist. "And why not?" She couldn't take him out, she knew. Not while he had that musket. But at least she could pretend. Try.

He unlocked the other shackle, then held the bonds at his side. "Who would you attack? You'll be here alone," he said.

Alone.

She let the word swallow her whole.

The first days were the hardest, until they weren't, the weeks worsening with passing time, eroding into new layers of hell. She bit her fingernails until they bled, disappeared. She screamed with despair, then rage, her voice echoing back at her in the dark. She sang songs to her growing belly in Irish, the meanings lost to her while the words and somber melodies still stuck to her mind. She counted the passing days of light slipping through the slats in the upper wall, then the nights. The bowls of slop and stale bread that left her more ravenous than before.

These conditions she might have weathered. Surely she'd been through worse than the gaol?

But the silence was wretched. The loneliness.

The waiting. To die, to go mad. She wasn't sure which would come first.

After two weeks, Anne lay in a sweaty heap on her cot. Jack's clothes clung to her like barnacles on a hull. She traced circles on her stomach, as if teaching her baby its letters—the way Da had taught her.

Anne came to attention when she heard steps coming down

the corridor. The sun was still bright, and she'd already had her morning slop.

She gasped as two guards led Jack to her cell, his head lowered in defeat.

"Ten minutes," one growled, kicking him inside and locking the door behind him.

"Jack?" She hardly recognized him, hardly knew how to feel. His torn calico shirt. His trousers stained with filth. The blond of his hair darkened with sweat and dirt.

She didn't know what to do, or why the Devil he stood before her now like a ghost.

"Bon," he said, taking a wobbly step forward. His irons clanged as he fell before her in a heap of convulsive sobs.

She swallowed, feeling the room spin.

A room she was in because of him.

Anne took a step back.

"They found me guilty, Bon," he said, trying to steady his voice. "I go to the gallows in an hour's time."

He leaned forward, his tears falling onto her bare feet.

"I begged them. I said, 'Let me see her. One last time, let me go to her.' A dead man's final wish."

Anne placed her hands protectively on her stomach. She let the horror sink in. What his body would become in a gibbet, tarred and then picked by vultures. His soul deprived of a burial. Her throat tightened, threatening to cut off her heartbeat.

"Say you forgive me, Bon," he said. "That's all I need, all I ask."

At this, her blood iced over. She refused to look at him. "I'm sorry to see you here," she paused, feeling heat rise to her face. "But if you had fought like a man, you need not hang like a dog."

He let out a bitter howl, beating a fist on the floor and fighting to compose himself.

"Please, Bon," he said, rising, searching her face.

She found his eyes. Those bottomless golden eyes she'd gotten lost in a thousand times. Now somber and sobered. The image of misery. Defeat. Anguish seared into his pupils.

"Who else?" Anne said, feeling the flare of anger waning to ash.

He swallowed, the knob of his throat bobbing. "Featherstone, Corner, Earl, Howell." He stopped. "Everyone, all of us, except for you and Mary."

Anne's attention sharpened. "You mean—"

"They'll try you separately."

Anne bit her lip, understanding. Putting her and Mary on trial beside the men created the ability to make an argument that it was their common-law husbands who'd influenced their "impressionable minds." It was a mistake Governor Nicholas Lawes would not make in his courtroom.

A separate trial would take her and Mary's sins into full accounting. No mercy, as Mary had warned. Now, they would answer for it all.

Jack stood, his trembling figure before her. He reached for her hands, and she didn't pull away.

He wouldn't die with her forgiveness. She couldn't grant that, and to say it would damn herself to follow him straight to hell. But curse them all, she still cared for him.

She'd cared for all of them.

Anne and Jack held each other and wept, their foreheads pressed together—all words and excuses spent—until the guards came and dragged him away.

CHAPTER 60

Spanish Town, Jamaica
November 28, 1720

One early morning, ten days after Jack appeared in her cell, five guards came to collect her for her trial.

And Mary's. The chance to see her again, to put their minds together, to get themselves out of this disaster.

The guards clamped the cold irons on Anne's wrists, then led her away.

They pushed Anne through a thick crowd gathered in some kind of square, a large common area flanked by redbrick buildings. The town hall, brilliant white with a crimson cupola, towered at the end of the lawn. The square was packed with Spanish Town onlookers catching glimpses and shouting. Gentlemen, noblewomen, elders, fishmongers, and prostitutes alike pressed together likes waves on the sea, craning to gawk.

Anne cursed, the staggering light of the sun blinding. "Is there always such a turnout?" she asked one guard. How long would it take to walk through this bog of sweaty bodies?

"Never," he grunted, pushing her at last inside the town hall building. They were met with a thick wall of heat.

In the single room with rows of benches, Anne saw hundreds of people, her eyes adjusting again. She blinked, scanning for the only person she cared to see. Then she spotted her, seated on the bench.

"Mary!" she yelled, squirming to run to her. A guard yanked her irons back, and she glared at him. "We're on our way over there anyway!" she snapped. She spun and found her friend's face again. Mary hadn't noticed her yet.

She looked a stone lighter since Anne had last seen Mary, her face gray.

Jesus, Mary, and Joseph. What have they done to you?

When she reached the bar, she grabbed Mary's hands. They were burning. "Mary?"

She turned, the corner of her pale mouth lifting. "It's so good to see you, Anne." Mary breathed a sigh of relief.

"What's wrong? Is it the baby?"

"No," Mary shook her head. Anne tried to press a wrist to her forehead, to judge the strength of the fever, but her chains prevented the movement. A guard then locked their shackles to the bench.

"All rise!" came an order, and the shoulder-to-shoulder crowd rose to their feet.

Anne turned from Mary to stare with astonishment at the number of people packed into a single room of the town hall. A spectacle. The smell of unwashed bodies. Then she and Mary stood, facing them all. Her stomach lurched.

In walked Governor Lawes, a wrinkled man in his final years. The former Chief Justice of Jamaica would oversee the trial. He looked grim—had to be, Anne figured, taking over as governor after his predecessor, Archibald Hamilton, was arrested for consorting with pirates. Ellen had been right about everything, the blurry line between them all. Pirates. Power. Pretenders. Governor Hamilton had stoked the fires of the most vicious privateers, brutes and torturers like the infamous Henry Jennings.

But in the end? A court in England acquitted Hamilton. He still continued on in politics, a prosperous career rolled out before him.

Anne watched Governor Lawes smooth out his papers on the table behind the bar. His powdered wig was starched and curled, and the thought of wearing it in this heat made her head itch. His spectacles hung low on his nose, his lined forehead creasing into folds as he croaked, "Order in the court."

To begin, he read the king's proclamation, "An Act for the More Effectual Suppressions of Piracy," the very document, Anne scoffed, that Bonny had used to justify turning in their companions on the *Swallow*.

"All piracies, felonies, and robberies committed in or upon the sea, or in any haven, river, creek, or place, where the Admiral or Admirals have power, authority, or justification, may be examined, enquired of, tried, heard, and determined and adjudged, according to the directions of this act, in any place at sea, or upon the land, in any of his said late Majesty's islands . . ."

So much effort—so many fancy words—Anne thought, for avoiding the appearance of barbarism.

". . . and to summon witnesses, to do all things necessary for the hearing and final determination of any case of piracy, robbery, and felony, and to give sentence and judgment of death this day."

The monotone preaching ended. A silence fell. Then, the trial began in earnest.

"The first witness," someone called out, welcoming a man to the stand. "Please step forward, Thomas Spenlow, captain of the *Neptune*."

Anne felt Mary stiffen beside her. Anne took her hand, squeezing. "Whatever Spenlow says, we can use it against him. If he calls us pirates for being aboard the *Revenge*, we can accuse him of being aboard the same ship for days." Anne faced her, voice low. "Whatever you say, do not change your plea to guilty. We have to appear penitent and demure, even weak, if it helps us gain their sympathy. Do you understand?"

Mary nodded, but a shadow passed across her pale face.

Captain Spenlow took the bench. He appeared clean, perfumed since she'd last seen him on their decks. What a pompous prick. She swallowed as the questions began.

"Tell us what you saw, Captain Spenlow."

He described how the *Revenge* took his schooner captive, making it trail after them for days while Rackham kept him aboard as a prisoner.

"And did you see women among the pirates? These ones, perhaps?"

"I did," Spenlow said, refusing to look Anne's way. "The one called 'Bon' worked as a leader among the rogues. She gave the men gunpowder and issued orders of when and where to shoot."

Anne tried to speak out, but then she remembered her own advice to Mary. Apparent weakness of mind might, among this crowd, prove favorable.

"Next witness," the governor called. "Mrs. Dorothy Thomas."

Anne's gut hit the floor, a string of curses pummeling her brain like grapeshot.

Damn you, Jack.

Dorothy smoothed out her skirts. She'd painted rouge on her cheeks, and the court watched with rapt attention.

"Can you tell us, Mrs. Thomas, of your harrowing account?"

Anne clenched her hands so hard she thought her fingers might punch through the other side.

"Two women"—she pointed—"who wore men's jackets and long trousers, and kerchiefs tied about their heads, stole me from my canoe and pulled me into their pirate ship."

Dorothy shot daggers across the courtroom, and Anne almost rose to her feet to shout. Mary put an arm out.

"They had a machete and pistols in their hands. They cursed and swore."

Guilty, Anne mused.

"But that one there . . ." She shook a damning finger at Mary. "I heard her. She said they should kill me! That if not, I'd come against them."

The court gasped, and Anne bit her lip hard enough to draw blood. The iron swelled on her tongue.

Mary did not move. She, of course, had foreseen it all.

Anne exhaled. If Jack wasn't already dead—the thought made her insides clench—she might push a sword through him herself.

Notetakers wrote furiously as the gathering glared at Anne and Mary with revulsion.

"Are you so sure they were these women you see here?" Governor Lawes said. "What you are describing—"

"I'm sure," she said. "I knew them to be women on account of the largeness of their breasts."

This seemed to put all doubts at ease. Anne's mouth went dry.

A series of debates followed—curious ones about whether or not women could be hanged like men and much tedious discussion about their nudity in battle.

Then at last, Captain Jonathan Barnet took the stand in his red uniform. A hush fell over the room. He looked no different than three weeks earlier when he'd taken them at Negril's Bay.

Sweet and Merciful Jesus. Barnet had seen it all. He knew what they were. And all doubts of that were dispelled as he eloquently described the scene and how, blow by blow, he crept upon the *Revenge* and took them captive.

"You are a seasoned privateer, are you not, Captain Barnet?"

"Served faithfully under Governor Hamilton, your predecessor. And I was rewarded generously by your excellence for capturing the stolen *William* with a nice sum of two hundred pounds and a substantial plantation near Montego Bay."

Anne didn't try to hide her disgust. Barnet had been given a plantation—worked and run by enslaved people—for her capture? And yet she was the one on trial, while he sat there in uniform?

If only she could call Ellen as a witness, or anyone she knew, for that matter. Firebrand Mam. Monsieur Perrin. The crew on the *Swallow*. All the friends she'd sailed alongside. Bloody hell, Anne wasn't innocent—not by a long shot. She'd long since shed the privilege of innocence some women could hide behind. But she had her reasons for her actions. She had not acted fairly, but life had not been fair either.

"Then you recognize a pirate when you see one. Tell us: Did the women you see before you engage in acts of piracy?"

He took a moment before responding. "I found them to be the bravest and toughest opponents I have ever faced in my career," he said with a tone of what might have been regret. "I was most impressed."

The murmurs escalated, and Governor Lawes ordered the court into silence. He turned to Anne and Mary. "You stand by your plea of 'not guilty'?"

Anne and Mary both rose.

"Not guilty," Anne said with emphasis. It was worth a chance, and they had very few of those. She looked to Mary.

"Not guilty," Mary followed, taking a seat again.

Anne's head swam. *What to do, what to do? Think, you fool.*

What else? What else could she do? They sat, speechless, the commotion rising in the room as the authorities deliberated. The tension so thick it would take a cutlass to slice through it.

"You, Mary Read and Anne Bonny, alias Bon, are to go from hence to the place from whence you came, and from thence to the place of execution; where you shall be severely hanged by the neck till you are severely dead. And God in His infinite mercy be merciful to both of your souls."

Not this.

The court gasped, the noise rising to a crescendo, at the unprecedented declaration. The British crown didn't hang women—everyone knew it. Even murderers.

But to them, Anne and Mary were worse, far worse, than common murderers. Her head pulsed. It didn't matter that Anne had never killed anyone. They were two women who dared to subvert the rules and roles of the world.

She tried to stand, but her legs failed her. Mary took her hand. *Not this. Think! You're a lawyer's daughter.*

"Do you have any reason why you should be spared the death sentence?" Governor Lawes asked.

Act. Now, or never.

Anne slammed her hands on the table, then stood. Her knees trembled, but she placed a palm on her stomach. Her very last defense.

"We pray that the execution of the sentence might be stayed."

The onlookers muttered with renewed surprise as Anne helped Mary stand, each still wearing the baggy breeches and men's shirts they wore while fighting in Negril's Bay. "We are both with child. We plead our bellies and ask that the court stay this sentence until matters can be arranged."

"Lies!" a gentleman screeched as Governor Lawes proclaimed this adjustment to the sentence.

What followed came in flashes. The bellows of outrage in the town hall. A woman crying, shrieking. Another fainting. Sweat slipping down Anne's spine, her heart thumping like a stampede. The guards ushering her and Mary away from the town hall, outside into the sunlight, hauling them back toward Middlesex Prison and its foul air, its despicable conditions. Its unending darkness and lancing solitude. That gut-churning, animal odor.

"How did you do it?" Mary asked as they wove through the pack of hungry wolves in the street, everyone gawking to see the hellcats as thoroughly advertised. A carriage stopped in their path, forcing the guards holding them to skirt it.

"I only bought us time," Anne said, panic punctuating her words. "But I'll think. I'll think up something. Mary, I'll—"

"Time is all I needed."

Hands grabbed Anne's shackles, dragging her from Mary now that they'd reached the garrison again.

"No!" Anne yelled, fighting off the guards. "Give us a moment, you miserable devils."

"The prison doctor must confirm if your statements are true."

As if it wasn't apparent? Anne threw out her elbow, then swung around, reaching for Mary.

Mary.

That strange glow on her features.

Calm, a steely face she wore well and often. That pained look behind a tiny smile.

But also something new.

Relief.

CHAPTER 61

Spanish Town, Jamaica
March 1721

The spasms in Anne's lower back grew stronger, more intense. A consistent rhythm mounted between each pulse.

She knew little about what to expect, just what Mam had told her about her own arrival. She knew enough to know it would hurt like the Devil. But what could hurt deeper than the past four months she'd spent rotting in this cell? She suppressed a scream as another wave knocked into her pelvis, its white-knuckle grip lasting for thirty miserable seconds before letting go.

Two guards approached with Captain Johnson. *Finally.* She raised her head, sweat pouring down her cheeks and an arm pushed against the stone wall.

"Are you . . . ?" Johnson removed his ostrich-feathered tricorn. His thin lips paled. "Guards, is there not a doctor? Don't just stand there! Call for the midwife."

They stared in astonishment for a moment, then scurried away to follow Johnson's orders. Once they left, Anne sucked air through her clenched teeth. "Stay," she said.

Captain Johnson blanched.

"Not for the birth, you blithering fool," she growled, then remembered herself.

The letters.

Damn this gowl. She needed him though. She needed him to deliver the—

"I only meant," she heaved, "that this baby will wait, I assure you. I've been at this for half the morning." She wiped her brow with her filthy sleeve. "Might not come until tomorrow."

"You need to be moved. I'll see to it," the captain said, making to leave and fumbling with his words, losing his polished composure. "These conditions . . ."

"Captain," she said, her eye catching his. "If you don't make a fuss, then I won't either. There is one more thing. One more—"

A cramp tore through her, cutting her off. "Please," she wheezed. "Sit. Before the guards return."

To her everlasting relief, he did, taking his usual stool. He looked cramped, shifty, and uncomfortable in his velvet waistcoat. But her body relaxed, waiting for the next swell to knock her over.

She'd use the time. If there was any time left, she'd use it well.

Clutching her stomach, she hobbled to retrieve the letters she'd hidden under the mattress. She took the stack of neatly folded papers and handed them to Johnson.

He studied them and the scrawled names, not saying a word.

"I've included instructions. Where these individuals might be reached."

He flipped through the stack, speechless.

Say something. Her desperation blinded her ability to read him. She was all out of cards.

"Captain," she said, taking a seat on the cot across from him. "I can appreciate the risks. But after everything I've shared with you, everything we've gone through—everything you'll no doubt benefit from as you write your book . . ."

"Do I want to know what these letters say?"

"Nothing that connects back to you. Let's just call it some final words to a few people of importance."

He frowned, massaging the crease in his brow.

Please, Captain.

He exhaled like he'd been holding his breath. "I came to tell you that I've been summoned back to England," he said, lowering the letters to his lap. "I make for London at dawn."

She felt a cramp rearing its head, ready to bite. She closed her eyes, letting it tear through her. "Then I guess this is goodbye?" she ground out.

"I suppose it is."

As the spasms released, she looked at him.

Please, she prayed. She was still a bloody papist. Whatever the hell that meant anymore.

"Thank you, Captain," she said. *In advance.* "You've been a boon to my spirit these past months." A partial truth. Though it surprised her, how that truth—however partial—had rooted into something deep within her.

He tucked the letters into his bag, then sprang to his feet quicker than she'd ever seen him move, as if he couldn't wait to be gone. He paused for a moment, then stretched out a trembling hand. She took it, shaking hard.

Clearing his throat, he said, "I hope—"

The sound of boots rushing down the corridor cut him off. They both turned, facing the incomers.

"How long has she labored?" a plain woman with gray hair asked the guard, who shrugged.

"Found her like this not five minutes ago," the guard said, rubbing his neck.

"Goodbye, Captain," Anne said with a nod as he backed out of the cell, his eyes wide and unreadable. She didn't break his gaze, even as the midwife ordered her to sit.

Johnson placed his hat over his powdered wig, then bowed, scurrying away and out of view.

Minutes wore on like hours. Hours like years of starless nights. The pummels came like breakers, crashing relentlessly, violently, her whole being fighting back. A dirk against a dozen pistols.

A room with white walls, sheets that smelled like ash soap. A birthing stool. The stern midwife at her side, holding her hand, ignoring a thousand ear-bleeding curses. Anne squeezed hard enough to break bones.

Jack, she called into the cavern of grief within herself. He should have been here—beautiful, stupid fool. He should have been a better man. Still living, still at her side. Still her life's greatest love.

Mary. Sweet Jesus, what of Mary? Anne rallied, throwing her crusted eyes open. Anne had to survive this. Had to—

A final push, teeth bared through a guttural scream. A child spilling out into the light.

CHAPTER 62

Captain Johnson felt many things. But most pressing of all, he felt ill.

He held a clean handkerchief to his nose, hurtling away from the garrison. He winced at the assault of the sun, bending over and steadying his ragged breathing.

He inhaled the fresh air. *Free* air. A light breeze through the palms on a brilliant blue day.

He raised his hands to his throat, rubbing the back of his very-much-not-broken neck.

Johnson had meant to pay Mary a last visit too, alas. But perhaps this turn of events was for the best. A nasty business, all of it. Besides, she no longer spoke in full sentences, just the occasional phrase or word.

He shivered, feeling bile rise. He quelled it, then tucked away his handkerchief. With any luck, he'd never have to visit the gaol again. That is, unless his publisher wanted future editions with more pirates worthy of attention.

Look at him, losing his mind with aspirations. He couldn't think this way, getting his hopes up.

When the queasy feeling in his gut abated, he straightened and walked back to his residence. Palms swayed and carriages zipped in and out of passersby. He had trunks of papers to load, notes he wouldn't trust outside of his possession. The sooner he could get out of Spanish Town, the better.

He passed St. Catherine's, its bell tolling. Spanish Town and Port Royal had never been the same after the earthquake three decades ago—or so he was told. But this church still stood, rebuilt.

He paused, listening to the clanging bell of the Anglican church. It wasn't much to look at. A plain, narrow, one-room design. Tall. Three tiers of brick. The white cupola with its red roof and weathervane. A crucifix, of course, as was customary. He knew the symbolism. He was a practicing Anglican, after all.

Then, with renewed horror, he remembered the letters in his possession.

He leaned into his stride and walked on, away from the tolling bell and its incessant chiming.

But what to do? Where to dispose of them?

His stomach churned anew, and he fetched a carriage. He had to get out of the heat. Gather his effects. All things done in their proper time.

Hours later, Captain Johnson paced his stuffy room, his clothes and materials scattered around him. He rubbed the bridge of his nose, then returned to the writing table.

He sat, poring over his notes. Which ones should he take on his person? Which ones should he stow away as baggage in the hold? Like this one, *just here.* He picked up the sheet of paper in question. His notes from the penultimate meeting he'd had with Mary. The ink was smeared from the speed of his quill.

Johnson squinted to make out the scrawl. But he remembered it well enough, asking her—as she lay on her side in the straw, curled over her stomach, those unflinching black eyes—why pirates risked so much.

Shifting his eye piece, he studied her response.

"As to a hanging, it is no hardship, for were it not for that, every cowardly Fellow would turn Pirate, and so infest the Seas, that Men of Courage must starve."

But what of death? Johnson pressed, even now, hunched over his notes days after their conversation. Was she jesting? Mocking him? She'd insisted that they'd have no punishment except for death, the fear of which "kept some dastardly rogues honest."

He read on, the script becoming more slanted, more desperate, in his attempts to snatch the record.

"Many of those who are now cheating the Widows and Orphans, and opposing their poor Neighbours, who have no Money to obtain 'Justice,' would then rob at Sea, and the Ocean would be crowded with Rogues, like the Land, and no Merchant would venture out; so that piracy, in a little Time, would not be worth following."

His pulse spiked, feeling the truth of the words leap at him from the page, though he didn't grasp their full meaning. Land rogues. Were these the cheaters she described? Those with money? Power? Or those without, thieving from their fellow men as they aspired for excellence? He quite liked the idea. But what was she suggesting? That the very basis of society was a kind of tyranny? That every person, in their own way, depending on their resources and level of courage, had the heart of a pirate?

If so, what manner of rogue was he?

Johnson's lip curved with delight. It would be a fine, fine book, he congratulated himself. Pamphlets would have nothing on what this volume could sell. Returning to stuff a pile of documents and the draft of his manuscript inside his bag, he flinched as if scorched.

Damnation. Anne's letters. They were still there.

Johnson sank into his chair and stared out the window, dragging a hand over his cheek. The fading light glittering over the Rio Cobre. The sky ablaze with yellows and pinks.

Some recipients were in England.

The others, more local. Reachable through the post? A ship or revered captain that managed such deliveries?

He rubbed his head, his wig and tricorn on the bed. He closed his eyes, but all he saw was Anne's assessing gaze. Her intensity and eloquence. Her stubborn loyalty. Her skewering judgments and tales so vivid, so harrowing, he wondered if anyone could survive them at all.

Would she survive this? Would the child, arriving even now, on the other side of town?

Anne burned through his mind. Her posture of victory despite her defeat.

He sighed, then crossed himself.

No one, he soothed himself as he resumed packing with haste, had to know it was he who'd sent them.

CHAPTER 63

Björn?

She felt him, the press of light around her heart.

Yet, she was fading.

Her body still, her breaths raspy.

I'm here, he said.

"There's nothing else I can do for her. Get the priest."

She pried her eyes open. A dark room. Three men standing above her. Two in red coats. One in brown. A doctor. With a medicine box.

She raised her hand, but it remained at her side. She tried again, her fingers twitching.

"She's awake again."

The men looked, one kneeling in the straw beside her with a crooked nose.

The doctor. His cold finger against her throat. Dull throb. Some instruments shuffling. The word "bloodletting."

"I already have." The doctor sighed. "But perhaps if I try again . . ."

With effort, she rolled her head to look at him. She overshot. Her eyes found the middle space between his boots and the stone wall.

Her heart quickened. She saw it then, a flicker. The pain leaching from the flames of her skin.

"Björn?"

A knife drawn. A pinch in her arm.

I'm here.

"I told you to stay," she wheezed, fighting for air, a laugh escaping her lips.

"What did she say?"

"Fever dreams. She gets 'em. I'll hold her down."

I never left, my love.

Björn reached for her, and she reached back. Leaning into him and his strength. She'd been strong alone for so long. She felt herself let go.

Then she startled. "I can't leave."

His fingers through her hair, a gentle kiss on her forehead.

Not yet, I know. Tell them. Tell them what you want.

Mary threw her eyes open. The men watching. The doctor with his knife.

You know it can be done.

Mrs. Lambert. That day in the war.

The knife. A flash of silver. The word came like an answer.

"Ces . . . arean."

The doctor froze. "Did you hear that?"

"More nonsense."

"No, I heard her. Shh!" The blur of his face came into view, the hard nose. "You want . . . a caesarean?"

Her throat rattled when she tried to speak.

"Nod if you can understand me."

Her head fell to the side.

"Never mind that. Blink! Blink if you can understand," he said with urgency.

She blinked.

"You want a caesarean?"

She blinked again.

"You understand what will happen? Your own fate, and likely that of the child?"

She blinked again. The warmth around her heart swelled, Björn keeping his promise.

The doctor cursed, throwing open his bag, shouting orders. Men moving, flying. Sails across her vision.

"Anne," she said, a smile resting on her lips. *Find her.* She strained to open her eyes.

"Anne?" the doctor said, leaning over her.

She blinked, then closed her eyes for the last time.

I'm still here, darling.

I'm here. No more hiding. No more pretending.

Nothing left to fight.

She breathed in, finding that deep well within, the place with water still and calm. Then she exhaled, letting go in a blaze of light.

CHAPTER 64

Spanish Town, Jamaica
April 1721

Anne had been warned about wanting to gouge out her eyes for lack of sleep. About the endless washing of soiled swaddles. About her body feeling like a wool shawl stretched out of proportion. They weren't wrong.

But no one had bothered to mention this: The ear print, the tiniest ear imprint left on her chest when her son pressed against her bare skin, falling asleep on her breast.

If this was a brand of motherhood, she'd take it.

Anne wore a fresh dress. They held her in a locked room with barred windows, but still—a room with windows somewhere outside the main garrison.

Sunlight.

She cooed to Mark as she sat in a slat-back chair, her voice a mix of humming and terrible singing. Her past came to her in snatches. An old Irish lullaby:

"Mo sheoid gan cealg, mo chuid gan tsaoil mhór."

My flawless jewel, my piece of the world.

"Seo iad aniar iad le glaoch ar mo leanbh | Le mian é tharraingt isteach san lios mór."

The song spoke about a thieving fairy. A warning. Anne would be damned before anyone tried to lure this child away from her, or she from him. If she wasn't already damned.

He was anything but.

It'd been a month since Mark's birth. She saw no one but the midwife and nothing but the water buckets and food trays.

The oak door pushed open with a creak. Anne stiffened, resisting the urge to tell the midwife that the baby was sleeping. But it wasn't the quiet old woman who stoked her unease—not after all her kindness. Every time the door opened, Anne's stomach lurched. Waiting.

She was so tired of waiting. Worrying her miserable guts out.

Then, an infant's soft cry. A baby, but not her son.

Anne's eyes alighted on the midwife, that meaningful look in her pearl-gray eyes. The wailing bundle in her arms.

Anne tried to stand, tried to breathe. To ask the question blistering on her tongue.

The midwife patted the bundle, then approached Anne with assured steps. Anne wouldn't, couldn't, look up again. The midwife placed a heavy hand on her shoulder.

No.

The words formed, cutting a hole through the better part of her heart. Her throat burned and tears burst the dam of her eyes.

I said, no!

"She needs to be fed. If she doesn't—"

The walls fell away, Anne's vision blurring with oceanic grief. Bottomless, endless salt. A world without Mary. The wind abandoned her lungs, leaving her bones washed upon the shore of this land of the living.

But the midwife paid no mind to Anne's trembling. She unwrapped the crying child. Those wrinkled toes. That snatch of black hair.

"The doctor believes—though he could not be sure—that Mary Read declared her intention for you to have her."

"Did Mary suffer long?"

Did she get to meet this child before . . . ?

We'll find a way—Mary's words, rising from the depths to meet her despair.

We'll look after each other. And the babies.

The midwife blanched and did not answer. Instead, she placed the fussing infant on Anne's breast beside the still-sleeping Mark. Anne shifted and tried to contain her guttural sobs, the anchor of responsibility dropping on her like an anvil. Did the letters arrive yet? How, how to fight for a life that belonged to more than just her now? The midwife aided Anne, positioning the baby to nurse. Good Lord, she was so small.

The wailing heightened, then stopped, replaced with the sound of suckling. The midwife exhaled with surprised satisfaction at the easy latch. "You'll need extra food and water to encourage your milk supply. I'll see to it."

Anne heaved in a raw breath of relief, despair—she wasn't sure which. She placed an arm around her wee little daughter.

"*Mo stór,*" she breathed. My treasure. "Jesus, Mary, and Joseph—you'll know how loved you are."

Even if it's the last thing I ever do.

One week turned into two, two into three. Anne's son grew, and so did her daughter. Every day, every hour, every second.

And as she counted, Anne also waited. Half with dread, half with hope like a flickering ember in the pit of her throat. Her resolve deepened as time marched on. Her plan *had* to work.

But what if it doesn't? She began to fear when three weeks passed. What if Captain Johnson failed to send the letters? The rotten man. Then she'd write them all again, and more letters, starting immediately. She'd write them again and again—procure more paper from the midwife, the boy who delivered the food trays, anyone. She refused to let them kill her, especially now. Not now.

And if that doesn't work? The question jolted her awake in the startling silence of the night.

She'd find another path forward. Anne had been stripped of her blades, but she still had her wits. Devil help the person who tried to hang her or take the children away.

It was a June morning when she was awoken by Mark's crying. At three months, he could roll himself over onto his belly—a position he found distressing. She forced herself to arise in the pink-purple air, scooping him up from the bed and placing him to her breast.

"Don't wake your sister," she soothed, glancing over her shoulder at the swaddled girl. She swooned at the sight of that tuft of inky, velvet-soft hair.

Anne paced with Mark, back and forth, rocking him in her embrace, then paused at the door.

It stood ajar.

Her pulse rose as she tiptoed toward it in the dawn, pale rays streaming in from the windows. She nudged her head out, down the long white hallway. The rising sun at the end of the tunnel. A garden terrace on the other side.

She jolted, almost tripping over a breakfast tray on the ground. *Strange.* She crouched, spotting the subtle but unmistakable glint of something through the pores of the bread.

She studied it, breaking apart the loaf, and the thumping in her rib cage threatened to burst through her skin.

Gold.

Bloody hell, the bread was laden with ingots of it! Her fingers shook as she picked up the loaf before spying the envelope that had been tucked beneath the food, still lying on the breakfast tray. She tore it open, her fingers shaking. A dagger fell out, wrapped in written instructions.

She stuffed her pockets as hope shot through her veins. *Who?* she breathed, reading the directions to safety.

She'd find out soon enough.

Anne quietly backed into the room, then sprinted for the girl.

Think, she calmed herself, eyes darting between children. She used the knife to rip the bedsheet in two. With one piece, she covered her notorious hair. With the second, she created a wrap for the babies. She tied her son to her back and her sleeping daughter to her chest.

Hands free, shoulders squared, Anne padded barefoot toward the door. She inhaled deeply, moving through the fear, searching for that still point within her.

Act.

Go boldly.

Head held high—armed with a sharp knife she now knew how to use—she stepped forward into freedom.

EPILOGUE

Undisclosed Location
1728

Anne inked her quill, hesitating for a moment before penning the name of the recipient:

> *Dear Captain Charles Johnson,*

She paused again, staring out the window of the single, second-story room. Merchants were closing for the day, their carts creaking down the road in the pinkening air. High tide was rolling in, sunlight glinting off the murky glass. The children would come home soon for dinner. They'd set out with little fishing poles, vowing to bring home a catch.

Anne let out a rueful laugh. She'd better think up an alternative meal plan in time. She'd brushed aside all her chores, the extra hours she *should* be putting in mending sails at the docks. In an uncharacteristic move, she'd stolen back her afternoon. She'd removed her boots and walked home barefoot, taking the long path along the grainy shore. Once inside, she'd paced the bright room until at last she found herself here, seated at her small oak desk.

Anne's attention flicked to her latest letter from Ellen. Another from Henry, who was eager to have them visit. Even Da had sobered up and now wrote the occasional letter.

Then her eyes landed on the leather volume: *A General History of the Robberies and Murders of the Most Notorious Pyrates.* She'd saved for months to buy a copy of her own. To turn the page and see her name, and Mary's, printed in bold.

Anne rubbed her temples. She owed everyone replies. And yet, it was Captain Charles Johnson who snagged her attention. She had his location now. It was a message she'd intended to write for seven years.

> *I hope this letter finds you in good health and in cheerful spirits. You are a difficult man to find. Forgive the lack of a return address—like you, I prefer my privacy. But if you are reading this, I'll delight in knowing my letter has found its intended reader at last.*

She opened the tome, combing through the most ridiculous quotes. She'd lost count of how many times she'd longed for Mary to be by her side, to have someone to mock it with.

How much she wished Mary were here for anything, for any reason.

> *I suppose congratulations are in order on your two volumes of* A General History of the Pyrates. *I found your accounting of my and Mary's "rambling lives" most curious. I'm glad what we shared was "exceedingly diverting" to you and your readership. Your embellishments (and, just between us, omissions) no doubt have been of service to your career. The latest I'd heard, you have published countless copies and are entering another reprinting. Is that so? My word, what will you do next, you clever devil?*
>
> *I'll spare you details of my current living situation, but suffice it to say that I am well settled with loved ones I adore. They rein in my "hazardous" ways you are so fond of commenting*

upon. I've made use of my odd assortment of skills—especially
needlework. Who knew! I suspect you would find my version
of happiness quite uninspiring, tedious, and dull. Not
"extravagant" enough to entertain your salacious readers. But I
have my ways and secrets, and I'm still allowed some of those.
*   And now, the real reasons why I write.*

Placing the quill down, Anne bit her lip. Jesus, Mary, and Joseph. What to call this strange fascination with voyaging through
others' lives? The prickly nature of empathy, masquerading as a
peculiar form of delight—sailing through someone else's misfor-
tunes while reclining comfortably beside the safety of one's own
hearth?

After some of my own investigations—trying to track you
down to give you my thanks—I came to learn that there is no
gentleman by the name of "Captain Charles Johnson" among the
members of London society, no man in England by that name
or description who has circumnavigated the globe by the age of
twenty-seven, and no direct relationship of someone by your
name connected with the former governor of Nassau. (You did
hear, of course, that your friend Governor Woodes Rogers was
imprisoned for debt? It seems he caused financial ruin during
his term. But he's been acquitted and promoted—as all men of
his power and rank are.) Your publisher will not let slip your
true identity, a position I can understand given the wild success
you've enjoyed.

She felt an itch to know, to unveil. To feel she was not alone
in having a past. Even if it was not the one the world would ever
know about. The real her, or the real Mary.

All the same, we spent so much time together in Spanish Town.
Delightful days, you are sure to remember. I failed to ask you
enough questions in return. You profess to know much about

*me, and on some points, perhaps you do. I know, at last, who I
am—which is what I find to matter. But still, I wonder what it
is you hide. And why? You've made a great effort to unearth and
publish the truth about me. But who, dear Captain, are you?*

Anne's ears perked. The trill of children coming down the road.
No. Not her own. She still had time. She scanned the words she
had written.
She could end it there. Be rid of this burden.
But her hand moved again.

Now, the second reason for my writing.

What *was* her real purpose for writing? The reason she still
thought of this man who did so little, yet so much?

*I want to thank you for sending the letters I gave you
seven years ago. One met its mark, and that has made all the
difference—to my life then, and now. I quite like how your book
phrased my disappearance: "But what is become of her since,
we cannot tell; only this we know, that she was not executed." A
fine, evocative ending. Hardly a full or determined accounting,
as you claimed in your premise, but one I appreciate—all my
snide remarks aside (in case you have forgotten the wit of an old
friend). Thank you for that discretion and for honoring my final
request of you. You've saved more lives than one.*

A knot caught in her throat. A flash of the face she saw daily
in her daughter's smiling, mahogany eyes. Anne inhaled, then
signed:

*Your Humble and Disobedient Servant,
Anne*

AFTERWORD

I can picture the scene of Mary and Anne in Negril's Bay well: fighting back to back as they took on an overwhelming press of armed men. It is a scene blazed into irrefutable court records, a scene of two women, pregnant, fighting for their lives while their drunken crewmates and ship leadership cowered in the hold. It is almost like these women had something more to fight for.

What *is* a female pirate? Before writing this book and studying the lives of Mary Read and Anne Bonny, I had my own casual notions—images informed by Hollywood movies and all manner of other media. Brutal, bloodthirsty women. "Floozies" who could hold their liquor but also sling a gun. And, most importantly, they were sexy—tantalizing, busty, and dripping with desire in their skin-tight leather bodices. They were never, heaven forbid, pregnant. There was often only one such "female pirate" per story, a token character, a feature of a pirate ship—like its sails, cannons, and seductive mermaid bowsprit—designed to make the life of the strapping male protagonist more interesting. Why would a plot need more than one of these women?

For the most part, filmmakers, screenwriters, and other writers have made their preferences clear. Of the two most infamous "female pirates" from popular history, they chose—time and time again—the quick-tempered, flaming hot Anne Bonny. Whether or not they ever called their character "Anne" or gave her fiery-red hair (we have no record of her true hair color, but red fits the part), many have perpetuated this trope and conflated the two women into a single caricature, all but erasing Mary Read.

Now, having written this book featuring two women who were many things but who *also* happened to be pirates, rather than reducing either Anne or Mary to "female pirate," I found far more questions than answers in my attempt to excavate these figures from three centuries of the male gaze.

In 1724, Captain Charles Johnson published the first edition of *A General History of the Pyrates*—the book that went on to immortalize Mary Read and Anne Bonny, alongside many other famed names such as John Rackham, Charles Vane, Edward Teach ("Blackbeard"), and Samuel Bellamy. Anyone engaging in pirate history and lore must contend with this book, which is sometimes called "the bible of pirate studies." As naval expert and pirate historian David Cordingly writes in *Under the Black Flag*, "Captain Johnson created the modern conception of pirates."

Who was this mysterious Captain Johnson, whose tabloid journalism has had such a profound influence on our popular opinions? For a while, some claimed it was a pen name for Daniel Defoe. When that theory got debunked, attention turned to Nathaniel Mist. Unable to verify the author, perhaps the more important question is not who wrote it, but rather, what was this mass-selling book up to? Johnson's introduction states there are times when the tales veer so far into the spectacular that they might have the "Air of a Novel." Some details in this collection certainly skew so ridiculous or cliché that they could only be read as fiction—representing a writer's desire to entertain, to sell a book so shocking that readers of pirate-trial pamphlets and even the most righteous churchgoers would be enticed to read its pages. And yet, a surprising amount of what Johnson wrote has since been verified by historians. His record is also one of the few, and certainly the most substantial, we have that discusses the lives of Mary Read and Anne Bonny.

If this is the famed bible of pirate studies, what do we make of its somewhat dubious stories that have not, or cannot, be verified? How do we separate fact from fiction when history itself, like memory, is a kind of fiction? These stakes are especially relevant in an era where women's histories—as well as those of poor folk, people of color, and other marginalized groups—were not well preserved.

The Determined is a work of fiction. I am not a historian; I'm a novelist. In a way, I did (though with different intentions, I hope) what Captain Johnson himself set out to do: to blend fact, invention, and myth together to bring to light the complex lives of these women for a reader. But unlike Johnson, I will divulge what has been verified as fact, what I relied on in his questionable record, and where I engaged my own imagination and speculation.

Let's start with the hard facts.

We have four legal records that speak directly about Mary and Anne. First, the proclamation from Governor Woodes Rogers issued September 4, 1720 (a lightly edited version appears in this book), and second, a similar proclamation made by the governor of Jamaica, Sir Nicholas Lawes.

Then there are the court papers that detail the trials of Rackham and Mary and Anne. They are available for free online. From these testimonies and other sources, I reconstructed the path the pirates took in their two months aboard the *Revenge*—who they raided, and the pitiful amounts they seized as the Golden Age of Piracy came to an end following Governor Woodes Rogers' mission and King George's 1717 proclamation granting amnesty to those who turned themselves in—and a reward for those who ratted out others.

The fourth irrefutable primary source is a burial record citing Mary's death on April 28, 1721. It was recorded in the Parish Registry of St. Catherine in Spanish Town, the same church that features in chapter 62 of this novel. Credit for this discovery goes to Tyler "Bioshock" Rodriguez, a YouTuber and myth debunker who was unsatisfied with all the speculation around this tale. His video

"The Legend of Anne Bonny," published in January 2021 on his channel Debunk File, disrupted many common myths about Anne and is well worth watching. He presents his original research and proposes his own ideas about who these women might have been. I can't help but love the irony of a twenty-two-year-old YouTuber publishing verifiable, cutting-edge research for the masses in a way historians and scholars have failed to do—especially when it comes to issues about class and pirates.

Rodriguez also discovered a St. Catherine's burial record for someone named Anne Bonny on December 29, 1733. Though we cannot confirm that this is *our* Anne, Rodriguez's work undid decades of snowballing assumptions that Anne's father was the one who bailed her out, bringing her back to the States where she married a man named Joseph Burleigh. If Rodriguez's discovery is correct, it implies that Anne never left Jamaica after her stint in prison.

We have no way of knowing how Anne managed to avoid her execution sentence. I find her escape especially surprising given the buzz surrounding her trial, one that held worldwide interest and collective astonishment at a time of relentless urgency to rid the seas of the scourge of pirates. This end of the Golden Age of Piracy was anything but golden. None were spared in Rackham's trial, including the potential recruits who claimed they were out "a-turtling." Even a whiff of being associated with piracy could get someone hanged, or worse, hanged then gibbeted like Rackham, where it was believed his soul would never find rest (that location, where people enter Port Royal, is still called "Rackham's Cay"). And yet, Anne was spared. How?

My novel speculates at some possible theories, many borrowed from Rebecca Alexandra Simon's book, *Pirate Queens: The Lives of Anne Bonny & Mary Read*. The most commonly accepted theory for many years was that Anne's father, hearing of the famous trial, bailed her out and brought her home to South Carolina. This has been a fan favorite for decades, with writers such as Phillip Thomas Tucker in *Anne Bonny: The Infamous Female Pirate* noting details such as Anne naming her child John, marrying again to a man named Joseph Burleigh, having seven more children with Burleigh, and living to a ripe old age in Virginia—long enough to see the American Revolution begin and end.

An alternative theory of what happened to Anne after her escape is that she was given reprieve, during which time she returned to Cuba to live with the people Johnson referred to as Rackham's "kind of family." This version speculates that Anne had a son.

Another theory, proposed by biographer Laura Sook Duncombe, was that the legendary pirate Captain Bartholomew Roberts, after hearing tales about Anne's famed courage, sprang Anne from jail—only to later reveal that Roberts herself was a woman, saying, "We women have to stick together, don't we? Come on!" Most find this idea impossible, but fun. I included Roberts as a letter recipient to nod to this speculation.

Whatever occurred that allowed Anne to escape the noose, I like to believe that she—the daughter of a lawyer—had some hand in rewriting her determined fate.

For my novel, I relied heavily on *A General History of the Pyrates* and took every one of Captain Johnson's details into account. As Johnson does, I'll start with Mary Read's portrait. He describes her childhood in England as a bastard and impersonating her deceased older brother "Mark" so her widowed mother could have, from her mother-in-law, "a Crown a Week for it's [sic] Maintenance." Then, Mary goes on to work other odd jobs, such as being a "Foot-boy" at the age of thirteen. The incident of forty-seven women appealing, without success, to Queen Anne to pardon their men accused of piracy is based on a 1707 event where the name "Ann Cantrell" shows up on the record among the other women. This Ann Cantrell was pleading on behalf of a pirate named John Read, and she had two children, one named Mary. In case there is any chance this was actually, in fact, our Mary's mother or Mary herself somehow, I've included it here.

According to Johnson, Mary's cross dressing continued as she served on a man-of-war, in the militia, then in the cavalry. He says "she behaved herself with a great deal of Bravery." From there, she "took on in a Regiment of Horse," earning the "Esteem of all her Officers," when a handsome Flemish soldier, her superior, caught her eye. I used key details from Johnson, such as sharing a tent with her love interest, and her breaking ranks to save him in battle, but tried to strip away some of the male gaze. Johnson said that her husband courting her to be his wife "was the utmost Wish of her Heart." The information about the Three Horse-Shoes inn after their marriage, and their happy life until his death, comes from his account.

Many have theorized that Mary's time in the military could only be fiction. But her path was more common than we might assume for women like Mary who had limited options. Rebecca Alexandra Simon cites an anonymous writer in 1762 who declared "that there were so many women in the British army that they should have had their own battalions."

I streamlined Mary's journey of getting to Nassau after Björn died. Johnson wrote about Mary's common-law husband (the court brief indicates that this was Thomas Brown), the duel Mary fought on his behalf, her anger and frustration at Rackham's over-confidence, her plea to kill Dorothy Thomas, and Mary's words and actions the night Mary battled alongside Anne at Negril's Bay. Mary is attributed with one of the most famous quotes about piracy, parts of which I adapted and included in her final words to Johnson in chapter 62.

For Anne's portrait, Johnson gives a lengthy commentary on her parentage—her father, a married gentleman and a lawyer, who falls for the maid. I highlighted these particulars in the backstory. Johnson describes Anne's upbringing in County Cork, Ireland, then Charles Town—which some records indicate she fled around the time her mother died and her father bought a plantation. The Gullah people's sweetgrass basket weaving, a tradition carried over from Africa and kept alive through today, dates back to the 1600s. The information Ellen shares about "the usual place" comes from historian Dr. Nic Butler's research. I found the chilling "Lot 4" slave action tag, excavated in what we now call Charleston, on display in the Heritage Museum of the Bahamas. Also factual is that the primary accusers of the crew aboard the *Revenge*—Woodes Rogers, Sir Nicholas Lawes, and Jonathan Barnet—were either actively involved in trading or owning enslaved people.

Johnson describes Anne's "fierce and couragious [sic] Temper," her willful nature, and an account involving a knife and "a young Fellow" trying to lie with her "against her Will," when "she beat him so, that he lay ill of it a considerable Time." He glosses over what happens next, or the effect of this attempted sexual assault on the rest of Anne's life. Johnson talks about her marriage to James Bonny (a man who was "not worth a Groat"), his cowardly betrayals, and his vengeful schemes while Anne fell for Calico Jack Rackham. He says she was "proved with Child" when Rackham sent her to Cuba, then nothing more comes of that storyline before they are back in Nassau—a shantytown self-governed by an estimated 1,000 pirates, who outnumbered the colonist population five to one. The local politics, place descriptions, and democratic "Articles" of pirates out of New Providence—including other details about life aboard—are accurate. Anne and Mary had to have both been pregnant by the time they took the *William*. Anne's damning parting words to Jack in his final wish to see her, that if he would have "fought like a man," he would not "hang like a dog," are taken directly from Johnson.

What, then, was left to speculation on my part? The cast of characters points to the particulars, but in broad strokes I tried to show that these were two distinct women. I consolidated contradicting timelines in some cases. Since we do not know who Johnson was, much less how he came by his information, we do not know if he ever met or interviewed Mary and Anne (Woodes Rogers was his likely informant). I added texture where there were gaps in the mother figures. I've never found a record that indicated that Mary and Anne, despite their outrage at Rackham, intended to strike out on their own. I invented what kind of sexual dynamic Anne and Rackham might have had, and we have little evidence that

Mary did not drink regularly—only that she and Anne were sober in the final battle in Negril's Bay when the men on the crew were anything but. There are no records of what happened to Mary's or Anne's babies, just as there are no definitive records of what happened to Anne after she evaded the noose. Mary may have died of fever before giving birth, or during birth, but a caesarean procedure would not be out of the question. It was a method used for many purposes. Its namesake comes from the time of Julius Caesar, when women were not to be buried while pregnant—it had nothing to do with trying to save the infant. Though a caesarean at the time was almost a guaranteed death for the mother, and likely the child, it has been a procedure for millennia. The first documented woman and baby to both survive a caesarean was in 1500.

As far as the wife sale, though that does not appear explicitly in Johnson's account, others have suggested it could have happened to Anne—and history confirms this was a real practice as a kind of pseudo-divorce. I took and adapted Bonny's speech in the town square from what another man named Joseph Thompson said while selling his wife in 1832.

Another point of speculation—a point that many have raised, ever since Johnson's embellished tale—dealt with the nature of Mary and Anne's relationship. Was their relationship queer? Or was it a powerful friendship, superimposed with the eroticized fantasies of a man reading into their already heinous, unthinkable behavior for women at the time—a man hoping to sell something salacious? Was their relationship something in-between? No historical evidence supports a queer connection, and any genuine evidence would likely have been missed or disregarded by primary sources at the time. Yet, in Johnson's second edition of *A General History of the Pyrates*, he expands in some skeptical ways, adding new material not previously there that suggested Anne had special feelings for Mary before she knew Mary was a woman. In this tweaked rendition, Johnson depicts a scene of Anne trying to discover Mary's secret just as Rackham walks in, spiraling him into a jealous rage until the truth comes out—which allows Rackham to disregard the perceived threat to his own relationship and masculinity. Since they were both women, he—like others at the time—could dismiss any validity to their intimacy because women could not, in his mind, have "sex." This added spice in a second edition, sprinkled on in hindsight, would no doubt sell more books for Johnson. I interpreted this scene in another way in my novel, but with the same particulars. To me, regardless of the relationship between Anne and Mary, a few issues arise that deserve analysis: Rackham's problematic response, alongside the flaw in Johnson's account that suggests that Anne could only have loved Mary while Anne thought her to be a "man."

Most historians, writes Rebecca Alexandra Simon, claim that, while these women "clearly loved each other," "there is little likelihood of a romance between Anne and Mary." Literary historian and essayist Rictor Norton, who specializes in LGBTQIA+ issues in literature, wrote that these women were "at most bisexual." In 1974, Susan Baker—a feminist writer at work during the women's movement—wrote a piece called "Anne Bonny & Mary Read: They Killed Pricks," which elaborated on this idea of the lesbian relationship (citing Johnson's revised scene) that has stuck around as an exciting, if factually unsupported, idea ever since. I'm captivated by what Jo Stanley, a feminist writer, described of female pirates, as making visible the terrifying power of unrepressed women. It is in this spirit of subverting the men's horror at their own sexual impulses (before then blaming women for stoking such evil desires), that I wrote some of the final scenes where Anne and Mary, true to recorded history, fought with their chests bare and hair down, using their female identities as a weapon. In sticking with the material presented to me, this book has certain depictions of gender that might not resonate with everyone. However, I have no interest in trying to essentialize or reduce the complex, wide spectrum of gender. I'm indebted to my trans and nonbinary early readers for their insights and feedback.

To honor the complexity of Mary and Anne, I chose to not further box them in by assigning their relationship or sexuality certain words or modern labels. Deep and abiding love does not need to be sexual; assuming it must have been, or must not have been, diminishes the depth of their affection. I didn't want to reduce them to something that would suit my personal agenda. As a queer woman, I am fascinated by this potential, but I did not want to repeat the mistake of Johnson. Instead, I leave this point ambiguous. But a reader can read the novel in many ways.

What emerged from this heart-labor of excavating these women from a history long since past? A thousand surprises. Though I didn't set out to write a story with menstruation, variations of sexual assault, miscarriage, the realities of pregnancy, or the grueling experiences of birth, that is what emerged on the page as I researched, studied, and wrote. Less "female pirate" stock footage, but also no "pirate queens" thumping their naked breasts and screaming for the world to notice and revere them. I saw a kind of pirate story I certainly had never heard of before, but also something that felt more recognizable, in these two women who lived real, brave lives—with just two months out of all of that brave time spent pillaging together on the high seas.

Mary Read and Anne Bonny lived specific and nuanced lives not determined by a "general history." To claim otherwise would be impossible. And yet, they *were* singularly determined—like many other characters I encountered while writing this book, particularly the women forced to make impossible choices, who could not afford the illusion and posturing of innocence. In the words of Rebecca Alexandra Simon, "Anne Bonny and Mary Read are the two most well-known female pirates of the age, but their lives represent the countless number of women who sailed the seas and were lost to history." The more we question and add to the record and tales of women like them—including in the realm of imagination—the more the story goes on, with new layers and complexity continuing to unfurl.

Cast of Characters

* Indicates a character using the name of a verified historical figure
† Indicates a character using the name and known depictions of a verified historical figure
‡ Indicates a character mentioned by name or otherwise in Captain Charles Johnson's *A General History of the Pyrates*

Cormac Family

"Da" / William Cormac‡
m. "Mam" / Mary ("Peg") Cormac‡
Anne Bonny†‡

Read Family

"Ma"‡
Unnamed sailor
h.b. Mark‡
Unnamed pirate‡
Mary Read†‡

Captain Charles Johnson*‡

Ireland Residents

Seán O'Brien
Aoife
Liam
Fionn
Mrs. Doyle
Mr. O'Neill
Mrs. Cormac‡
Granny Cormac‡
Granddad Cormac
"a blacksmith" who fancied Peg‡

England Residents

Mrs. Dalton
Captain Southwick
Mr. Robert
The Goodwins
Lady Barton and her daughters
Miss Marlow
Master Tansley

Charles Town Residents

Monsieur Perrin
Ellen Fulworth
Dr. Ashby
Peter Fulworth
Nathaniel Fulworth‡
Mr. Bull
Mrs. Fulworth
Mr. Fulworth

Continental European Residents

Henry Danby
Björn Van Acker‡

Sergeant Gorst
Mrs. Lambert
Lord Van Acker

Sailors, Pirates, and Privateers

Mr. Taylor
James Bonny†‡
Captain Eford
Alby
Dutton
Murphy
John Rackham / "Calico Jack"†‡
Charles Vane†‡
Henry Jennings†‡
Fletcher
Captain Spenlow†‡
Captain Dillon†
Captain Jean Bondavais†
Captain Jonathan Barnett†

Nassau Residents

Governor Woodes Rogers†‡
Boris
Mr. Huxley
Old Wentworth
Benjamin ("Ben") Hornigold†‡
Thomas Brown*‡
Captain John Ham†

Cuba Residents

"where Rackham kept a little kind of family"‡

The *Revenge* Crew

Jack Fenwick / "Old Dad the Cooper"*
Richard Corner (quartermaster)*

Thomas Earl*
George Featherstone (shipmaster)*
John Howell*
Daniel York‡
Thomas Baker*
John Eaton*
Edward Warner*
Thomas Quick*

Jamaica Residents

Dorothy Thomas†
Governor Sir Nicholas Lawes†

Political and Military Leaders Referenced

Queen Maeve
Furbaide
Grace O'Malley / Gráinne Ní Mháille†
Black Oak†
Donal O'Flaherty†
Queen Elizabeth I of England †
King Charles II of Scotland†
Joan of Arc†
"Dauphin" Charles VII of France†
Queen Anne of England†
Marshal Villeroi†
Duke of Marlborough†
King George I of England†

Tried individuals aboard the *William* who were not depicted specifically in this book

Andrew Gibson*
John Davis*
Noah Harwood*
Patrick Carty*
James Dobbin*

John Cole*
Benjamin Palmer*
Walter Rouse*
John Hanson*
John Howard*

ACKNOWLEDGMENTS

I wrote this book during the most difficult era of my life. Like Mary and Anne, it was the women who saw me through. I've said this before, but I'll never stop saying it: my relationships are my greatest treasure. I've never needed my crew more, and I'm humbled to have known such remarkable people and to have enjoyed such deep and meaningful friendships, to regularly witness their unapologetic power and the thousands of ways they "make the whole earth shake."

To Maggie Christensen, Victoria Hartman, Margaret Olsen Hemming, Brittney Jenson, Mariya Manzhos, Kim Matheson, Katie Ludlow Rich, Toni Tugenberg, and Carol Ann Litster Young—thank you for your deep and abiding support, both on and off the page. This also includes Mikaela Benson, Barbara Jones Brown, Kami Coppins, Kim Ence, Kim Green, Lisa Van Orman Hadley, Brenda Heaton, Rachel Keränen, Heather Last, Rachel Morse, Leslie Nielsen, Megan Nordquist, Gloria Pak, Megan Palmer, Stefani Philp, Kim Rohrer, and Eliza Wells.

To my (coincidentally) all-female publishing team at Kensington Books: Elizabeth Trout, my brilliant and unfailingly kind editor, deserves heaps of gold. So do Jesse Cruz and Michelle Addo-Chajet for their publicity work, as well as Lauren Jernigan and Kate

Johnson for their help navigating the wild seas of social media. To everyone at Kensington Books, including Carly Sommerstein for the beautiful layout, I tip my tricorn to you. Thank you also to my team at Inkwell, Kimberly Witherspoon and Maria Whelan.

To my trans and nonbinary readers, whose friendship and feedback have been a treasured gift: Ash Rowan, for his writing and bone-deep way of seeing and experiencing the world; Sam Layco, for their nerdy and social justice heart; Andee Bowden, for their fantastic insights on everything from gender to historical clothing; and Dani, who is as beautiful as the name she chose for herself.

To Ryan Palmer and Rich Nielsen, for your invaluable feedback on this book, but even more importantly, for who you are.

To rem, for sojourning with me through thick and thin.

To my brilliant early readers Julie Allen, Stefani Anderson, Alixa Brobbey, Cynthia W. Connell, Linda Hamilton, Megan Hamzawi, Thomas Sorensen, Carole Turley, and Steven Young—a thousand thanks for your time and care and thoughtful comments. They made all the difference.

To Thomas McConkie, for helping me—as Mary must throughout this book—find the "still point." Thank you for your work at Lower Lights and for your podcast, Mindfulness+.

To Mollie, the passionate teacher at Irish With Mollie (irishwith mollie.com). *Go raibh míle maith agat.* I'm forever indebted to your expertise and admire everything you do to champion the Irish language. Thank you also to Fiona Byrne, my favorite Irish pal, for her fantastic comments and early reading.

A legion of people helped me name the *Swallow*'s ship dog. When Willa Nielsen said I needed a pirate dog, I had no idea how many would rise to the task of helping me name this spaniel. Through this collaborative effort, the dog really came alive to me, and in turn, to Anne. Thank you to Emily Kim from Em Doodles (emdoodlesandstuff.com), for coming up with the name "Toddy Mops." With your magic ability to name, doodle, and make people laugh, you are the best thing on the internet.

To everyone else who provided a middle name or nickname

for Toddy Mops that features in these pages: Melonie Cannon, Shayna Cox, Carmen Sleight Crawford, Natalie Cutino, Tarah Everett, Cheyenne Gavin, Valerie Green, Megan Hamzawi, Kara Hess, Jennifer Jones, Katie Meek, Debbie Nash, Briahna Nelson, Heather Oman, Ryan Palmer, Amber Palmer, Mallory Perry, Katie Ludlow Rich, Sarah Rosenthal, Sarah Rueckert, Ella Seybold, Amy Stoddard, Heather Sundahl, Heidi Thompson, Emily Waldo, and Eliza Wells.

The adventure didn't stop there. Since the dog naming went so well, I had my newsletter subscribers also nominate names for the taverns featured in this book. Thank you to "Cici" Juliet Wendel—aka Lady Cici of the Sartorial Prowess—my friend, volunteer stylist, and creative at Ciella Studio, who named the Jubilee, where Mary and Anne meet.

Credit for other establishment names throughout the novel go to Valerie Anderson, Andee Bowden, Bridget Fawcett, Carin Griggs, Christian Hales, Victoria Hartmann, Margaret Olsen Hemming, Lara Niedermeyer, Heather Oman, Katie Ludlow Rich, Jessica Sagers, LuAnn Walters, and Kim Ellen Warnick.

To my newsletter followers—who make up my "hype crew" and constantly vote on my writing-related things, such as names for pirate dogs and taverns—my deepest gratitude. (Join my newsletter if you want in on the fun! rachelrueckert.com/newsletter)

To Gary Campbell and Soren Campbell, for your insights about sailing.

To Renee Ormsbee at Reneesance, for making the most incredible custom pirate hats.

To the Exponent II community, for creating space and amplifying voices, and for always having my back.

To Taylor Swift, for providing the soundtrack to my healing.

To independent bookstores, who have helped my writing career set sail. Thank you for the priceless work you do and the magical spaces you create.

A special thank-you to my family, my biggest fans. They have embraced me as well as my lifelong pirate obsession. To Pappy for his unfailing confidence in me. To my mom, for taking me, since before I could consciously remember, on all those daily walks to the open sea. I'm also indebted to my nieces, Hadley and Sloane—the best things to have ever happened to this planet—for reminding me that the world is a wondrous marvel.

To all my dear ones, mentors, and teachers—and many more whom I wish I could name in full—thank you, from the depths of my heart. You have my love and loyalty forever.

READING GROUP GUIDE

Discussion Questions

1. Who do you think may have saved Anne? What theories do you have about her escape?

2. Before reading this book, what was your understanding of female pirates? Has your perspective changed?

3. What fascinated you the most in reading the afterword?

4. Mary and Anne subverted roles for women during their time. How has their story challenged your own ideas about gender, in the past but also at present?

5. What do you think the title means?

6. Who were your favorite side characters? Were there any, in their own way, who also lived with determination?

7. What do you make of Captain Charles Johnson? Why do you think the author made the choice to include him as a character?

8. In what ways has the male gaze impacted Mary's and Anne's legacies?

9. Mary and Anne make impossible choices amid limited options and difficult circumstances. When was a time you made an impossible choice? Did it feel like a choice?

10. The women in this novel face assaults and vulnerable hardships. When they speak about their experiences, characters respond in many different ways. What can we learn from their various reactions?

11. Who would you cast in a film adaptation of *The Determined*?

12. Compare Mary and Anne with other historical figures, such as Grace O'Malley and Joan of Arc, mentioned throughout this book. How are they similar or different?

13. Mary is credited with a famous speech about the courage of pirates in contrast with the "Rogues" who govern land by "cheating Widows and Orphans, and opposing their poor Neighbours." Her quote is lightly adapted in chapter 62 of this novel. Do you agree with her perspective? Why or why not?

14. What do you make of the quote from *A General History of the Robberies and Murders of the Most Notorious Pyrates* that prefaces this novel? In what ways is the medium of writing and storytelling challenged and engaged with this as a theme?

15. Mary and Anne, though inked into history, represent untold numbers of women who also sailed the seas but whose histories were not recorded. How can we best serve them, and all women's history, to honor their stories?

Visit our website at
KensingtonBooks.com
to sign up for our newsletters, read
more from your favorite authors, see
books by series, view reading group
guides, and more!

Become a Part of Our
Between the Chapters Book Club
Community and Join the Conversation

Submit your book review for a chance to win exclusive
Between the Chapters swag you can't get anywhere else!
https://www.kensingtonbooks.com/pages/review/